P 2.50

THE KING OF ATHELNEY

In the second of his three Saxon novels, Alfred Duggan portrays quite brilliantly the greatest king of the period, Alfred, an inspiring leader who came to the throne unexpectedly and committed himself and his people to secure freedom at last from the pirate invaders who came, year after year, to fight, steal and destroy.

ALFRED DUGGAN

Alfred Duggan died in 1964. In his youth and early manhood he had the reputation of being something of a rake and he was forty-seven before he published his first novel. His substantial life's work was produced over a period of just fourteen years, having emerged, in Evelyn Waugh's words, 'with his mind acute, his remarkable memory unimpaired and a prose style already perfectly fitted for his use'.

D0915800

*By Alfred Duggan and also published in this series of
Methven's Classic Historical Novels*

THE LITTLE EMPERORS
Britain and the Collapse of the Roman Empire

CONSCIENCE OF THE KING
The Saxon Invasion of Britain

THE CUNNING OF THE DOVE
Edward the Confessor and England before
the Conquest

GOD AND MY RIGHT
The Life and Death of Thomas Becket

The King of Athelney

by

Alfred Duggan

METHVEN'S BOOKSELLERS
Woking, Surrey

British Library Cataloguing in Publication Data:
A catalogue record for this book is available
from the British Library

© The Estate of Alfred Duggan 1961

ISBN 1 902894 02 2

First published in Great Britain by
Faber and Faber in 1961

This edition published in 1999 by
Methven's plc
43a Chertsey Road
Woking
Surrey GU21 5AJ

Typeset by
Avon Dataset Ltd, Bidford on Avon, Warwickshire B50 4JH

Printed and bound in Great Britain by
Mackays of Chatham plc, Chatham, Kent

1

A Child in Rome

A group of chamberlains and chaplains stood before the palace of the Lateran, enjoying the last rays of spring sunshine and making plans for tomorrow.

'Mass at St. Peters, another visit to the new walls while we are on that side of the river, back here to dine, then spend the afternoon at paper-work in the Curia. Does that satisfy everybody? It gives the Holy Father an easy day, and we can fit in anything urgent that happens to turn up.' The Master of Ceremonies looked round the company, seeking agreement.

'We must arrange a Confirmation soon,' answered one of the chaplains. 'We usually have one about this time of year, and there is quite a crop of children waiting.'

'A Confirmation before the weather gets too hot,' the Master of Ceremonies agreed. 'That's easily arranged, so long as we warn the candidates in good time. Now is there anyone special we ought to invite to dinner tomorrow?'

'I don't know about dinner, but there's a new arrival who ought to have a private audience,' said a Frankish clerk. 'A King's son from the barbarous north, come on pilgrimage and bringing splendid gifts.'

'Then why not dinner? That's the usual thing.'

'He happens to be four years old. He couldn't sit still to the end, even if he could cope with the food. Also he's not his father's heir, just the youngest boy in a long family. I don't know why they sent him. I suppose to fulfil a vow of pilgrimage by deputy. But the gifts he brings are very fine indeed.'

'Then he can have his private audience, but he won't be asked to dinner,' decided the Master of Ceremonies. 'Is his family devout? Will he behave properly? Where's his father's kingdom, anyway? What do they want of the Holy Father? They must want something, or they would never have sent this boy. I suppose they are not schismatics, or excommunicate?'

'I can tell you all about this embassy,' said a young chaplain, whose Latin had a Germanic throatiness. 'I saw them this afternoon in Our Lady of the Saxons, where they were giving thanks for their safe arrival. They are men from my own island. I spoke to them in the church.'

'More of those northern eccentrics,' groaned the Master of Ceremonies. 'Do they follow the Roman rite, or have they brought their own calendar with them? Is the King who sent them a man of any real importance?'

'They are faithful Romanists. They come from the south of Britain, which was converted by our Augustine and has always followed our rite. The child's father is a genuine independent King. In fact *his* father was the most powerful King in the island, though things have changed a bit recently. As you are aware, the Northumbrians are the greatest nation in Britain, and their royal house was the most noble and the most holy . . .'

A chamberlain interrupted. 'We know that indeed. All your ancestors were Kings, Saints, and Martyrs, who fell in battle against the heathen or the schismatics of the west. You need not recite the whole history of Britain. Just tell us about the King who sent these gifts, and his youngest son with them.'

'He is King Ethelwulf of the West Saxons, son of King Egbert who defeated the Mercians. His line goes back to Woden, as noble a pedigree as any German can boast. The West Saxons are the third people among the Germans of Britain, less notable than the Northumbrians or the Mercians. But theirs is the only Kingdom still ruled by its ancient royal line. Now that the Mercians and my

2

own Northumbrians are ruled by upstarts, the Kings of the West Saxons are the most noble rulers in the island.'

'Save for the Welsh, whose Kings all trace their descent from Noah,' put in another chaplain, proud to display his knowledge of northern affairs.

'I do not admit the exception. The line of Woden goes back to Sceaf, a son of Noah born actually in the Ark. But surely we are all descended from Noah, or we wouldn't be here. It's just that some of us cannot trace our pedigrees.'

'What does it matter,' said the Master of Ceremonies with a snort. 'British pedigrees! Each one a mile long and stuffed with heathen gods! My forefathers were here when Alaric came, and you can't have a better line than that. I suppose they were descended from Romulus, though they forgot to leave their genealogy on record. The point is that this Saxon King is a man of importance in his own country, so we must honour his son. I wonder why he sent his youngest to represent him, and such a baby too? It would have been more practical to send the heir, and let him see the world before he begins to rule.'

'A vow, I suppose,' the Northumbrian answered. 'This Ethelwulf is a good Christian, for a King. He nearly went into the church instead of being King. The story goes that he took minor orders in his father's lifetime.'

'He went into the church when he was baptized,' said the Frank smugly. 'But if he is descended from Woden he is well born. We must see his little son properly honoured.'

It was comforting to feel that no one around him was frightened. They were flustered, of course, and on their best behaviour; as any sensible man would be when he is about to be presented to the Vicar of God on earth. But the feeling that his elders were on their best behaviour made it easier for a small boy to behave well also. Everyone said that the Pope was a kindly old man. He must kiss his hand gracefully, and answer a few of the

3

questions grown-ups were always asking. Then he could go off and see the sights, and mother would be pleased with him when he got back to Winchester.

During part of the long journey through Frankland the grown-ups had been very frightened. Of course they had not said so, and indeed they had tried to hide it. But even a four-year-old takes notice when warriors loosen their swords in the scabbard and fuss over their saddle-girths at every blind corner on the road. When the guide questioned local peasants the fear had been plain in his voice, even though he spoke a foreign tongue.

The warriors of the young prince's escort were right to be afraid. They were King's companions, bound in honour to safeguard his life with their own, and to die on the same field if he should be slain. Yet if they encountered the Army a four-year-old could not gallop away; they would have to form the shield-wall and die where they stood.

That summer the Army was plundering up the valley of the Loire. Heathen men sacked Nantes, Angers, Tours, Poitiers. St. Martin himself could not protect his servants; at the pillaging of Marmoutier his monks were killed by the hundred. Luckily the Army moved in one body, to overawe the Franks. The English pilgrims had journeyed cautiously from the coast, and then ridden swiftly by night across the belt of devastation. During that fearsome night the child rode on the saddlebow of a well-mounted King's companion, silent, gritting his teeth lest the pain of the jolting should make him cry out. It had rained all night, so that his wet trousers made the discomfort more painful. His bottom was still sore, and getting worse instead of better; though once they had reached the foothills of the Alps they had travelled softly, the child in a padded pannier slung to the side of a quiet mule.

In the Alps there were brigands, of course, and more brigands in Lombardy; pilgrims bearing rich gifts to Rome were the prey they sought. But the warriors of the escort had no fear of brigands. No common brigand loves gold well enough to be killed trying to win it.

The Army was different. The heathen men of the Army loved gold well enough to die for it; that was what made them invincible. No one could guess what the Army would do next, and no sensible ruler tried to fight it. Some twenty years ago it had come out of the unknown north; since then it had ravaged Christendom without ceasing. Wherever it went it made a desert; the whole world was not ruined only because it was very easy to pay the Army to move on.

A sensible hardworking Christian will pay such men to go away, rather than lay down his life in defence of his trumpery earthly goods. Of course all heathen men are not invincible. The warriors of Wessex had won great glory when they wiped out many shiploads of heathen at Aclea only two years ago. But those men were not the Army. The Army was stronger than ever, for every summer more heathen came south to join it.

So far, the Army had not ventured into Italy. Here the danger came from another kind of heathen, the infidel Saracens who now held Sicily. Less than ten years ago they had pillaged Rome. Now Pope Leo had built new walls, to protect the Christian shrines across the river from the ancient city. The infidels could not get in again. In Rome everyone felt safe.

The child had heard a lot about these new walls. Last night the pilgrims in the Saxon School had talked of little else. Of course the whole party lodged in the hall of the Saxon School. He himself ranked as founder's kin, since the hall had been endowed by his great-great-great-great-uncle, King Ine, brother to his grandfather's grandfather's grandfather; this Ine had been buried in the church of Our Lady of the Saxons after he had abdicated to end his days in the Holy City. A King's son knows his ancestry, even when he is only four years old. The Saxon School, the corporation of Saxon residents and pilgrims in Rome, had been allotted a section of the new walls and a postern, as its share in the defence of the City.

This morning, secure behind the new walls, they had heard Mass in their own Saxon church and breakfasted in the common hall of the School. Now they were putting on their best clothes, in readiness for their audience with the Pope.

There had been a little trouble over these clothes, for the Saxons were accustomed to dress in bright colours. Sigenoth, captain of the escort, shone like a kingfisher in stripes of blue and green; but when Cutha the chaplain appeared in a mantle of sky-blue one of the priests of the School took him aside.

'The Pope likes the clergy to wear dark colours. It's in one of the Canons somewhere, I believe, though I forget the reference. Have you a brown mantle, and perhaps a dark-blue tunic?'

The chaplain was hurt in his dignity.

'This mantle was dyed in woad to get it to a clerical colour. Then I washed it a bit, so that it wouldn't look dingy. At court all the clerks wear yellow tunics.'

'Yes, but this is Rome. Remember St. Augustine's advice. I can lend you a dark tunic, and we'll send a boy to fetch a black mantle from the nearest cloister. Monks always wear black here. Don't take offence. We often have this trouble with newcomers from Britain.'

Grumbling, Cutha removed the mantle which it had taken him months to fade to a pleasing colour.

The child wore a scarlet hood and scarlet trousers. His tunic was grass-green, over a white linen shirt; the same green was repeated in the cross-gartering of his trousers, and in his shoes. Round his waist was a green leather belt; over his shoulder a baldric of soft white leather bore a purse of green silk and a little gold-hilted knife. On ceremonial occasions a King's son should wear a sword. But he was too small to carry a real sword and his father had decreed that it would be wasteful to make a miniature for a single function. At least all his companions were properly armed.

They would ride to the Lateran palace on the far side

of the river, in the old Rome of the pagan emperors. It was not a long journey, but to walk would be undignified. That fitted in very well, because a servant could walk all the way and lead the quiet horse that had been chosen to carry him. He could not be sure of controlling his horse, especially in a crowded and noisy city; but he might enjoy the dignity of riding alone, instead of being hoisted on a warrior's saddlebow or carried in the pannier of a mule. Shortly before midday they set out.

The companions stared curiously about them, talking together in low tones. Rome was not so thronged and prosperous as gay, German-speaking Pavia, where they had rested so pleasantly after crossing the mountains; but even a northern warrior could see that it had once been the greatest city in the world.

'How sheer that wall stands,' said Sigenoth. 'Look, it must have been smoothed with the chisel from top to bottom. And what are those marks high above the street? Can they be letters? An odd place to put writing.'

'Yes, letters, they must be,' answered the chaplain. 'Though we don't form our letters in that way nowadays. Let me see. I can just make out IMP TRIB, but there's moss over the first word. It's the name of an emperor, and perhaps a date.'

'But why stick it up in the street?' Sigenoth persisted.

'I suppose because at one time everyone who lived in this city could read. Amazing to think of, isn't it? But then Rome is an amazing place even now.'

The child listened with awe. A city in which everyone could read! Perhaps they could fly as well, and turn stones to gold?

Then he was being helped off his horse. The dismounted escort formed up round him, and they all marched into the great hall. At the far end, on a dais, was a table covered with a clean white cloth; and behind it on a carved marble throne sat the Vicar of God on earth.

Leo, Bishop of Rome, was a good man, even a child

7

could see that; so he did not feel frightened. But this was the most important of all the grown-ups, so you listened to him carefully and took pains with your answer. He had glanced at a tablet before he greeted you, which went to show that so many King's sons came to see him that he found it hard to keep track of them. But he found the right entry on the tablet, and his greeting was kindly.

An interpreter repeated his words in clear Saxon.

'You are the youngest son of the King of the West Saxons, in Britain? I see you bring splendid gifts. I hope you will be happy in Rome, and that as you dwell among our holy relics your virtue will increase. Now tell me your name, young prince.'

He knew from the poems how such a question should be answered. In a strange hall you declared not only your name but your descent, so that your host could do you fitting honour. He took a deep breath and recited:

'I am Alfred, son of Ethelwulf, son of Egbert, son of Ealhmund, son of Eafa, son of Eoppa, son of Ingild, son of Cenred, son of Ceolwold, son of Cutha, son of Cuthwine, son of Ceawlin, son of Cynric, son of Creoda, son of Cerdic, son of Elesa, son of Esla, son of Gewis, son of Wig, son of Freawine, son of Freothogar, son of Brand, son of Baeldag, son of Woden, son of Frealaf, son of Finn, son of Godwulf, son of Geat, son of Taetwa, son of Beaw, son of Sceldwa, son of Heremod, son of Itermon, son of Hathra, son of Hawla, son of Bedwig, son of Sceaf, who was the son of Noah and born in the Ark. My father is King of the West Saxons, in the German parts of Britain.'

'This is the answer of the Pope,' said the interpreter, after he had put all this into Latin:

'You have a very noble ancestry. You must take care to be worthy of your ancestors. You are also a clever child, to remember so many names. His Holiness does not ask you to dine with him, because the food will not be suitable for one of your years. But he asks you to see him this evening, after supper, when he will talk with you about the problems of your Kingdom.'

'Please tell the Pope I'm the youngest. I shan't ever be a King. There's my brother Ethelbald and my brother Ethelbert and my brother Ethelred. I came just to bring my father's greetings and to learn the ways of the civilized world.'

He saw that his companions were pleased with his modesty, though the interpreter put it all into a very short Latin phrase.

In the evening he sat at the Pope's feet on a little stool. There was no one else in the chamber, except the interpreter and a page lounging by the door. At first the Pope spoke to him of the welfare of his soul, and he did not listen very closely; for there was nothing to be said on that subject which he had not heard from the priests at home. Presently Leo began to make plans for his stay in Rome, and that was more interesting.

'Now what can I do for you? Your father does not wish you to be a priest, so I can't give you holy orders. You were baptized years ago, and you are too young to be married. But there is no reason why I shouldn't confirm you. You are a bit young for it, but you know your catechism. Yes, that's it. Confirmed by the Pope in person. Not many boys in Britain can boast of that, though of course here in Rome it's common enough. Is there anything else we can do for him?' he added, speaking directly to the interpreter. 'Do you think he would like a Consulship?'

'For a King's son, my lord?' said the interpreter, raising his eyebrows. 'Rather a lowly honour, don't you think? Half a dozen of the notaries in the Curia have been Consuls, and the last one we promoted was a common Greek silk-merchant.'

'Never mind. In Britain there will be no other Roman Consuls. I can't anoint him King, since he has three elder brothers. He will enjoy being made a Consul. See if you

9

can find a sword small enough for him. It's obvious he feels ashamed to carry nothing but a knife.'

Then Pope Leo went back to his conversation with this enterprising little King's son; he told him of the relics and history of Rome, and suggested what he ought to see before he went back to the misty north.

There were a great many other children to be confirmed, and the ceremony went on and on until all he could feel was a blur of fatigue. St. Peter's was too big for the eyes of a child to take it in. He had an impression of groves of stone columns stretching away into the gloom, of candle-light shining on gold, of walls painted with figures and palaces. From the roof Christ in Majesty frowned down on the sinful world. When he first saw the mighty figure he cowered, imagining that he saw God reigning in Heaven; then he plucked up courage to peep through his fingers, and presently understood that the design had been made by thousands upon thousands of coloured marble squares. More evidence of the mastery of these astonishing Romans.

Now the Pope was being carried away in a litter, and the other children were making for the west door. But as he got to his feet the interpreter approached, beckoning him to follow the Pope into the sacristy.

By now Leo seemed an old friend. A kind man, holy, elderly, and fond of children; and at the same time a worshipful hero, who could design a mighty wall and if necessary hold it against the infidel. That he had to speak with him through an interpreter somehow made the conversation easier; it was less frightening than speaking direct into the ear of God's Vicar.

Of course the Pope spoke first. What he said must be important; for the interpreter transmitted the message formally like an ambassador, instead of repeating the gist of his words in Saxon.

'His Holiness wishes to confer on you the rank of a Consul of Rome. Long ago these Consuls ruled the City.

Now that our Bishop rules us a Consul has no duties, though he takes oath to defend Rome if need be, and to obey the Holy Father. Will you take such an oath?'

Pope Leo interrupted, as though to remind the interpreter of a further point.

'His Holiness will invest you with the insignia of your office and show you to the people in the portico of this church. That is all the ceremony. He will do it partly because you seem to him a good boy, partly as thanks to your father for his splendid gifts. Are you willing?'

The interpreter's careful explanation went over his head. He was too tired to understand it. He must swear to obey the Pope; but everyone ought to obey him, so that was easy. Now they were taking him back into the church, and down the nave to the portico at the west end. He followed meekly.

All the Saxons of his escort were waiting in the square, and most of the residents from the Saxon School. But there were only a few Roman loiterers; this Consulship was not such a very great thing after all.

Then a group of magnificent chamberlains were handing the Pope the insignia. A deacon spoke in Latin, slowly and distinctly, and he saw that he was expected to repeat the oath after him. It is unchancy to swear in a foreign tongue; you may be promising anything. But Pope Leo was a holy man, to be trusted; and anyway he was utterly in his power. He repeated the words of the oath, as well as his tongue could stumble through the outlandish combinations of consonants.

A muttered, perfunctory cheer rose from the little group of Romans who could understand what he was saying; and the Saxons cheered more loudly, because they were in the habit of cheering anything done by a King's son. As the Pope stood over him he sank uncertainly to one knee.

This was better than he had expected. A tunic of purple silk was slipped over his head, and a short cloak of purple wool fastened on his shoulder. Then the Pope bound a narrow fillet round his brow, a ribbon of white silk embroidered with gold thread; and, oh glory, the tall old man was bending down to fasten round his waist a red leather belt from which hung a real though miniature sword. He grasped it for a moment, to make sure it was not a dummy. It moved easily in the scabbard, and he saw an inch of sharp blue steel.

He was the Pope's man, there could be no doubt of it. He had accepted from him clothing, jewellery and arms, the gifts of a lord to his war-companion. Never mind. Soon he would go home, and in Wessex he would be fighting for the Church whenever he fought against the heathen. The Pope would not fetch him all the way from Britain to fight for Rome here in Italy.

Now the ceremony was over, but of course he might keep the robes and the sword. He wished he might ride in state through the streets of the City; but St. Peter's was only a short step from the Saxon School. Since he felt very tired he went back in comfort, carried on the shoulder of a warrior of his escort.

They let him stay up for supper, because it would have been cruel to undress him so soon after he had been girt with his first sword. He sat in the place of honour at the high table, while all the Britons in Rome crowded the hall of the Saxon School.

Of course they gave him nothing to eat but thin porridge, since roast pork at bedtime is not good for little boys; and the wine they brought him in a silver cup had been copiously watered. That was how it had been when he stayed up for other formal feasts on the journey. The surprise was the ceremony that accompanied the wine-cup.

Sigenoth, captain of the escort, bore it with his own hands, and presented it on bended knee; at the same time all the company shouted: 'Hail to the King.' Alfred burst into tears, for he thought they were mocking him. Godgifu, his nurse, came bustling from the pantry to comfort him. She carried him off in her arms, and put him straight to bed in the middle of supper; which made the sense of humiliation even worse.

But when Godgifu came back to the hall to rebuke the escort Sigenoth had his answer ready. 'Of course I wasn't mocking the child,' he said stoutly. 'We hailed him King because he is a King. Remember what the Pope has done to him today. He anointed him, didn't he? And then he fastened a diadem round his brow, and buckled a sword at his waist. I don't know how many times he gave him a special blessing, praying for his good fortune. Finally young Alfred repeated the King's oath, swearing to do justice and protect the weak. Or at least that's what they tell me he swore.'

'That's true,' Godgifu admitted, 'but it wasn't done all at once. The anointing was for his Confirmation.'

'He was anointed and crowned on the same day, in the same church, all in a matter of an hour or so,' Sigenoth persisted. 'Neither he nor the Pope left the church until all was done. That makes it a single ceremony, as I see it; and our companions think as I do. The Pope has made our little atheling a King. It's true that he hasn't a Kingdom as yet; perhaps we can win one for him as we travel home through Frankland.'

The captain of the escort saw it as an amusing coincidence, a humorous quibble. Some others in the hall, especially the foreigners from Mercia and Northumbria, were more impressed. They did not believe that the Pope had crowned Alfred as King of the West Saxons; but they supposed that Fate had foreshadowed a mighty destiny for him. Thus it had been in the old heathen days, when Woden visited the cradle of future hero.

Settled among his sheepskins, the tired little atheling fell asleep, muttering that he was not a King and half-wondering whether he was.

Before snow should close the passes they were on their way home again. The Pope had given them precious relics, a golden cross for the minster of the West Saxons at Winchester, and a letter to King Ethelwulf. So the journey had been completely successful.

For several days they halted in Pavia, where they could understand the German speech of the Lombards. It was the best place to buy mules to carry their baggage over the mountains. A Saxon monk who called on them, for you met Saxon monks in every town of northern Italy, insisted on showing the young atheling the grave of a Queen of Wessex. She had died a few years ago, penniless and alone; they would have buried her as a pauper if the community of Saxon pilgrims had not arranged a proper funeral. The monk had seen her buried, and daily he prayed for her soul.

'She was a very wicked woman, much in need of our prayers,' he explained. 'But she had been a very great lady, and the Saxon race would be dishonoured if she lacked a royal tomb. She was Eadburh, daughter of the mighty Offa, King of the Mercians. She was married to Beorhtric, King of the West Saxons, but she poisoned her husband and fled to the Franks. Charlemagne would not receive her at his court, though he made her abbess of a rich convent. Then she fled with a lover to Italy. After he had deserted her she lived here in Pavia as a harlot. She was penniless when she died.'

'We know the story,' Sigenoth interposed. 'Her husband had seized the rightful inheritance of our little atheling's grandfather. Egbert also took refuge with the great Charlemagne, until at length he succeeded to the Kingdom. In Wessex we shall never forget the wicked Queen Eadburh. In memory of her crimes we have had no other Queen. The wife of our King is known only as the Lady Osburh. She never wears a crown, or sits on a throne, or takes the chief place at a feast. We have no Queens, for fear that our luck might change. But this is an old story, from the days when King Egbert was young. It seems strange that you, who are not an old man, should have seen the burial of this wicked woman.'

'What you do in youth is never forgotten,' said the

monk. 'The wicked woman lived on for fifty years after her crime. When I knew her she was poor and old and very ugly. But men still pointed at her as the wicked and beautiful Queen of the West Saxons.'

During this exchange of reminiscences the atheling had said nothing, but seemed only interested in kicking a pebble round the edge of the grave. But that evening, as he rode to bed on Sigenoth's shoulder, he said: 'She was very bad, that beautiful Queen, wasn't she?'

'*Very* bad, atheling,' answered Sigenoth, wishing that the monk had been a little less explicit about Queen Eadburh's sins in the presence of his young lord.

'She was bad to my grandfather. But my mother is beautiful and she is very, very good. When I get home I shall give her my diadem because she has no crown. But *no one* can have my sword that the Pope gave me.'

2

The Lady Osburh

The shabby old house at Wantage could not compare with the royal hall at Winchester; but to all the family it was their real home. King Ine had given it to Ingild his brother, who was King Ethelwulf's grandfather's grandfather's father; and his heirs had continued to hold it even when Berkshire was subject to the King of the Mercians. All King Ethelwulf's children had been born there; the lady Osburh seldom left it, though the King must continually ride through his dominions. The escort of warriors was dismissed when they reached Winchester, but Alfred did not consider his journey finished until he had arrived at Wantage.

Mother was there, of course, and most of her children. In fact seven of the twelve children she had borne would never leave it, for they lay in the little chapel, awaiting the Resurrection. The Cerdingas were an unhealthy stock. Wise old men shook their heads and muttered that a family sprung from Woden, the devil who had led the heathen Saxons to Britain, could not prosper now that the land was Christian. All the same, Wessex was proud that her Kings still came from the ancient royal line, while the other German Kingdoms of Britain had fallen into the hands of usurpers sprung from nowhere. And it could not be denied that, if Cerdingas died young, those who reached manhood lived their brief lives with amazing energy.

Father was in Winchester, discussing the news brought by the embassy and trying once again to concert measures

17

against the Army with the King of the Franks. That was
a will-o'-the-wisp which kept him busy and careworn.
Anyone could see that international action was the best
way to drive back the Army to its northern home; but
when it came to the point it was much easier to pay the
Army to move into the next Kingdom, instead of fighting
the heathen again and again until your warband was
destroyed and you were weaker than your greedy neighbours. The Army always went away honestly when it
was paid, though of course it might come back again.

Alfred's eldest brother, Ethelbald, was also away. He
lived at Canterbury, where he ruled as his father's deputy
the dependent provinces of Wessex: Kent, Sussex, Surrey
and Essex. But then Ethelbald, at twenty-three, was a
man full grown, so much older than his brothers that
they scarcely regarded him as one of themselves. After
Ethelbald had come the seven dead Cerdingas, so that
the next one living was Ethelswitha.

At fifteen she was on the point of joining the grown-
up world. Soon after harvest she was to marry King
Burhed of the Mercians. But the younger boys thought
of her as one of themselves, or at least as much of a
companion as a mere girl could be. She was very wise,
and if you followed her advice you could nearly always
get out of scrapes when you had offended against the
incomprehensible code of the adult world.

Thirteen-year-old Ethelbert was the natural leader of
the children, including his elder sister. He and eight-year-
old Ethelred did everything together; but they had a
strong sense of family solidarity and they made room for
four-year-old Alfred. Many ties bound them together.
They were Cerdingas, of the race of Woden, better born
than any of their play-fellows; but they were far from the
succession, and could never expect to be more than sons
or brothers of a King. When they grew up it would be
their duty to fight for Wessex, and to advise the King if
he sought their advice. They would never hold the
absolute responsibility of Kingship.

Alfred was his father's favourite, and his mother's also. There was no disguising the curious fact. But they were sensible children, willing to forgive him an unfair advantage which he had never done anything to earn. He did not tell tales, or blatantly attempt to curry favour. Grown-ups have these curious fancies, and a wise child accepts them as he accepts the cold of winter. When Alfred came home they were all genuinely glad to see him, and eager to hear his stories of the great world.

Alfred was destined to be the clever one of the family; so much could be learned from his name. There must have been some prophecy at his birth, as in the old stories of Woden appearing at the cradle of some ancient hero. When he was a baby no one could have known whether he would be clever or stupid; and yet they had named him Alfred, Supernatural Counsel, instead of giving him the usual Ethel-name that denoted his royal descent. Neither mother nor father would ever explain how they had known, before his baptism, that one day the little baby would be wise.

Meanwhile there was a great deal to be learned, in a very short time. Cerdingas died young; but in compensation they lived hard in their youth. Their cheeks glowed pink and their eyes bright; they could not keep still, and their minds were as darting and alert as their bodies.

Alfred was already beginning to ride, which meant that he must learn about horses. Grooms feed a horse and keep him clean; and athelings can count on devoted service from the lower orders. But even a veteran groom does not know how much a good horse can do if he must, how much he has left in him when he seems utterly exhausted, what sort of rough country he can get over at a pinch; because grooms do not ride to war and trust their lives to a horse when they are in a tight place. Even if you are too young to carry a sword, you can learn these things by riding for long hours in all weathers.

Every day Alfred went hunting with his brothers; it

was exciting, and falls from his small pony seldom hurt him. Learning to manage hounds, and especially hawks, called for more patience. Hounds must be treated fairly, and you must never lose your temper with them. As for hawks, you must be prepared to sit endlessly under a tree, waiting for the tiresome creatures to remember their training and come to your lure. Sometimes it could be very tedious, but it was disgraceful for even a five-year-old to come home without his bird. Luckily his elder brothers were skilled huntsmen, always willing to help him; they said, in their kindly patronizing way, that he promised very well and might even one day surpass them.

In all his outdoor pursuits, as on every formal occasion, he was handicapped by a weakness not shared by any other member of the family. His bowels were always loose; from moment to moment he never knew when he would have to retire. It made things very awkward, especially during long services in church. The leeches held that it was the result of his long wet ride when he crossed the path of the Army on his way to Rome. At his age the infirmity was excusable, but if it persisted it would disable him.

With so many skills to be learned there was little time for formal lessons in the schoolroom. An atheling should be able to read; it was mildly discreditable to attest a charter without knowing what was in it. Even more important, an atheling should be able to hold his own at the supper table, when gleemen sing of the deeds of mighty ancestors. He must know the history of all the Cerdingas, and something about the other heroes of the German race: Dietrich of Bern, who ruled in Italy, and Beowulf, who ruled on the borders of the Danes. It was easy for Alfred to learn these heroic stories, since everyone he met could tell them by the hour; not only his brothers, but any casual groom or forester, could recite the lay of the death of Horsa at the battle of Aegelesthrep, or the heathen myth of the killing of Balder.

There was so much of wonder and splendour in the

world. His mind reached out to take in all that was offered: hunting, hawking, coursing, horsemanship, the qualities of a hero and the duties of a Christian.

Mere reading was more difficult. There was no reason why A should be shaped like a pyramid, or B like two buns; the eye which could so quickly recognize the track of a hare, the mind that so easily remembered intricate patterns of verse, had nothing to bite on. There was no sense behind the alphabet, it was purely a matter of remembering by rote. Try as he might, he could not remember it. His brothers, though they were older, were not much more at ease with their letters.

In the autumn the whole family assembled at the border town of Chippenham for the marriage of Ethelswitha to King Burhed of the Mercians. The bridegroom brought a great train of companions, very well armed and splendidly dressed. But Mercian nobles could never be the equals of West Saxons, for in Mercia they had overthrown the ancient line of Woden-descended Kings, submitting themselves to the rule of the strongest sword. A West Saxon gleeman had put it very effectively, in an unkind jingle which Alfred repeated proudly to his brothers; Ethelbert capped it even more unkindly, saying that if Burhed was indeed the strongest sword in Mercia the Mercians must be in a very bad way.

All the same, Burhed was a decent young man, with a kind expression and pleasant manners; he was said to be a good Christian and a man of honour, who would give his young Queen all the respect that was her due.

In this gathering of noblemen and athelings the Cerdingas showed as a race apart, distinct from the ordinary Germans of southern Britain. All had the same bright pink cheeks, whether their skins were browned by the sun or white from sitting over embroidery in the ladies' bower; their hair was the same shade of pale gold; all were slender, though tall and vigorous. The older they were the thinner they became. King Ethelwulf, at forty-seven, was much slighter than Ethelbald, his twenty-three-year-old heir.

But the real distinguishing mark of the family was a peculiar barking cough; as they sat together at the high table the sound of their coughing, and of their eager conversation, would tell any stranger that this was the hall of the West Saxon King. Mercians by comparison seemed stolid and peasant-like.

Looking at those dark, heavy-jowled Mercians, 'like so many bag-puddings', King Ethelwulf decided to wake them up by showing them what a Cerdinga could do, even a very young Cerdinga. 'You there, young Alfred,' he called down the table, banging with his drinking horn for attention.

'Sir!' Alfred jumped to his feet. Now that he was no longer bolstered up on a pile of cushions his head was not very far above the table.

'It shall be your turn next. Let's hear how you sing. One of the old lays, you know them all. Choose which you like, my boy.'

The child's head whirled. How unfair of father to call on him, the youngest, to entertain this grand company! His brothers would only forgive him if he did it superbly. What should he sing? He looked round at the company. Ethelswitha smiled and nodded encouragement. A lot of pig-faced Mercians crowded behind her. He knew what he would choose.

'Well, Alfred, what's it to be?'

'The Lay of the Death of Cynewulf, sir.'

He saw Ethelred give a little start of comprehension; these Mercians would hear how West Saxons kept faith with their lords.

A thane lifted him on to a stool. He threw out his hand in a gesture to the harper and began to declaim. With short plucked notes the harp marked the rhythm of the verse.

The poem opened with a flowery description of the glorious land of the West Saxons, and of the riches and power of Cynewulf, its King. In highflown language, so highflown that it was hard to understand unless you were familiar with the epic style, the lay told how Cynewulf had won the throne from his kinsman Sigebert; and how Sigebert lurked as an outlaw in the Weald until he was murdered by a swineherd, who was himself avenging the murder of his lord. But Sigebert left a brother, the atheling Cyneheard.

All this was the introduction, in which the poet strove to impress his hearers by the number of strained metaphors he could invent. Now came the story proper. The poet told it baldly and laconically, leaving his hearers to supply appropriate sentiments from their own hearts.

The boy stood straight on his stool, his eyes fixed on the sooty roof. His voice rang clear and high, without obvious expression. This is how things fell out, it said, this is life as it is lived by the heroes.

'The King went to Merton to visit his leman in her bower. The atheling Cyneheard heard of it, and came there with his companions. Before the King's men were aware of them they had surrounded the bower. Alone, the King defended the door of the bower, until he recognized the atheling. Then the King rushed out and fought with the atheling, and wounded him. But the atheling's companions killed the King.

'In the hall the King's companions heard the keening of women in the bower. They ran out, each man as he armed himself. The atheling offered them quarter if they would flee, and money if they would serve him. But they fought until all were killed; save for one Welshman, a hostage, and he was sore wounded.

'In the morning other companions of the King heard of it. Their leaders were Wigfrith the thane and Osric the alderman.' (He smiled at his mother, for he told of her grandfather.) 'The atheling offered them money and land if they would serve him as King, and reminded them that among his companions were many of their kinsmen. They answered that no kinsman was dearer to them than their lord, and that they could not serve his slayer. But they offered to allow their own kinsmen to go free and unharmed.

'Their kinsmen among the companions of the atheling answered: "We shall not yield, any more than did your comrades yesterday who were slain with the King." Then the companions of King Cynewulf stormed the gate, and killed the atheling and all his companions; all except one, who was the godson of Osric the alderman. Osric saved his life, though he was sorely wounded.

'Cynewulf the King is buried at Winchester and Cyneheard at Axminster; two athelings of the right line of Cerdic.'

The boy's voice was silent. The last note of the harp died away. In silence the company reflected on the obligation of loyalty as it was understood in Wessex.

Ethelwulf was very nearly a great King, but somehow his wise plans never took effect. Perhaps that was because he planned so carefully for the future that he neglected what must be done today. This new alliance with Mercia ought to have strengthened the West Saxons; in fact they were asked to help the Mercians against the Welsh, and themselves got no help in return. By the time Alfred was six he had grown used to hearing mild grumbles against his father's policy. Aldermen complained that the King was too clever by half. All these alliances were a waste of time and money. When Wessex alone had fought the heathen, at Aclea a few years ago, the heathen had been destroyed. Fight small parties of heathen, and if the whole Army comes pay it to go away; that was the best that any King could do. Even Charlemagne had not been able to drive the heathen right away from Frankland.

But these negotiations with foreign powers made the royal household a more lively place. Envoys paid frequent visits, and a most fascinating foreigner came to live permanently in Winchester. This was Felix, the Frankish clerk in charge of the King's Latin correspondence. Felix had been born in Flanders; he easily picked up the Saxon form of his native language. But he knew Latin so thoroughly that he could translate into Saxon as he read; just as he could take dictation in Saxon and write it down in Latin without ever pausing to fumble for a phrase. During that summer all the children were with their father in Winchester, since there was no campaign; Alfred would sit in the office, hearing the queer jumbled black marks come alive as Felix read them. Such a power of reading and translation seemed to him the most wonderful talent in the world.

It was a difficult business, and to learn it took a very long time. Felix never rode to war, or went hunting. It seemed that if you wanted to write well you had no time to do anything else; and he himself had to learn all the duties of an atheling, in the forest, in the stables, and on the battlefield.

The boys had a tutor of their own, who was supposed to teach them to read Saxon. They heard so much Latin in church that they knew the meaning of a good many words, without bothering about grammar. But their reading, even in Saxon, went very slowly; it seemed they would never make the big jump between recognizing single letters and combining them into sentences.

King Ethelwulf did not care. His heir, Ethelbald, could read Saxon well enough; for the younger athelings such learning was superfluous, though a good thing if they could manage it. The lady Osburh took the situation more to heart. One morning, as they sat down to a brief half-hour of lessons before joining the hunt, she came into the chamber. Each boy had a prayer scratched in large letters on the tablet before him, and tried to say it over to himself. It was hard to find fresh prayers for them to read, since of course they knew the usual ones by heart.

'Oh dear, you never seem to get any better, and the horses will be round in a few minutes,' Osburh said with a sigh.

'It's because these prayers are so dull,' complained Ethelbert. 'There's no shape to them, if you see what I mean. I have to read each letter separately, and can't guess what the next word will be.'

'I suppose they are dull, when you're not really praying,' his mother agreed. 'But it would be wasteful to give you real books, when you would only cover them with dirty finger-marks. Besides, people don't write interesting books in Saxon; all the good books are written in Latin, so you couldn't understand them even if you could read them. Clerks who can write well think it a waste of time to write down our poems, though I like to read them when I get the chance. Would *you like to read them?*'

The boys brightened at the suggestion. They knew a great many poems by heart, as every nobleman should; but when you forgot a passage it was tiresome to track down someone who could remind you of it, and even worse to try to bridge the gap with your own composition. A book of German poems would be a valuable treasure.

'I have a book here,' their mother continued, 'a book of heroic poems in our own Saxon. I bullied a clerk into writing it, though he complained that such stuff was beneath the attention of an educated man. There are pictures at the bottom of each page, and in the margin; and the initial letters are painted crimson and gold. I will give this book as a prize to the first of you who can tell me the poems in it. Do you agree? It will encourage you to get on with your reading.'

'The one who can first say all the poems gets the book?' asked Alfred.

His mother smiled assent, and his brothers murmured their gratitude. But at that moment grooms brought round the horses and they all made for the door. German poetry was interesting, and a painted book was a very fine prize; but nothing ought to interfere with the serious business of hunting.

That same evening Alfred got hold of the beautiful painted book. He took it off to the stuffy little chamber where his tutor was copying a despatch. He persuaded the man to read the poems to him, over and over again; that was a much quicker way to learn them than to try to read out their long words, letter by letter, with his own eyes.

All these poems followed the same pattern. A hero lived in great prosperity, usually at the court of some wealthy King. Then honour compelled him to fight a dangerous foe. Perhaps he was victorious, but if so some other task must be performed immediately after the victory. In the end the hero, overmatched, went down fighting gallantly. For every one of those old stories had an inspiring but unhappy ending.

Once you were at home in the rich epical language half of the narrative could be filled out from stock. The King's hall, the hero's sword, armour and horse, were always described in much the same string of stately adjectives. What you really needed to remember was the hero's name, the name of the King he served, and the names of his enemies; and the pictures and initial letters of the book called these easily to mind.

That night Alfred went to sleep chanting to himself the lay of Alfred Cerdinga, a young hero who lived in the hall of King Ethelwulf until he went out to fight the heathen pirates; in his mind the words fell into place with hardly an effort, though the white, silky-coated charger who bore the young hero to battle, decked in the red leather trappings he had seen on the Pope's mule, bore no resemblance to the sturdy hunters which filled his father's stable.

A week later the lady Osburh dropped in again to see how her sons were getting on with their lessons. Springing to his feet, Alfred launched into heroic poetry. As he recited he turned the leaves of the gorgeous painted book, partly to help his memory by a glance at the pictures, partly to encourage the transparent pretence that he was

27

reading. He continued without faltering until the last page; and since he held the only copy no one could check his deviations from the text.

When he had finished his mother had to admit that he had fairly won the prize. Nothing had been said about reading the book, though that was what she had meant. She was glad to know that a son of hers shared her delight in the poems which praised the mighty ancestors.

His parents doted on Alfred, and even his elder brothers thought him less tiresome than most small boys. He was handsome and graceful, though not especially strong; his singing voice was true, and he played the harp better than most children of his age. But what was most remarkable about him was that sometimes he questioned what was told to him by his elders.

'The *were* of a King is five thousand mancuses. You must remember that, or you will not know all the *weres*, which would be disgraceful in an atheling.'

'But no kindred could pay five thousand pieces of gold. There isn't so much gold in all Britain. Besides, who would accept *were* for a slain King? If my father were killed do you think his companions would hold out their hands for money? In the story of Cynewulf and Cyneheard both sides offered money and land, but the companions fought on. It's silly to talk of *were* for the killing of a King.'

'Never mind. The *were* of a King is five thousand mancuses. Everyone must have a *were*, or the law would not be complete. An atheling must know the law, so you must learn the *weres*.'

King Ethelwulf went about Wessex telling his subjects what a clever boy he had in his youngest son; and the lady Osburh did not hide her belief that he was more intelligent and charming than his brothers. Little Alfred became intolerably conceited.

One day at dinnertime a deputation of ploughmen sought an audience with him. They were peasants from one of his own villages and they brought him a present of gaily-coloured finches in a painted wooden box; in return they wanted their six-year-old lord to make their village masshouse into a real parish church, with a lodging for a priest who would always be on hand to shrive the dying and baptize the new-born.

But it was dinnertime, and he was hungry. He told the steward to chase away the smelly group of yokels who came between an atheling and his dinner. 'I am a Woden-born Cerdinga, and I should pass my time in the company of thanes and King's companions. Those ploughmen are not worthy to come into my presence. This is a royal hall, where only noblemen are welcome.'

A grubby, horny, chapped hand boxed his ear most painfully, and he jumped round to see a tall monk standing over him. He recognized the monk and knew he had every right to be there, even by the standard he had just laid down. This was his cousin Neot, a Woden-born Cerdinga and a monk of St. Benedict. He had come to Winchester, as he came often, to beg for his minster.

'That was base, little Alfred, and a disgrace to our kindred. These are your men and you are their lord. If you will not hear their plea to whom can they bring it? But your conduct was worse than ignoble, it was wicked and unchristian. These men are also your neighbours. You have been guilty of a grievous sin. If you repent the sin will not bar you from Heaven, but none the less you must atone for it. In the next world your punishment will be very heavy, unless God is gracious enough to punish you in this life. That may come to pass. Perhaps one day you will find yourself homeless and penniless, landless, with no fine clothes, no warm hall, no savoury smell of dinner waiting for you, your only companions peasants such as these men whom you have despised. If that should happen, then thank God, and the monks of St. Benedict, that you are avoiding the pains of Purgatory by making atonement for your sins during your brief life on earth.'

Cousin Neot looked very terrible, standing there in his coarse black cowl, pointing with a grimy, broken-nailed forefinger. Everyone knew he had been granted the gift of prophecy, and at that moment he looked as though he were in God's intimate confidence. Weeping, little Alfred rushed to the privy. The looseness of his bowels had come back in full force, as usual at any critical moment.

Henceforth Alfred took special pains to be gracious to his social inferiors. Within a few years the effort had become second nature, so that those who knew him in after life found it hard to believe that a holy man had been driven to rebuke him for the sin of pride. The prophecy was not so easily forgotten. All Wessex remembered what Neot had foretold, that one day the atheling Alfred might be friendless and penniless. But that kind of thing came to many of the race of Cerdic; in the meantime he was the King's favourite son, and a likeable child. Courtiers smiled at him, and even his brothers were not jealous.

In those days the Army still ravaged in Frankland. Britain was an unlucky hunting-ground for pirates. At Aclea King Ethelwulf and the warband of Wessex had killed them by thousands; and far off in the north, it was said, King Aelle of the Northumbrians had thrown the famous pirate Ragnar Leatherbreeks into a pit filled with serpents, where he perished miserably. In Ireland the heathen carried all before them, and they plundered the coast of Wales. But southern Britain, where they got more hard knocks than booty, they avoided.

3

Travels with Father

Since there was no pressing danger to his realm King Ethelwulf decided to perform his long-delayed pilgrimage to St. Peter. His journey would take him through Frankland, where he could conclude that alliance with the King of the West Franks which was the chief aim of his foreign policy. The atheling Ethelbald, now twenty-five-years old, could govern Wessex as his deputy. The King wished to take his lady with him, but Osburh was in poor health. In the end he decided to take only one member of his family, the six-year-old Alfred. The boy would profit by a second journey, now that he was old enough to understand what he saw; and his intelligence was already evident.

Rome was the destination, but a meeting with the King of the Franks was equally important. A day's journey inland from Quentavic they found King Charles waiting to receive them. They had passed by roofless halls and ruined churches, but the mud cottages of the peasants had been repaired and there were men working in the fields; for the Army had moved on to fresh pastures in the south-east.

King Charles was the grandest personage Alfred had ever seen, far grander and more imposing than the Pope. He sat on a tall throne of carved wood, surrounded by jewelled warriors; his robes were of silk, a gift to the great Charlemagne from Greekland; and his golden crown and golden bracelets had also been worn by the mighty Emperor. But the crown was an open circlet, so that above it you could see the King's bald skull; for he had never achieved the closed crown which was the mark of the Emperor of the West.

While he knelt to watch his father receive the formal embrace that Kings grant only to their equals Alfred fouled his trousers. The courtiers made allowance for his age; he was smuggled out quietly to wash and change his clothes. But the accident made him miserable for days after. His servants tried to comfort him, suggesting that he had not got over the effects of his hurried ride in wet trousers during his first journey; but he himself felt that God had sent this special affliction to punish him for his sins. He feared that all his life he would be humiliated by this absurd weakness of his bowels, which attacked him whenever he needed to look dignified. At six years old he could count on forgiveness; but when he was a grown and responsible atheling he would have to keep away from ceremonial functions.

Apart from this disgusting mishap, and the constant apprehension that it would come again at the most inconvenient moment, he enjoyed his stay at the court of King Charles. It was a long stay, for that highly mobile household journeyed with the King of the West Saxons all the way to the border of Septimania.

His father and King Charles got on well together. They rode side by side on the short stages of the daily journey, and sat in deep discussion after supper. No one would pretend that the Kingdom of the West Saxons was as powerful or important as the Kingdom of the Neustrian Franks, but King Charles took the view that all independent crowned Kings are equal to one another. Alfred did not know what they talked about; but it seemed likely that father was not making much progress with his scheme for united international action against the Army.

Of course Alfred could not follow the conversation of nobles from Burgundy and Aquitaine, who spoke the same Romance dialect as their peasants; but the ancestral Frankish of Neustria and Flanders was near enough to

Saxon for a quick-witted boy to pick it up in a week or so.

Ordinary Frankish courtiers seldom spoke of the Army. This year the lands by the Loire were undisturbed, for the heathen were plundering the valleys of the Meuse and the upper Seine. No one in Frankland proposed to do anything about it. The Franks seemed to regard the Army as a natural disaster, like hailstorms at vintage. Victims of heathen rapacity were deserving objects of charity; but the Army was just one of the facts of life in a fallen world, and Christians were wasting their time if they plotted to destroy it.

Though they did not discuss the Army, the courtiers talked incessantly of war. What interested them was the prospect of reuniting the wide realm of Charlemagne by the conquest of Lotharingia and Austrasia. That might happen at any moment, if only their King would show a little more energy in making war on his kindred. All experienced politicians knew that the Army was invincible; you paid it to go away, you did not fight it.

The court had drifted slowly as far as the Rhone when a weary messenger brought news from Wessex. King Ethelwulf and his clerks studied the letters in a little chamber behind the hall; presently the King came out alone to the sunny porch, and sent for his son.

'There's bad news for us both, my boy,' he began, in the gentle unnatural tone some adults use in speaking to children. 'Distressing news, but also important for our future. We must think it over prudently, and not give way to unmanly grief. Ethelbald writes that your mother took to her bed with a fever; after three days of illness she was dead. Bishop Swithun shrove her. By this time she will be buried in the minster at Winchester. Poor Osburh, she was young to die; younger than me, and I am not an old man. But this sad event alters many things, and in particular the future I had planned for you.'

Ethelwulf's bumbling voice died away. Normally he

was so interested in his own conversation that he did not notice its effect on his hearer; now even he could see that young Alfred was not listening.

The boy sobbed passionately, his hands clasping a pillar of the porch. While he was away his mother had been stolen from him. Every day he noted some new thing for the pleasure of telling her about it when he came home; and now he would never speak to her again. She had been *his* mother, in a very special sense; his brothers were indeed her children, but he had been the favourite, as they themselves admitted without envy or rancour. She had been closer to him than any other human creature, and he had been her chosen companion. He was old enough to recognize that in the nature of things he was likely to survive her; but this sudden death when he did not know that she was ill, this burial when he could not even see the closing of the tomb, the knowledge that he had been feasting in Frankland while she was in her last agony, made it all seem peculiarly poignant. And now father was talking as though this was merely some political upset on which the Cerdingas must take counsel together. That was the final crowning sorrow. Suddenly he saw King Ethelwulf as a doddering fool, and reminded himself sharply that God had commanded him to honour his father. But the same commandment bade him honour his mother also, and he felt that his father was honouring her too lightly. He gulped down his tears and looked up at King Ethelwulf. Never again would he see his father as the representative of Cerdic the Conqueror, leader of the potent warband of the West Saxons, the victor of Aclea. Henceforth the King would be in his eyes a silly old man who mumbled trivialities when he ought to be mourning the lovely dead.

Luckily the court was moving on and he could sit his pony or lie in his litter, alone with his grief among a crowd of servants. Until the evening he could pray for his mother's soul, recalling her grace and wit and kindness.

When his father again sought him he was lying in his narrow pallet-bed, munching his child's supper of sweet cake and watered wine. Soon would begin the formal supper in hall, and next day they would take leave of King Charles. So although King Ethelwulf had plenty to say he must be brief.

'As I told you this morning, my boy, this sad news makes a difference to my plans for both of us. We are making this journey to pray at the tomb of St. Peter; but even more to strengthen the Frankish alliance. Poor Osburh and I had talked it over. We had agreed that, if King Charles approved of you, we should ask him to find a baby Frankish princess for you to marry. The little girl would be brought up in Wessex, and that would forge a bond between Franks and Saxons. It seems there is no baby available. That's the sort of thing you never find out unless you visit a foreign court in person. The clerks who draft official despatches can never bother to keep track of baby girls.'

The King had been gazing mournfully at his son. Now he twirled his moustache and squared his shoulders.

'But while I talked with King Charles this afternoon – we rode quite alone, even the bodyguard was out of hearing, which I take as a very high compliment to the West Saxons – as we talked together King Charles pointed out that I am a widower, free to marry again. It so happens that he himself has a daughter, who is very nearly ready for a husband. Of course that makes her too old for you, my boy. In short, he proposed that on my way back from Rome I should marry his daughter Judith, who will be thirteen in the spring. The wedding will of course take place next year. Think it over, my dear boy, and be ready to give your stepmother a welcome when you meet her. Now I must hurry back to the hall, or I shall keep King Charles waiting. That would be bad manners from the guest of honour at our last supper in Frankland.'

Alfred lay awake, staring into the rafters of this foreign

chamber. Not only was his mother dead; his father had already forgotten her. He was preparing to replace her with a strange young princess, a princess young enough to be his daughter.

In high summer King Ethelwulf and Alfred his son reached Rome. For the honour of the West Saxons they brought rich gifts. For St. Peter there was a golden crown, two basins of gold for the handwashing during Mass, and two little golden images of saints. In the treasury of the church Ethelwulf placed a sword with a golden hilt, four silver lamps, and many lengths of embroidered silk. For St. Paul, whose shrine lay outside the walls, there were four silver sanctuary lamps. The King gave purses of gold to the nobles and higher clergy of the city, and his companions scattered silver pennies among the poor. The church of Our Lady of the Saxons, and the hall of the Saxon School, were lavishly repaired and redecorated.

But there was no papal reception for the royal pilgrims. The saintly Pope Leo was lately dead, and the whole city was disordered by the threat of a disputed election. Crowds suborned by foreign gold rioted in support of the wicked Cardinal Anastasius until the Schools were mustered in arms to keep order. At length the electors did their duty, and in the course of a hot and stormy September, Benedict III was chosen to fill the Chair of Peter.

Through the following winter and spring the Cerdingas remained in Rome. Young Alfred could observe the magnificence of the Church's liturgical year, as it was celebrated with the most elaborate ritual in the west. He saw the quiet penitential waiting of Advent, the sudden glory of Christmas, the long gloom of Lent, the fasting and mourning of Holy Week that gave way to the miracle of Easter. In the great churches built long ago by Constantine the ceremonial was performed with imperial dignity.

Much of old Rome, on the left bank of the Tiber, was

far gone in decay; grass grew thick round the paving-stones until squatters grazed their cattle in what had been the Forum. But on the right bank the new city of the Popes, the city fortified by the holy Leo, was visibly the busy centre of Christendom. From Ireland, from Spain, from the newly won lands by the Elbe, bishops, pilgrims, and great rulers came to pray at the tomb of Peter. Everyone who came from lands north of the Alps complained of the ravages of the Army; but no one was willing to fight it. The Army might be a scourge sent by God as punishment for sin, or it might be an agent of the Devil, who has power to afflict mortal men on earth, according to the point of view of the speaker. But the Army was *there*. By heavy payment you might persuade it to move into the next Kingdom; it was futile to withstand it with the sword.

What really interested Roman politicians was the death of the Emperor Lothar, and the division of his wide realm. Perhaps King Charles of Neustria might yet draw together all the dominions of the mighty Charlemagne. Intelligent men could discuss that sort of thing with learning and subtlety. No one could foretell the movements of the Army; it was an unpleasant topic anyway, best left in obscurity.

Under Pope Benedict there was a fair degree of public order; or at least the armed men who rioted through the streets were political rebels, not brigands, and unlikely to molest a young pilgrim of royal birth. Alfred visited the famous relics of antiquity, the tall many-columned temples and the long porticoes heavy with deep-cut carving. These were very fine things, such as no man of this degenerate age could imitate. But what really took his fancy were the little modern churches. These were small enough to be comprehensible; you could even translate their brick and marble into the timber and clay of Wessex. Within, their walls glittered with pictures of saints, made with little cubes of marble. Underneath the pictures were written the names of these saints, for the people who prayed in these churches could read.

Now there was a thing you might copy at home. Not the mosaic, of course, for in Wessex we have no marble. But surely you could paint such pictures on a white plaster wall? The men who had drawn and coloured that lovely book of poems, his book, the book his mother had given him for a prize, the book he would keep for the rest of his life in memory of her – those skilful men could paint a wall as well as they painted a sheet of vellum.

He would make it his task to see that the churches of Wessex glowed as splendidly, in their provincial plaster and paint, as did the churches of Rome, glorified with marble. For that he must foster learning, he must make artists his friends. When he was grown up, and one of his brother occupied the throne of the West Saxons, he would be rich enough to support many painters.

Unless, indeed, the Army should come to Wessex and reduce all the house of Cerdic to beggary. That also might come to pass.

At Pentecost King Ethelwulf took his following to pray at the tomb of his predecessor, King Ine. This tomb had the place of honour in the church of Our Lady of the Saxons, the church rebuilt more than a century ago by Ine's munificence. Only a great and wise King can leave his people in peace and prosperity while he prepares for his end near the shrines of the Apostles. That King Ine had ended his days peacefully in Rome, while Wessex continued in peace during his absence, was the greatest glory of the West Saxons.

Then, with the blessing of Pope Benedict, King Ethelwulf set out for Frankland.

Presently they found the court of King Charles, who had come specially to meet them. Once more King Ethelwulf was received in great honour; and while the wine went round at the end of a lavish feast the lady Judith was produced for inspection by her prospective husband.

Young Alfred saw her also, though he had no seat at the feast. Gossip among the servants had told him that she might appear, so he squatted down behind a serving table in a corner of the hall. It was past his bedtime, but his servant was a shy man who would hesitate to break into a royal banquet. That was one of the advantages of increasing years; the nurse who had looked after him on his first journey abroad would have snatched him away under the eyes of a dozen Kings.

He saw Judith enter, bearing a cup of wine for her father's distinguished guest. A waiting woman walked beside her, and she did no more than present the cup with a curtsey and walk straight out again; for the later stages of a long drinking-party is no time for a young girl to dally with the men. She came only to be seen; Alfred saw her well, and disliked what he saw.

Judith had the pink-and-white complexion, blue eyes, and golden hair that are expected in any German princess. She was thirteen, but her figure was that of a child. She moved gracefully, her composure mingled with enough maidenly shyness to make all the grown men feel pleasantly protective. King Ethelwulf in particular was delighted with her.

But to Alfred she seemed a sulky girl, a greedy girl, a selfish, conceited, proud, unfriendly little rival for the affection of his foolish father. It was unbearable that she should steal the place of his darling mother. Surely even the grown-ups, their sensibilities blunted by years of over-eating, over-drinking, and over-boasting, could see her as the horrid little minx she really was.

He crept back to the buttery, where his servant found him and hustled him away. The servant, who had been drinking the health of the new Lady of Wessex, blundered as he prepared his lord for bed. That was another black mark to add to Judith's score.

In bed he lay crying quietly to himself. Before his eyes he called up the image of mother bending over him to settle him for the night. He tried hard to picture her in

Heaven, where she must be (though he had just been praying dutifully for the welfare of her soul in Purgatory). But he found it impossible to picture what the saints in Heaven did with their time while they waited for time, and the world, to stop. He was sure that mother was watching him, and doing what she could for his welfare. But how could she be happy in Heaven while her children were unhappy on earth?

He would not hate his father. That would give pain to mother, who had loved her husband as she had loved the rest of her family. He would do his best not to hate even this Judith, for hate is a mortal sin and mother grieved when her children sinned. But he would judge Judith fairly, not making the excuses that an honourable man makes for the failings of his kindred. Judith was not his kin, and an atheling of the house of Cerdic owed her neither favour nor filial affection.

King Ethelwulf was a devout Christian, who kept the commandments to the best of his ability. In his youth he had made a suitable alliance with the daughter of a noble Jutish house, and as a husband he had been a great deal more faithful to his marriage-vows than were some Kings with the same opportunities. He had been fond of the lady Osburh, and now that she was dead he missed her. But she had not been remarkably beautiful, and the fact that she was more intelligent than he did not endear her to him. She had been a good wife; but then, thank God, Wessex was full of good and dutiful wives. He could not see that to his children she had been the most important person in the world, when to him she had been no more than the Lady he had chosen from half a dozen young women of appropriate rank.

A Christian King cannot flaunt a mistress, especially when he has just made the pilgrimage to Rome. But a vigorous King aged forty-eight does not want to sleep alone for the rest of his life. He had found a suitable replacement, of even higher rank and with valuable family connexions. Luckily she was also personally attractive, though he would have married her if she had been humpbacked and squinting. He told himself that he expected his son to see the matter in the same neutral, unexcited light.

But he could not avoid embarrassing moments. The morning came when young Alfred, blushing with shyness, but his eyes bright and hard, asked to speak privately with him. Alone with his father he rushed breathlessly into speech.

'I know, sir, that you don't like us to tell tales, but there is something I must tell you that Judith, I mean the lady Judith, keeps on doing.' Seeing his father scowl, he hurried on.

'I'm sure she means no harm, sir. She's a Frankish princess and doesn't know our customs. But she says she's to be Queen, she calls herself Queen of the West Saxons – I heard her, truly I did. And her ladies too, they go about talking of "our Queen Judith". And they shouldn't should they, father? Because we *don't have Queens in Wessex*.'

'Well now,' Ethelwulf shuffled uneasily, 'you seem to be getting very excited over nothing. It's true as far as it goes, of course. We don't have Queens. But it's a modern rule, quite modern, introduced to deal with a particular case. The King may change the customs of his court, especially in little matters of this kind. Remember, I won't be introducing anything new. The really ancient custom is to honour the King's wife with the title of Queen. No one can object when I bring the custom of our mighty ancestors.'

'We haven't had a Queen since the wicked Eadburh. Mother was never styled Queen, and you didn't mind.'

'It's only seventy years since Queen Eadburh came to Wessex. There are men living who saw her as an old woman in Pavia. You can't call that a really ancient custom. Your mother was not exactly of royal birth; her father was steward to the Kings of Wessex, and he could

41

trace his line back to the Kings of the Jutes who once reigned in the Isle of Wight; but it is a long time since there have been Kings in the family. Judith has been a princess since she was born. Her mother is Queen of the Western Franks. Her father takes it for granted that when she gets to Wessex she will be a Queen, and if I don't give her the title he may break off the match.'

'Father, the West Saxons won't like it. And my brothers . . .'

'Never mind who likes it and who doesn't,' the King burst out. 'I'm your King and your father, and you'll obey me!'

'Yes, father, we must obey you.'

'Of course you must. I should think so, indeed. Just because you have been twice to Rome you are a great deal too free with your advice, young Alfred. You will give your stepmother all the deference due to a Queen. And don't go telling the Franks that we have no Queens in Wessex. King Charles knows nothing of that bad recent custom, and I don't want him to worry about it.'

There was no more to be said. Alfred bowed acknowledgement of his father's command. This wicked stepmother, younger than some of her stepchildren, would have privileges that his own mother had lacked.

But someone among the large West Saxon escort must have tattled. King Charles learned of the difficulty that might face his young daughter, and took steps to overcome it. When the court reached Verberie on the River Oise he planned a marriage ceremony that would ensure all due honour for his daughter. Archbishop Hincmar of Rheims would marry Judith to King Ethelred, and at the same time place on her head a golden crown. The universal church would see her as a Queen, and then the remote and barbarous West Saxons must follow the precedent.

The wedding was a gorgeous and elaborate affair. To the atheling Alfred was granted the honour of bearing the Queen's train. For this he was dressed in a tunic of fine red wool embroidered with gold thread, and a cloak of blue silk. At his waist he carried the short sword Pope Leo had given him.

When it came to the point the West Saxon escort cheered as loudly as any Frank. Afterwards there was a very lavish feast, though the food had been brought from afar because the country round about had not yet recovered from the ravages of the Army.

On their journey to the coast King Ethelwulf showed himself to be a besotted and undignified husband. His wife gave him orders, even in the presence of veteran warriors. She was loaded with jewellery, and over her kerchief wore the golden circlet that marked her as a Queen. But her women whispered to the maidservants, who passed it on to the warriors, that this was still no true marriage; in body Queen Judith was still a child.

4

Brothers United

Judith hated the sea, so they made the short crossing
from Boulogne to Dover instead of taking the usual route
from Quentavic to the Solent. They all reached Dover
safely; but even in July there was something of a storm,
and the ships were scattered. It was decided that the
royal party should assemble in Canterbury, and there get
ready for the state entry into Winchester.

But at Canterbury Archbishop Ceolnoth had assembled all the chief men of Wessex, and King Ethelwulf
could go no further until he had conferred with them.
It was not immediately apparent that he could not go
on to Winchester anyway, unless he were willing to
begin a devastating civil war; but that was what the
chief men of his Kingdom had come to Canterbury to
tell him.

Alfred was too young to be admitted to the council,
and so was his next brother Ethelred. But Ethelbert, now
sixteen years of age, had just taken up the duties of a
warrior. Girt with the sword that denoted his status as a
man (though the sword of such a young man was bound
to its scabbard by heavy peace-strings) he called his
juniors into conference in the evening after the first
meeting of the council.

They met in a guestroom of Christ Church minister, a
private room with the rare luxury of a chimney and horn
windows. It was nearly as comfortable as the guestrooms
in the Saxon School at Rome.

Alfred was excited by this summons to discuss serious

politics with a nearly grown man, and of course that meant they must wait while he dashed to the privy. His chronic disability was most humiliating; but at least, he consoled himself as he sat in the stinking outhouse, he could never be expected to make up his mind in a hurry.

When at last the three young athelings were seated on stools before the fireplace Ethelbert launched out into a prepared speech.

'This matter concerns the royal house of Wessex, and though the aldermen say you are too young to sit in council I thought you ought to know all about it. Have you noticed that Ethelbald hasn't come, though all the leading men of Wessex are here in Canterbury? He's in Winchester, with his companions; and he says he will hold Winchester against father.'

'Then we burn Winchester over his head,' said the eleven-year-old Ethelred. 'I suppose I can have a sword for that? Alfred already has the sword Pope Leo gave him. How soon can we be ready to march?'

'Do you want to kill your brother?' asked Ethelbert shortly.

'I wouldn't mind killing Ethelbald. I don't like him. But of course when you put it like that I see that brother should not slay brother.'

'Surely it's our duty to fight for father, even if it means killing Ethelbald,' said Alfred. 'Besides, father is the King, and we ought to obey him.'

'If it comes to war of course we must fight for father,' said Ethelbert gloomily. 'We couldn't stay out of it. When there is fighting athelings must fight. But I sent for you because perhaps if the three of us stick together this quarrel may be ended without fighting.'

Alfred sat up straight and stuck his thumbs in his belt. At eight years old he was helping to decide whether there would be peace or war in Wessex.

'What is Ethelbald after?' he asked. 'Does he want to be King in Hampshire?'

'No. He plans to displace father and reign as King of all the West Saxons.'

'Then there can't be peace. We must fight him to the death. Why, it's *dishonourable*. Father is his lord. And he is breaking God's commandment – you know, "honour thy father and thy mother". All the honourable warriors and bishops will be against him. He won't have a chance. Couldn't we make him climb down and save his life?'

Ethelred looked curiously at the youngest of the family. Alfred was doing more than his share of the talking, as usual; but then he saw everything so clearly, and made up his mind so quickly. The advice of baby brother might be worth hearing, though that seemed to be an odd reversal of nature.

'There is something to be said for Ethelbald,' Ethelbert answered, 'and it's worth bearing in mind that if it comes to fighting he will probably win. That's no reason why we should give in to him, if we think him in the wrong. But Alfred has been abroad for two years, and he doesn't understand the feelings of the ordinary warriors. Most of them support Ethelbald, and so do at least some of the bishops. In fact the men who organized the revolt are alderman Ethelwulf and Bishop Ealhstan. I'm told the alderman Eanwulf backs it also, though he has stayed in Somerset instead of coming to Winchester.'

'And Bishop Swithun?' asked Alfred.

'He's father's friend, and he hates civil war. But if Ethelbald succeeds he will recognize him as King.'

Alfred sat silent. Before he went oversea these great men had been nothing but names to him, just grown-ups like all the other incomprehensible grown-ups. Now he was trying to see them as people. Instead he saw them as forces, like the draughtsman who has reached the back row and so become more powerful than his fellows. Bishop Ealhstan was the greatest man in Wessex, Bishop of the half of the Kingdom that lay west of Selwood, chief minister and almost viceroy during King Ethelwulf's absence oversea. In company with Eanwulf, alderman of

Somerset, he had long ago won a great victory over the heathen. These men were the landmarks of the Kingdom, and it would be dangerous to oppose them. Then he remembered something derogatory to alderman Ethelwulf; he mentioned it at once, chiefly to see what answer his brother would give.

'This Ethelwulf is a foreigner, a Mercian. King Boerhtwulf made him alderman of Berkshire. When Wessex beat Mercia he forsook his King to keep the government of his shire. Surely the West Saxons won't follow a Mercian and a turncoat?'

'They will follow the three great warleaders of Wessex,' said Ethelbert. 'Alderman Ethelwulf is a foreigner, but he's well born and honourable; any warrior may follow him without shame. And since the Bishop of Sherborne leads the plot they will not fear the censure of the church.'

'But why, why did it happen?' asked Alfred. 'Why should great warleaders betray their lord? It isn't as though father were no use on the battlefield. Didn't he kill more heathen pirates than have been killed since first they began to ravage in Britain?'

'That was at Aclea, years ago,' said Ethelbert drily. 'It's stale news now. What the warriors remember is that the heathen wintered in Thanet recently, and in Sheppey only the year before last. That's something new here in Britain. They used to raid in the summer and then go home. Though Kent looks to Wessex for protection father chose to go off to Rome instead of fighting the invaders.'

'They were small bands. The Army is still in Frankland,' said Ethelred in extenuation.

'That makes it worse. It would have been easier to beat them,' answered Ethelbert. 'There are other things as well, all sorts of complaints. Some thanes don't like this new scheme for quartering one pauper on every ten hides of land. They say it amounts to a new tax, which is a new custom. I've heard bishops complain that father's gifts to Rome should have gone to our own minsters. No

48

church in Wessex can expect anything of value for years to come, since the hoard has been emptied to glut the Pope, who already has finer jewels than anything we can give him. And then, of course, there's *Queen* Judith.'

He spoke the hated title with a sneer.

The younger brothers exchanged glances. This had been in their minds since they heard of Ethelbald's revolt. They had not dared to mention it; for they could not speak of it without condemnation, and that would seem like disloyalty to their father and lord.

'Well then, there's something to be said for Ethelbald, as you mentioned just now,' Ethelred agreed hesitatingly. 'What exactly is he after? Does he want to send father back to Frankland without a crown? That would be shame to all the Cerdingas.'

'That's what he'd like to do,' answered Ethelbert, 'no sense in taking two bites at the cherry. Anyway, if he is to be guilty of robbing his father, why stop at robbing him of half his goods? But he might compromise, if compromise would avert a civil war. He would leave something, say Essex or Thanet, so that father can go on calling himself King.'

'And Judith can call herself Queen,' added Ethelred bitterly. 'But that's not much of a compromise. Essex is a very poor realm, and Thanet must be quite valueless since all those heathen wintered there.'

'If Ethelbald would give up Essex or Thanet I think he'd give up more,' said Alfred with sudden decision. He was offering advice to his elder brothers, and they might very well tell him to shut up. But he saw it all so clearly in his head that he plunged on reckless of snubs. A peaceful solution was so desperately important.

'Look, Ethelbert, can't you go to Ethelbald and tell him that he can have peace, and very nearly everything he wants? Or he can have war against all the other Cerdingas. Tell him he can be King of the West Saxons, but father must have all the rest.'

Ethelbert looked judicial; his young brother was

running away with the council. But Ethelred snatched eagerly at the idea.

'That's a good plan. For Ethelbald all Wessex, both sides of Selwood, with the shires by the Thames that used to be Mercian. That leaves for father Kent, Surrey, Sussex and Essex.'

'And father can live in Canterbury, which is really a fine city though of course it's not so fine as Rome. And he'll be quite rich, and a King, and Judith can be his Queen, for they don't mind Queens here in Kent. Ethelbert, do say you think it's a good plan.'

Ethelbert smiled. 'I do think it's a good plan. It might even work. If it doesn't we must think of something else, for anything is better than civil war. I haven't been to Frankland, as Alfred has, but I know that in grandfather Egbert's day it was the mightiest realm in the world, and look at it now.'

'They tell you it's because of the Army,' said Alfred, eager to display his knowledge of foreign parts.

'I expect they do, but that's not the reason. It isn't because Franks can't fight, either. But King Charles spends all his time plotting to overthrow the other Kings his kinsmen, and so the Army ravages unhindered. We can't have that here.'

The three Cerdingas leaned forward on their stools. In appearance they were amazingly alike: pink spots on the cheek, blue eyes flashing under a thatch of golden hair, straight but narrow shoulders. The short barking coughs were all on the same note, a family inheritance.

Ethelred joined in. 'And the worst kind of civil war is when brother fights brother. If we stick together we can make Ethelbald see reason. But now that the three of us are united let's go farther than that. Let's take oath, here and now, that we shall never fight against our own kin. No civil war among the Cerdingas of Wessex.'

'We can take a better oath than that,' said Alfred. A wonderful idea was taking shape in his mind, though as yet he could not see the details clearly. His brothers were listening to him as though he were a grown man. 'Let's take an oath that so long as we live we shall obey whoever is the King of the West Saxons. Tomorrow that will be Ethelbald, and he isn't the King I should choose for lord. But the King of the West Saxons is the head of our house, and everyone knows that is the most noble house in Britain. I'm such a lot the youngest that I suppose one day I shall have to serve Ethelbald's son when he has one, and I shan't think twice about it because the King of the West Saxons is the lord I'm going to follow. I swear it now, on the hilt of this sword the Pope gave me.'

Ethelbert started, seeing his youngest brother tugging at the peace-strings on his toy sword. Yet what Alfred was doing appealed to a half-forgotten sentiment deep in his mind. The heathen heroes of old had taken oath on their swords; such an oath was more binding on a true warrior than any promise sworn before the altar. It was clever of young Alfred to get the best of both worlds. Ethelbert, a warrior and a Christian, leaned forward to lay his hand on the swordhilt sanctified by Pope Leo.

Next day all the athelings, even the boys Ethelred and Alfred, came to the council in the Archbishop's hall. King Ethelwulf accepted the compromise suggested by his second son, and Bishop Ealhstan ratified it on behalf of the absent Ethelbald. King Ethelwulf, and Judith his Queen, would reign over Kent, Sussex, Surrey and Essex; on his death his dominions would pass to his eldest son, now ruling over the West Saxons. The two Kings would take solemn oath never to make war on one another.

Since the Mercians had overthrown the ancient Kentish royal house the south-west had often been ruled by an under-king. Now the under-king would be the father of his suzereign, which seemed a little odd; but the ordinary Kentish-men would hardly notice the fact. King Ethelwulf bore his diminished dignity with a great display of

Christian forbearance, but in fact he found the change rather pleasant than otherwise. In Kent there was no trouble about according Judith all the honours of a Queen; and Canterbury, constantly in touch with the Continent, was a more comfortable residence for a Frankish household than tradition-bound Saxon Winchester. The heathen raiders had been paid to leave Sheppey, and had honestly kept their bargain. The King of Kent might take his ease in the wealthiest and most civilized province of Britain.

The three younger Cerdingas remained united. To avoid taking sides in the family dispute they retired to live together at Wantage, the home of their childhood. There was good hunting round about, and Ethelbert conscientiously engaged a tutor to continue Alfred's education. But Alfred spent most of his time hunting.

The brothers were very happy. They were so alike in mind that they seldom quarrelled; and Alfred was so much the most intelligent that the difference in age was hardly noticeable. Considering that they were boys on their own, with plenty of money, they were remarkably well behaved. There was a tradition that younger sons of the house of Cerdic should live quietly.

In Winchester Ethelbald lived rather more riotously; but he did not interfere with his brothers. He was something of a tyrant; but a vigorous tyrant, who allowed no one else to bully his people. The little groups of heathen who raided into Mercia from Wales dared not cross the Thames into Wessex, and the Cornwelsh of the west were quiet and obedient.

When Alfred was nine news came to Wantage that King Ethelwulf had suddenly coughed blood and died. No one was particularly surprised; he was in his fifty-third year, a ripe age for a Cerdinga. His body was brought to Winchester for burial, and after the funeral his sons sat amicably at the high table in the royal hall.

King Ethelbald was elaborately gracious to the three younger brothers ranged at his left hand. They sat solemn and glum, looking absurdly alike and answering in chorus when he spoke to them. On his right sat Bishop Swithun, and beyond him the widowed lady Judith, who had left her royal crown in Canterbury.

When they had eaten and the time had come for drinking King Ethelbald told his cupbearer to take the King's cup to Ethelbert; this cup was the long curved horn of a wild German bull, and round its middle was a circle of beaten gold like a crown.

'Pledge me, King Ethelbert,' Ethelbald called solemnly so that all might hear. 'I give you Kent, and all the other dominions of our late father, to be your realm as under-king to the King of the West Saxons.'

'He is very young,' said Bishop Swithun, too surprised to keep his opinion to himself.

'He is eighteen, old enough to use his sword in the front rank of the warband. That is the chief duty of an under-king. But you needn't take it, Ethelbert, if you think it will be too much for you. Accept or refuse, whichever you like.'

'Of course I accept,' answered Ethelbert stoutly. 'My place is in the front rank of your warband, whether I am a King or no. I am old enough to do my duty, which is to help the head of the house of Cerdic. Where would you like me to live? Canterbury will be crowded, with Queen Judith and another King in it. Or perhaps Queen Judith will be going back to Frankland?'

Simpering, Judith looked up through long eyelashes. During the funeral she had worn a solemn expression, but no one had expected her to display the grief felt by the true kin of the late King Ethelwulf. Now her face broke into a cheerful smile. She began to speak, and then checked. 'You tell them, Ethelbald,' she murmured.

'Ah yes, another formal announcement,' said Ethelbald, and cleared his throat as though uncertain how to begin.

'Queen Judith will not be staying on in Canterbury, neither will she go back to her father in Frankland. As a matter of fact she will be here in Winchester, as my wife and my Queen.'

Bishop Swithun gave a little jump, his whole body rising; but his face remained expressionless and his hands were hidden in his lap. He turned his head stiffly to gaze at King Ethelbald.

Alfred's squeaky voice broke the astonished silence. 'You can't marry father's wife. That's incest.'

'A nasty word, incest,' said Ethelbald with a frown. 'I didn't think anyone would use it to my face, but I feared some of you might be thinking it. That's why I am telling my kindred before the marriage. I shall explain, very briefly. Judith has never been married. She will come to me a maiden.'

Swithun relaxed with a sigh of relief, but Alfred continued:

'Father was very fond of her. I saw them together in Frankland, and I know. It's very odd that she should have remained a maiden so long. But I believe there are ways of proving these things.'

Ethelbald went very red in the face, but he kept his voice low.

'My wife will not submit to examination by a jury of matrons. She has given me the word of a Queen, and that is sufficient. I add my oath to hers, and mine is the heaviest oath in Wessex. Are my brothers the athelings convinced by the word of their King, who is also the head of their house? Ethelbert, what is your opinion?'

When Ethelbald spoke so formally he must be very angry indeed. 'Of course I agree with you, brother,' said Ethelbert soothingly. 'If you wish it I shall add my kingly oath to yours, and if you need more oath-helpers Ethelred and Alfred will join with me.'

'I need no oath-helpers. I am not on trial. The Queen and I have explained the matter to our family, solely to put an end to uninformed gossip. Bishop Swithun, will you marry us tomorrow?'

'I wish you had chosen another bride. You will give

scandal, even if you do not sin. But a maiden may marry any man not related to her, either by blood or by a spiritual relationship. And I for one believe the oath of my lord the King of the West Saxons. I will marry you.' The holy Swithun was fearless before Kings, but he was also a patriotic and loyal West Saxon.

'Well, it's done, and we are committed to support it. But what on earth possessed him to choose Judith? It's a blot on the record of our house, and we shall be years living it down.' Ethelred spoke in anger to his two brothers, as soon as they were back in their lodging after the wedding.

'I suppose he was always jealous of father, and now he can prove that he's the better man.' Ethelbert was judicious and very grown up.

'Perhaps he is just being old-fashioned.' Alfred also tried to speak like an elderly statesman. 'Judith isn't merely a princess, she stands for the Frankish alliance. In the old heathen days it was quite usual for a King to marry his young stepmother, to show that he would continue the alliance made by his father. I expect that's it, you know. After all, she *says* she is a maiden.'

'And Swithun married them. Since he countenances it the church can't object. There's no Bishop holier or stricter than our Swithun,' said Ethelred with relief. 'But when you go to Canterbury you must take Alfred and me with you. We shan't want to live in a court ruled by *Queen* Judith.'

'She's not a Queen in Wessex,' said Alfred automatically. 'But I also want to live in Kent, away from both of them.'

Alfred thought of the move to Canterbury as the end of his childhood. All his memories of the nursery and of his mother were bound up with the old hall at Wantage; in Canterbury he saw his brothers ruling their people and holding weighty councils with the Archbishop. He had put away childish things as they had, and must apply himself to the duties of an atheling.

He was still handicapped by that unfortunate weakness of the bowels. At his father's funeral, and at Judith's second marriage, he had been driven to run out of the hall in a manner humiliating to his adolescent dignity. But save for that weakness he seemed to be the healthiest member of the family. Ethelbald grew thinner and thinner; his energy was boundless, but he kept himself going on great quantities of strong wine. Ethelbert was a competent under-king; but when he must hear long speeches in a lawsuit, or reckon up accounts, or do anything else that entailed close thought, his head ached abominably. Ethelred caught cold very easily, and then must lie in bed and nurse his fever. Only Alfred could go hunting in all weathers, and then sit up half the night singing of the ancient heroes.

His education was finished. He could read a Saxon charter, because most of it was common form and he knew these legal forms by heart. After he had squared his elbows and stuck out his tongue he could write a simple message. He knew the meaning of many Latin phrases after hearing them continually repeated in church, and of course he could say his own daily prayers in the vulgar tongue. He was in love with the chant, as he heard it sung daily by the monks of Canterbury in their minster; and when these psalms had been translated to him he thought some of them finer poetry than anything he had heard in German. He got hold of a clearly-written psalter and in secret, for fear of ridicule, copied out a few passages in a little book of his own. He could copy Latin well enough, so long as he did not have to work out the spelling in his head. He carried his book about with him, hidden under his tunic; when he was alone he would pull it out and sing his favourite verses. There were still a lot of blank pages at the end of the book, but he would fill them presently. There were Latin poems other than the psalms; and perhaps when he was older reading and writing would come more easily to him.

At eleven years old he saw himself as a grown man. Ethelbert found him useful; for a King, even an under-king, never has enough intelligent subordinates who will tell him the truth. Alfred could inspect a muster, or examine the management of a royal estate, and after-wards report exactly what he had seen. Even though he could never represent the King at a ceremonial function, he was still a most valuable servant of the state.

The Army ravaged in Frankland. But the Saxons of Britain must keep good watch; for every year small fleets of 'summer pirates' cruised along their coasts, men who came south for a season's plunder before returning to their homes in the unexplored north. In the summer of 860, for the first time since their great defeat at Aclea, a detachment from the Army tried its luck in Wessex. These were Weland's men, who had been plundering the valley of the Somme; they left Frankland because the peasants of those parts had nothing left.

They must have had spies in Britain, for they chose their time well. When King Ethelbald lay sick at Sher-bourne beyond Penselwood the heathen landed near Portsmouth. Instead of scattering to plunder they hastened inland, and sacked Winchester before the warband could muster to oppose them. But the burgesses had warning of their coming and fled, so that though they took rich spoil they did not kill many Christians.

The brothers at Canterbury dared not leave Kent undefended. They gathered their men, and then waited in an agony of suspense for more news of the raiders.

When the news came it was most heartening. King Ethelbald might be lying sick, but he had kept his realm in good order. As Weland's men straggled back to their ships, many of them drunk and all burdened with plunder, Osric of Hampshire and Ethelwulf of Berkshire fell on them with the warbands of two shires. The heathen shieldwall was broken, and most of the pirates killed as they fled. Wessex was still a dangerous land for heathen men; the lesson would be remembered by the main Army in Frankland.

The brothers were especially pleased that these two aldermen had gained such glory; for Osric was their cousin on the mother's side, and they knew and admired the Mercian veteran Ethelwulf, their neighbour at Wantage in the old days.

Then in January 861 they heard that King Ethelbald lay dead. He was buried where he had died, at Sherbourne; for sacked Winchester was in no condition to stage a royal funeral. Alfred felt no grief, and pretended no more than a decent solemnity. He was now nearly twelve years old, and he had never thought of Ethelbald as a real genuine brother. To him infancy meant mother, and mother alone; his boyhood was the company of Ethelbert and Ethelred at Wantage.

As the athelings stood in the cramped chancel, watching the closing of the tomb, Ethelred spoke for himself and his younger brother. Turning to Ethelbert, he bowed. 'Hail, King of the West Saxons, of Kent, Sussex, Surrey and the East Saxons,' he said. 'The house of Cerdic is united to obey you. We remember the oath we swore at Canterbury when father was alive. You are our King and we shall serve you.'

'Well, since Ethelbald left no children that sounds reasonable,' answered Ethelbert with a shrug. 'Perhaps dear Judith is still a maiden. But we can talk of these things after the funeral feast.'

At the next meeting of the council all was arranged as Ethelred had suggested. Judith, who might have been a nuisance, luckily went home to Frankland; where King Charles, disturbed at the reputation she had gained in Britain, sent her to live in a convent of nuns. Ethelbert was proclaimed King of the West Saxons. Because Ethelred, at fifteen, was too young to be an under-king, the separate Kingdom of Kent with its appurtenances was united with Wessex. The three brothers continued to live together in great friendship; and Ethelred and Alfred, though they were given no provinces to govern, remained the most trusted and honoured of the King's companions.

5

Heathen Men in Britain

After five years the family was still united in friendship;
a remarkable tribute to the loyalty and sobriety of the
two young athelings, King's sons who lived quietly at
court and helped their brother to govern his realm. At
the Easter council of 865 Alfred, aged sixteen, for the
first time took his place at the board.

His brother Ethelred, aged twenty, was the second man
in the Kingdom and King Ethelbert's trusted helper. Soon
a wife must be found for him, for the King would never
marry. At twenty-five Ethelbert was already not far from
the grave; he had grown very thin, and sometimes he
coughed up flecks of blood. It would go ill with the West
Saxons if the King left an infant heir. No one put the
proposition into blunt words; but King Ethelbert took
pains to make it clear that his successor would be his
brother Ethelred.

The council had met in Canterbury to deal with an
emergency. Archbishop Ceolnoth was present, because it
was impossible to meet at Canterbury without him;
otherwise it was a gathering of warriors. King Ethelbert
took the head of the table, with the Archbishop on his
right; on his left sat his two brothers, and down the table
stretched the aldermen. Bishop Ealhstan sat among the
warriors; though it was twenty years since he had wiped
out a band of heathen raiders he was still the greatest
warleader in Wessex beyond Selwood.

The King frowned as he rapped on the table to open
the meeting. 'We are here to discuss the heathen men in

61

Thanet,' he said with irritation in his voice. 'Why they are still there, after a winter spent in plundering my subjects; and the best way to kill them before they sail away.'

Alderman Ethelwulf answered at once, speaking as crossly as the King.

'They are there because Thanet is a strong fortress. We can't get at them behind the Wansum. If we want to be rid of them we must pay them to go away.'

'That would be shameful,' said young Ethelred hotly, and Alfred muttered agreement.

'It may be shameful,' Ethelwulf replied, 'though better men than the Cerdingas have done it in the past. The King of the Neustrian Franks, and even the Emperor, have paid the Army to go away. But it has one great advantage. If we pay these scoundrels they will in fact go away; they keep their bargains. Of course they may come back again. We can't stop that. When you reproach the heathen for coming back after being paid to go away they always explain that this is another band, not the one that was paid; even though you see familiar faces in it. By their own standards they are speaking the truth. If they choose another warleader, or even take in a few recruits, that makes them a different band in their own eyes.'

'In other words,' said the King, 'alderman Ethelwulf advises us to bribe these men, and in the same breath admits that bribery won't get rid of them. I say we ought to attack their camp.'

'If you lead, my lord, I must follow,' the alderman answered stubbornly, 'though I don't suppose all the thanes of Berkshire will march with me so far to the eastward. Try and picture what happens after that. We go up against their camp, a strong palisade behind an awkward river. We don't have by any means the whole warband of Wessex, because most of our men will stay at home to guard their own borders. The King leads the attack, as a young King should, and his brothers charge beside him. Bishop Ealhstan and alderman Osric and I won't be far behind you, I don't have to tell you that. Then the assault is beaten off, and the leaders killed as their men flee. It's happened time and again. That will be the end of the house of Cerdic, which has ruled in Wessex since the Saxons left Germany. Remember that not one of you has sons to come after him. But it will be the end of Wessex also – no alderman in Hampshire, no alderman in Berkshire, no warleader west of Selwood. The next King to rule in Winchester may well be a heathen pirate.'

'If the heathen win a victory in Thanet they will sack Canterbury,' added the Archbishop. 'In Kent we obey Wessex, but in return Wessex owes us protection.'

'Don't you see, you silly old man, that we are trying to protect you?' shouted the angry King.

'Of course you are, but you are going the wrong way about it,' said the alderman of Hampshire, trying to lessen the heat of the discussion. As an elder kinsman Osric could talk to Ethelbert more freely than could the Mercian Ethelwulf.

'We all agree,' he went on weightily, 'that the ideal solution would be to kill the heathen in Thanet. The trouble is we don't think it can be done. You won't get your thanes to march to the far north-east of your dominions. The heathen hold a tremendously strong position. They are too wise to come out and fight in the open field. As Ethelwulf has just told you, we are in no position to risk even one bloody defeat. It's bad luck that the dynasty consists of three young unmarried men; but while that is so we must be cautious.'

'We shall have to pay these brutes to go away,' said Bishop Ealhstan, 'and I for one think it unlikely that they will come back again. Thanet must be utterly ruined by now, not worth further plundering. If they come back to Wessex they will choose some other district, perhaps a district where we can get at them. And if we levy a tax on all Wessex to raise the money we shall have done more than our duty to Kent. These Kentishmen ought to defend their own frontiers without always calling on our help.'

Round the table there was a mutter of agreement. It was gratifying to West Saxon pride that Canterbury, the mother-church of Britain, should look to Winchester for protection; but it was tiresome that these Kentish Jutes were never able to stand on their own feet.

'Hengist's first foothold in Britain was Thanet,' said young Alfred. 'He held it against all the power of the Welsh. That was the beginning of the conquest of the island. There's an old song about it.'

It was neatly said. He was too young to volunteer advice to his elders; but he had given them something to think over. In one breath he had reminded them that Thanet was reputed impregnable, and that warriors secure in Thanet had once advanced to the conquest of the island. They might take it as they chose.

Bishop Ealhstan was not to be side-tracked into historical discussion. 'We are agreed then,' he said firmly, 'that we levy a tax to pay them to go away. They will come back somewhere, but not to Thanet. Then we shall kill them.'

'That is best,' agreed the Archbishop. 'Remember, this is just a small band. It isn't the Army, which is still plundering the Franks. To pay them to go away won't cost very much. If the tax is levied carefully the King may find himself with money in hand when it's all over.'

That was a good bait, though produced a little clumsily. But the King and his brothers still glowered at their councillors. Young warriors who have never seen a battlefield do not like to be told to pay up instead of fighting.

'I must do as you say,' the King agreed grudgingly. 'Does anyone know how much these scoundrels are asking?'

'They are really quite moderate,' said the Archbishop. 'After all, it's a small band. Don't be surprised that I know their demands,' he added as the King stirred angrily. 'I haven't been negotiating with the enemy. But there are still two priests in Thanet, and the heathen allowed them to send me a letter.'

'Very well. We'll raise a tax and pay them. I shall leave the raising of it to the clergy. You are best at adding figures. Don't make Wessex pay it all. If the Kentishmen can't be bothered to fight for their homes they may as well contribute most of the ransom. Now my brothers and I will ride after a stag, and try to forget this sordid business.' Without waiting for an answer the three athelings swept out of the hall.

They were still angry as they rode on the open down, with the huntsmen and bodyguard out of hearing behind them. 'Greater men have paid ransom in the past,' said Alfred as calmly as he could. 'Father paid ransom for this very Thanet, and so did Ethelbald. You couldn't do anything else, when all the warleaders advised against fighting.'

'In the past Wessex has paid ransom, after fighting first and getting a beating,' the King answered fiercely. 'I wouldn't mind that so much. This is the first time we have paid up without even gathering the warband. Of course the heathen will come back again. By midsummer they may be asking ransom for Winchester.'

'You can't fight without followers,' said Ethelred, 'though of course if you try Alfred and I will fight beside you. I have fifty companions and Alfred has thirty. How many have you, two hundred? It isn't enough. Unless indeed you think we ought to get ourselves killed to shame the West Saxons into defending their borders.'

'It's too late for that now, after father paid ransom so often,' Alfred put in before the King could answer. 'It would have been a good law to lay down, that Wessex never pays ransom. But if we tried it now no one would understand.'

'No, let these Kentish Jutes do what they really wish to do,' the King decided with a shrug of contempt.

'Perhaps we would be better off if we gave Canterbury back to the Mercians. Then they would have the shame of paying ransom for it.'

'It's an honour to appoint the Archbishop of all Britain,' Alfred pointed out. 'All the same, the Mercians obey our Archbishop, and they should help to protect him. Couldn't we come to some arrangement with them, an alliance against the heathen wherever they may land?'

'That's been tried, and it didn't work. When Ethelswitha married that ass Burhed father agreed to help Mercia against the heathen. They sent for him that very summer, and he came with the warband of Wessex. But they only wanted us to fight thieving Welshmen, so the warband came home and father went off to Rome instead. I suppose you were too young to remember, but the aldermen haven't forgotten it.' The King shrugged moodily.

'Then let's pay up and forget it. One day we may catch a band of heathen in the open. Hallo, they've found a stag at last.'

It was not easy to pay ransom to the heathen, even though the King and all his councillors had agreed to the regrettable project. The tax was levied, and by midsummer the money was ready. The aldermen and their companions had gone home to guard their own frontiers, and there were few warriors in Kent. At the last minute the heathen decided that they might do better by foraging for themselves. Breaking out from Thanet, they ravaged Kent to the Medway and then escaped oversea while the warband of Wessex was mustering at Winchester.

King Ethelbert had publicly offered to pay ransom; then he had seen a province swiftly and efficiently plundered before his warriors could gather to defend it. All Britain laughed at the angry young men in Winchester, who talked so bravely and were so easily deceived. What made it even worse was that the heathen could not be reproached with treachery. When they broke out no treaty had been concluded; it was just that the treaty seemed so near that the warriors had gone home without waiting for the final oath-taking.

The harvest was good, and at Wantage the court might feast in splendour. King Ethelbert had been tricked by a band of heathen, but that might happen to anyone. It was perhaps more serious that the King's health was failing; he ate very little, and felt tired all the time. But for the last year his death had been expected, and discounted. He had been a competent, honest ruler; but his next brother was ready to step into his shoes, and since he was unmarried there would be no infant athelings to complicate the succession.

A warrior of good birth should not cling to life, or lament in an unmanly fashion because inevitable death is near. But the surviving children of Osburh felt that they had much to talk about, and they wanted to get it all said before they were parted. Ethelswitha, Queen of the Mercians, came for a short visit to say farewell. She came without her husband; they got on together as well as most couples who have married for reasons of state, but King Burhed had a weak, complaining character, and his Queen was still childless after twelve years of married life. The race of Cerdic was dwindling to extinction.

Alfred was sorry to lose his brother, but not shocked. Every day children die in their cradles, and no one can do anything about it; Ethelbert had been granted twenty-five years of life and five years of Kingship, which was better luck than came to most men. His strongest emotion was gratitude that Ethelred remained in robust health; he still had a brother to carry the burden of Kingship in these unquiet times. He and Ethelred must marry soon, to beget more Cerdingas. But that might not be too irksome. The brides would probably be Mercians. Wessex was not what it had been a generation ago, and to ask for Frankish princesses might be to invite a snub. The East English were now an insignificant community, and the feud-torn Northumbrians lacked a recognized royal line. Unless you did something eccentric like marrying a girl from Wales or Ireland that left only the ladies of the several Woden-born lines which made up the aristocracy of Mercia.

Rather to his surprise, Alfred had been very little bothered by the lusts of the flesh; which were supposed to be a dangerous temptation to young athelings. He liked the look of a pretty girl, and young women seldom say No to the handsome younger brother of their King; but that shaming weakness in his bowels always came on when the affair was working up to a climax. It is impossible to conduct a seduction when at short intervals you must retire behind the nearest bush. After two or three false starts he found it prudent to keep away from the ladies of the court, even when they threw themselves at his head with determination.

At Wantage they hawked for partridges among the stubble, a gentle amusement to suit an invalid King; or crouched in hides in the greenwood to shoot deer driven past them. But for most of the time they sat by the fire, passing the harp from hand to hand. It comforted the last of the Cerdingas to rehearse the mighty deeds of their ancestors.

On the morrow of Michaelmas the three brothers and their sister sat in an empty hall. The feast of the previous day had ended in hard drinking, and most of the companions were recovering in private. The open door of the hall faced westward, and a flaming sunset sent reflections dancing up the long narrow room. Queen Ethelswitha was secretly bored by the warlike songs of her brothers, though it would be shameful to admit it. To change the subject she said idly: 'I wonder how Judith is getting on? It's odd to think that I barely knew her, when here in Wessex even the peasants sing of her beauty and wickedness. She can't be having much fun, shut up in a convent; even though they call her the Abbess.'

'You didn't miss anything by going to Mercia before

she came to Wessex,' King Ethelbert answered. 'Of course all the songs say she was beautiful and wicked. You can't make a song about a girl who was clumsy and fresh and so ordinary to look at that now I can't recall her face. As to wickedness, the poor foreign child wanted to be the King's wife for as long as she lived among the West Saxons. I'm glad she has gone back to her own people. If they make her comfortable in her convent I suppose we shall hear no more of her.'

'Oh, but there's another song about her, and quite a good one,' Alfred said eagerly. 'Only it happens to be a Flemish song and round here no one knows it. At yesterday's fair I heard a Flemish pedlar singing it.'

'Trust Alfred to pick up all the new songs, even the foreign ones,' remarked Ethelred.

'Well, mother liked me to learn poetry,' Alfred continued, 'but this was really a most interesting song. Since she left Wessex Judith has had all sorts of adventures. Three years ago she eloped from her convent with a warrior named Baldwin, a man of no family but a great warleader among the Franks. Her father was furious, of course, and sent men after them. But they found a priest to marry them, and friends to hide them from the King of the Franks. Then the Pope took their side, and persuaded King Charles to see reason. This Baldwin has been made alderman in Flanders, and they live together in great splendour at Bruges. Judith has borne children, so perhaps her story that father left her a maiden was true after all. Otherwise she would have given us some half-brothers.'

'You must sing me the Lay of Baldwin and Judith before I go home,' said Ethelswitha. 'But not now, because I want to look at the sunset. What's the saying? "A red sky at night is the shepherd's delight?" We shall have fine weather. But you can't see it properly from here. Come out with me to the porch.'

From the porch they could see all the western sky aflame. Then, as the light faded, clouds overhead glowed a burning pink and Alfred stepped clear of the porch to see the whole heavens.

'Hallo,' he remarked. 'Over to the north-east there is something burning. Surely it's not dry enough for a stack to catch? Is there a house over there? Ought we to go and help?'

But Wantage had been the home of his childhood, and he identified the light just as his brothers shouted the same explanation. 'It's Beacon Hill,' he cried. 'They have lit the alarm. Shall I have the horns blown to muster the companions?'

'Wait a minute,' said the King sharply, and the obedient young Cerdingas waited for the head of the family to issue his orders. 'That beacon is in the north-east. In other words, it's passing on a warning from Mercia. Oh, I know it was laid to give warning of Mercian raids, but here's the Queen of the Mercians standing beside us. Anyway, the Mercians are our allies. So there's no need to sound the horns and call out the whole countryside. Perhaps the Mercians are in trouble and calling for our help, perhaps they are passing on an alarm from even farther afield. Ethelred, tell the companions to stay awake, with their arms handy. Alfred, slip down to the stables and pass the word to keep the horses saddled until further orders. Not all of them, mind, just enough to give fresh mounts to messengers. But have all the horses driven in from pasture and stabled, even though it means feeding them hay. Hang the expense. Perhaps the warband will be riding tonight. But we can't do anything more until we hear from King Burhed.'

'It isn't Welshmen, with the alarm coming from the east,' murmured Ethelswitha, familiar with all the troubles of Mercia. 'I suppose it's heathen ships off the east coast, hundreds of miles away. A chain of beacons is a good way of spreading the alarm, but you can't stop until you reach the end of the chain.'

The Cerdingas did not return to the hall, which was filling with restless and excited companions. Instead they

70

went off to a little parlour beside the King's bedchamber. Servants carried in a brazier and horns of ale; one of the under-butlers brought the precious harp, carefully cradled in his arms. Soon they were lounging on the benches, listening to Alfred's rendering of the new Lay of the Lady Judith.

Alfred sang well, considering the state of his nerves. He was fortified by the conviction that his bowels could not trouble him again this evening; on the way back from the stables he had been doubled up by a spasm and now he was as hollow as an empty ale-cask. But the order to mount and ride to the first battle of his life would bring on the trouble again, even if he were quite empty. He wondered savagely whether any other warlike young prince had been cursed with such a comic and disabling affliction.

Twice dogs barked in the distance, and the music ceased while they listened for hoofbeats. But it was not until after midnight that King Burhed's messenger rode up. It was good that the waiting was ended, but his message left them not very much wiser.

The alarm had travelled right across Mercia, as Ethelswitha had pointed out was the weakness of this method of sending news. It had originated in East Anglia, so that no one could say more than that it meant pirates on the coast. Perhaps a watchman by the shore had seen a solitary heathen ship; and the chance of a fine evening had sent the warning travelling from hilltop to hilltop until it reached the western sea.

Next morning Queen Ethelswitha rode home with a strong escort, to be beside her lord if he must prepare for war. There was still no real news, though peasants were telling remarkable stories. The Scots had overrun Northumbria and burned York: a single pirate ship had broken London Bridge: a great fleet had come ashore among the East English: there was plague in Lichfield, so that armed warriors barred the roads. Alfred, sent to listen to this gossip because he had the knack of making

71

peasants talk freely in his company, guessed that among this spate of rumour he had heard the truth. Peasants picked up news of disaster out of the empty air, so that well-mounted messengers were astonished to find their tidings known before they arrived; but it was impossible to say which of these many tales was true.

All that day the companions sat about in hall, looking to their weapons. All day horses stood at the picket-ropes, so that good autumn grazing was wasted and precious hay consumed before winter. King Ethelbert's clerks counted the silver in the royal hoard, and listed the serviceable swords and shields. The young athelings climbed to the highest point of the downs, but nowhere could they see the smoke of burning thatch or the dust of a marching warband. At dusk they rode round the outlying farms, to reassure timid peasants who might otherwise drive their cattle westward and leave Wantage hungry. Before midnight another messenger arrived from King Burhed; but all he could say was that East Anglia continued in a state of alarm, though no enemy had been seen on the border of Mercia.

After Mass on the second morning they had definite news. The alarm had been raised in East Anglia when a great heathen fleet was sighted; by their course the ships had come over the open sea, not coastwise from London River or the shore of the Northumbrians. That was the official news, sent by King Burhed; gossip added that the heathen had put into harbour, landing in such force that the East English dared not dispute their disembarkation.

'Thank God they didn't come back to Thanet again,' said King Ethelbert cheerfully. 'It's the duty of King Edmund to get rid of them, or to call for help from his Mercian overload. It's not my responsibility. And yet it may be partly my fault. If I hadn't offered ransom for Thanet they might not have come back again to Britain.'

'You are too scrupulous,' said Ethelred to comfort him. 'Small squadrons of heathen raid the east coast every year. They may dig themselves in for the winter, if

72

they find a position strong enough. But they haven't come because it paid them to ravage Thanet last year. They have come because they have quarrelled with the sons of Ragnar who lead the Army. They want to pick up a little silver on their way home to the north.'

'Yes, while the Army stays in Frankland we are safe,' added Alfred. 'These heathen may not even pillage the East English. Sometimes a few shiploads come ashore for beef and fresh water. I've heard that they will actually give silver for food, if the defenders muster in force to oppose them.'

'If a West Saxon sells them anything, no matter what price they offer for it, I'll burn his house over his head,' said the King savagely. 'These heathen are the enemies of the whole human race, and the silver they offer is stolen. All our men know the penalty for trading with the heathen, but perhaps I had better put out a fresh proclamation to remind them.'

Next day the companions went back to their normal hunting and gambling, and the horses were put out to grass. Without any fresh news, the King and his brothers had convinced themselves that the danger could not be serious; each said what he wanted to believe, and was confirmed in it when the others said it also. This was a descent by a little party of heathen stragglers; they would steal or buy a few oxen, and then sail away again.

They were still at Wantage in October, when the Englishman came to court. It seemed odd that a churl of such low rank should bear an official message; a free man certainly, but a peasant who drove the plough on his own land. He rode clumsily.

Alfred was chosen to question the uncouth messenger and set him at his ease, while his brothers stood quiet in the background. But the messenger needed no urging. He told what he had himself seen, and he was bursting to tell it.

'Heathen ships came to shore on my land, so early in the morning that we did not see them coming and there

73

was no time to run away. By the shore is a hollow howe, the tomb of some hero; it was robbed long ago, though my kin didn't rob it. For three days I hid there, on the very edge of the heathen camp; until I stole away along the shores where they had set no guards, swam down the coast and ran to tell King Edmund. This is what I saw – this is what I told him – this is what he said I must tell to all the Kings of the English and the Saxons . . .

'I can't number the heathen. In bright sunshine I counted three hundred ships, but there were more. They have dug a trench across the Ness, and built huts of turf inside it. They live quietly, keeping good discipline, and they carry more wealth than you can imagine, in arm-rings and collars of silver and gold.'

'You say they were quiet and well-ordered.' Alfred spoke gently to reassure the nervous peasant. 'What were they doing? Did they all obey one leader?'

'They were collecting horses, as far as I could see. Bands went out everyday, and came back with more horses. I don't think they bothered to kill the peasants, or take them as slaves. There were few captives in the camp, and when the foragers came back they did not carry the heads of dead men. As to their leaders, there were four of them, for I saw them often together. I don't mean that there were four separate warbands. These four men together commanded all the warriors in the camp.'

'In fact they might have been four brothers, as the King here has two brothers to help him? Did you happen to see a banner carried before these four men, a special banner with a special design on it?' Alfred heard his brothers gasp in dismay. This was the crucial question.

'Oh yes, my lord, those leaders might very well be brothers, though one is sickly and the others are strong. There was a special banner, though it was carried behind them and not in front. A big banner with a black raven on it.'

'Thank you. We understand. It's my belief the heathen knew you were there, and let you get away so that your news would strike terror into all the warriors of the English. Even so, you have been brave, and you tell your story clearly. While you eat supper the King of the West Saxons will choose a suitable gift for you. Tomorrow morning you shall have a fresh horse for your journey. Now we wish to discuss your news in private.'

Alfred spoke formally, very much the atheling giving orders to a churl; but he had the knack of doing it in a friendly way. Like all his fellows, this Englishman believed in a hierarchy of rank, and would have felt embarrassed and miserable if a King's son had talked to him as an equal. He went out smiling, to a good supper and the prospect of a royal gift.

'A greater fleet than he could count – four brothers to lead it – a banner bearing a raven,' said the King in an awed voice. 'God have mercy upon us.'

'The Army it must be,' echoed Ethelred. 'The Army which even the Franks dare not fight, the Army which has pillaged all the realm of Charlemagne. I wonder why they left Frankland? No more to be stolen, I suppose. If the Franks had beaten them in the field we should have heard of it. All the same, perhaps one of their leaders has been wounded. The man said one of them looked sickly, but they are all mighty warleaders.'

'Oh no, that helped to convince me,' Alfred replied. 'Haven't you heard of Ivar, Ragnar's eldest son? I heard the story when I was in Frankland. The four brothers are all mighty warleaders. Ivar's men win great spoil because he tells them what to do, but he himself can hardly lift a sword. They say that Ragnar married the fairest lady in the north, and she was eager to marry such a famous warrior. But on the marriage-night she wished to sleep alone, because it was the wrong time for her to sleep with a man. Ragnar, who could not bear to be thwarted in anything, raped her all the same. So Ivar was engendered on a menstruous woman. He came from her womb shapeless, with gristle where his bones should be. Ivar the Boneless he is called, and he looks very horrible. But his men have sacked more cities and taken richer plunder than any other band of heathen. It's the final touch which tells us that the Army is among the East English. There is only one Ivar the Boneless, and where he is the Army must be also.'

'The Army in Britain! God have mercy upon us!' King Ethelbert repeated, staring with blank eyes.

6

Mercian Alliances

It seemed an anticlimax that the dreaded Army did nothing throughout the winter, except to sit still in the strong fortress it had constructed. Young King Edmund of the East English set scouts to watch the heathen, but he dared not challenge them to battle. When the sons of Ragnar had fortified their camp and gathered enough horses to mount their followers, they opened negotiations. In return for an appropriate payment they would not ravage the lands of the East English, and when spring came they would ride away. King Edmund gave them the money they sought, since he could do nothing else.

Meanwhile the other Kingdoms of Britain were arming as best they could. The Northumbrians were engaged in another of their fierce civil wars, and had no energy to spare for the heathen; but the Mercians, and even the Welsh, sought the alliance of the West Saxons.

King Ethelbert died soon after Christmas, as had been expected for the last six months. He was twenty-five years of age, which was young for even a Cerdinga to die. He was buried at Sherborne beside his brother King Ethelbald, and his younger brother Ethelred reigned in his stead.

At the council which proclaimed King Ethelred it was suggested that Alfred should be under-king in Kent. That seemed a neat solution to the problem of finding honourable employment for the young brother of a young King; for if Ethelred lived until he had a grown son to succeed him Alfred might be tempted to rebel against his nephew unless he had a province of his own. But King Ethelred, in the most flattering terms, declared that he needed his brother's help; Alfred would be second-in-command and King's deputy throughout the whole land of the West Saxons, not under-king in a mere corner of the realm. He added that Alfred must be considered heir to the throne, at least for so long as the King was unmarried.

In the spring the brothers rode along their northern border, to inspect the warbands and the alarm-beacons. Ivar kept his promises, and he had promised to depart from the East English; he might lead his men through Mercia to the rich farms of the Thames Valley.

Alfred kept his eighteenth birthday as they rode by the northern fringe of Selwood. He was getting to know every ridge and marsh and ford in Wessex, as a warleader should know them. Long ago poets had observed that battles are often fought on old battlefields, and he began to see why; there are only so many ways into a Kingdom, only a few defiles where warbands can wait for the invader. When he shut his eyes he could summon up the shape of Wessex as an eagle might see it: the long coast on the south, full of havens where the pirates might shelter; the knot of chalk ridges in the centre, easy marching even in wet weather; the desolate moors of the far west and the marshes of the far east, with Selwood like a wall dividing the whole land. It was just as well that he could imagine this picture, for the only map he had ever seen had been a circular sheet, showing Europe, Asia, and Africa as three limbs of a Latin cross.

He was content with his position as second in the Kingdom. He and Ethelred thought alike in everything, so that they never quarrelled; and there was no reason to suppose that he would not outlive his brother. If the time should ever come when he must be ruled by a nephew, he would be old enough to accept retirement.

The brothers were always busy. With Wessex on a war footing they must travel continually, and besides the business of ruling there was the management of the royal demesne. Every peasant who had no other lord paid food-rent to the King, and some of them farmed their land very badly unless the King showed them how to do it.

The veteran advisers who remembered King Ethelwulf were leaving the scene. During the summer died Bishop Ealhstan, who for fifty years had been the King's deputy west of Selwood, the originator of the revolt against Queen Judith. He had been too powerful for a subject, and not always truly loyal; but a landmark vanished with his dying, and it was hard to fill his place.

Within a fortnight died Eanwulf, alderman of the Somersaetas, who long ago had joined with Bishop Ealhstan to destroy the heathen raiders by the River Parrett. Of the great fighting aldermen only Ethelwulf of Berkshire and Osric of Hampshire were left, and they were old. The young King and his younger brother journeyed as far as the Land's End, to reinforce their authority over the restless Cornwelsh. They were agreeably surprised to find excellent hunting in the foreign land of Cornwall; they decided that it would be wise and pleasant to ride through it each spring, hunting the red deer and reminding the Cornwelsh that they were subject to the West Saxons.

The Army remained among the East English until full summer; then in early June the heathen kept their promise to seek fresh fields, as they always kept their promises if they were paid in full. Their ships coasted north to the Humber, but the warriors rode overland to York. After sacking the most holy and splendid of all the cities of Britain they settled down to live there in comfort until their plunder should be consumed and they must ride farther to overthrow another Kingdom.

With all Mercia between them and the foe the West Saxons felt safer. But terrible news reached them in the spring. The proud and turbulent Northumbrians were too proud to offer ransom, and too turbulent to compose their differences in face of invasion. The two contenders for the crown united their warbands for a joint attack on the heathen. In March they went up against York, and were utterly defeated; King Osbert and eight aldermen were slain on the field but his rival King Aelle was taken alive. The sons of Ragnar carved the war-eagle on his living body; for it was said that his father had killed the mighty Ragnar by casting him into a pit of snakes.

After that there were no rulers among the Northumbrians, save for the heathen who lived riotously in York. Even such a wide land could not support the Army for longer than a single summer; in the autumn the heathen rode south to Mercia and fortified their winter quarters in the town of Nottingham. Ivar offered the usual terms: if the Mercians would pay him throughout the winter he would not ravage their land, and when spring came he would seek another hunting ground.

The Army had lived in this manner among the Franks. A wise King paid the Army to go away, since resistance was hopeless; if there was any doubt on that point it had been proved once again by the slaughter of Northumbrians outside York. But King Burhed was married to a proud Cerdinga; Ethelswitha persuaded him to seek help from her brothers.

The Mercian envoy found King Ethelred keeping Christmas at Winchester, and spoke to him alone. But the atheling Alfred was the second man in the Kingdom, and matters of state could not be kept from him. As soon as the interview was over the brothers discussed it together.

'Burhed will take a crack at the Army, if we bring the warband of Wessex to fight beside him,' said the King. 'I didn't think he had the courage for it, but I suppose he feels cornered. And just to make sure that we really fight hard he offers each of us a noble and wealthy Mercian bride. What shall I answer?'

'Fight the Army? Everyone says it's suicide.' Alfred feared to give advice on such a great matter, and took refuge in repeating common opinion.

'Yes, but now the Army is here in Britain someone will have to fight it. Britain is smaller than Frankland. If York and all Northumbria cannot feed the heathen for more than half a year then soon all Britain will be starving. It's just as much suicide to watch them take your harvest as it is to fight them. There's always the chance that we might win. The Army beat the Northumbrians. It can beat the Mercians. But Mercia and Wessex combined might give the heathen a shaking.'

'Oh, I didn't know you were willing to fight. When do we start? We can't muster the warband until the thanes have sobered up after Christmas. But must we get married as well? It seems to me a pointless distraction.'

'Why not marry? We are the last of the Cerdingas. We must marry, or see our line disappear. Since King Burhed is anxious to keep our friendship he will choose good brides for us; and Ethelswitha will advise him. Have you a girl-friend? No, don't tell me. But if you have there's no need to get rid of her just because you make a marriage of convenience.'

'No girl-friend,' said Alfred with a grin. 'You may not want to know, but if there was one you would have heard of her. It's everyone's business to see the King knows that sort of thing. I haven't found anyone I like well enough.'

'Then we shall get married together, as soon as we join the Mercians. We can begin to muster the warband when Christmas is over.'

Alfred frowned.

'You are the King, but you can't order me to get married. I would rather fight my first campaign as a bachelor, especially since there is a good chance that it will be my last. I don't want to leave a fatherless son, and that's what may happen if Burhed's battle goes wrong.'

It was the King's turn to frown. If the warband of Wessex were defeated in a set battle it was unlikely that either of the young Cerdingas would leave the field alive;

but it was unpleasant to be reminded of the future so bluntly.

'Very well,' he said after a pause. 'A King can't command his subject to marry. I myself shall marry a Mercian girl as soon as we arrive, just to show Burhed that we are genuinely his allies. You can put off your wedding, if you like, until after the war. But take a look at the girl chosen for you, and if you don't dislike her you might consent to a betrothal. You can't do better. Burhed will find someone worthy of our family. Then if all goes well you can start to raise children in a year or two. If the Kingdom of the West Saxons is to continue we must have more young Cerdingas.'

'Then that's settled,' said Alfred, relieved. 'Now all we have to do is to muster the warband. During the twelve days of Christmas we must drink with our companions or they will take offence. When that's over I shall ride for Cornwall. The Cornwelsh fight well enough if you can get them into field, but they don't like us enough to join the muster without being fetched.'

'Right, you gather the Cornwelsh. You have the knack of keeping them in a good temper. I shall summon the thanes east of Selwood, as far as Kent. If we start after Epiphany the muster should be complete by Candlemas. We'll join Burhed while the Army is still in winter quarters, and see whether for once God will defend the right.'

The Cornwelsh were quite willing to fight the heathen. They had disliked old King Ethelwulf for giving Cornish land to Saxon monks, but King Ethelbald had protected them, and they had nothing against his younger brothers. Without trouble Alfred mustered his warband.

It was a small band, since it was to campaign in a foreign country; only men of some standing, who had peasants to work their land for them, could set out on a long expedition. The followers of King Burhed would be more numerous; for the fyrd, the levy of every able-bodied man, came out against invaders. But untrained, half-armed peasants were of little use on the battlefield, and it would be expensive to feed them on a long march.

Those Cornwelsh who had been chosen were soon riding eastward, and Alfred found spare time to hunt the red deer on Dartmoor. It gave him an opportunity to be alone, and to set his thoughts in order. He had not told his brother the true reason why the idea of marriage filled him with revulsion, because it seemed so absurd that he could not speak it aloud. All the same, he felt in his heart that marriage had been denied to him by the humiliating affliction he had picked up on his journey to Rome. He was a noble warrior, a Woden-born Cerdinga, brother to a King; what would his bride think when he dashed from the marriage-bed to sit in the privy? That would happen, he was sure of it. And what of the wedding itself? The trouble came on him whenever he felt himself the centre of attention.

Marriage was denied to him, even though so few Cerdingas were left in the world. It was most unfair that a painful pilgrimage, undertaken solely in honour of God and His Apostles, should bring such dire consequences. But God's ways are mysterious, and seldom appear fair. In a sullen mood he ordered his huntsmen to leave him, and continued alone across the moor.

Perhaps it was not God's will that he should be thus punished? Perhaps it was a wile of the Enemy? An odd sort of wile, which had preserved him from fornication. He was slightly ashamed of his lack of enterprise, and hid it from his closest companions; but the truth was that in his nineteenth year he was still a virgin. He had been brought up to keep the Commandments, and that had something to do with it; but an even stronger incentive had been his fear of making a disgusting fool of himself.

Now it was his duty to marry, for the welfare of the West Saxons as well as for his own peace of mind. The royal line ought not to depend on the children of his brother alone, when the family was so unlucky that out of four strong young men two were already dead.

Very well, if it was his duty to marry then God must remove this affliction. He would pray for it; why not pray for it here and now? He saw in a little valley a tumbled pile of stones, the tomb-chapel of a local holy man, St. Gueryr. Cousin Neot had spoken of it as a lucky place, where prayer came easily. His horse slithered down the slope, and he left the beast free to graze among the gorse.

The beehive-shaped hut contained nothing except a square altar and in the floor the tomb-slab. Probably Mass was said there only on St. Gueryr's feast, after the Celtic manner; Celts did not think a congregation necessary, to them a holy place was an end in itself. But this was a church where God's Body had been offered for the sins of the world, as holy as St. Peter's in Rome. He pushed back his hood, stood his sword in a corner, and knelt on the bare floor.

He ought to begin by meditating on the virtues of St. Gueryr; but he knew absolutely nothing about the life of that servant of God. His fancy called up a picture of a squat scowling man, bearded to the eyebrows, who tinkled a little bell to warn off the profane; probably an inaccurate picture, but that was how pilgrims from Ireland looked as they passed through Britain on their way to Rome. Then he controlled his distraction, and began to see the immensity of God's Majesty and the insignificance of Alfred Cerdinga. That was wrong too, he reminded himself with a jerk. Alfred Cerdinga mattered as much as any sparrow; God cared for him, personally.

He prayed, his mind clear and his thoughts in order. God had visited him with an affliction, so presumably he had deserved it. This affliction had preserved his chastity through the troubles of adolescence; it was not really an evil thing after all. But now the King who was his lord wanted him to marry, and the welfare of the West Saxons demanded it. He might without selfishness ask God to change his affliction for some other, even though it would be presumptuous to ask for it to be removed altogether.

That was a dangerous prayer. Suppose the weakness in his bowels were cured, and in exchange he became blind or leprous? A frightful disablement might send him safe to Heaven, and at the same time render him useless to his brother and his people. 'O God,' he prayed, 'leave my body strong and active. Let me still be fit to lead the warband. I shall submit to any other goad You may set in my flesh.' Perhaps he was bargaining with God, like a huckster at a fair; but he knew that he was also praying from his heart.

He stiffened in alarm, at a hot breath on the back of his neck. He groped for his sword; then saw that his horse had wandered into the chapel, frightened at the loneliness of the valley. Night had fallen; he had been in the chapel for many hours.

As he picked his way over the rough moorland he felt curiously certain that never again would he have to rush from some great ceremony to the privy. There had been no tangible answer, but God had put into his mind the knowledge that his body would be fit for all the duties of his station.

King Burhed, looking round at the numerous fyrd of the Mercians, was disposed to patronize his brothers-in-law who brought from Wessex such a scanty warband. But in fighting quality the companions and thanes of the West Saxons were superior to the Mercian levy, its ranks swelled with half-armed and untrained peasants. Alderman Ethelwulf was in his element; delighted to be in company with fellow-Mercians after his long exile, but proud of his companions from Berkshire.

Of course King Burhed took command. This was his land, and his was the larger following; besides, the Cerdinga brothers were absurdly young for responsibility. King Ethelred was indeed a full-grown man with the beginnings of a beard; but you never saw him without the eighteen-year-old brother who advised him in everything.

The allied host lingered at Tamworth. It was known that the Army would remain in Nottingham at least until the spring, and there was no point in making war while the weather was still wintry. Besides, King Burhed had other business, and it might as well be concluded before they marched. There was a great feast of welcome for the royal guests. Early in the evening, before anyone was drunk, charming young ladies passed among the benches bearing wine.

Next morning everyone was bleary-eyed and short-tempered. But Ethelred, combing out his fluffy beard in the chamber he shared with his brother, spoke fairly cheerfully: 'I've seen my fate, and it might be worse. Godgifu is as pretty as most ladies of royal blood, and there can be no doubt of her descent from Woden. Another advantage is that she comes from a big family, so her parents won't spend all their time with her. There's nothing more tiresome than having a mother-in-law continually round your neck.'

'I suppose that's a warning,' answered Alfred, 'because my Elswitha is an only child. You forget that I am not a King. The alderman of the Gaini has as heavy respon-sibilities as any atheling of Wessex. He will stay in Mercia to govern his people. Mucill's descent will pass, though he doesn't stem from Woden; his ancestors were petty chiefs ruling the Gaini before the tribe merged with the Mercians. But on her mother's side Elswitha is descended from the old Mercian royal line, which is as Woden-born as the Cerdingas. Have you met Eadburh, my future mother-in-law? A great lady, and pious, and educated. In fact she reminds me of mother, which is the highest praise I know.'

'Yes, but you aren't marrying your mother-in-law. What do you think of the girl?' asked the King with a chuckle.

'I've nothing against her. She has been properly

brought up and won't bother me. It would be foolish to expect more from an alliance of this kind. How many girls are there in Britain, my equals in blood and not betrothed to someone else? Elswitha has a straight back and two arms and two legs, and no one would call her positively hideous. My job is to fight for Wessex, hers will be to produce royal Cerdingas. We shall be too busy to get on each other's nerves.'

'A tepid way to approach marriage, but at least you won't be disappointed. Now my Godgifu is a cuddly little thing. I shall get married as soon as King Burhed is ready. Won't you change your mind and make a double wedding of it, or are you still set on waiting until the end of the campaign?'

'Fighting first and marriage afterwards,' said Alfred shortly. 'I'll drink at your wedding and gladly. But I don't think it right to widow a girl within a month of her wedding.'

That reminder of the future wiped the smile from King Ethelred's lips. In silence he continued dressing.

On the day before King Ethelred was to marry the lady Godgifu, Alfred made his formal offer for the hand of the lady Elswitha. Alderman Mucill received him kindly, and there was no difficulty over the dowry; for King Burhed, anxious to strengthen the alliance with Wessex, added silver from his own hoard. Alfred, or perhaps the hoard of the West Saxons at Winchester, would gain greatly by the match. There was one minor blemish, but it could not be helped; Mucill of the Gaini was a vulgar man, whose effusive manner grated on the nerves of his future son-in-law. For more than three hundred years his ancestors had been petty chiefs in an obscure province; he was thrilled to know that his daughter was to marry a Cerdinga of Wessex, brother and almost colleague of the King of the West Saxons. He showed his delight too openly, with much slapping of Alfred's back and some facetious bedroom jokes.

Then Alfred was presented to the lady Eadburh, and she quickly effaced the impression of her husband's vulgarity. He found her sitting at her embroidery, in an attitude that reminded him of his mother; there was a book on her knee also, and his mother was the only woman he had ever seen reading for pleasure.

He tried to puzzle out the title of her book; but it was a long title, and in Latin, and upside down.

'Do you read?' she asked casually. 'This is part of Livy's *History of Rome*. Now that the Army has come it gives me courage. The Romans wouldn't give in, and in the end they won.'

'In the end they lost,' he answered without thinking. 'I've been to Rome, and seen the ruins. But it's true that the Romans were stubborn, and perhaps one day their city will recover. No, I can't read Latin. I can barely read Saxon. I was staring in surprise, which is rude of me, because so few ladies read.'

'Ah, but I was brought up to be an Abbess. My father was too poor to give me a dowry, but I had an aunt who was Abbess of her own foundation. She promised to leave me her convent in her will, and that meant that I must learn to be a nun. The life would have suited me. But then Mucill made an offer. He wanted a Woden-born wife, even without a dowry. A come-down, perhaps. I might have been the bride of Christ, and instead I married a rustic alderman without a single heathen god in his pedigree. But then perhaps my aunt was wrong to promise me her convent. By the letter of the rule nuns elect their superior.'

'By the letter of the law,' said Alfred, 'the West Saxons elect their King. But they always elect a Cerdinga. Besides, no one would found a convent if she couldn't dispose of it by will. I've often heard the point argued. At least you were studying to be a real nun, instead of taking the revenue and living in the secular world. That ought to be forbidden.'

'Yes, that's going too far. We ought not to ignore the

rule, even if in this imperfect world the wishes of the founder carry great weight. I was only explaining how I came to read Latin. You ought to take it up some day, when you have time.'

'When I have time –' exclaimed Alfred. 'I shan't have any spare time until I am too old to ride, and then I shall be too old to learn Latin. But I'm glad that your aunt's plan came to nothing. If you were an Abbess there would be no Elswitha, and I want to marry her.'

'You don't want to marry her, young man,' the lady said calmly. 'You've got to marry, because there are no young Cerdingas growing up. With this new alliance it's prudent to marry a Mercian. So you look for a Mercian who has Woden among her ancestors, and King Burhed finds my daughter for you. Don't protest. That's the truth, isn't it? Well, there are worse reasons for marrying, and you look like a man of honour. Remember, you will make promises before the altar. Do your best to keep them.'

'So far I have kept the promises I have made,' he answered stiffly. 'Your daughter will enjoy the respect and protection of an atheling of the West Saxons.'

'But not his love. I see. Well, you can't promise it if it isn't there. Bad times are coming. A young girl may need honest protection more than she needs love. Keep her safe while you live, and if you happen to get killed don't leave a brood of bastards to dispute her inheritance. We can't ask for more in a fallen world.'

Alfred felt at once embarrassed and attracted by this outspoken old lady. She would be a stimulating mother-in-law. But for the moment her conversation was too much for him.

'Now that I have your permission to pay my addresses, and the permission of alderman Mucill, I shall go at once in search of your daughter.'

He escaped from the bower; but instead of seeking the lady Elswitha he wandered off to King Burhed's stables. Eadburh had shown him where he stood.

Hitherto he had not realized that he was offering marriage without love. It would be a true marriage, all the same. In his view adultery was treason to the lady a husband had sworn to serve, just as rebellion was treason to a lord. His honour would keep him faithful – though he must be careful not to fall in love with anyone else.

The wedding of King Ethelred and the lady Godgifu was celebrated hurriedly but with adequate ceremony, and the allied force marched up against Nottingham. There was no time to waste, for the peasants of the Mercian fyrd were eager to get back to their fields. But with so many unmounted men the march was slow.

They arrived before the town, and sat down to look at it. It was not an encouraging sight. Within a loop of the Trent loomed a steep earthen bank, crowned by a palisade. From the mound fierce heathen warriors, resplendent in byrnies of linked mail, mocked the Christians.

It became apparent that King Burhed did not know what to do next. He had brought against the heathen the strongest warband mustered in Britain for many years. If the heathen would come out to fight him he might beat them decisively. But the heathen sat firm behind their palisade, laughing at him.

A council of war broke up in anger and indecision. It was unfortunate that the leaders of the expedition had far less military experience than their subordinates. The King of the Mercians had conducted some inconclusive skirmishing against the Welsh, and his prowess as a swordsman in single combat was well known; but he had never commanded in a battle, or even been present at one. King Ethelred and his brother had seen no fighting at all.

But the West Saxon aldermen, Ethelwulf of Berkshire and Osric of Hampshire, had destroyed dangerous heathen warbands; and there were Mercian aldermen with an equally good record. These lieutenants were reluctant to carry out the instructions of their untried leaders, though among themselves they could not agree on any other plan.

For several days in succession the Christians drew up in battle array, challenging the heathen to cross the river and attack them. The heathen remained behind their strong palisade. Without telling the Kings, Ethelwulf set out by night with his own companions. Some miles upstream they crossed the Trent, and at dawn appeared to the north of the heathen defences; but before they could reach the palisade they were driven off by a heavy shower of arrows and javelins. After their return to the Mercian camp Ethelwulf explained that he had been testing the strength of the palisade, and had never intended to breach it; which seemed to Ethelred and Alfred a very silly way of getting brave men killed, though the other veterans agreed that it was a recognized manoeuvre in the intricate art of war.

From their camp on the south bank the allies closed the river to shipping; but overland the heathen could draw unlimited supplies from conquered Northumbria. The allies were fed from Mercia; but the Mercians were free men who paid lawful taxes, and there was a limit to the amount of beef and bread they were bound to send to their King. Even more important, the peasants of the Mercian fyrd could not be kept under arms indefinitely, or there would be no harvest.

After a week of stalemate King Burhed called another council; and by this time everyone was so disheartened that the meeting listened to him in decorous silence.

'In ten days the fyrd must go home,' the King began, 'though of course the companions can stay all summer. So I propose that we set the peasants to dig a bank right round the heathen camp. When it's finished the companions will hold it. Then the heathen must surrender as soon as their provisions run out.'

'Wouldn't a double entrenchment be better?' asked alderman Ethelwulf mildly. 'There are other heathen in

Northumbria, and they might march to the relief of the Army.'

'A sound idea,' the King agreed. 'We shall make another bank, facing outwards. That will be hard work for the peasants, but they can do it in the time if we keep them at it.'

Alderman Osric spoke slowly, almost as though talking to himself: 'Each face of the heathen camp is half a mile long. Our inner palisade will stretch for at least two miles. The outer palisade must of course be longer, to allow room for our huts. Say five miles of entrenchment in all. But the River Trent runs through it twice, in and out. By rights we ought to build fortified bridges, though at a pinch two ferries might do. Let's break it down into furlongs. How many men do we need to hold a furlong of palisade? Remember, the heathen can attack any point in it without warning, so every yard must be held all the time. In addition we shall need two central reserves, one on each side of the river; unless your peasants can build two broad bridges.' His voice died away into a sigh.

'That's that, my lord,' said a Mercian firmly. 'Osric has shown us that your plan is beyond our means. Suppose the Army marched out to fight, would you draw up your men in a line five miles long, divided by an unfordable river?'

'But the Army won't come out to fight us. What are we to do?' wailed the King.

'We must attack their camp, before your peasants go home.' King Ethelred spoke with decision. 'The peasants will carry earth to fill up the ditch, and brushwood to burn the palisade. The companions will protect them while they work. When we have made a breach we charge in column, and fight among the heathen huts.'

'They'll beat us, you know,' Ethelwulf objected.

'Very likely. But they won't beat all of us, because only the head of the column will get inside the palisade. The rest can withdraw when they see things going badly. Then next day we try again, and the day after that.'

There was silence, until King Burhed exclaimed in wonder:

'But why go out of your way to fight when you know you will lose?'

Ethelwulf interrupted with an impatient gesture, in spite of the respect an alderman owes to a King.

'It might work in the long run,' the veteran said slowly. 'The heathen won't enjoy a battle every day. After a month or so they might go off to plunder in Frankland, or somewhere else where they can get silver without fighting. But how many of us would be left when that time came? Kings fight in the front rank, and so do aldermen. Today there are only two Cerdingas in the world. Who would feast in Winchester next Christmas?'

'Does that matter, if the Army leaves Britain?' asked Ethelred.

'It does matter,' Burhed answered with heat. 'I'm willing to lead my companions against the invader, because that's the first duty of a King. I'm not willing to throw away my life, on the chance that a battle every day may eventually weary the enemy. I'm not sure it wouldn't be suicide, a mortal sin. Anyway, the plan wouldn't work, because my own people would get tried of it before the Army did. For your third battle, my dear Ethelred, you would find yourself marching alone.'

'West Saxons follow their King,' grunted Osric. 'But by the third day there would be very few of us left. And since honour demands that we fall on the same field as our King none of us would return to Wessex. You ask too much of us, while Wessex is prosperous and un-ravaged. I'll die as bravely as the next man, when all hope is gone. Don't order me to get myself killed just to make things a little easier for the Mercians.'

'That's enough. King Ethelred's plan is rejected by the council,' said King Burhed. 'It's a gallant suggestion, such as we might expect from a gallant young King – whose sword has never drawn blood. But aside from other objections it would be doing the heathen's work for them.

They would like nothing better than to kill all the trained warriors in Britain, and then make the peasants plough for them as slaves.'

'Well, what will you do?' asked Alfred, since no one else had anything to say.

'I shall treat with the Army, now, while the allied force is still in position. Of course we shall have to pay them something. But we shan't have to pay very much, while they can see us eager for battle. They will accept moderate terms – and when they come back again, in a year or so, we shall catch them in the open and cut off their heads.'

'You are prudent and farseeing,' said King Ethelred with exaggerated politeness. 'It's the best that can be done, with the force we have available here. I beg you to conclude your treaty as speedily as possible. I am anxious to get back home, and we must not be a drain on your resources when you will need all your silver to pay the sons of Ragnar.'

As the two Cerdingas walked together to their hut Alfred spoke anxiously: 'Should you have shown your contempt quite so openly? Perhaps Burhed isn't a coward; it may be that he knows he leads a warband of cowards. Anyway, everyone pays the Army to go away. All the Kings of the Franks do it. We did it ourselves to get them out of Thanet.'

'That wasn't the Army, just a small band of pirates. And we didn't call up our allies to watch us do it. If he didn't mean to fight why did he summon us from Wessex? Everyone says you must pay the Army to go away, because you can't fight it. I know that. But *I* say everyone is wrong. The only way to make the Army go away is to fight it again and again, day after day. Put yourself in the place of those heathen. If they like fighting they have plenty of it at home. They come to Britain because here they can win silver without drawing their swords. They don't want a battle, even if they win it. The most famous victory can be dangerous, and hard work as well. Any sensible man would rather plough for his bread than fight every day for it. If the Army comes to Wessex we must fight them so long as a single West Saxon can stand on his feet. And we must never offer silver.'

'Well, you'll have Ethelwulf behind you, and Osric, and me of course. That's four of us. Some thanes may offer ransom privately for their own estates, after we have lost a few battles. Still, there doesn't seem to be a better way of dealing with the heathen. Perhaps they will conquer Britain whatever we do.'

'Then we shan't be alive to see it,' answered Ethelred brusquely. 'I wish now I hadn't saddled myself with a Mercian wife. I can't break with Burhed, no matter how much we despise him. Will you go through with your marriage after this?'

'I think so,' said Alfred after a pause. 'You are married, so we can't live together in the old way. I must start my own household, and that's easier with a wife. Elswitha is Woden-born, and I quite like her. Perhaps it would be better to say that I don't dislike her. But I definitely look forward to seeing more of her mother, and I can't do that if I jilt the girl. We'll be married as soon as these Mercians have fixed up their contemptible treaty. That means a feast, with King Burhed present. To the common people it will look as if we part friends, which is all to the good.'

For his marriage in Lichfield minster Alfred wore a byrnie of linked mail, and carried in the crook of his arm a burnished helmet. King Burhed had offered him clothes more suitable to a peaceful ceremony, but he answered that he had come to Mercia to fight and that while in that country he would wear armour. His long yellow hair hung in curls to his shoulder, and his cloak was of crimson silk; so that even in war-dress he made a fine figure of a bridegroom. He rode confidently to the church. Since he had prayed in the chapel of St. Gueryr his old affliction had not troubled him. Then he remembered that he had prayed God to change it for another, not to remove it; and he wondered uneasily what would be the form of his new trouble.

Very soon he found out. Walking up the nave he wanted to run away and hide. A King's son, and the cleverest of the family, he had been used all his life to the stares of the crowd. Now he was in an agony of shyness; only the swordhilt in his wet palm and the weight of the helmet on his wrist gave him the courage to continue. Sweat poured down his face; his stomach was full of wind; his legs were so tense that he could hardly keep his balance. Summoning all his fortitude, he stood swaying by the altar while Ethelred at his elbow gazed at him curiously. Then the bride entered the church and all eyes turned to her. With a pang Alfred acknowledged the new affliction that God had sent to him. For the rest of his life the turned heads of a gaping crowd would set him quivering with self-consciousness; there was never an hour when he did not fear lest shameful shyness should leave his mind a blank and his body a trembling mass of nerves.

Elswitha was a pink-and-white doll, in the white linen of a bride and the scarlet silk of a princess. She was happy, of course, because this was her wedding day; but she was happy because she was being married, not because she was to be Alfred's wife. He understood that with relief. He feared that he would not make her a loving husband.

Then he saw Eadburh smiling at him; and that cheered him. He was being yoked for life to a girl who meant nothing to him; but he was gaining a mother-in-law whom he would value as a friend. When it was time to exchange vows he spoke up with a smile, and smiled again at the little figure beside him as he slid the ring on her finger.

Afterwards he drank wine enough to drown his shyness; and the wedding night passed off fairly well, considering the lack of experience in both parties.

Elswitha was content with kindness. She did not demand or expect devotion. She would do.

When the West Saxons returned to their own country the lady Godgifu was lodged in the royal hall at Winchester; and by a masterpiece of tact King Ethelred made over to his sister-in-law the second royal hall, the comfortable establishment in Canterbury. In theory these were also the homes of the two young husbands; but a King can never stay long in one place, and while the Army remained in Britain the frontiers must be constantly inspected. The brothers passed their time riding from Kent to Cornwall and back again, comrades and colleagues as they had been in the days when they were yet unmarried.

They found time to do their duty to their ancestors. Soon after Christmas the lady Godgifu was delivered of a son, who was given the royal name of Ethelwold. Shortly afterwards the lady Elswitha bore a daughter, which was a disappointment. But the child was healthy and the mother came through without danger, so that it was reasonable to expect sons in plenty later on. The baby was christened Ethelfleda.

Alfred stayed in Canterbury for his wife's confinement, though he grudged every day of separation from his brother. It was a consolation that Eadburh was there also. Whenever he saw her she reminded him of his mother; but she was a more stimulating companion even than dear Osburh. For besides virtue and learning and insight into the minds of others she had an astringent wit his mother had lacked.

After the christening they walked together through the city to look at the ancient church of St. Martin, which had been the private chapel of a Christian Queen when the Jutes still worshipped Woden and Thor.

'A wonderful place, Canterbury,' said Eadburh. 'I can just remember the time when we Mercians had the duty of protecting it. Or at least I was brought up with the idea that it ought to be under Mercian rule. I hope your brother will protect it properly, especially now that York has fallen to the heathen.'

'I suppose York and the north in general have more saints of native stock. But Canterbury stems from Rome. I'm quite sure my brother will never let it go. He's of the right line of Cerdic, and knows the duty he owes to his people.'

'You are rather unkind to King Burhed,' said Eadburh with a smile. 'He does his best, you know. All the same, there must be a difference. No one really believes that Burhed is descended from a brother of the great Penda. I can trace my own descent from Creoda, and from Icel who led the English to Britain, and from Offa who reigned over them in Germany, and so back to Woden.'

'Since you are sprung from Woden you will agree with the Cerdingas that a King should fight for his people, and offer ransom only after he has been beaten. Sometimes I wonder about Woden. He wasn't a god, because there is only one God. But if he was just a devil from Hell the lessons he taught his descendants aren't devilish.'

'I have wondered too. Perhaps he was simply a brave and noble warrior, so honourable that he has never been forgotten.

It's glorious to be descended from him, isn't it? But it can be a burden, too. Well, let's see if they let me into St. Augustine's. You are not quite a King, but they might stretch a point for you.'

The monks were delighted to show the lady Eadburh over their minster. The rule against females within the enclosure did not apply to Queens, and she was nearly a Queen. Besides, she impressed them by reading from the book of homilies which stood in the refectory.

No one could ever take the place of Osburh, but Alfred felt he had added to his kin a loved companion.

Throughout the year 869, until the harvest had been reaped, the Army remained quiet in York. The Northumbrians had submitted, save for a few stubborn warriors who held the rock of Bamburgh in farthest Bernicia. King Burhed could congratulate himself that by paying quite a small ransom he had saved Mercia from plunder. Deira was a waste, and Bernicia a battleground; but the rest of Britain was unravaged.

7

The Battle-Winter: Reading

The heathen of the Army were professional fighting-men, who never did any other work; it had become their custom to seek new raiding-grounds at the onset of winter, just when honest men hang up their weapons. In November 869 thousands of horsemen rode out unexpectedly from York. With neither baggage nor followers to slow their march they passed swiftly through Mercia, and sacked Thetford in East Anglia before the English could muster to defend it.

All over Britain beacons flared and warriors gathered. But presently the Cerdingas heard that the Army had settled down in Thetford for the winter, and the thanes were dismissed to keep Christmas in their own homes.

'In the spring King Edmund will seek our help,' said King Ethelred. 'I suppose we must march if he summons us.'

'The East English look to Mercia for protection,' Alfred objected. 'We need not move until we hear definitely that King Burhed is in the field.'

'There's no obligation, but we shall march,' his brother answered firmly. 'The warband of the West Saxons will help anyone who fights the Army, even a Welsh chieftain.'

'Welsh chieftains may fight, because they have no silver to pay ransom. But after Burhed's bad example young Edmund will pay up, mark my words. The East English are a puny people. They won't stand a chance against the Army.'

'Puny perhaps; but stubborn, or so they say. Young

Edmund has a sense of duty. And since he's the weakest King in Britain we can put ourselves under his orders without damaging our dignity.'

'He has never been on campaign. He rules a rich land and few warriors. He'll pay,' Alfred said again. He was sure of it. In all Britain there was no other King like Ethelred his brother; those others would always pay sooner than fight.

Vague rumours of war came from East Anglia, and presently the full story was known. Young Edmund had marched against the Army with the warband of his own small Kingdom only. Contemptuously the Army had come out from its ramparts to squash the presumptuous patriots. When the English fled King Edmund, fighting to the last, had been captured alive.

Ivar the Boneless killed him, slowly and painfully. There is no point in asking ransom for a King when you already hold his realm; you may take his life and his silver also. In Wessex they shrugged their shoulders and tried to forget it. Young Edmund should have sought allies before he challenged the Army to battle; and as for the story that he might have saved his life by denying Christ to worship Thor, the heathen were not trying to spread their idolatrous faith. They wanted Britain to continue as a Christian land, so that there would be plenty of rich minsters for them to plunder.

King Edmund was killed in November, and by Christmas few men spoke of him. It was more widely remembered that the Army had destroyed the famous minster at Peterborough, slaughtering the abbot and his monks. Then stories began to circulate of miracles wrought by the martyred King. During the summer of 870, while the Army lay at ease at Thetford, Ivar the Boneless died suddenly; it was recalled that he had killed Edmund with his own hand. Other miracles took place at the King's tomb. It was said that even the heathen feared the vengeance of the holy young man they had murdered, and were anxious to quit his realm.

About that time Archbishop Ceolnoth died also, and King Ethelred appointed Bishop Ethelred of Wiltshire to fill his place. Archbishop Wulfhere wandered homeless on the Yorkshire moors, and what remained of the hierarchy of Britain must be kept up to strength. All the clergy agreed that King Edmund had gained the crown of martyrdom. That was curious, for he had done no more than the bare duty of a King; he had fought to the death to save his people from invasion, just as Aelle and Osbert, whom no one honoured as martyrs, had fought to the death outside York. But the miracles proved that such was the Will of God, which fallible mortals cannot fathom.

Everyone wondered where the Army would go next. The heathen had conquered Northumbria and East Anglia, and taken tribute from Mercia. It was likely that they would invade Wessex.

King Ethelred and his brother made what preparations they could. They sent their wives to remote Somerset, where they might take refuge on the western moors if the heathen came round by sea. That year Godgifu had miscarried, so that she took with her only young Ethel-wold; Elswitha had borne a second child, a boy, whom Alfred had caused to be christened Edward. It was a strange name for a Cerdinga, but the son of a younger son might more easily stay loyal if his name did not remind him of his royal birth. The women went willingly to their rustic exile. They did not expect to see their husbands in wartime, and they thought first of the safety of their children.

Immediately after harvest the warbands mustered; but they could not be concentrated in one body, for the Cerdingas had a desperately long frontier to defend, from the mouth of the Severn to the mouth of the Thames. The heathen had horses, and might ride south-west to Cotswold; but they also had ships, and might prefer to pillage the rich churches of Kent. The King and his brother lay with their companions at Wantage, more or less in the centre of the line. They could ride swiftly to any threatened point.

In November the Army moved. After crossing the middle Thames the heathen dug a fortified camp on the tongue of land where the Kennet met the Thames, at the royal hall of Reading.

The two Cerdingas rode side by side on the windswept Berkshire chalk. King Ethelred's purple cloak was held round his neck by jewelled pins. Over his byrnie he wore a loose cassock of grey frieze, and the long sleeves of his tunic were pulled down over his hands. Under his helmet a woollen scarf was wrapped round his ears. Sheepskins had been strapped to cover his thighs on the saddle. Nonetheless, the north-east wind brought water to his eyes and a drop to the tip of his nose; he coughed continuously.

'In that get-up it will take you ten minutes to draw your sword,' said Alfred reprovingly. 'But I suppose it's safe. On this open down there's no cover for an ambush.'

'It's this horrible wind,' answered his brother. 'Only heathen from the frozen north would make war in such weather. But if I've got to fight in midwinter I must keep fit to lead the warband. You know what happens when I get chilled; the fever takes away my senses. It would be a fine thing if I lay wrapped up by the fire while the West Saxons march to the first battle of my reign.'

'Well, we none of us look very soldierly,' said Alfred, glancing back at the column of companions, huddled in the saddle with heads bent against the wind. 'My fingers are so cold I doubt I could hold a sword. Hallo, someone's lit another beacon.'

'Those beacons seemed a good idea while the Army was in East Anglia,' the King said pettishly. 'But they don't tell us anything except that there are raiders about, and that we have known for the last four days.'

Ribbons of smoke showed on both sides of the ridge,

smearing the trees of the Thames valley and the denser forest to the south. The new one, a little south of east, was also bent flat by the gale, so that it was hard to make out where it rose. Alfred drew rein and looked carefully round the horizon. He stood the cold better than his brother, and wore over his byrnie only a long cloak wound twice round his shoulders. In front and on both flanks stretched a screen of scouts, picked horsemen riding in a scattered line; four hundred yards away, on the right, a scout stood in his stirrups and held up his shield.

'Someone coming,' grunted Alfred. 'The scout thinks they're friends, but we'd better be careful.'

The King halted; his companions formed on each side of him, and a few enthusiasts threw back their cloaks to free their sword-arms. But while the King kept his saddle there was no need to dismount. Twice yesterday they had dismounted to form the shield-wall, only to find that the approaching warriors were West Saxon reinforcements.

A knot of horsemen zigzagged up the slope. They were not more than a dozen, so they must be friends. The scouts resumed their advance, and the warband once more shook out into column.

'It's old Ethelwulf,' Alfred said again. 'I recognize that Mercian cob he always rides. I suppose if he governed Berkshire for a hundred years he would still buy Mercian ponies. He hasn't got his warband with him, so I suppose he's come to tell us the news. Good news, by the look of him. He's waving his arms and sitting up very cheerfully.'

'Your eyes are better than mine, especially in this wind,' the King said regretfully. 'Yes, that's Ethelwulf all right. And he's very pleased with himself. Let's gallop up and hear what he has to say.'

'No, wait for him here where our companions can hear his story. The old boy likes an audience, and if he brings good news he deserves one. Make sure there's a gleeman within hearing. Ethelwulf loves fame, and we must show him that he can earn it as well among the West Saxons as among the Mercians.'

King Ethelred halted. He was always ready to follow Alfred's advice, even when it was expressed in a form very like a command. Alfred could see into the mind of any warrior, and keep him in a good temper; where a busy preoccupied young King might drive straight ahead without noticing disappointed feelings. 'Don't let's overdo it,' he muttered all the same. 'Ethelwulf drove father into Kent. He may do his best for his adopted country, but he hasn't always been loyal to his lord.'

'He's a Mercian. They don't know the meaning of loyalty. How can they, without a proper royal line? But he's on our side against the Army, and he was killing heathen when I was in my cradle.'

Alfred smiled grateful recognition as the alderman of Berkshire rode up.

Dismounting with a swagger, the veteran glanced swiftly round. He was obviously pleased that the whole warband of the King's companions was grouped where they could hear him.

'First blood to the West Saxons, my lord,' he announced, beaming. 'Down in the forest I have a wagonload of swords and shields. It's spoil taken from the heathen. Yesterday the fyrd of Berkshire met them at Englefield, and at the end of the day we held the place of slaughter. We killed quite a lot of them, too, before they broke; though the fugitives got away faster than we could follow.'

'That's great glory for you and for Berkshire,' the King replied graciously. 'I hope you took spoil of gold and silver besides weapons. If you did, of course your men may keep it as the reward of their valour.'

Alfred smiled. When the alderman offered only weapons as spoil his brother had been quick to take the hint. By making a spontaneous gift of what these men would keep anyway he had done his best to preserve the royal authority.

'I suppose it wasn't the whole Army you beat, alderman?' he asked. 'That would be too much to hope for. I take it the main body of heathen are still at Reading?'

Ethelwulf composed his features. He was no longer the joyful bearer of good news, but rather the responsible veteran reporting on the events of the campaign.

'No, atheling, it wasn't the Army,' he said quietly, 'foragers, I should say. But a strong foraging party, with some famous warriors. Two Earls led it, as we could see from their standards. Best of all, one Earl was wounded; he was carried from the field on a shield. The heathen lost heavily. In Reading they won't be feeling very cheerful.'

'Splendid news,' said the King with enthusiasm. 'We shall attack the camp as soon as all our men have come up. Attack the heathen every day. Never mind if they hold the place of slaughter at nightfall, but attack again the next day. That's the only way to show them that plundering the West Saxons doesn't pay.'

'Your men are down in the forest?' Alfred inquired.

'They are, atheling, and if the King commands it they will join your march. Though they need rest,' said Ethelwulf.

'Of course the warriors of Berkshire must join us. The presence of these heroes will encourage our recruits. That's my royal command, alderman, so pass it on to your companions. We shan't go much farther today, and I suppose they have horses. I shall give the whole fyrd a day of rest before we attack the heathen behind their palisade. Your followers will be rested before the next battle, my dear Ethelwulf; and the glory they have already gained should inspire them to even greater efforts.'

'You see how it is,' Alfred added. 'Your men can't take their spoil home and rejoin us when they feel like it. The King has formally commanded them to remain in the field. If they go home after that they may lawfully be proclaimed *nithing*.'

'Then send some of your companions with me when I go back to my warband,' said Ethelwulf with a grin. 'Heroes don't like being kept in the field after victory. They may forget the full tale of their exploits if they can't tell them at once to the old women at home.'

'If they argue,' said the King, 'say that I myself will come to inspect the spoil. What they won from the heathen must have been taken from Christians in the first place, and if we can find the rightful owners we ought to return it.'

'But not if they come willingly to Reading,' said Ethelwulf quickly. 'I shall tell them that, and they will come willingly.'

'In fact they are coming already,' Alfred pointed out. 'I see horsemen leaving the wood. Of course they want to tell us of their great deeds, and I suppose they have safely buried their gold and silver in the forest.'

'They can't bury the cattle,' Ethelwulf grumbled. 'I expect you will squander the beasts by killing them to feed your men. But that's better than giving them back to their rightful owners after we have won them in battle.'

'We shall eat your oxen, but we shall pay for them,' said the King shortly. Ethelred saluted and rode to join his followers.

That evening they halted only a short march from the heathen camp. Most of the warriors of Wessex east of Selwood were already before Reading, and when they had been joined by the King's followers from the west they would be a mighty host. The peasants of Berkshire had gathered also; they were not well enough armed to fight in the front rank, but they could look after horses and gather fuel for the camp, so that Wessex might fight at full strength. The heroes of Ethelwulf, with a splendid audience, boasted far into the night.

Alfred found the alderman sitting in front of his hut with a great fire before him. A gleeman was already singing of the victory at Englefield, while Ethelwulf listened critically and put in small corrections of fact. Most of his companions were incapably drunk, but their elderly leader was careful of his health; he held a long horn of ale, but he was still sober.

'I'm sorry I was short with you this morning,' Alfred began, 'but we must keep the warband united for the great attack on the Army. After victory every hero wants to go home. If I hadn't spoken most of your men would have vanished. The King, who has never seen war, forgets these things. I have never seen war either, but I know from the old songs how heroes behave. It's because I have never seen war that I want to talk to you. Are the heathen really fiercer than the West Saxons? How do you go about beating them? You have made war for more than forty years. I want your advice.'

That was the right approach to a veteran. Ethelwulf beamed.

'The heathen are no fiercer than we are, no harder to kill than a Saxon. But they are professionals, who make war all the year round for every year of their lives; while our companions spend most of their time drinking. The heathen don't fight better, but they work harder. When it's a question of entrenching a camp they dig with their own hands, instead of rounding up peasants to dig for them. If they are posted as sentries they stay until relieved. You can't surprise the Army. It never falls into an ambush. It marches farther and faster in a day than any band of Christians. You might put it this way: the heathen go on after they are tired, our men stop. That's quite a big handicap.'

'And of course there's the reputation of the invincible Army,' Alfred continued moodily. 'Were your companions reluctant when you led them to attack that party of foragers?'

'Some were a bit slow on their feet, perhaps,' Ethelwulf admitted, 'but there was less hanging back than I had expected. We followed after the raiders, we didn't meet them. So my men had seen the burned farms and the desecrated churches, the women with their bellies ripped open and the children with their heads smashed in. They were not my own kin, since I am a Mercian; and I have seen many wars. But the fyrd of Berkshire felt very strongly about it.'

'That's how my brother feels. These people are our kin, every one of them. But some of the thanes from Somerset or Sussex haven't the same stake in victory. I hope they follow us when the horns sound for the onset.'

'You can never tell beforehand,' said the alderman with a shrug. 'I've seen battles lost that ought to have been won – and the other way round, of course. We shall know the day after tomorrow. Until then it's a waste of time to prophesy. But if I may give you a word of advice: don't linger obstinately on a lost field. There are only two full-grown Cerdingas. There's no shame in running when everyone runs.'

'Is that how a noble of Mercia sees it?' answered Alfred hotly. 'In Wessex athelings fight to the last.'

'Never mind about me, young man. I have ancestors, just as you have, and I also must be worthy of them. Before you were born I carried a sword, and now that I'm old my legs are too stiff to run away. I'm telling you for your own good.'

'I'm sorry, alderman. Of course you will gain great glory tomorrow, as the day before yesterday you gained great glory at Englefield. All the same, I shall pass on your warning to my brother. We must have leaders in Wessex, no matter how the battle goes.'

Alfred went away thoughtful. Ethelwulf had greater experience of warfare than anyone else in the host, and it was evident that he expected the assault to end in defeat.

But when at first light the horns roused the defenders of Wessex most of the warriors felt confident; it was only four days since two heathen Earls had been defeated at Englefield, and the tale of that famous victory had lost nothing in the telling. Peasants laughed cheerfully as they lit the fires for breakfast, and warriors whistled and joked while they gave a final polish to their mail.

At sunrise the chaplains would offer Mass. Until then everyone was busy, except for great men who had plenty of servants. Alfred snatched at this rare moment of solitude, a few minutes when he might walk alone with his thoughts.

He was twenty-one years old, and he had never drawn his sword in anger. Perhaps it was even more remarkable that King Ethelred, aged twenty-five, was equally a novice in arms. The host of Wessex must win by hard fighting, without help from skilled leadership. The heathen of the Army had been fighting since they were weaned; and their leader was King Halfdan, eldest surviving son of the great Ragnar.

How would it feel to fence with an angry, foreign man, who was trying to kill you? Would he be so paralysed by the strange experience that he forgot the artificial parries he had been taught at exercise? Would he be killed easily and contemptuously, in the first ten minutes? Worse still, when the shock came would he feel afraid? He had a vision of himself running away, while the assembled hosts mocked him. The horror of the vision nearly brought on another bout of the shyness which had unmanned him at his wedding. His hands shook, his knees knocked together, he could scarcely breathe. That brought him some consolation; if he felt thoroughly frightened he would be physically incapable of running away. He must behave well, or leave his bones on the field. But it was absurd that a nervous young atheling, with a fuzz of boy's beard, should lead grown veterans into battle. Yet he was a Cerdinga, and the children of Cerdic were brought into the world to lead their kin into battle. When the swords crossed he would do his duty – his ancestors would see to that. Meanwhile until Mass began he would kneel in the chapel-tent, and pray for courage . . .

The leaders came out of the chapel as all the other field-Masses were ending. King Ethelred gave his orders in a self-conscious but military voice: 'Parade in an hour, ready for action. Let the men breakfast now, and encourage them to empty their bowels if they can. That's a good thing if they get wounded. I myself will place the standards. The men will form on them when the horns sound. Any questions?'

'Do we all attack? Who defends the camp?' asked Ethelwulf.

'I was coming to that. Thank you for reminding me. We shall form in three divisions. I take the right, naturally. My brother Alfred commands on the left. Alderman Ethelwulf, with the fyrd of Berkshire and all the peasants, grooms and able-bodied servants will form behind us. If the worst comes to the worst they will defend our camp; but it's not likely that we shall be driven right off the field. If the attack goes well the reserve will reinforce us when we are over the heathen palisade; if we give ground the reserve will charge to allow us to disengage and reform for another attack. These are my instructions, mind you. I can't give definite orders before the battle begins, and once it has started I shall be too busy to look behind me. The movements of the reserve are left to the discretion of alderman Ethelwulf, the victor of Englefield and the most experienced veteran in my host.'

There was a murmur of satisfaction; when the King was present he could not delegate his command, but this untried novice had shifted most of the responsibility to a proven leader.

'There's just one other point,' Ethelwulf put in. 'We have ample supplies, including plenty of wine. Let every warrior have a cup of wine at breakfast, and if he asks for it give him a second. It puts heart into a man. But don't allow anyone more than two cups. A drunken man feels brave; but his hand moves slowly, and he easily gets killed.'

As the two athelings squatted side by side before bread and cold bacon Alfred was amused to see the servant lay out four cups of wine and no more. In this host even the King obeyed Ethelwulf. Then his nerves took charge of him, and he found himself shaking all over. Would he falter when he reached the heathen palisade? How would he feel as his sword sank into living flesh? He picked up his second wine-cup and shook his head brusquely. Within an hour all these questions would be answered. There was no escape from destiny.

'Neot gave up all this, to eat cabbage and drink water and kneel for long hours every day. I wonder if his was the wiser choice?' said Ethelred half to himself. Alfred knew that his brother was enduring the same trial.

'We are Cerdingas, born to lead our kinsmen,' he answered stoutly. As soon as he began to encourage the King he felt braver himself.

'I must place the standards. Check the men's weapons as they form up. If you find a peasant with a byrnie put him among the companions. We can't waste a single well-armed man.'

As he walked to his post Alfred checked his own equipment. He had a good plain sword, a steel blade with bronze hilt and bone hand-grips; it balanced well and he was used to it. The wood of his round shield was covered with red leather and the bronze boss decorated with enamel, so that it marked him as a person of importance. His byrnie also was worthy of an atheling; proof against spear-thrusts, yet of small supple links. Under it he wore a padded tunic, to save his ribs from bruising. His trousers were white, padded against the cold rather than against sword-cuts. He looked again at the fastenings of his shoes, but they were as firm as his servant could tie them; a loose shoe might trip its wearer at a critical moment, but a tight one might lame him. He was not quite satisfied with his helmet. In his baggage he had an ornamental affair of gilt bronze decorated with spreading oxhorns, a trophy his father had taken from the heathen long ago; but a glancing blow on a horn might leave its wearer bareheaded. Instead he had chosen a plain steel cap, conical and highly polished. It sat firm on his head, but critics might call it too plain for an atheling. It would be a pity if enemies could whisper that he feared to be noticed on the battlefield.

Suppose his sword stuck when he tried to draw it? He pulled it out to make sure, and then put it back with a blush as he saw veterans slouching empty-handed to the standards.

At long last the war-horns sounded and he set off at a steady plod towards the heathen palisade. Behind him plodded the thanes of the shires beyond Selwood; for the King of the West Saxons must lead into battle the warriors from the ancient core of his Kingdom.

There had been no attempt at surprise. It was considered more important that the troops should make ready at leisure, after a good breakfast. As they drew near the palisade they saw the Army waiting for them.

Sixty yards from the ditch Alfred halted his men to dress the line. Behind the ditch an earthen bank rose five feet from the frozen mud, and on it bristled a shoulder-high palisade of sharp outward-sloping spikes. Behind it the heathen held their great axes resting on their shoulders; most of them had no shield, for they needed both hands for the axe. They were tall men, very well dressed and not at all frightened. How on earth could you climb over that fence, using both hands to grasp the spikes, without being cut in half by an axe wielded by a man who stood firm on his feet with nothing to distract him from his butchery?

But the horns bellowed; javelins and arrows flashed through the air. He set his teeth and ran blindly forward. The ditch was just not too wide to be jumped, if you ran at it properly. He landed on the far side, halfway up the bank; and blinked, ashamed to find that he had jumped with his eyes shut.

There was room for a swordblade between the stakes. He must drive back that tall hero, naked to the waist, whose mouth spattered foam on the long yellow plaits

114

of his hair. His sword darted through and the pirate retreated a pace.

The bank was lined with Saxon warriors, others jostling in the ditch. A brave man jumped, to balance for a moment on the stakes, his head within the hostile camp; an axe crashed down on his spine, splitting the linked byrnie as though it were wool. That mode of attack was sheer suicide.

A man standing in the ditch had wrenched at a stake and pulled it nearly flat. Something might be done that way. Slinging his shield on his back, Alfred tugged at another stake; until he saw an axe poised above him and jumped back in haste.

A javelin glanced from his byrnie. It was madness to stand so close, a mark to be shot at and unable to harm the foe. Most of his followers had already withdrawn out of arrow shot. With his shield on his back he walked slowly away from the unharmed palisade.

On his right he could see his brother's men also retiring. The assault had failed all along the line. But the battle had lasted for hardly ten minutes, and there were still six hours of daylight. The West Saxons could not admit defeat so early. He must try again, if he could hit on some more promising plan.

As the line reformed a messenger found him. 'From alderman Ethelwulf,' he gasped out. 'Here is a wood-cutter's axe. He is taking them for the peasants of the Berkshire fyrd. It's no good sending peasants into the front line, but with these axes your companions may cut a gap in the palisade.'

'A pity we didn't think of that before,' Alfred muttered. 'We shall never manage another charge as brisk as the first. But it's a good idea,' he added in a louder voice. 'Thank the alderman for me. As soon as the axes arrive we shall try again.'

For four hours they tried again, in charge after charge. Each attack was beaten off in a very few minutes; for under the hail of arrows and javelins no one could live in the ditch. But each attack knocked a few holes in that menacing palisade, and some heathen were killed by thrusts between the stakes as they ventured too close. Alfred himself had killed a man, and was surprised that such a landmark in his life left such a slight impression. His old foe, the baresark with the yellow swinging plaits, had reached out to hew at him over the palisade; he felt very brave as he jumped forward under the blow, so that the axe-haft hit him on the shoulder while his own sword darted between the stakes to sink into the naked sweating chest. Later, when he tried the same stroke a second time, an axe swinging on the far side of the palisade knocked his sword clean out of his hand. Luckily the plain sword bore no mark of ownership. Some heathen had taken valuable spoil, but he would not boast that he had disarmed an atheling of Wessex.

There were plenty of ownerless swords in the ditch. The blade he picked up was of soft Wealden iron instead of Baltic steel; but he could kill a man with it, if only the heathen would come out from behind their stakes and fight honestly in the open.

The sun was a red ball in the south-west. In an hour the early dusk of November would come down. All round the wooded horizon a white haze was gathering, but over the camp lay a smear of steam from sweating frightened bodies. If the West Saxons were to withdraw in daylight there was time for only one more assault.

Alfred was summoned to confer with his brother. King Ethelred was unwounded, but he wore a leather cap instead of the fine helmet which had been knocked from his head. He was very tired, and his streaming nose had smeared his face rather disgustingly.

'Look here, Alfred,' he said between gasps and wheezes, 'we will try something new for the last assault. Have you noticed that the heathen have split into two wings, to meet our double attack? All their best men have been drawn to the flanks, and their centre is thin.

So this time I shall take post with the best of my companions on the left of my division, and you will take the right of yours. As we charge we incline inwards, until we reach the palisade side by side. I shall order Ethelwulf to charge behind us. We can't leave him standing on the field all day without striking a blow. Now go back and wait for my signal. This is the last charge of the day. Put all you've got into it.'

Barely half of Alfred's companions still followed him; though he hoped that some of the missing had been taken wounded to the rear. Everyone was tired, and the November wind stiffened sweat-soaked bodies. But the enemy would be just as tired and shaken. He took post before a clump of axemen. If they cut a gap in the palisade an atheling ought to be the first man through. He seemed to have been leading these charges all his life. He knew exactly what he would do, and how it would fall out.

But this time things went differently. They had cut a gap of several yards in the palisade before the enemy noticed the change in the weight of the attack. Alfred went through beside his brother. It was comforting to be fighting on level ground, and for the second time he killed an adversary; by a swift thrust in the belly while the two-handed axe was heaved up. Perhaps these great axes were not such dangerous weapons after all; a sword made a more deadly wound. The best thing of all was that he had grown accustomed to fighting hand to hand; in fact it was hard to remember that his life was in deadly danger every moment of the fight.

The heathen rallied when their supports ran up from the flanks. Alfred saw his brother stagger as an axe beat on his shield; the West Saxons were going back, pushed off their feet by the weight of the charge. His brother had given ground; he also must retire, or be cut off among the heathen.

For a few minutes the Saxons hung on to the gap in the palisade. If only Ethelwulf would come in, while they were still on the crest of the bank! But more and more heathen pushed at them, in a crescendo of hate and fury. These trained professionals fought as fiercely in the evening as at the first onset.

Abruptly the aspect of the battle altered. The Saxons were on the defensive, and it was doubtful whether they could defend themselves much longer. As they were hustled down into the ditch some turned their backs to the foe. Two elderly companions pulled King Ethelred by his belt to hasten his retreat. Alfred was in danger of being cut off, until half a dozen of his men turned back to help him. Then they were all outside the camp, reforming as they had reformed a dozen times during the long day.

But there was no time to reform. The heathen poured through the gap in the palisade in a decisive counter-attack. The Saxon line wavered, a few men ran back in terror. King Ethelred stood his ground, alone, until Alfred ran over to stand on his left. With their companions clustering round them they retired at a fast but collected walk, turning to make a front when the heathen pressed too closely.

The heathen did not press hard because there was easier prey on either side. The bulk of the Saxons were frankly running away, and direct pursuit was safer and more enjoyable than another push at the athelings who still fought back. The King spoke to his brother in savage disappointment: 'I never thought my own kinsmen would desert their King on the field. And the day began so well!'

'Our men haven't really been beaten,' Alfred consoled him. 'It's just that suddenly they stopped trying. I suppose that can happen to any warband at the end of a long fight.'

'If they aren't beaten, how fast would they run if they had been?' asked the King bitterly. 'By dark they will be scattered. We must pull back behind Selwood, and set about raising a fresh warband.'

They halted and turned about, to form a ragged front

against their pursuers. Suddenly there was a great outcry behind them, and scattered pirates ran by on their way back to the heathen palisade. The athelings took a fresh grasp of their swords and prepared to renew the fight. Then the fyrd of Berkshire charged up on both sides of them. They saw old Ethelwulf, white hair flying, running like a youth as he chased the heathen.

'Saved!' gasped the King. 'But we must call him off before he begins another battle. You, run and tell the alderman to rally on our camp. We have done enough for one day. The men will break again if we let them fight on.'

The messenger ran forward while the King continued his retreat.

In the Saxon camp frightened grooms were loading frightened packhorses. The King encouraged them to hurry. 'Thanks to Ethelwulf, our warband has been saved,' he told Alfred. 'But tonight we must fall back a long day's march to the westward. We'll move by the chalk ridge we used for our approach. It's open country, and firm enough for the baggage to make good time in the dark. I must find dry clothes, and get warm by a fire, or I'll be down with fever tomorrow. So I'll go ahead as soon as they find me a horse. You take over the rearguard. Save as much of our baggage as you can. What you can't move give to the Berkshire peasants who saved us this evening. Don't forget to tell Ethelwulf to come to me so that I can reward him for his heroism today.'

Night was falling, and the heathen remained quiet behind their palisade. But there could be no rest for the beaten West Saxons until they were beyond reach of attack. Alfred did not know how to set about organizing a rearguard among shaken troops who clung together chiefly because they were afraid to venture into the woods by themselves. But his own companions would stand by him whatever befell, and the companions of Ethelwulf would be even more useful, since they had left the field victorious after a brief engagement.

There were more than enough horses, with so many warriors dead. The retreat was going smoothly, and the night was so dark and windy that the enemy were unlikely to interfere. But he could not find alderman Ethelwulf, though he had spoken with a few Berkshire thanes.

He sent messengers to search for him, though he was reluctant to publish to his nervous men that such a famous warrior was missing. The messengers could not find even the companions of the alderman of Berkshire. It was very odd. Surely the whole band had not set off with some wild idea of joining their old comrades the Mercians? Then he found among the wounded one of Ethelwulf's companions, and learned what had happened to the missing hero.

A northern axe had hewed deep into the Mercian's shoulder. He was conscious, and could sit a horse if he was held on it; but the gash was too wide to heal, and when inflammation set in he would die. He was ready for death.

'My lord was killed at my side,' he said with a grimace of pain,' and a true companion should not survive his lord. Ethelwulf was too old for swordplay. He didn't get his shield down in time and a heathen Earl cut him in the thigh. I saw it, and I recognized the Earl. He's the man they call Sidroc the Elder, father of Sidroc the Younger whom we wounded at Englefield. You know who killed my lord. I shall never fight again, and I leave to the West Saxons the duty of avenging him. Ethelwulf died quickly, for the axe cut the great vein in his leg. Then we charged to catch Sidroc, and I got my wound. The other companions took up Ethelwulf's body and carried it off for burial.'

'Then where are they now?' asked Alfred. 'We shall make a great tomb for Ethelwulf at Sherborne.'

'Oh no, atheling. Ethelwulf of the Pecsaetas will be buried beside his ancestors. When his companions have buried him they will come back again to Wessex to fight

120

the heathen. It was all decided while your men were loading the baggage.'

'So that's what became of them. But how can they do it? The Army lies between Wessex and the Peak, and all the land round Derby is held by the pirates.'

'They'll do it. They wouldn't let me come with them, because I can't walk. They will kill a sentry or two, and slip through the heathen lines. We remember the song you sang at King Burhed's wedding. We want to remind the West Saxons that Mercians also can keep faith with their lord.'

'You have done honourably. I myself will tell the gleemen, and so long as this war is remembered the devotion of Ethelwulf's companions will be remembered also.'

'Thank you, my lord. Then I need not worry about dying, for my honour will live after me.'

Alfred rode on, stumbling through frozen mud, until the column reached the open chalk and could move more easily. The tale of Ethelwulf's death had shaken him, and even more the desperate undertaking of his Mercian companions. He himself had been responsible. The poem he had sung as a child, choosing it merely to score off men who changed their Kings so lightly, had sent brave warriors into deadly peril. That is what it is to be an atheling, whose lightest word is never forgotten. And cousin Neot, who had the gift of prophecy, had said long ago that because of his haughtiness he would one day find himself alone and forsaken. To be an atheling is a very heavy burden.

8

The Battle-Winter: Ashdown

Four days later the fyrd of Wessex was once again assembled within sight of the Army. But this time they were far to the westward, on the edge of the chalk ridge of Ashdown. For the heathen, encouraged by victory, had ridden westward to plunder in untouched country.

Dawn came later, and the weather was even colder. The Saxons had slept in the open; though King Ethelred, who was coughing badly, had sheltered in a cottage. While his servants strapped him into his byrnie he talked over his plans with his brother.

'We shall attack them again, as soon as the men have eaten breakfast. I suppose they will beat us, as they beat us at Reading. But the only way to discourage the Army is to fight it again and again. The heathen don't want to fight, especially in the middle of winter. They came here to win plunder, not to conquer Kingdoms. If we keep on fighting them they will go away. The only danger is that our men may be too frightened to rally when next I call them to the muster. But I don't think things have reached that pitch – yet.'

'They'll rally again, even after another beating,' Alfred reassured him. 'It needs more than two defeats to take the heart out of a West Saxon. Besides, we are in the middle of Wessex, and their homes are at stake. We got most of the women and children away, but they have seen a few bodies where the heathen passed by. That will make any man eager to fight.

'Then that's settled. We attack in two divisions. You

123

take the left wing and I take the right. I wish we had some trustworthy veteran to command the reserve. But we haven't anyone with the right experience, and anyway all the thanes will want to serve under an atheling. I miss Ethelwulf more every day.'

'Could Bishop Heahmund command the reserve?' asked Alfred. 'The thanes will obey him. But he has not seen a great deal of warfare. You would have to send orders when you want him to advance.'

'The Bishop of Sherborne? That's not a bad idea. A Bishop who goes to war is always popular, and the touchiest hero won't mind serving under him. But a commander who can't move without orders is no use to me. Later on, when he has seen more service, I shall give him a command of his own. Today we'll have no reserve, just the two wings. You take the men from west of Selwood, and the South Saxons as well to make our numbers equal. I shall have the men of old Wessex, Kent, and Surrey. If we are driven from the field we shall hide in the woods, and rally again twenty miles to the westward.'

'When do we attack?' asked Alfred.

'Mass at sunrise, of course, and then breakfast. But with the enemy so near we shan't take any chances. Let the men form their ranks first of all, then the priests can say Mass before them. They can breakfast in rank as well, so we shan't be caught in disorder. Have you seen the enemy camp? Is it strongly defended?'

'I haven't seen it myself, except from the foot of the hill. I have spoken to scouts who got very near it last night. The heathen posted sentries, and patrolled so carefully that there was no chance of surprising them. But then you can never surprise the Army. Oddly enough, they haven't dug a ditch. With no trees on the hilltop they can't make a palisade, so I suppose they didn't bother to make a bank.'

'Perhaps they propose to attack. Better watch for it,' said the King.

'That's not likely, when they have a strong position on

a steep hill. Besides, they are not eager for battle, and we are. But I shall keep my eyes open.'

'Then that's all, and the best of luck in case we don't meet again before the fighting. By the way, I shall hear Mass in this hut, to keep out of the wind as long as possible. Once swords have been drawn I don't feel the cold. Excitement keeps me warm, I suppose. But it's too cold for me outside just now. So if you want to send me a message the man will find me here.'

Alfred would have liked to embrace his brother; there was a very good chance that they would never meet again. But a farewell now might be discouraging. He saluted as stiffly as if he had been taking orders from a stranger.

While his wing of the host formed in rank he gazed at the Army on its foggy hilltop. Last night some Christian captives had managed to escape, and after questioning them he had a fair idea of the strength of the enemy. Their numbers were not too frightening; the fyrd of Wessex would slightly outnumber the Army. But every heathen warrior was a veteran of long standing, who had done nothing but fight for many years; while many peasants of the fyrd came to the field with sickles and scythes. Even the thanes, who had good byrnies and swords, spent their time in hunting and farming, not in war. It would be a fight of professionals against amateurs.

The leaders of the Army were the best warriors of the north. Now that Ivar was dead his next brother, King Halfdan, was without a rival among the pirates; his colleague, King Bacsaeg, was said to follow him loyally. Besides the two Kings there were enough Earls, with their companions, to make up half the Army. They had been plundering great cities when the athelings of Wessex were in their cradles.

The only advantage possessed by the West Saxons was that God ought to be on their side. That should be decisive, of course. But as Alfred considered the point he saw that of recent years God had not helped His servants against the unbelievers. The Army had pillaged Holy

Ireland and the great minsters of the Franks; another kind of heathen held Jerusalem. Four centuries ago his own heathen ancestor Cerdic had won Wessex from the Christian Welsh. To fight in defence of God and His Church might earn you heaven after death; it was no guarantee of victory in this world.

As the priest muttered the first words of the Mass he suppressed the impious thought. All round him his companions fell on their knees.

Kneeling, he tried to fix his mind on God. Success or failure was utterly unimportant; what mattered was that he should do his duty until the end of his life. Even if the Church were extirpated from Britain that might be in accordance with the Divine Plan. At the first Pentecost all the Christians in the world had gathered in one upper room; the Church might diminish to that number again. But the Church would endure until the end of the world, because God had promised it. He, and all these companions and kinsmen round him, would fight the heathen for as long as they could lift their swords; and after defeat they would fight again, because that was what King Ethelred his brother had taught them to do.

The priest hurried through Mass at a great pace; he followed Bishop Heahmund, and was anxious to get back to his lord's warband. Without breach of decorum Alfred could look again at the Army on its hill, though he might not yet rise from his knees. He was surprised by what he saw. The Army had come out from the camp and mustered in line, though the sun was barely risen. Against the sky he could make out a jagged outline of brandished axes and swords.

Then the outline blurred, and he rubbed his eyes. But it was certainly not so easy to see the helmets and weapons of the heathen. Why was that? Because the background was no longer grey November sky but sodden grass. At this distance he could not make out moving feet, but undoubtedly the Army was advancing downhill to charge the waiting West Saxons.

He considered. His men were drawn up on level ground at the foot of the chalk ridge. They would meet the heathen charge at a stand. In the first ten minutes the line might break; the heathen would come fresh to the pursuit, and would do great execution. After such a bloody defeat it might be that his men would never again come to the muster; those who got away would flee to Wales or even to Frankland.

The right move, he was sure of it, was to charge uphill and meet the Army on the move. But in the King's presence the King's brother could not order the host to advance. The order must come from Ethelred. He ran to the cottage where the King heard Mass.

As he ran he had time for doubts. A month ago he had never seen war. He was a novice, survivor of only one battle and that a defeat. If a counter-charge were the obvious move some veteran would have already suggested it. But it *was* the right move. He was the King's brother and closest adviser. When he knew what ought to be done he could not keep silent.

He burst into the cottage at the very moment of the Consecration. A few companions looked round in alarm; but the King, rapt on his knees, frowned at the interruption. 'The Army is charging and we must meet it,' Alfred whispered urgently. 'Don't interrupt,' snapped Ethelred. 'We may all be dead by midday. I must receive Communion.'

'But the battle is beginning,' Alfred persisted.

'What of it? My West Saxons can hold firm in their ranks until Mass is finished. I shall be with you as soon as I can.'

Alfred flung out of the cottage, with a perfunctory bob at the newly-consecrated Host. In a way, King Ethelred was right; at a votive Mass before battle a King ought to have the good manners to wait for the *Ite*. His men had their orders, and they were properly drawn up to meet the Army's attack.

But the right thing to do was to charge against the

Army's charge, he was sure of it. And the men would obey his orders, for they would assume they were the King's. As he left the cottage, amid the frowns and stares of the devout congregation, he felt for a moment the sense of collapse that came with his attacks of self-consciousness. But in the open his assurance returned. In the presence of the King, without authorization, an untried atheling would move the combined host of the whole Kingdom.

As he ran to his post he pulled his shield from his back to the fighting position on the left arm. Arrived before his own wing he did not check his pace but turned towards the approaching Army. With a roar of war cries and horns the fyrd of the West Saxons charged behind him.

The heathen host charged also in two divisions; on his right he could see the Raven banner and two crowned Kings advancing before it. On his own front a separate corps was led by a cluster of gold-collared warriors who must be Earls. Yes, they were the Earls, for one of them had a bandaged shoulder; Sidroc the Younger who had been wounded by the gallant Ethelwulf. He ran towards him, thinking he had found an easy victim whose downfall would hearten the West Saxons. Then he decided that a wounded man was not a worthy antagonist for a Woden-born atheling, and instead chose as his adversary a bearded warrior whose great two-handed axe gleamed with gems and polished silver.

He was wildly excited and yet perfectly cool. He could feel his legs moving more quickly and accurately than ever before in his life; he had the comforting certainty, which comes sometimes to young athletes, that for the next hour or so he would be right on top of his form, stronger and faster and more agile than on ordinary days. As the Earl swung up his axe Alfred bunched his feet and leaped; his swordpoint sank into the soft bearded throat before the axe could descend.

The first blow struck in this battle had killed a great

Earl. The Saxons charged with renewed enthusiasm; dressing their ranks, the heathen stolidly prepared for a long fight. The two hosts settled down to hew at each other over the war-linden on the slope of Ashdown.

Half a hour later a tremor went through the ranks; the heathen gave ground just a little. King Ethelred and his companions, come straight from Communion to fight for Christendom, had given just that extra push which turns a standing battle into a stumbling advance. Step by step the heathen retreated, hoping to break off the engagement and dress their ranks afresh. But the Saxons followed them closely.

It was nearly midday when suddenly the heathen ran back and got clear of their adversaries; only practised veterans could have obeyed orders so neatly in the heat of battle. But they were not yet ready for retreat. By a solitary thorn tree just below the crest of the down they reformed their ranks and returned to the charge. Yet as they retired the Saxons had seen clearly the bodies of the slain, and a joyful cry went up that a King of the great Army had fallen.

For two hours which seemed a lifetime Alfred fought in the shadow of that solitary thorn, without retreating or advancing a step. While he was fresh the point of his sword flickered so swiftly that no axe could harm him, but as he tired he found it more and more difficult to dodge clear of those slow ponderous two-handed swipes. The heathen fought as fiercely in the afternoon as they had fought in the November sunrise; they were professionals who had been fighting all their lives.

Suddenly it ended. Like starlings wheeling together the heathen turned and fled. Most of them were not really afraid, but they had had enough and wanted to end the battle; they ran fast, hoping to get clear of pursuit.

But they could not get clear. They might be professionals, but the Army had little experience of retreat. They wanted to get away from those darting sword-points, to rest and draw breath and form up again in their ranks; and they were denied the respite they needed. They ran faster and faster, with no time to seek their waiting horses. Presently they began to panic.

No Saxon could feel tired with the back of a frightened pirate just out of reach of his sword. Alfred ran without effort. It was impossible to catch up with the fleeing Army, but there was a constant dribble of injured or exhausted pirates who turned with bared teeth to die among their pursuers, and an occasional coward who squealed as the avenging sword caught him shamefully in the back. For miles they ran over the bare chalk down, the watery sunset fading behind them.

It was so marvellous, so unexpected, such a merciful deliverance, that no Saxon could think sensibly about it. The sun had set and there was barely light to see the ground when a groom who had his wits about him brought up a few horses. Of course King Ethelred was the first man mounted, and then a grinning companion was holding a stirrup for the atheling and second in command. It was too late. After a mere half mile of bloody slaughter the winter dark closed down until it was impossible to see a sword's-length ahead. Groaning with vexation, the King ordered the horns to sound the recall. While the Saxons stumbled wearily back to camp the Army fled by a clear road to Reading.

Alfred was too tired to ride back to his baggage. He slept wrapped in his cloak under the thorn tree where the fighting had raged most fiercely. His companions wanted to hew down the tree to make a fire, but he forbade it; in after years he would come back to that tree, and live again the happiest moment of his life. In the morning he woke elated, and then recalled that he must face an awkward interview. He must explain to his brother and King his reasons for taking command of the host.

It was a thing no ordinary King would forgive – the most famous victory of modern times, and all the credit and glory stolen by his younger brother. But Ethelred was not an ordinary King. When Alfred sought him out he was embraced on both cheeks. Then the King gave him the splendid sword, decorated with amber and pearls, that had been found under the body of King Bacsaeg. 'You are the second man in the Kingdom of the West Saxons, and that's high honour,' he said with a grin, 'but on Ashdown you were the first, and I shall never deny it.'

It was wonderful to serve such a brother.

They spent a happy day gathering the spoil. From the thorn tree to the end of Ashdown the grey grass of winter was dotted with the bodies and weapons of the heathen. West of the thorn tree the ground was heaped with corpses, but half of them were Saxon and it was depressing to wander among them. The burial of the defenders was left to the local clergy and peasants, assisted by the companions of the lords among the fallen. The bodies of the heathen were collected for burning, which is less trouble than burial and was after all what their own comrades would have done with them. (King Ethelred was careful to explain that he intended no dishonour to the corpses of brave men who had fallen honestly in a hard-fought fight.) Most of these pirates had plundered throughout Christendom for many years, and since they had no homes they carried all their wealth into battle. Each body was worth searching carefully, for finger-rings and arm-rings and neck-rings, for belts set with gems, for purses stuffed with silver. Their armour and weapons were better made and more richly ornamented than anything worn by companions or thanes among the West Saxons.

King Ethelred persuaded his men to set aside most of the unbroken armour and weapons. The West Saxons had lost heavily, but in their camp were peasants who needed only byrnies and swords to stand in the host beside well-born thanes. A few years ago nobles of good ancestry would have gone home in a huff if they had found churlish peasants set in the ranks beside them; but the coming of the Army had made men willing to forget the claims of birth. After the new recruits had been armed King Ethelred would command a host stronger than that which had fought at Ashdown; but the Army, shut up in inland Wessex, would not be so easily reinforced.

'The Army marched out and we beat it. At nightfall the West Saxons held the place of slaughter, while the Army fled to Reading,' King Ethelred repeated in wonder as he looked at the wreckage of the retreat.

'The Army,' he went on in a singsong voice, 'the great Army, the Army of the sons of Ragnar. The Army that plundered all the lands of the Franks, Neustria, Flanders, Burgundy, Austrasia. The Army that sacked the shrine of St. Martin and slew the monks of Marmoutier. The Army that martyred King Edmund of the East English. The Army that holds York and all Northumbria. The Army that receives tribute from the Mercians and the Welsh. The Army marched against the West Saxons. The heathen men sought battle, they were not taken unawares. Next day the King of the West Saxons stood at his ease, counting his spoil in the place of slaughter.'

'Yes, there's a poem in it, as good as any of the epics,' said Alfred with a grin, as pleased by his brother's happiness as by the outcome of the battle. 'Shall we work on it together? This evening I'll take the harp and hammer out a refrain, so that we remember the words we string together. But to fill out a good poem we want plenty of names, long lists of terrible rolling heathen names so that our grandchildren see the menace and the power of the Army. Those dead men look very ordinary, lying on the muddy grass stripped of their arms, waiting to be burned on a bonfire as dead leaves are burned in the autumn. Have you noticed how even the mightiest hero looks insignificant when there is no breath to hold his ribs apart? Take this man, for example. See, he turned to face us when we caught up with him. He took the edge of a sword on his collar-bone, and then the point in his belly; as good an end as any heathen can make. Yet

132

now he looks like a dead rabbit. How many monks did you kill, in Frankland and Northumbria? How many altars have you defiled? Did you burn great cities? I wish we knew his name. You can't make a poem without names.'

'Perhaps we can find out their names,' said the King, excited by the new idea. 'I shall send a messenger to ride through the camp, offering five gold pieces for every wounded heathen who can still speak. There may be some of them who have not yet been finished off.'

'Don't waste gold. Offer the reward for the first heathen brought to you. We shan't need more than one,' said the prudent Alfred.

Within an hour a suitable prisoner had been produced. He could talk rationally and understand what was said to him, for he had not been wounded. While fleeing in the dark he had broken his ankle. A groom had found him crawling towards the forest; the unarmed groom had been wondering how to kill his prize when he heard of the King's offer.

The dead were scattered over five miles of chalk ridge, but the more valuable of their weapons had been gathered into a single heap. The pirate was brought to look over these trophies, more easily recognized than the stripped and gashed corpses. He sat sideways on a pony; but his arms had been bound behind his back and the groom held the end of the rope.

Alfred could understand the man's speech, which sounded like Northumbrian English spoken with a slow unaccented burr. He addressed him politely, as a warrior speaks to a foe of equal birth. The pirate was cold and tired and hungry and in pain, but he answered with dignity.

'It's the last and best service I can do for my old comrades,' he said proudly. 'If you are going to put this battle into a poem their names must be remembered correctly. A dead man is dead completely, but one part of him never dies: the good repute he leaves after death.'

'We disagree on that point,' said Alfred, recalling his Christian duty. 'Have they explained to you that if you will accept baptism you will be permitted to live, as a slave among the West Saxons?'

'It has been explained. Thor has given me many happy years of plunder among the Christians. I do not choose to desert him at the end. Now show me the weapons, and I will name the leaders among the mighty dead of yesterday.'

He recognized many weapons. He named the owners under his breath, tut-tutting at the mischance which had brought so many good men to early death. But he was a cultivated man, for a pirate, and he knew that no poem can find room for hundreds of names. At the end he thought for a moment, going over the list in his mind. Then he spoke formally:

'These are the most famous of the heroes of the Army, who met death at the hands of the West Saxons on the field of Ashdown. First I must tell of King Bacsaeg, a great King from far to the north-east, from our border against the Finns. Yet though he was a King he came only as a summer pirate, he was not a true veteran of the Army. He was the friend and faithful follower of King Halfdan.'

'We shall burn his body unmutilated, as his own companions would burn it had he died at home,' said Ethelred. 'That is honour enough for any pirate, even for a King of the pirates. Now tell us of the other great men who fell.'

'I have seen the weapons of five famous Earls. Of these Sidroc the Old was the most venerable, and Sidroc the Young the mightiest warrior. They were father and son. Sidroc the Young was wounded in the first battle we fought here in Wessex. If he had come whole to Ashdown no Saxon could have killed him.'

'That's the man alderman Ethelwulf wounded at Englefield,' muttered the King. 'I'm glad we finished him off. Ethelwulf's work was not wasted.'

'The other Earls were Harold and Fraena and Osbjorn, famous men who had taken great plunder from the Franks. Osbjorn was at the killing of that young English King whose ghost now comes back to seek vengeance on us.'

'So the heathen are still afraid of the holy martyr Edmund,' Alfred whispered. 'But we need not put that into our poem. He will be remembered for ever without us. What other great men fell?'

'There are no more to be named here and now. One King and five Earls are enough for the most famous victory. There fell thousands of brave pirates, and thousands of brave Christians also, for the killing was not all on one side. But your poem will be a sufficient memorial for them without mention of their names. Their grandchildren can say that they marched to Ashdown and remain there, and that will be enough.'

'I thank you for your help,' said the King gravely. 'You also came to Ashdown and will not leave it, and my poem will be your memorial. Now get off that pony and sit on the ground. If you bend your head that man behind you will strike with his axe, and you will feel no pain.'

'An uncouth suggestion,' said the pirate in anger. 'I help you with your poem, and you propose to kill me from behind as though you had caught me running away. Your groom will bear witness that I turned to face him when there was no hope of escape. With this tiresome leg I can't stand alone, but I have a right to die on my feet, with my face to my adversary. I shall lean against this pony while the young prince runs me though with his sword.'

They helped him off with his byrnie, so that a single thrust would kill him quickly. As he balanced on one leg, with his eyes open and his lips firm, Alfred split his heart.

The Epic of Ashdown was a good poem of its kind, though on the long side. It quickly became popular, so

135

popular that at the time no one bothered to write it down. In after years the clergy disliked its tone, which seemed to them to betray too much admiration for heathen courage, so they never put it on parchment. Then other things happened, which were even more worth writing about; and within two generations the Epic had been forgotten.

9

The Battle-Winter: King Ethelred

Both sides had lost so heavily that for a fortnight there was no more fighting. King Ethelred and his brother rode swiftly to Somerset, to tell their families of their exploits; and then returned to the muster a few miles west of Reading.

The famous victory of Ashdown brought no concrete gains. The intangible advantages were many: the thanes were in good heart, eager to continue the war at a season when their ancestors had settled down in the chimney-corner to wait for spring; the heathen had been shaken by the bloody check. But the pirates still held their impregnable position in the heart of Wessex; they had ample supplies, and reinforcements could reach them by way of the Thames. Perhaps the elimination of King Bacsaeg had strengthened the power of King Halfdan, for there were no signs of divided counsels in the mighty Army.

'But if only our thanes can endure the weather this kind of campaign does us less harm than fighting in summer,' King Ethelred said cheerfully as he discussed the future with his brother. 'There's nothing else we ought to be doing at this time of year; no ploughing, no lambing, no threshing. The warriors will be as happy drinking ale by the camp fire as they would be at home with nothing to do and no one to talk to. Deep snow or an outbreak of disease might stop the campaign, but if the heathen in their marsh can stick it so can we on dry ground.'

'Disease is the danger,' answered Alfred. 'I'm not thinking of the warriors. It's hot weather, not frost, that brings sickness to crowded camps. But you must take care of that chest of yours. You are coughing worse than ever. If you go on riding about in the rain, drenched to the skin, the West Saxons will soon be looking for another King.'

'It's a risk that must be taken,' Ethelred shrugged. 'If our ancestors had been afraid of the weather they would never have conquered Britain. If I am laid up for a time you must take charge of the host; and if I should be killed, well, I have a son to succeed me.'

'That's just it. Of course I can take a temporary command. But your son is a baby and we are at war. If tomorrow you get killed, who leads your companions on the next day?'

'You do, of course. It's a nagging temptation to be the younger brother of a King, I know. I was one myself. But we both managed to keep loyal to Ethelbald and Ethelbert, and I can trust you to be loyal to your nephew after I am gone. I suppose they will make you King; the idea of a regency is too complicated for our simple thanes. But we are not a long-lived race. By the time young Ethelwold is grown up you will be ready to retire. So it's all quite simple and we have nothing to worry about.'

'It sounds simple as you put it. Of course I may be the one to be killed in battle, and you may reign until Ethelwold is old enough to succeed you. What worries me is the fate of my own baby son. Brothers trust one another, cousins don't. I'm afraid that your Ethelwold will be jealous of my Edward, though I took care to give him a name which reminds him that he will never be King. Children may be brought up as friends, and change their minds when they grow up.'

'Then you and I will take an oath of friendship for our children,' said the King. 'We don't need it for ourselves. We haven't quarrelled since I took your rattle while you were crawling on the floor. So I swear here and now, by the honour of our ancestors, that I shall safeguard the rights of your son for as long as I shall live. Now you take the same oath, and we need not fear the future.'

Alfred swore. There were no witnesses and no relics. But the surviving sons of King Ethelwulf could trust one another.

'There, that's over,' said Alfred with relief. 'Now what shall we do to make the Army sorry that ever it marched into Wessex?'

'We shan't attack their palisade again,' the King decided. 'While they stand on the defensive they are still too strong for us. But I don't suppose they are enjoying their stay by the muddy river, and we shall fight them when next they come out into the open.'

A bare fortnight after the great battle of Ashdown the stubborn Army sent out another foraging party. The West Saxons were alert; King Ethelred with his whole levy met the invaders at Basing, a day's march south of Reading.

The Saxons were confident; at the last battle they had seen the backs of their enemies, and they attacked gaily in expectation of another victory. But the heathen were a picked force, every man in good armour; while many Saxons, cloaked against the biting cold, had left their byrnies in camp.

Both sides charged. For less than an hour they stumbled among the frozen clods, Saxon sword against heathen axe; then suddenly, without warning and for no obvious reason, the Saxons broke.

Alfred commanded the left division of the host, as was the custom when the King took the right wing. He felt the infection of panic as it swept through his men, the desperate urge to get clear and calm down before renewing the struggle. It was not exactly fear of imminent death; but rather a certainty that the battle was going wrong, and must be stopped and started again if they were to hope for success. But the heathen followed up so fiercely that the only way to get clear was to run at top speed.

An atheling might not flee at top speed. Half a dozen of his companions stood by him as he withdrew at a swift but dignified walk. On the other flank King Ethelred formed a similar rearguard. The heathen battered on the shieldwall, but would not loosen their ranks for pursuit; one of their own stratagems was a feigned flight, and they suspected that the same tactics were being used against them. At the edge of Basing field they halted to dress their line and the Saxons broke off the action.

With curses and prayers the brothers got their men together, and once more advanced cautiously. By this time the December sun was low in the sky and a mist was rising. All they found on the field of ruined Basing were the naked bodies of the slain. The foragers had already set off for Reading.

'So much for the glory of Ashdown,' said Alfred bitterly. 'Why did our people run away? The heathen have recovered their confidence, and we must begin all over again.'

'Nobody knows why men run away,' answered King Ethelred. 'It happens sometimes, and you must be ready for it. Next time they may fight like lions. You never can tell. But the battle wasn't completely useless, even though we lost it. We made the heathen fight for a few cows. A single battle gave them all Northumbria, a mere skirmish gave them all East Anglia. They have been six weeks in Wessex, they have lost a King and many Earls, and they hold no more land than is covered by their camp. This is the grimmest winter the Army has endured since it came to Christendom. Perhaps in the summer it will go away.'

'Then we say no more about the panic, but just get ready for the next battle?' inquired Alfred.

'That's about it. I wish we could see the sun. I'm more bothered by this cold than by the Army. But I shan't attack that palisade a second time. Christmas is near, and luckily the heathen keep their Yule about the same time. We'll send the levies home for a holiday, and keep watch with just our own companions. They feast with us at Christmas anyway. After Christmas we shall fight every heathen foraging party. Fight them again and again, and never mind how often you get beaten. That's the only way of persuading the Army to move to a new hunting ground.'

During the glum brief days of midwinter the Army remained behind its palisade. There was always a Saxon warband outside Reading, and the heathen had to fight for each stolen ox; but most of the Christians had a chance to go home and see their families. Within a day's march of Reading the land was a desert, but the greater part of Wessex had been preserved from plunder.

The court kept Christmas at Sherborne, with good horses standing saddled and a watchful eye on the beacons. Alfred had to make friends with Elswitha all over again, as though they met as strangers. It seemed to him that she had changed during her exile in the Somerset marshes; he did not see that the change was in himself, a young veteran of two months of bloody winter warfare.

He sat on the floor as often as on a bench; his table-manners and his language had coarsened; his hands were rough and calloused, and he did not always remember to wash them. He had very little to say to any woman, and he stared at every grown man in a considering way, wondering what strain he could take before he turned and ran. But his notched sword shone bright from many scourings, and he was the hero of Ashdown. All the women, Elswitha included, looked after him in silent worship.

Candlemas had come, with driving snow and a hint of lengthening days, before the Army stirred from its encampment. Suddenly all the heathen rode out in a body, leaving only a small garrison of sick and wounded to hold their camp. The small Saxon warband before Reading dared not oppose them, and it was three days

141

before King Ethelred could collect his full force. By that time the Army had penetrated deep into the land, though they rode too fast to burn the farmsteads as they passed. The Army was challenging another set battle. The West Saxons accepted the challenge.

In council someone suggested that it might be wiser to march on Reading and capture the heathen camp in the absence of the Army. King Ethelred and his brother united to condemn the proposal, which seemed to them pusillanimous. An ordinary foe might retreat if his base was threatened; but the Army had no base and no home; the women in Reading were not honourable wives, but slaves taken from ravaged villages whom they would willingly discard for fresh concubines. It was even more decisive that while the Saxons were capturing Reading the Army would be free to ravage Wessex. King Ethelred repeated his theme: that only repeated battle would persuade the Army to go away.

Next morning the Saxons drew up in the open field, beside the little village of Merton. There was no attempt at surprise, no concealment of reserves. Here were the defenders of the land, eager to fight; the Army marched to the attack with equal ostentation.

It was the largest force that the West Saxons had ever put into the field. A few thanes had come even from distant and ruined Thanet, and the Bishop of Sherborne led the full levy from the lands beyond Selwood. All southern Britain, from the Foreland to Land's End was gathered to strike a blow at the invaders. King Ethelred took the right wing and Alfred commanded on the left.

Already battle had become a habit, even for a young man in his twenty-first year who four months ago had never drawn his sword. Alfred walked steadily forward against the advancing foe, and quickened to a run as he saw the heathen begin their charge. Charge must be met with charge, unless you had a palisade to help you; and it was waste of time to build a palisade when the heathen would merely walk round it and go on to ravage elsewhere.

There was nothing to be done but to run up against a running pirate and bash with your sword against his axe. At Ashdown that had brought victory, at Basing defeat; here at Merton they had an even chance, and anyway such straightforward tactics seemed fitting for a Woden-born Cerdinga. Raising his shield, Alfred broke into a trot.

By right of birth he charged ahead of his men. But his post was not so exposed as it seemed, and it did not make him unduly nervous. Behind him were his chosen companions, and every man of them would sacrifice his life to save his lord's. If he were knocked off his feet, if his shield-arm should drop, a companion would stand over him until he recovered. There was not even the normal danger that a foeman eager for glory would make a special set at an atheling. That would happen in a battle against civilized men; but the heathen of the Army were hardbitten professionals, who fought for profit and not for glory.

Everything was going as well as could be expected. The veterans of the Army kept good order as the charge crashed home, but so did the wary and confident West Saxons. Alfred thrust with his sword, kept his shield high, and shouted his war cry; in this press the most experienced warleader could do no more.

Such a battle could last all day. Both sides had every man in line, with no reserve; there was no attempt at manoeuvre. Perhaps they would still be fighting on the same ground when darkness fell; perhaps some man, heathen or Christian, would turn his back in panic and infect his fellows until the lines dissolved into a cloud of fugitives and pursuers. Meanwhile Alfred and his companions fought prudently and cautiously, taking as much care to guard themselves as to strike at the enemy.

Alfred stumbled over a heathen corpse, and cringed under his shield awaiting the stroke from a heathen axe which was the penalty for a misstep. As he straightened himself unhurt he saw there was no foe within reach. The heathen line stood as firm as before, but it had moved back a few paces.

His own companions formed in a close knot, and he led them forward at a run. The heathen fought back, but they gave a little more ground. Perhaps they were trying to disengage? But evidently they were retiring under orders, not because they had had enough. With some difficulty Alfred halted his followers, and stood watching to see whether the enemy would break off the fight. That would be a most satisfactory ending to the day, even if there were no pursuit; if the Army admitted a second defeat many pirates would go home in disgust.

When his men were in good order he charged again; again the heathen stood to meet him. Were they keeping him busy while some disaster overwhelmed his brother? In that crowd it was hard to see what was happening on the other flank; but the line seemed straight and from the right came the clamorous roar of equal battle, not cries of victory. Perhaps these disciplined veterans were truly about to leave the field in defeat.

It must be right to keep up the pressure. His men were excited and it was hard to hold them in line; but by leading another charge he made sure they were all behind him. A tall pirate came out to meet him, swinging a sword instead of the usual axe. The fellow used the point almost like a civilized man, instead of the customary blind swipe with the edge. Alfred fenced with him, seeking to stab below the shield while the heathen thrust at his throat.

Suddenly his adversary was out of reach, running away as hard as he could. The whole heathen line was in flight; delirious Saxons gave chase at top speed.

There was something odd about this unexpected victory. As Alfred ran after those fleeing backs he felt the oddity but could not explain it. Suddenly he understood; that man fencing with him had been perfectly cool, not a bit frightened. It was just possible that some disaster further down the line had broken the Army's formation; but men who must retreat because their comrades have given way do not run in that frenzied fashion.

He grabbed the nearest Saxon. 'Get back into line,' he shouted. 'Can't you see that this is a feigned flight? The heathen will turn on us when we have scattered.'

He managed to stop that one man; who immediately lost interest in the battle and squatted down to rob a corpse. A few more Saxons, poor thanes or promoted peasants, were also busy robbing the dead while the fight still raged. But his own companions were strung out in line like a riotous pack of hounds as they followed in the tracks of the enemy. Alfred ran on; he was the leader of these men and he must keep up with them.

All happened as he had feared. After a mile of pursuit the Saxons were scattered; many of them, thinking the battle over, had slowed to a walk or stopped to rest. But the heathen still ran in a thick line, so close together that few of them had been cut down. Suddenly they halted and faced about.

Alfred had been expecting it, and beside him were a group of companions, level-headed men whose first thought was to protect their lord. In good order they made their way steadily back to the wood beyond the old battlefield where they had left their horses. The Army, with plenty of terrified fugitives to pursue, did not bother them dangerously.

In that stubborn fight at Merton neither side was overcome by fear. The heathen fled to lure the Christians into a trap; the Saxons fled because they were attacked when scattered. Presently the Christians reformed their line. Men who had loitered found the battle coming back to them, and since they were not afraid they took their place in the ranks. As darkness fell the Saxons drew off in good order. The heathen held the place of slaughter, but if they wished to continue their plundering of Wessex they must fight again next day.

145

Instead, when dawn came, they rode back to their camp at Reading.

'The heathen made us look very silly,' said King Ethelred as he examined the tracks of the retreating Army. 'We ought to be ashamed of ourselves, deceived by a feigned flight after a winter of campaigning! But on the whole it was worth it. We lost some good men, but so did they. And they turned back leaving most of Wessex unravaged. If we can keep it up they will go away in the summer.'

'If we can keep it up,' Alfred answered doubtfully. 'I'm afraid our men will desert if we offer them nothing but daily battle without the glory of victory. And though the rumour runs that the army lost another Earl we shall find it hard to replace Bishop Heahmund. No one else can bring out all the thanes from beyond Selwood.'

'That's not quite true. The westerners follow the Bishop of Sherborne, not the holy Heahmund in particular. If I can find another brave clerk to be Bishop in his place no harm will be done. In fact it will be an inspiration. Heahmund died in battle against the heathen, so his monks may count him as a martyr. He is just as much of a martyr as King Edmund of the East English, that nowadays everyone makes such a fuss about.'

'Yes, it's tiresome that Edmund should be a saint, after one fight against the heathen and that a defeat; when no one invokes the intercession of the King of the West Saxons, who has fought the heathen all winter and once actually beat them,' said Alfred with a chuckle. 'Seriously, though, young Edmund did more than get killed fighting the heathen. They offered him his life if he would worship Thor. When he refused they killed him. That makes him a genuine martyr, even though it would have been shameful for a man of his birth to answer differently.'

'Just as it would be shameful if men of our birth should stop fighting, while the Army is quartered among our kinsmen,' said King Ethelred. 'Your companions and mine will stick by us, even if the thanes go home to attend to their ploughing. I shall fight the heathen so long as I have ten men to follow me. The Army lost an Earl, and a good many warriors, even though we couldn't count them because we had been driven from the place of slaughter. This must be the hardest winter they have endured since they left the north. Plenty of fighting and very little plunder. I don't suppose recruits will throng to King Halfdan when the summer pirates come south this year.'

But the next news that reached the court of Wessex was disappointing in the extreme; a band of pirates had come ashore near London and pushed up the Thames to join King Halfdan in Reading. After all its losses the Army was stronger than when it had first arrived in Wessex.

King Ethelred redoubled his exertions. With his companions and the few thanes who still followed his standard he attacked every band of foragers who left the heathen palisade. He rode all night and fought nearly every day, through the driving rain of spring and the enervating fast of Lent. Alfred with his own companions operated independently. The brothers were too weak to meet the whole Army in the field, but luckily the Army as a whole did not leave the shelter of Reading.

On Maundy Thursday, 12 April 871, the athelings rode south to keep Easter in the peaceful and unravaged minster of Wimborne. For a week only scouts would watch the Army; but the heathen had grown cautious, and might not notice the absence of defenders until they were back again. A Christian King must keep Easter even when there are invaders in his land. Godgifu and Elswitha came from Somerset to meet their husbands, and on the evening of Holy Saturday they feasted as they had not feasted since the old days when the Army ravaged in Frankland and Britain was at peace.

At daybreak on Easter Monday the companions mustered to ride back to the war. The athelings had risen late, but that was to be excused at the end of their brief holiday. While Alfred was getting into his byrnie, thinking out an apology for keeping his King waiting, a servant told him that King Ethelred would not be riding that day.

He found the King in bed, feverish and wandering in his speech. Godgifu and little Ethelwold were praying by the bedside. Ethelred recognized his brother; but though he talked to him with the urgent loquacity of fever he kept on forgetting where he was, and the need to return to the outposts near Reading. Presently a leech arrived, a man famous in those parts for his skill; but he explained with a regretful smile that in April he could not find the herbs needed for his draughts. He could cure any fever, but only in high summer. A monk brought razors, and suggested bleeding. He could not say that it would help the patient, for no one knew a cure for this fever; but if it was to be done he could do it.

Everyone looked to Alfred for instructions, since it is a grave matter to draw blood from a King. In his twenty-second year he must take control. Godgifu could suggest nothing but prayers for her husband's recovery, which were already being offered in the minster. Alfred did not know what ailed his brother; the most skilled physicians could not have found out. At a guess he supposed that riding in the rain had brought on a feverish cold. At random he gave orders that the King should be bled; because it is more comforting to do something to a sick man than to do nothing. He waited until the nick in the arm had been bound up, and was reassured to see the fever diminish. At nightfall he told the royal household to obey the orders of Godgifu, whom he left in charge; and then rode through the darkness to join the warband. If Ethelred had been well enough to give orders that was what he would have desired; the King of the West Saxons was the guardian of his people, and the defence of the realm was his first duty.

The Army lay quiet in Reading; but after six months of

winter campaigning the West Saxons needed an atheling to keep them at their post. Alfred must spend his days talking to the thanes, reminding them that their homes stood unburned only because they continued in the field. His men were tired of this unending war, a defensive war that could not promise plunder or conquest.

On the evening of Easter Saturday, 21 April 871, he came back from the outposts to change into dry clothes, eat supper, and go round the night sentries again; the dreary task that had continued all winter. At his hut a messenger was waiting. King Ethelred had died that morning, and Godgifu summoned the last atheling of Wessex to arrange his burial.

10

Wessex Pays Tribute

The monks of Wimborne filed from the nave into the choir, to continue the chant, God's work which must go on day and night even if heathen men were now riding to sack the minster. Alfred rose from his aching knees. As he left the west door he turned for a last look at the freshly-mortared stone which covered the body of Ethelred, King of the West Saxons.

He had stayed behind after the others, even Godgifu and little Ethelwold, had gone back to the hall. He had asked them to leave him, and they had instantly obeyed. Any King is obeyed without question on the first day of his reign.

As soon as Alfred had reached Wimborne he had been chosen King. He had expected it, and he had not attempted to refuse; though it was a small, unrepresentative council that chose him, while the best warriors watched the Army in Reading. He was in his twenty-second year, and the victor of Ashdown. There was no other adult Cerdinga to dispute his claim; while fighting continued it would be absurd if the West Saxons chose a child to rule them.

All the same, young Ethelwold must be King one day. That was what he had promised to Ethelred, when Ethelred promised to look after little Edward if the war should leave him fatherless. Alfred had become King by accident, to the detriment of the nephew who was his rightful lord. But if all the time he remembered that he was King on sufferance, preserving the realm of the West

Saxons until its rightful ruler was old enough to take command, no harm would come of it.

Kingship was a minor worry. It would not last for ever, and it was not very different from the kind of work he had been doing as second in command of his brother's Kingdom. In less than twenty years he might abdicate in favour of his nephew, and perhaps end his days in the holy air of Rome; for an ex-King was better out of the land he had been accustomed to rule. Grief and loneliness were greater afflictions.

Of all the brothers Ethelred had been his closest companion; in childhood they had played together, and for more than four years they had ruled the West Saxons almost in partnership. During this terrible winter of invasion, the battle-winter as gleemen already called it, they had seldom been separated. Even though they had discussed prudently what the survivor should do if one of them were killed, at the back of his mind he had taken it for granted that Ethelred would be beside him when he was an old man.

All his life he had thought of himself as the King's brother; it was the station in life to which he had been called. The Cerdingas prospered because they did not quarrel among themselves. That was why they still ruled in Wessex, after all the other Kingdoms of Britain had fallen under the sway of new lords sprung from nowhere. Loyalty to the head of the family had been the great imperative by which he guided his life. Now there was no one to claim that loyalty.

It was impossible to believe that he had no brothers. Always there had been someone to share his lodging, someone he could speak to without formality, someone who would tell him frankly that his ingenious plans were nonsense. He had lived among a group of equals; now he was alone.

As a King without brothers he would have no intimate friends. More than that, he had no trusted counsellors. Osric of Hampshire was dead, and Ethelwulf the Mercian whose companions had dodged their way through a host of enemies to bury their lord in the tomb of his ancestors. Bishop Ealhstand had died before the battle-winter, the old hero who had vanquished the heathen long ago; the See of Sherborne was again vacant after the death in battle of Bishop Heahmund. Alfred was not yet twenty-two, and he must govern the West Saxons by his own unaided wisdom.

In the hall he found the royal household assembled, and felt a stab of self-consciousness as his sister-in-law signalled to the ladies to rise and curtsey. Elswitha seemed more of a stranger than ever, standing there humbly with her hands on her breast and her eyes cast down. But a King must govern, even when his subjects distract him by untimely etiquette. In future he must give orders without waiting to be asked for them; his mind might be uncertain, but he must speak as though it had been made up.

'Ladies,' he said firmly, 'this evening you must make ready, so that tomorrow you can ride to the safety of the Somerset marshes. The abbot of Wimborne will see to the Masses and Dirges for my brother. Don't protest, Godgifu. I know you ought to be present when Masses are sung for your husband. But that's only a form; they will be as effective without you. While I fight the heathen I cannot be looking over my shoulder to protect my brother's family, or my own. Tomorrow I must return to the warband before Reading. Wimborne will have to take its chance. We can't spare warriors to protect the minster. If the thanes outside Reading do their duty no heathen will come raiding so far to the south. You understand, all of you? I must defend Wessex as a whole. My own family will be as well defended as the rest of my people, and no better.'

There was a murmur of assent, though he could see that the royal ladies did not like his orders. At this rate he would never make friends with Elswitha, never be the

153

loved and trusted playmate of his children. Life would be much easier if he could take his family to their refuge and see them comfortably settled; but such self-indulgence was forbidden to a chosen King.

For the rest of the evening he sat alone in his chamber, or walked alone in the gloom of the porch. There were so many orders to be given, so many plans to be made. When he spoke he must speak without hesitation, as though what he commanded were the only sensible course. And since he had no counsellors, he must think out his plans and decide them before he opened his mouth.

Long after dark he sent a page to fetch his blankets, so that he could sleep by the fire in the council-chamber. Tired out, he wrapped himself in a cocoon and slept soundly. Somewhere at the back of the hall was a soft warm double bed; but Elswitha would be in it, and tonight he must be alone with his thoughts and his sorrow.

Bad news awaited him at the camp. The heathen knew all that passed among the West Saxons, as was natural when every day they bought cattle from double-dealing apostate Christians. The heathen guessed that many West Saxon warriors would attend the funeral of their King, and on the very day of the burial they sallied out to the attack. The West Saxons were worsted, and many good thanes killed. The survivors were shaken and disheartened, anxious to get beyond the reach of their enemies. After inspecting the camp and talking with his most trustworthy companions King Alfred gave the first military command of his reign: the West Saxons were to retire to the westward, exposing all central Wessex to the ravages of the Army.

But it seemed that the Army was now bent on conquest, not plunder. Instead of sending out foraging parties King Halfdan marched westward with all his force. Hampshire was spared, and the new tomb at Wimborne;

but if the heathen defeated the warband of Wessex, now regrouping at Wilton, the whole Kingdom would lie at their mercy. One month after he had been called to the throne Alfred must fight yet another decisive battle.

His men were discouraged, and there were not very many of them; for spring had come. These thanes had kept the field all winter, a thing unheard-of which their descendants would recall with pride; but spring was a season when prudent lords looked after their own fields. From harvest to the first snow was the proper time for fighting; no one could be expected to keep at it all the year long.

But the heathen of the Army marched against Wilton in their thousands, so that there was nothing to do but to offer battle. King Alfred mustered his men and marched to meet them.

He had no advisers. He drew up his men in a single body, for lack of a trustworthy subordinate to command the reserve. But the magic memory of Ashdown still retained some of its power; he was surprised to find that his men faced battle in good spirits, though they were more eager to end the campaign than to win another famous and fruitless victory.

Leading the whole warband was not very different from leading one wing of it. He would not be taken by surprise, as Ethelred had been surprised at the opening of Ashdown. His chaplain hurried through a field-Mass in the open air, with the men standing ready in their ranks. Before the Mass was finished the Army came in sight, marching steadily to the attack.

Alfred enjoyed one small tactical advantage; all the best warriors of Wessex were grouped among his companions. Of course he had inherited the companions of the late King, who had himself inherited the surviving companions of his elder brothers. Within eleven years three Kings of the West Saxons had died in the flower of their youth; but not one of them had been killed in battle, so that their companions might honourably live on to seek new lords. In the centre of the Saxon host, behind the King, were hundreds of trained professional fighting-men, each as brave and skilled in arms as any heathen pirate.

When the two hosts encountered it seemed at first that the story of Ashdown would be repeated. The King's companions halted the heathen charge and forced back the centre; then both sides hewed at each other over the war-linden, fighting stubbornly where they stood. They fought on level ground, with no advantage of position. It was just the kind of battle which the heathen most disliked: bloody hand-to-hand fighting against a brave foe, with no opportunity for manoeuvre or trickery; the kind of fighting which cannot help a hard-working pirate to earn a living. After two hours of it the heathen centre yielded more ground, and the wings must retreat in haste to keep the line unbroken.

Alfred fought with caution. He was the only adult Cerdinga alive, and if he were killed the realm of the West Saxons would dissolve. But now he gathered his companions for a final, reckless charge. His leadership had brought victory at Ashdown, but then he had been second under his brother. How splendid if the first battle of his own reign should end in an equally famous and more decisive victory!

The charge succeeded. The heathen fled. But they did not forget the training and discipline which had brought them through so many years of warfare; their wings, scarcely pressed by the peasants of the fyrd and a scattering of country thanes, fled at the same speed as the centre so that the line remained unbroken.

King Alfred's first battle was ending in his first victory. It must be so. All his brothers had made it plain that they considered him the best warleader in the family. Another really good push would break that obstinate shield-wall. Even if the heathen had planned a feigned flight a vigorous pursuit might hustle them off their feet and break their formation. He was aware of his companions

roaring and pounding behind him, but he saw only the
few pirates directly in his front; there was no time to
look round at the wings. For two miles he pressed the
pursuit without turning his head.

Of course it was another feigned flight, carried out as
only practised war-hardened pirates could do it. After an
advance of two miles the Saxons were in disorder; many
had lagged behind to plunder the slain. The heathen
shield-wall was still unbroken when suddenly the Army
turned and came back to the charge. At sunset Alfred
drew off his remaining companions as a rearguard to his
beaten forces, and the Army passed the night on the
place of slaughter.

All the same, after plundering the Christian dead the
Army marched back to Reading. While the Saxons held
together in a single host the heathen could not go out
in small raiding bands, and they got no profit from
remaining deep in hostile territory. At Reading they had
plentiful supplies, replenished by convoys from Northumbria and by Mercian traders who did not inquire into
the origin of the silver with which they were paid. By the
midsummer of 871 both hosts held the positions they
had held in November 870.

Alfred saw that the stalemate could not continue. Every
day some companion who held land would seek permission to attend to its farming, every day thanes were
missing who had not waited to seek permission. The
lawful food-rents had long been eaten, though peasants
sent beef and ale to their defenders rather than see it
stolen by the heathen. Sentries and scouts watched for
raiders as eagerly as before, since the safety of their own
homes depended on their watchfulness; but when the
warband was mustered in force the men fell in sulkily.
Alfred never saw anyone grumble, but behind his back
he heard a continual mutter of grumbling.

Unless the King ended it soon the war would end of
itself.

In the camp before Reading the King slept in a wooden hut, which was weather-tight but otherwise utterly lacking in comfort. There had been no time to recruit a proper royal household. Ethelred's servants had gone with Godgifu to Somerset, and his own servants were with Elswitha. His numerous war-companions came into his hut unannounced, as was their right. They were brave fighting-men, not war-leaders; if he asked their advice in public he got nothing but tedious competitive boasting, and if he managed to consult one in private the man could recommend nothing more subtle than another assault on that impregnable palisade.

Duduc, his chaplain, had been well educated in Frankland. But his education had ended a very long time ago, and he had no books with him in camp save his Missal. The senior war-companion, Egwulf, was upright and honourable and utterly fearless; he had killed great numbers of the heathen in single combat, and returned in glory from many set battles. But when swords were drawn he thought only of what he himself would do and never looked at the men beside him; a good man to lead a charge, but too impetuous to be trusted with the command of a detachment.

It was late June, and beyond the scene of war they would be cutting the hay, when the heathen made their first overture for peace. A Northumbrian churl slipped out from the palisade, which was not at all unusual. There was a steady trickle of these English peasants from Northumbria or East Anglia, who would rather leave their holdings and live as labourers in Wessex than continue to serve their heathen masters. But when this deserter was questioned by the guards he asked to be taken to the King, and showed as credentials a copper arm-ring engraved with heathen runes.

He was an ignorant peasant, who could tell nothing of the Army except that the heathen had plenty to eat and were feeling bored by the fruitless campaign; which the West Saxons could have guessed for themselves. But

he repeated the message he had been told to pass on: if a
thane, or better still one of the King's trusted war-
companions, would come to the river-bank wearing this
arm-ring, one of the heathen would parley with him
from a skiff and arrange time and place for a meeting of
more eminent men.

It was the standard opening. The heathen knew the
rules for a peaceful parley, and often observed them if
their enemies were prudent. If they could not conquer a
realm they wanted to be paid to go away; the fixing of a
ransom needed honest negotiation. But it might mean
more than that. Never before had the Army been held
for so long in one place; never before had it fought battle
after battle throughout the winter. There might be
divisions in the camp. Perhaps some discontented pirates
could be bribed to betray King Halfdan. Alfred kept the
news secret from his war-weary men, for if they knew
that peace was on the way they would all go home at
once. He himself, in a plain tunic and a cheap leather
helmet, went alone to the meeting-place by the river-
bank.

He knelt among the reeds, his helmet showing above a
shield stuck in the muddy ground. He had a hunting-
bow beside him, with good straight arrows, and he had
reconnoitred a path by which he could slip away to a
tangle of thorns. An escort was hidden not far off, who
had been told that he was scouting the river route by
which the heathen drew their supplies. He ought to be
safe from treachery.

But the heathen envoy came openly and honestly,
alone, standing upright to pole his narrow dugout. When
Alfred waved the arm-ring on the end of a spear the man
poled in close to the bank and hailed him.

'West Saxon ahoy, we want to talk with one of your
leaders. It will be worth your while. We may go away if
you pay us well enough.'

'Pirate ahoy,' Alfred answered. 'We want you to go
away, and we are willing to talk it over. We won't pay

you, but we might let you go in peace with the plunder
you have taken from other countries. Who will speak for
you? King Halfdan?'

'Of course not. We are not seeking mercy. But if you
send a noble war-leader we shall send an envoy of equal
birth. Earl Oscytel has done this sort of thing before. He
has a good memory and reports accurately what he has
been told. He is one of King Halfdan's counsellors and
war-leaders, so you must send someone as noble and
well born.'

'We shall send a war-leader of equal birth, whose word
can bind the King of the West Saxons. Let the meeting be
here, at noon tomorrow. Your Earl may come ashore
with six warriors for his escort, and we shall have ale
and beef waiting for him in a tent.'

'Not here. Too much cover in those reeds. There's a
meadow half a mile upstream, a nice open stretch where
no ambush could be hid. The Earl will be rowed to it in
a galley, so that you see him coming and see that he
comes without a warband. But you mustn't count the
rowers as part of the escort. Only his bodyguard of six
will step ashore with him.'

'Tomorrow, at noon, in the meadow. No hostages from
either side. You will see us ride openly to the river-bank.
We shall bring servants with ale and meat, but only six
warriors for a bodyguard. Do you want this arm-ring
back? Stick out your punting-pole and I'll slide it down
to you.'

The pirate, who stood as firmly in his narrow dugout
as though he were on dry land, poled back upstream
with the arm-ring. Alfred picked up his bow and dodged
back to his waiting horse.

As he rode he thought over the mechanics of the
meeting. He was right to parley with the invaders, of
that he was certain. The men of Wessex could not be
kept under arms much longer, and a treaty of peace was
a better ending to the war than a forlorn assault on that
impregnable palisade. But he must not let his men know

that he was negotiating with the pirates. No one wants to be killed in the last skirmish of a war. They would all go home if they saw him talking quietly with a pirate Earl. Perhaps the pirates knew it, and planned to deceive his men into deserting? No, that wouldn't do. If they knew the feelings of the Saxons they would know also that another month would see the break-up of the warband of Wessex without any negotiation. The great heathen Army must itself be dissatisfied and ready to break up. King Halfdan needed an end to this stalemate as urgently as did King Alfred.

Even if the negotiations were genuine that did not solve the problem of keeping them secret. He must go himself to meet this Oscytel, of course; that was not so much to preserve secrecy as because there was no one whom he could trust to negotiate on behalf of the West Saxons. It was just the kind of mission that a King entrusted to a brother; if Ethelred had been alive Alfred would have represented him. But King Alfred was alone.

He might take a chance and go to the meeting unescorted. But the heathen were not genuinely honourable, they negotiated honestly solely because that was the easiest way of getting the silver they craved. From their English and Saxon slaves they must know something of the state of Wessex. They would know that the King had no grown heir to take up the defence if he were killed; with the King out of the way the West Saxons would collapse, as the Northumbrians had collapsed. The temptation to murder him would be more than many Christians could withstand. He must take an escort.

He would choose the most discreet and close-mouthed of his companions, but the news that he was treating with the enemy was bound to leak out. Therefore he must begin the meeting knowing that in the end he must make peace, for his warband would not follow him if the campaign were renewed. But the heathen could not be sure of that. It only meant that he must negotiate very carefully.

As soon as he reached his hut he sent for Egwulf and told him everything. The veteran took it calmly.

'So the war's over,' he said. 'For the first time in my life I shall be glad of a peace. There has been enough fighting even for me.'

'If the heathen could hear you say that they would demand such a great ransom that we should have nothing left. Or better still they would treat for a month and then renew the war. Remember, it was they who asked for peace. King Halfdan wants to leave Wessex with a whole skin. But he must give his warriors something, a few cows or a handful of silver, or else the Army which is his Kingdom will break into fragments. Don't you see, Egwulf? We are the victors. The heathen crave peace from us. But they will fear us only so long as they think we are ready for further war.'

'Well, my lord, we aren't. I am a King's companion, and I shall fight whenever my lord leads me into battle. The other companions will follow you if they must, but they don't look forward to it any more than I do. The thanes and the peasants of the fyrd might try to stop a band of raiders, but if you lead them against that palisade tomorrow very few of them will follow you.'

'That's sad, but not fatal so long as the enemy don't know it,' said Alfred with a grimace of disgust.

'You can't keep it secret, my lord. We are private here, I am old enough to be your father, and I must talk to you frankly for your own good. I am a warrior by trade, just as much a professional fighting-man as any heathen pirate. I can judge another warrior by looking at him, especially when he is chatting off his guard; it's part of my trade, and an important part. If the escort of the heathen Earl are sick of this war, unwilling to fight another battle, I shall see it in the way they hold themselves. The heathen Earl can learn as much from looking at your escort. It doesn't matter if the men of the escort don't know what you are discussing; though unless they are half-witted they must know that you meet a

162

heathen Earl only to make peace. They don't want to fight, and it shows in the way they stand. If you meet this heathen you must make peace. If you want to continue the war don't meet him at all.'

'If I don't meet him can I continue the war?'

'I think not, but you can never be absolutely certain. Courage ebbs and flows like the tide. Even the peasants might follow you if they happen to be feeling brave that morning. The most I can say is that probably we would be beaten.'

'Thank you, Egwulf. You have given sound advice and admitted that you can't foretell the future. That's greater honesty than you find in most royal councillors. If I meet this Earl you shall be captain of my escort. But I still haven't made up my mind whether to go to the meeting.'

Until sunset Alfred stalked through the woods behind the camp. He was within a few weeks of his twenty-second birthday, he had been King of the West Saxons for less than three months, and he must take the most important decision of his reign without consulting his council.

Again and again Ethelred had said that Wessex must never pay ransom, that the only way to get rid of the Army was to fight it and go on fighting it. Ethelred had been his favourite brother and his worshipped hero; what he said must be right. But Ethelred had campaigned through the bitter winter, suffering hardships that brought him to early death, because a Cerdinga must make any sacrifice to preserve Wessex. Unless peace came soon Wessex would break in its King's hand. His companions would follow him into battle, as Egwulf had said; but they would expect defeat, and therefore they would be beaten. The thanes and peasants would not even follow him. The warband of Wessex would be scattered, while the King and his most faithful companions stood in the shield-wall to meet inevitable death. On the next day there would be no Kingdom of the West Saxons.

The Roman heroes of old, whose legends he had been told in his childhood, had believed that death was better than slavery. If he fought tomorrow there was an outside chance that he might win, as Egwulf had agreed; and if fortune went against him he would be dead before his people were reduced to slavery.

There was some attraction in the prospect. Alfred enjoyed battle and did not greatly fear death if it were sufficiently heroic; on the other hand he dreaded negotiation with wily and experienced heathen, who would almost certainly make a fool of him. To make matters worse, he was sure that in the middle of the parley he would be attacked once again by his ridiculous self-consciousness; he would stammer and sweat while the Earl bullied him into paying a greater ransom than Wessex could afford. That was final. He would not go to the meeting. Tomorrow, or at the latest on the day after, he would seek death or glory.

But if he took that course he would be failing in his duty, and failing merely to gratify his private self-esteem. He would be throwing away the lives of his companions, not to save Wessex but only because he feared to make a fool of himself in public. His first duty must be to ensure the continuance of Wessex, even if its King should be cozened by veteran pirates. He would go to the river-bank, to see what terms he could get from the enemy.

His decision once taken he returned to the camp and made it public. There was no chance of secrecy anyway, and if all his men knew that he was going to negotiate they would not let him change his mind in the morning. He ordered Egwulf to choose five other companions to make up the escort, and summoned the captains to a council of war. Within an hour the news was all over the camp, and there could be no drawing back.

The council met in a buoyant mood. Now that the war was as good as over everyone felt full of courage. When the King made the formal announcement that the enemy had begged for a parley the councillors cheered and banged their swords against their shields; someone at the back struck up a war song. In a burst of enthusiasm they advised unanimously that Wessex should offer the Army safe passage down the Thames and nothing more; not a silver penny, not a sheaf of oats, should be given in ransom. Of course the pirates must jump at such lenient terms; had they not sought this parley because they feared for their lives?

One thing Alfred had not told his followers: that the Army expected a war-leader, not the King in person, to represent Wessex at the conference. If he had let that out all the captains would have quarrelled among themselves, each seeking the post of envoy; and it would have been awkward to explain that he did not think any one of them competent to fill it. This Oscytel was by all accounts one of the greater Earls among the heathen; the escort, unless they gossiped with their pirate counterparts, would perhaps mistake him for the mighty King Halfdan. Anyway, the King was sole guardian of the honour of Wessex. Since nothing could be concluded without his consent it would save time if he in person conducted the negotiations.

In the morning he dressed himself with care. His sword, shield and byrnie were excellent of their kind, but his tunic was of plain scarlet wool and he wore no ornaments of gold. He looked a leading warrior, but there was nothing to indicate the King.

He still felt in his heart that this negotiation was shameful; Ethelred would have died before he parleyed with an armed invader. But he knew very well that he must bring back peace from the conference, or continue the war to inevitable defeat.

The seven Saxons just had time to dismount before the heathen boat came into sight. It was only a flat-bottomed river-barge, but the Army had decorated it with shields hung along the rowlocks and a painted dragon-mask on the bow as though it were a war-galley. There were eight rowers a side, tousleheaded naked slaves; but Earl Oscytel and his bodyguard of six were dressed in all the splendour of successful pirates.

Oscytel was older than the young King, a burly warrior in his late thirties. His yellow hair hung in long plaits, his fair beard spread over his chest. He carried a gold-hilted sword and a shield that glistened with enamel; on his head was one of those impractical but imposing helmets embellished with spreading ox-horns which among the heathen were a badge of grandeur. That was a comforting sight, implying that the pirates expected fair play and no bloodshed; no sensible warrior would risk his life under a helmet which could be knocked flying by a single stroke. Beneath their byrnies the seven pirates wore tunics of scarlet wool, and their clean white trousers were cross-gartered with narrow strips of matching scarlet; their shoes were of soft red leather.

Of course the Army must demonstrate its splendour, to remind the Saxons that every sensible ruler paid it to go away. Alfred glanced back at his own escort, their weapons dulled and nicked by long campaigning, their grubby woollens sodden after seven winter months in the field. The heathen had scored a point. They did not look like emissaries from the party that had first sought peace.

Oscytel and his bodyguard disembarked. The boat was backed into midstream, where the steersman stood erect with a bow in his hand. That had not been agreed in the preliminaries, but it was not worth arguing about; the rowers were unarmed slaves when they might have been warriors, so the pirates were not really stealing an advantage.

The two bodyguards halted a hundred yards apart, to stare at one another in frank curiosity. So that is what an enemy looks like when he isn't fighting; perhaps there will be a chance to talk to him and find out if he is a real human being.

Alfred and Oscytel met alone in the middle of the meadow, where they could talk without being overheard. Oscytel opened the conversation, speaking in a mixture of English and Danish which any Saxon could understand after he was used to the accent.

'Hallo,' he said in cheerful surprise, 'you are the King of the West Saxons. I didn't know this was to be a meeting of commanders. I'm not supreme commander of the Army. But King Halfdan has given me full powers, and he will hold himself bound by any agreement we can hammer out together.'

'I am the King, as it happens,' answered Alfred, blushing with that maddening self-consciousness which afflicted him at the most inappropriate moments. 'But I am not here as King. I come as an envoy from myself, if you see what I mean. There's no one I can send to represent me, as Halfdan trusts you to represent him. My brother died in the spring, and most of our veteran war-leaders have fallen in battle. If I sent an alderman he would have to consult me at every step, so I thought it quicker to come myself. Treat me as an equal. I don't want royal honours.'

'That's frank, my lord. After such a good opening we shall quickly reach agreement. The Army also lost a good many war-leaders in battle, but perhaps we started with more of them. At present I am an Earl, but one day I shall be a King if I gather enough companions. So by birth I am worthy to talk with you, though I have never commanded the Army in battle. Well, let's get down to business. Suppose you tell me your offer, and we can go on from there.'

This was not how they negotiated in the epics. Oscytel ought to have begun with a eulogy of the might and prowess of the Army, to which Alfred could reply with an expression of undaunted defiance and a denunciation of the wickedness of piracy. But they were speaking in prose, Alfred reflected. The epics were essentially true to life, but everyday life was not always consonant with epic truth. He dismissed from his mind the rhetoric he had prepared, and answered baldly.

'The Army seeks peace, not the West Saxons. Therefore you should state your terms first. But you are bound to ask for more than you hope to get, so we may as well cut out all that. What I offer can be stated shortly: safe passage from Wessex in return for an oath never to come back.'

'Fair enough, and of course that's what we want. By sunset we shall have fixed up this treaty. But there will have to be a few trimmings, as I shall explain. Do you mind if I sit down?'

He spread his cloak on a log of driftwood, and patted it to indicate that the King should sit beside him. It was hard to remember that this pleasant young man was a ferocious heathen pirate.

'It's like this, my lord,' he said easily. 'King Halfdan and all the leaders want the Army to move. We haven't enjoyed our stay in Wessex, and we must find some other land where there are richer pickings and fewer hard knocks. But though some of us are called Kings and others Earls our men are not our natural-born subjects. They join us for profit, and if we don't give them plunder they look round for another leader. Our men have endured a very hard campaign, and they won't end it without a little silver in their purses. If you want us all to go away, and I agree that this would be the best solution, you must give us some sort of ransom. Quite a small one would do.' He smiled pleasantly and waited for Alfred's answer.

'It's not my business to keep the Army united,' said the King with a shrug. He found it astonishing that he should talk so frankly with a savage foe of civilization, but the interview had begun on this footing and he could not now alter its tone. 'My final offer is safe passage down the river, with your plunder. If some of you accept and others refuse we shall kill those who stay behind.'

'Will you? I wonder. Since November you have killed

a King and eleven Earls. But you haven't got inside our palisade.'

'We shall go on trying until we succeed.' Alfred got to his feet, to show that the parley was ended.

'Wait a minute, my lord, and think it over.' The Earl tugged at his cloak and he sat down again.

'Your men are as sick of this war as we are,' Oscytel continued coolly. 'I can see it in their faces, and so can you. Think of what will happen after the Army disperses. There will be little groups of pirates all over Wessex, and Mercia too if that is any concern of yours. Your men will go home to get in the harvest. Some pirate, somewhere, will gain a petty local success. Then he will set himself up as King, and all the other pirates will join his standard. The Army will be reconstituted, right in the middle of your dominions. If it goes on long enough your land-owners will pay ransom for their own lands, and perhaps cease to obey you as King. Whereas if you give us three silver pennies a head we shall all go down river in a body; and if you make it ten pennies a head King Halfdan will swear eternal friendship with Wessex.'

'I don't want King Halfdan's friendship. One day I shall kill him, unless someone else saves me the trouble. A man of your experience can see that the Army is going downhill. You plundered Frankland because the Franks thought you invincible. The West Saxons have proved that you can be withstood, and wherever you go in future the Christians will fight you. You may win plunder, but you will lose men by the hundred. It's not much of a prospect. Have you ever thought of settling down? If you would accept baptism and swear the right oaths I could find a place for you in my warband, with a good holding of land and peasants to till it for you when you grow too old for fighting.'

'You are gracious, lord King. But I am a pirate by trade and I like the life. So I suppose we go on with the war? I shall take back your refusal of peace to King Halfdan.'

169

It was Alfred's turn to tug at a cloak and persuade the other to continue the parley.

'No, I want peace, and so does King Halfdan. If you should go down river now, all of you, after taking oath to leave Wessex, how long would you consider that oath binding? I ask you as a man of honour. Give me a true answer.'

The pirate shrugged, spreading his hands wide. 'The Army lives in the present, my lord. Our trade doesn't call for careful planning. If King Halfdan takes oath to leave you he will keep his word. He will fortify some camp outside Wessex, and live in it for the coming winter. Next spring he must look for another hunting ground, and he himself couldn't tell you which hunting ground he will choose. Perhaps the men of the Army will do the choosing for him. All I can say is that after this battle-winter Wessex will be pretty low on the list. But the Army keeps its bargains principally because it never bargains for longer than one year at a time.'

'I see. I shall be buying one winter of peace, and perhaps more. How much do you need, to give every warrior three silver pennies?'

'King Halfdan leads ten thousand warriors,' said Oscytel, looking straight ahead from under a frowning brow.

'That may have been true last November. You are repeating your instructions, and I don't blame you for it. But it's my belief that if I hand over ten thousand silver pennies that will be enough to pay every warrior now under the Raven Banner.'

'Not nearly enough. Twenty thousand might do.'

They settled down to haggle, a task in which neither was skilled. After a few more exchanges they agreed that eighteen thousand silver pennies would be sufficient to pay the ordinary warriors at the rate of three a head, and leave something extra for the leaders. In another hour of argument they settled the machinery of payment. The money would be handed over in three equal instalments, and on receipt of each payment one third of the Army would move. Alfred would have preferred to pay each pirate separately, and Oscytel wanted the whole sum in advance. This compromise ensured that two-thirds at least of the Army would carry out its promise, and at the same time avoided the danger of leaving a small rear-guard who might be massacred by vengeful Saxons.

On Michaelmas Day 871 King Alfred watched the burning of the palisade which stretched from the Kennet to the Thames on the royal manor of Reading. Three days ago the last of the heathen had left, and with curiosity and awe the companions of the royal warband had explored the deserted camp. Perhaps it was wasteful to destroy such a strong fortress; but it did not block the river route by which the pirates were most likely to return, and anyway it was such a hateful reminder of the worst trial Wessex had ever endured that no one wanted to preserve it.

Wessex was free, eleven months after the invaders had first occupied Reading. The West Saxons were still ruled by the right line of Cerdic, a most unlikely and fortunate ending to the bitter battle-winter. But Wessex had paid ransom to the pirates, in spite of the warning of King Ethelred who had given his life to keep his people free. All the Saxons praised Alfred, the unconquered and unconquerable King. He himself felt deeply ashamed.

11

The End of Mercia

On his twenty-second birthday Alfred was undisputed King of an independent Wessex. But the land was poor and ravaged, and not yet truly at peace; for the Army had settled in London, and the borders of Kent and Surrey must still be defended. King Halfdan seemed inclined to make London his base for further raids in Britain, another Jomsburg in a land that had been Christian for generations. In the autumn of 872, when the harvest-rents were paid, Alfred's treasurer showed him a silver penny with the mintmark of London and the monogram of the King of the pirates; a Kentish thane had sent it as part of his rent-silver. Of course the coin, and any others like it that reached the royal hoard at Winchester, were at once melted and coined again as sterling pennies of Wessex. But that Halfdan should strike coins, as though London were his permanent capital, was a very evil omen for the future.

Throughout that summer Alfred did his best to rule his people. He rode into every shire to preside over the lawcourt; for the best part of a year everyone had been too busy to judge suits, and there were hundreds of causes to be settled. There was hardly any money to support the royal household; but luckily the companions did not expect presents in peacetime, and he was able to live very simply. Elswitha helped him to economize; as a girl she had been poor, and she had no ambition to live grandly.

In other respects she was very little help to her busy husband. She was a good woman, but a stupid one. Her pride of birth kept her from showing fear, but it was obvious that she expected the Army to conquer Britain in the end, though an honourable King must fight on until he was beaten. She shied away from any discussion of the future, and sometimes spoke wistfully of the security of exile in Rome or Pavia. She had left her Mercian home for a foreign land, and it seemed that she would be as happy, or as unhappy, among alien Italians as among alien Saxons. She got on well enough with her husband, and certainly there was no other man in her life; but only when she was playing with her children did she ever smile or speak without being spoken to.

Loneliness was Alfred's worst affliction. With all his brothers dead there was no one to share his private thoughts. Such a young King could not easily confide in a veteran councillor, and anyway no veteran councillors were left; the battle-winter had weeded out the infirm and slain the courageous. Planning was more difficult because his private plans were not clear even to himself. He was dissatisfied with the Wessex he saw as he rode from one shire to the next, a Wessex of poverty and insecurity, a land of ruined buildings patched up to last another year, a land governed by ignorant inefficient aldermen, promoted because there was no one better qualified to take the place of some hero fallen before Reading. Even bishops and abbots were not as he remembered them in his father's time, but clumsy virtuous uneducated men barely able to stumble through the Missal. Wessex was not what it should be. But what should it be? He was unable to say, except that it ought to be more like the Rome he remembered from his childhood.

His people were proud of him, but he was not really beloved. He was the most valiant King in Britain, but all the same Wessex had paid ransom to the Army. There was very little to show for all the suffering and expense of the terrible battle-winter. A few months ago Alfred had been the hero of the famous and almost miraculous deliverance of Ashdown, the warrior who had led the charge while his brother and King was praying on his knees. But since then he had fought again and again, and had lost as often as he had won. He was a stubborn King, a leader to boast of; but perhaps Wessex would have been less ravaged, hundreds of good men slain on the field would still be alive, if he had been quicker to see that the only way to get rid of the Army was to pay it to march off. His companions let him see that they longed for peace; the thanes of the countryside grumbled as they repaired their half-burned halls. All the sufferings of the last year had been thrown away in the end. Now King Halfdan minted the ransom of Wessex into shining London pennies.

In the summer of 872 came heartening news; the North-umbrians had risen against their heathen overlords. Perhaps one day the English would join with the Saxons to free all Britain from the pirates. On the other hand, the insurgents had driven out not only their puppet-king, but also the Archbishop of York who supported him. King Egbert and Archbishop Wulfhere sought refuge with the Mercians. King Burhed wrote worried letters to his West Saxon ally pointing out the danger of provoking the Army to new activity.

The Army marched north from London, though a garrison was left to hold the port. That was clear gain for Wessex, since a danger had been removed from the Kentish border; but in another sense it added to the general discouragement, for the invincible Army made short work of the insurgent Northumbrians. After a few weeks the pirates left the ruined north to take up winter quarters in the Mercian town of Torksey. King Burhed paid them a large ransom, so they stayed quiet in their camp and the land was saved from pillage; but he could not offer enough to persuade the heathen to leave his Kingdom.

In Wessex, after a good harvest, there was enough to

eat. But East Anglia was under heathen rule, Northumbria was almost a desert, and the Army lived secure in Mercian Lindsey. Elswitha bore Alfred a second son, named Edmund; but he died when he was a few months old. It was altogether a gloomy year.

In 873 the exiled King Egbert died in Mercia, and the stubborn Northumbrians chose one Ricsige to rule over them. The Army did not bother to reconquer the wasted moors of the north, and before winter Archbishop Wulfhere was back in York. For the moment Northumbria was free, though the Army might reoccupy it whenever it chose. The heathen were very comfortable in Torksey, where the Mercians paid them a monthly ransom.

In the autumn the Army marched unexpectedly to Repton, a favourite residence of the King of the Mercians. King Burhed mustered his warband, but during the winter there was no serious fighting.

In June 874 the King of the West Saxons kept his twenty-fifth birthday at Wantage. There was a great company, and a due degree of splendour; for the land was recovering from the heathen ravages. Elswitha presided over the women's table; Alfred, at the high table, felt lonely and bored. Beside him were aldermen, thanes and bishops, and in the body of the hall a great band of companions; but none of these people were really his friends. If he had followed his own inclination he would have dined with Ethelfleda and Edward in the bower; for he loved his little daughter, and his baby son was a sturdy impudent brat. But a King can seldom follow his own inclination.

Fires glowed on the northern skyline, but no one paid much attention. There was fighting throughout Mercia, and someone was always nervously lighting a beacon. During all that spring and summer there had been smoke in the northern sky, and it was just as likely to come from a burning homestead as from an alarm signal. The heathen liked to burn houses, even when they gained nothing by it.

One of the scouts who watched the frontier was the first to bring news of unexpected visitors.

'Horsemen from Mercia, my lord. They ride as hard as tired beasts can carry them, and they wear byrnies. But it seems to me that they come in peace. They keep to the road, without plundering, and with them are pack-horses and I think a few women. My captain is watching them from a hill.'

'I suppose it's a beaten English warband,' said Alfred half to himself. 'They are unneighbourly to seek refuge in Wessex, when they would be safe enough among the mountains of Wales. Now the pirates will follow them here.'

'Not yet, my lord,' answered the messenger. 'We watched the road behind them, and there is no pursuit. They look more like some rich thane fleeing with his household. They are riding for Wantage, and my captain suggests that you speak to them yourself.'

'If it's a thane deserting King Burhed I shall send him back to his duty. But you say you have seen women and baggage. Perhaps some lord wants to put his family in safety before he returns to the fight. Very well, let them come here in peace. In Somerset we have plenty of room for Mercian ladies. Then the men must go back and fight for their lord before the pirates notice they have fled.'

The King drank until he had emptied his horn, and stood to show that the feast was ended. The companions grumbled as they strapped on their byrnies, for they had planned to sit drinking until they slept on the floor, as is right on the birthday of a great King. But it is elementary prudence to wear a byrnie for the reception of unheralded visitors. The women, on the other hand, went off gladly to prepare guest-chambers; to sit for hours drinking ale bored them and was bad for their figures. Though it was the only respectable way to celebrate the King's birthday

177

they were pleased at an excuse to drop it, and at the prospect of hearing fresh gossip from strangers.

An hour later the tables had been cleared from the hall. The King of the West Saxons sat in state, surrounded by his companions and counsellors, ready to receive guests of noble birth. As usual, Alfred was worried. In these days unexpected news was always bad news; and he foresaw that it might be difficult to combine the traditional hospitality of a Christian King with the duty of returning frightened deserters to their lord. Any men he sent back would probably be killed by the pirates. But then the King of the West Saxons would probably be killed by the pirates before his beard was grey.

In the yard there was a noise of many horses, and all the bustle of dismounting. This waiting tried the nerves, and Alfred felt a twinge of his old familiar self-consciousness. Life would be much easier if unexpected guests were announced before they arrived; but to question a stranger before he volunteered his name and ancestry would be a shocking breach of civility. Besides, the messenger might make a mistake in the guest's genealogy, and bloodfeuds have arisen from lesser misunderstandings.

Then a familiar figure appeared in the doorway, and a well-remembered voice announced: 'King Burhed and Queen Ethelswitha of the Mercians, come in peace to visit the King of the West Saxons.'

'My dear Burhed,' exclaimed Alfred, so surprised that he forgot to feel self-conscious, 'what a pleasure to see you again, and my dear sister also. You come in a good hour, when Wantage is filled with food and drink for my birthday feast. I suppose you have some urgent mission, to leave your land in time of war. But politics can wait until you have eaten.'

It was gratifying thus to patronize Burhed, who looked rather battered and had cheered up visibly at mention of food. The pause while the guests dined would give Alfred time for thought. It was a tricky situation, and he might have to make up his mind immediately, without consulting his counsellors.

Only one mission could bring a King from a realm at war, a desperate search for allies. In the course of the evening Burhed would beg the West Saxons to march. It was the plain duty of his neighbours to help him against the Army, but Alfred was reluctant to see the warband of Wessex committed to a fresh campaign. For one thing, in his own land Burhed must command, and he was not a good war-leader; for another, Alfred's own thanes might be unwilling to go abroad, reopening the war against the pirates and at the same time leaving Wessex exposed to invasion. To refuse would be dishonourable; to accept, and then find that his own men would not follow, would be most shameful. Why hadn't Burhed sent an envoy, to present a request which might be refused? The tiresome fellow never had any tact.

All the same, it was good to see his sister. There were so few people with whom he could talk about his dead brothers.

But it was unfair of Burhed to have brought her. He must know that Wessex needed to keep out of his war; he had made his wife come with him only to exert unfair pressure on his brother-in-law. On the other hand, Kings married the daughters of other Kings only to have a chance to exert this unfair pressure. It was all very difficult. Wessex was still too weak to renew the war. But how could the King of the West Saxons say so without holding himself and his people up to public contempt? Gleemen would compose bitter songs about the victorious King who refused to help a brother in his utmost need.

These thoughts whirled through his head, while the visiting King and Queen put down great quantities of tepid boiled pork and expensive French wine. They were as tired as they were hungry; they must have endured a very rough journey.

At last dear Ethelswitha shut the lid of her drinking-horn. As she held out her greasy hands to be washed she caught her husband's eye. King Burhed also closed the lid of his horn, reluctantly and with a comic little sigh of disappointment. That was a good sign. Ethelswitha still ruled the family. She could be counted on to see that a King of the West Saxons must put the interests of his people before even the sacred duty of helping an ally. In the painful interview that was coming she might mediate between the two Kings.

The three retired to the little parlour behind the hall. The sun was setting, and they sat side by side on a bench before the fire, for even in June the evenings were chilly. In silence they stared into the flames, until at length Alfred took the plunge. This conversation would be unpleasant, but he must get it over.

'If you want supplies, my dear Burhed, just ask for them, and pay when it suits you. If a few hundred warriors will turn the scale I will come myself with my companions. But with affairs as they are I can't ask the warband of Wessex to go abroad, and if I did ask them I would not be obeyed. I can't bring you all my power; as my brother brought his power to that unlucky campaign before Nottingham. Mercia must fight without Wessex.'

'There are limits to the power of any King, as we know very well,' said Ethelswitha. 'But we have not come to seek help.'

'We would be grateful for help with our journey,' Burhed put in swiftly. 'I should explain that I am no longer fighting the Army. It's hopeless, anyway, just leading good men to their death. I am on my way to Rome. I'm an old man, and I shall make my soul beside the tombs of the Apostles. Ethelswitha will follow later, if the Pope receives me properly. Of course we left Mercia in a hurry, and we didn't bring very much with us. So if you will feed my household until we cross the Channel you will be aiding a pious pilgrim. But I must say honestly that I shall never be able to repay you.' He shook his head mournfully.

'Good God, have you forsaken your people?' Alfred was too amazed to choose a more courteous form of words.

'If you like you can put it in that way. Others will. But the truth is that the Mercians have forsaken *me*. I did my best, I assure you.' Burhed waved his hands while the words tumbled out of his mouth. Alfred was reminded of a guilty man explaining away his offence to a lawcourt. 'I led my warband to battle, and in the charge I killed half a dozen pirates. You know I was always considered a good swordsman. But it wasn't enough; at the end of the day the heathen held the place of slaughter. Then we skirmished for a bit with their foragers, until I decided to try my luck a second time. Half my thanes never came to the muster, and the other half expected to be beaten. To lead such men against the Army, led by Halfdan son of the mighty Ragnar, would have been suicide. I heard a rumour that if I led my men to a second defeat they themselves would kill me during the rout. What could I do after that? But if I can't save my people I can still save my own soul. So I gathered my family and set out for Rome.'

'Since you can't fight the Army can you make peace with them?' asked Alfred, trying to understand this novel situation.

'I myself can't. They want a bigger ransom than I could raise from my plundered Kingdom. Perhaps someone will make peace later on. Some lords have fled with me. The others I suppose hope to buy peace for their own holdings, one at a time.'

'But what is happening in Mercia? Or don't you know?'

'I can tell you that,' said Ethelswitha, smiling an appeal to her brother's forebearance. 'Poor Burhed finds it hard to explain. The Mercians are trying to choose another King, in agreement with the chiefs of the Army. The plan is to buy peace from the pirates by giving them land, since they have already taken all our silver. It might even work, who knows? But I don't envy the next King of the Mercians.'

'I see. Now there's nothing between the Army and the frontier of Wessex. Thank you for warning me in good time. Well, it's a sad business, but nothing can be done about it. Of course I shall help you on your way to Rome. I hope Ethelswitha will stay with me until you have arranged her lodging in Italy. You must be very tired. Go to bed as soon as you like.'

It was a brutal dismissal of a crowned King; but Burhed might as well begin to get used to the treatment he would receive as an exile in Italy. Ethelswitha rose as her husband slunk off, but at a gesture from Alfred she sat down again.

'So he ran away even before all his people had been conquered! I nearly called him *nithing* to his face, though he's my guest. But he knows without being told that he is *nithing*. You can see it in the curve of his spine. Well, "for richer for poorer, for better for worse, in sickness and in health", and I suppose in disgrace also. You do right to go with him, though I should have forgiven you if you had stayed behind in Mercia.'

Alfred stared at his sister with a puzzled frown, awed by this unprecedented disaster.

'You mustn't be too hard on poor Burhed. They tell me he fought very bravely. But he can't plan a campaign, and he lost heart when he heard his own sworn companions grumbling about his muddled leadership. Perhaps there was nothing else he could do. Perhaps it really is futile to resist the great Army.'

'Victory or defeat have nothing to do with it. In any war someone must be on the losing side. Edmund was beaten, but he died King of the East English. Our brother Ethelred died King of the West Saxons, though in the end I had to pay the heathen to go away. Burhed might have died fighting the heathen, the best death for a Christian King. Instead he slinks away to Rome without even buying peace for his people. A warrior who deserts his lord in the field is *nithing*. Burhed has deserted his lord, the people of Mercia. There can be no excuse.'

'It was unanimous, you know,' said Ethelswitha with a shake of the head. 'The people of Mercia also deserted King Burhed. They had a choice, and they chose to seek peace from the Army. Whether they will get it is another question. Perhaps the pirates will kill them all . . . But does everyone have to be a hero all the time? Is it never right to be prudent, to save your own life when all else is already lost? Burhed can't stop the heathen conquering Mercia, though perhaps a better King might have done it. No one would blame him if he fled from a lost battle. Is he wrong to flee all the way to Rome from a lost campaign?'

'You know he is wrong. In sticking up for your husband you are doing your duty, and I don't blame you for it. Would you have suggested flight, if he had been willing to fight on?'

'I am Woden-born, of the right line of Cerdic,' said Ethelswitha without pausing to think.

'And Burhed isn't? But he fought his way to his throne.'

'Don't set too high a standard,' his sister answered sharply. 'Suppose your own own people should refuse to continue the war? Would you fight on alone, to certain death?'

'I should see it as my duty. I might lack the resolution to carry out my duty. No one can be sure beforehand that he will withstand temptation. But that's enough about King Burhed and the fate of Mercia. On that you and I will never agree. At present your husband is my guest, and you I hope will stay with us at least until next summer. You are very tired. Shall we meet again in the morning?'

'Very well, I shall go to bed. By the way, there's something I forgot to tell you. Alderman Mucill was killed in the battle, and Eadburh has joined our party. She talks of going to Rome with Burhed, but I know she would be glad if you asked her to stay with her daughter in Wessex.'

Alfred brightened. 'Of course she must stay with us. Or rather, she must make Wessex her home. She's the Queen's mother and grandmother to the heir. Her proper place is here with us.'

Two such openings were more than Ethelswitha could resist.

'By the custom of the West Saxons Elswitha is no Queen, and the atheling with the best claim to be your heir is your nephew Ethelwold, son of Ethelred. But I'm glad you welcome Eadburh. She's a dear, and very good company. Good night.'

Alfred managed a friendly smile. Any brother knows that in an argument his elder sister will have the last word.

Next morning Alfred talked business with Burhed. The exile needed silver for his journey, but Alfred's hoard had been emptied three years ago when he paid ransom to the Army. In the end they agreed to barter. Burhed had brought with him the royal Mercian library, which would be almost valueless on the continent. Alfred offered a fine illuminated Gospel, which any Roman banker would be pleased to buy, in exchange for a curious document, a set of Easter tables in which long ago someone had entered the chief events of the Saxon conquest of Britain. Easter tables have a blank half-line every Leap Year, so the battles and deaths, arranged at four-yearly intervals, could not be completely accurate. But the ancient parchment took Alfred's fancy. Carefully used, it would provide a framework for the old heroic epics. One day he might commission a real written history of the deeds of his mighty ancestors. Wessex was the only Kingdom in Britain still ruled by the line of the original conquerors; before it was too late his people should have a record of how they came to occupy their land.

Then Burhed and his resentful, dispirited bodyguard set off for the coast. But Ethelswitha and Eadburh remained in Wantage, where everyone made them welcome.

At Wantage they heard how the Mercians, in consultation with Halfdan the heathen King, had chosen a thane of no particular ancestry to rule over them. The most shameful part of the transaction was that this miserable Ceolwulf had agreed to share his realm with the heathen whenever they should ask for it. But at least he was a Christian; it was just a little bit better than living nakedly under the heathen yoke.

The most exciting news came during harvest. After having held together with astonishing discipline for nine years the great Army was rent by an internal quarrel. King Halfdan wanted to march north, to pillage the thrice-pillaged Northumbrians. Some of his captains wished to go to East Anglia, which had lain undefended since the martyrdom of King Edmund. Alfred noted with pride and pleasure that no party among the heathen was in favour of another invasion of prickly Wessex.

'But the heathen must journey farther, or else change their way of life,' said Eadburh, as she discussed the future with her son-in-law. 'A pirate finds golden chalices and silver candlesticks. A few years later he comes back to the same minster for more. He doesn't see that he has stolen the accumulation of centuries; he thinks Christians perpetually renew their offerings. Sixty years ago every pirate went home laden with gold. Now they must be content with corn and horses and slaves. Perhaps presently they will get tired of raiding, and stay at home.'

'By all accounts their homes can't support them,' Alfred objected. 'It's odd that suddenly there should be more of them than their land can feed, when their own legends say they have lived in the north for many generations. But there are countries they haven't yet raided. They may leave Britain and move on to Italy or Spain, or perhaps Greekland.'

'They are afraid of the Greeks, and rightly,' said Eadburh. 'The Emperor has a great host of mail-clad men who fight on horseback, or so I was told by a pilgrim home from Jerusalem. In Italy the walled cities would bar their way, and in Spain they would face the Moors. For the pirates it's Britain or Frankland or Germany.'

'Then they will be raiding Britain when my grandsons carry swords,' said Alfred with a shrug. 'I hope the West Saxons stick it out to the end. They have a long war before them.'

'If the great Army breaks up the pirates won't be so formidable,' Eadburh consoled him. 'Perhaps some of them will realize that there are no more golden chalices, and settle down to plough the land they have conquered.'

'They would rather cut throats than plough, that's why they are here. We must go on fighting them. The trouble is that if the war lasts long enough the West Saxons may themselves end up pirates, as bloodthirsty as their enemies.'

'Of course, I had forgotten. You want to make Wessex into a civilized land. What bad luck, my poor Alfred, that after you became King so unexpectedly you should find yourself doomed to perpetual war.'

'Every King spends most of his time fighting, or getting ready to fight. All the same, I may get my story of the Coming of the Saxons written some day. It's a matter of finding the right men to do it. I don't need a great many helpers, so long as they are intelligent enough to write what I have planned.'

'And not so intelligent that they insist on writing something different? In the end you will have to dictate it yourself. But it's a worthy plan, and I hope you bring it off.'

'If Wessex holds out I shall. If the Army wins there will be no point in writing it. Slaves have no history.'

'Here comes Ethelswitha. Don't talk about slavery

where she can hear you. It's hard to be bound to a husband who left his people enslaved and ran off to safety.'

By Christmas all Britain knew that the Army had split. King Halfdan with his band encamped near the mouth of the Tyne, and raided westward into Strathclyde and northward among the Picts; but these northerners had very little worth stealing. The greater part of the Army marched to Cambridge in the land of the East English, under the leadership of a King named Guthrum.

In Cambridge the pirates lived quietly, never raiding beyond the borders of the East English. The conquered realm of St. Edmund paid ransom enough to keep them in comfort for one winter; but the rent demanded was greater than the land could produce year after year, and it was evident that soon the Army must move to fresh hunting grounds.

In the spring of 875 a letter came from King Burhed. He was settled comfortably in the Saxon School in Rome, and he commanded Ethelswitha to join him. As soon as the sailing season opened she prepared to set out. Alfred rode with her as far as Wight; she was the last companion of his childhood, and he knew that after she had gone oversea he would never meet her again.

They rode through a Wessex of peace, where fat cattle grazed on the waste as though there were not a pirate in Britain. But at Yarmouth in Wight the war caught up with them. Oslac son of Osric, the young alderman of Hampshire, was there to warn them of pirates in the offing.

'How many pirates?' asked Alfred.

'How many? They come and go, hanging about on the horizon.' Oslac shrugged his shoulders. 'Yesterday a fisherman saw seven of them in company, and cut his nets to bring the news; but there may be a dozen within call. I can guard Hampshire, I can't guard the sea.'

'But I can,' said Alfred gaily. 'It seems to me that the

King of the West Saxons should patrol the sea as well as the land. When I was in Devon I had ships built for me, and I have sent for half a dozen of them to come here and escort my sister on her voyage.'

'What an extraordinary idea,' Ethelswitha exclaimed. 'I always think of the sea as belonging to the pirates. There isn't another King in Britain who has ships of his own. Will your fleet seek out the pirates and fight a great battle?'

'No battles,' answered Alfred with a rueful shake of the head. 'The West Saxons can't maintain a strong warband and build a great navy at the same time. I have about twenty ships in all, dotted round the coast from Kent to Cornwall. And very expensive they are, because the steersman and other experts have to be hired Frisians, paid all the year round. The six ships which will meet us here are all I have near Wight.'

'Then why have any, if they can't fight a battle? Isn't it a waste of money?' Ethelswitha asked bluntly.

'I don't think so.' Alfred answered his sister as an equal, though Oslac looked a little shocked at such plain speaking.

'You see,' the King went on, 'the pirates don't come in a great fleet unless they intend to land, and then we can fight them on shore. But these little groups of pirate ships can be a great nuisance, much more of a nuisance than say two hundred plunderers on horseback. A handful of them are cruising off Wight, and here is the alderman of Hampshire with all his companions riding up and down the shore to guard against them when he is urgently needed near London. What do you think about it, cousin Oslac?'

'A very good plan,' said the alderman. 'When your ships go out to look for these pirates I shall be on board with my companions. No need to carry food and water for a long voyage, so each of our ships can hold as many fighting-men as a whole squadron of pirates.'

'And the pirates won't know that, and will be willing

to meet us,' said the King cheerfully. 'Well, why are we waiting? As soon as my squadron arrives I shall go on board the flagship. I'm sorry to displace you, cousin Oslac, but when the King is afloat he takes command. Of course you will be captain of the ship.'

'May I come with you?' asked Ethelswitha.

'Better not, but we shall use you as bait all the same. We send out the roundship that should have carried you. There's a flat calm, and she will have to creep along with the sweeps. When the pirates come down on the empty roundship my longships dash out with their oars double banked. I've never fought at sea. Do the pirates wear anything special when they come ashore to burn a village?'

'Bare feet or goatskin shoes with the hair left on, so they don't slip on a wet deck,' answered Oslac. 'It seems that you fall overboard only once if you wear a byrnie. I'll see you have the right shoes. Otherwise I suppose it's just like fighting on land.'

The children and cousin of the lady Osburh laid their plans with something of the old gaiety of their childhood.

Three hours later the ships were manned; in fact overmanned, for they carried the King's companions and Oslac's in addition to their normal crews. Alfred stood by the steersman in the stern of the flagship. It was astonishing to feel these long narrow fighting-machines moving through the water, quite unlike the sluggish wallowing of the roundships which had carried him across the Channel long ago. Of course it was not a bit like fighting on land. His warriors were divided into handy little packets, and he could signal where they should go. But dear cousin Oslac, though brave, was not very bright.

The plan worked perfectly. The longships hid behind a headland, their oars ready in the rowlocks. Presently the pirates appeared out of the gauzy summer mist. A watcher on the cliff lit his beacon; but that was standard procedure when pirates were sighted from the shore, and the raiders suspected nothing. At the flash of the first spark the longships set off, their oars beating the foam.

There were seven pirates against six sail of Saxons; but the raiders saw they had been ambushed, and assumed they were trapped by overwhelming force. They fled in a body; until their commander hoisted a signal at his masthead and they scattered singly on divergent courses.

'Damn their careful tactics. They are better drilled than any honest men, because they have more time for it,' Oslac muttered into his silky young man's moustache. 'In this mist they will get away.'

'Not all of them. Stick to the leader,' Alfred answered cheerfully. 'Unless our oars break we've got her. Come on, all hands to the oars. The crew will be encouraged to see us do a little pulling.'

Even in his excitement he kept his head well enough to go forward to the bow oar. The travels of his childhood recalled to him that an amateur can stop any boat by trying to row stroke. Soon the King of the West Saxons and the alderman of Hampshire were pulling raggedly just behind the foaming beak of their ship.

When he saw that he could not escape the pirate commander turned at bay. He swung his ship round in a tight circle, hoping to ram the leading pursuer. But while he turned the other Saxons caught up with their King, to ram the pirate amidships before he could use his own beak. Rammed again in the stern, the longship opened out into a cluster of splintered planking. Most of the byrnie-clad raiders went straight to the bottom, and the few who clung to wreckage were an easy mark for arrows. There were no survivors.

'One sunk and six frightened,' said Alfred with satisfaction, reporting to Ethelswitha who had waited on the beach. 'Though the pirates reckon their ships in hundreds it will make them more cautious about raiding the Channel.'

'It's a good beginning,' his sister agreed. 'In fact most

remarkable. I can't remember that anyone recently has sunk a pirate ship, except another pirate of course. Christians always fight them on land. Isn't it an enormous expense to build ships and hire crews just for fighting? What made you think of doing it?'

'I'm very proud of my new idea. Even the great Charlemagne never built a special navy for fighting. But really it's a very old idea. In Rome I saw a platform decorated with the beaks of warships; the old Romans had them in hundreds, and so did the old Greeks before them. I was thinking about the pirates and how to cope with them, and suddenly I remembered what I had seen in Rome. As for the expense, it doesn't cost much more than keeping the same men idle on land as King's companions. It's war that costs money, not ships in particular.'

'Soon I also will see all the wonders of Rome. I wish I were going on a more respectable errand, but it will be exciting all the same. Do you realize that every year thousands of pilgrims see Rome, and you are the first who got the idea of building warships from it? You were always supposed to be the clever one of the family.'

'The way to find new ideas is to think about the past. Nothing that we can imagine is really new. It's just that things go out of fashion, and then they are forgotten.'

After he had said good-bye to the sister whom he would never see again Alfred still glowed with pleasure from her praise. He really did try to think things out, instead of doing what had been done last time; and he had discovered that the best way to find new ideas was to imagine how the ancients would have solved the same problem. What a wonderful world that had been into which Christ was born! Could a just and victorious ruler do anything to bring back that world again? Not if he had to spend all his time defending his realm from pirates.

12

A King Forsaken

The Army was most dangerous in the late autumn. Then
movement was easy, over stubble and short grass; and
every steading was stocked with food from the harvest,
so that foragers might fill their sacks anywhere. When
everyone felt rich, seeing the bulging rickyards, the
heathen sought fresh victims; that was the time when
Kings could most easily be persuaded to pay ransom.

In any case the Army must move once a year; if the
same peasants lost two harvests in succession they would
lack seed corn, and even robbers would go hungry.

Most of Britain had been laid waste. The Army must
travel far if it was to find a rich land to feed it through
the winter. In that autumn of 875 the pirates suddenly
rode out from Cambridge, across the south country by
way of the desolate Chilterns and the open heaths of
Dorset, until they reached the Channel at Wareham.

The West Saxons mustered swiftly. But Alfred found
that many of his thanes were content to hustle the
heathen across their land without trying to bring them
to battle; raiders in a hurry could not stop to burn the
ricks. There was plenty of hard riding, and a few brushes
at the outposts; but the heathen were fortified in a strong
camp between the Frome and the Tarrant before he could
attack them in force. There was nothing for it but to
settle down to another long blockade, as at Reading five
years ago.

It was the dullest, most unpleasant form of warfare.
The heathen might sleep soundly behind their trench,

watched over by a few sentries; but the West Saxons must continuously stand to arms, since the enemy could break out at any moment. There was none of the excitement of battle, no chance to win plunder. Everyone could see the need to pen the raiders into the fortress they had chosen; if they got out all Wessex might be ravaged. All the same, bored thanes tried to slip away to enjoy the comforts of Christmas at home, though none of them would have shirked a set battle.

Alfred remained in camp, to keep his men up to the mark. This was all the harder because for the first time since his marriage he was beginning to enjoy family life. Eadburh made all the difference. In her mother's company Elswitha was cheerful and talkative; and though what she had to say was not very interesting her children were stimulated by their mother's happiness. Ethelfleda was a sturdy little tomboy; Edward all that a King's son should be, straight and tall and handsome, with courteous manners and a grave smile.

At any moment the war might take a turn for the worse. Already the Army had shown that it could move faster than the defenders, and if it broke out of Wareham it might pillage any part of Wessex. After long and serious thought Alfred once more sent his household to the marshy fastnesses of Somerset. Such a move was bad for the morale of his men, who saw that their King feared disaster; but the more intelligent thanes could see that for themselves anyway. Occasionally Alfred rode over from Wareham to Somerset to spend a few hours with his wife and children, though he was conscious that this set a poor example to the men who were reluctantly maintaining the siege.

By the summer of 876 learned clerks were comparing the blockade of Wareham to the ten-year siege of Troy. In June Alfred kept his twenty-seventh birthday among the huts of the besiegers. For five years he had been King of the West Saxons; and the affairs of his Kingdom were in very much the same state as when he came to the throne, with the Army in Wareham instead of Reading.

But though Wessex was no better off there was a slight improvement in the condition of Britain as a whole. King Halfdan's followers were no longer a danger to peaceful Christians. Oddly enough, the court of Wessex received first-hand news of the affairs of Northumbria. A young English warleader named Edwulf rode right across Britain to seek the alliance of the King of the West Saxons.

Alfred found the young man in Somerset, with Ethelfleda and Edward standing in silent worship before his weapons. Byrnie and sword lay on a stool, fine pieces but dinted and scarred in battle; the great attraction was the heavy battle-axe he had taken from a chief of the pirates.

Alfred was pleased to be talking seriously with a man of his own age. The youngest of his aldermen, Ethelnoth of Somerset, was in his late forties.

Edwulf was very conscious of the battle-axe, not quite sure he had done right to bring such an implement into a Christian home.

'The English of the north have taken to them,' he said anxiously. 'Handy things in a skirmish; no second blow needed. We don't make them, of course. We use only those we pick up on the battlefield.'

'A handsome thing. I might use one myself one day. But don't get them made by your own smiths. I expect the heathen sing spells when they temper the steel, spells forbidden to Christians. But you didn't ride through the lands of the heathen to show me your weapons. What's your news?'

'Ah, that's worth telling indeed. The northern wing of the Army is out of the war! King Halfdan's men complained to him that the pickings they won from the Picts and the Strathclyde Welsh were not worth the risk of their lives. But they wouldn't go home, or face a long voyage to another land. After a lot of high words and a few blows they parted from their leader. King Halfdan has gone off to Ireland; his followers have shared out the land near York and will live by farming it.'

'That's bad news. We shall have them in Britain for ever.'

'Yes, my lord, but not as pirates. Usually they will be too busy to go raiding, and if they attack us we can ravage their land in return. They will be easier to live with. Perhaps one day they will become Christians.'

'It's possible. They are the same kind of men as our ancestors. But it will be for our grandchildren to deal with that. It's clear gain that they won't reinforce Guthrum this year. Thank you for riding so far to tell me.'

'That was not the only reason for my coming.' Young Edwulf coughed. 'I need friends. Now that Halfdan is gone some of the Northumbrians have chosen Egbert to be their King. He's a good man, though he will never win York from the heathen. But I hold the rock of Bamburgh far to the north, almost on the border of the Picts. I defend my own against all comers; King Egbert can neither help nor harm me. Yet I need a friend in the free and civilized south. If I become the sworn follower of the King of the West Saxons will you help me as a lord should help his man?'

Alfred hesitated. The offer was tempting, though he knew it was his duty to refuse it. Then he thought of a way out.

'I will take you, and gladly, as one of my companions. But only if you come to live in my hall. Bamburgh is a fortress of the Northumbrians, and I cannot steal the subjects of a friendly and Christian King. I suppose you don't want to leave home? Of course not. Then you cannot be my companion. But there is no reason why we should not be friends. That's it. Go back and hold Bamburgh as a loyal subject of the King of the Northumbrians; and as the friend of Alfred Cerdinga, who happens to be King of the West Saxons. You won't be deserted on your northern rock. Yet we do not rob King Egbert.'

Edwulf brightened at the suggestion. Instead of kneeling to a new lord he embraced Alfred as his equal. Next day he set out on his long ride home, on his arm a gold ring which was the pledge of the friendship and protection of Wessex.

In the camp before Wareham Alfred told his companions that the warriors of King Halfdan had become peaceful land-owners. It was good news, but Alfred himself had gained a further advantage.

'This is the first time an Englishman has offered to serve a Saxon King,' he said proudly. 'My father was lord of all the Saxons and Jutes in Britain, since even the East Saxons paid him tribute. But I am the first of my line who can call himself a King of the English.'

The heathen could not break out from Wareham. Throughout the summer they tested the force of the besiegers, but would not face a set battle. By autumn they were beginning to feel hungry. As was their custom, they sent envoys to negotiate.

Alfred refused a formal parley. There was to be no truce, no bodyguards, no interview in a neutral open space. At length Oscytel came to him alone and unarmed, led with bandaged eyes over the trench which cut off Wareham from the open country. But since it is hard for one man to argue with a numerous council King Alfred agreed to meet him alone.

Without his weapons the young pirate looked seedy, which was a good beginning; he was thin and careworn, to prove that the Army was on short rations. Alfred opened the discussion with a high hand.

'We cannot storm your camp,' he began, 'but you can't get out over our trench. If you could you wouldn't be here now. Very well. You wish to leave and we don't want to keep you. But you get no payment for going away.'

Oscytel stood and thought. 'This is something new. The Army is always paid to go away.'

'King Guthrum does not lead the great Army. Half the Army is farming in Northumbria. King Guthrum and his half of the Army have been beaten. The most I offer is a safe retreat.'

The pirate frowned as his hand stole down to his belt. His jaw tightened when he felt that he wore no sword.

'You are right,' he said after a pause. 'We have been beaten, or at least we have been held. That has never happened to us before, and now it is fair that we make peace on novel terms.' He opened his hands in a friendly gesture. 'We accept your offer of a safe retreat, for we should be foolish to refuse it. Even so, there are terms to be agreed. The promise of a King, of such a King as you, will be enough for King Guthrum. But some of his followers are rough ignorant men, and perhaps not very honourable themselves. Before we leave our palisade you must give us hostages, and swear after your Christian fashion that you will allow us to ride from your Kingdom unharmed.'

'That's out of the question. You are the beaten side. You have sued for peace. If you like I will swear to keep my word, but you get no hostages.'

For half an hour they wrangled, until Oscytel suggested a compromise.

'Would you give hostages if the Army gives you hostages? There is another thing we have never done before, but never before have we been in such a tight place. Don't push us to the point of despair. We can die fiercely when we know there is no escape.'

'I know the old poems of my people, who were very like you before they became Christians. I know that when all hope is gone heroes die fighting, and I want to find a way out for you. But the whole world must see that Wessex has gained the victory. We must have hostages, and we will give you hostages in exchange.'

'And you will take oath not to harm us on the march?'

'Again, in exchange for your oath.'

Oscytel protested. The heathen were honourable men,

whose gods punished a broken promise as the Christian God punished perjury. Besides, they had no sacred objects on which they could swear, as Christians swear on holy relics.

Alfred could answer him. 'While my ancestors were heathen they worshipped the gods you worship now. It's all in the old poems. When a heathen King is about to do justice he swears on a holy arm-ring. Let King Guthrum do so, and I shall exchange oaths with him.'

'But that is the arm-ring of Thor, on which Kings take oath only once a year, at the time of the annual lawmoot. It can't be used to ratify a private promise. Thor would feel insulted.'

'If you incur the enmity of Thor I shall be delighted. King Guthrum will take oath in my presence, and he will do it before I swear.'

Alfred could not be moved from his decision, and in Wareham the heathen were hungry and afraid. After further argument Oscytel gave way.

In the open ground between the two palisades a Christian altar was built; and beside it a trophy of helmet, shield and sword which represented Thor. King Alfred knelt to kiss the sacred relics of his altar, but King Guthrum merely placed his right hand on the magic ring he wore on his left arm. Then the hostages came forward in two self-conscious groups. They were sustained by the knowledge that they had been chosen as the best warriors among their people; if they came alive out of this exchange they would be held in honour for the rest of their lives.

The hungry Army rode forth from Wareham. By evening they had covered twenty miles, as far as the northern border of Wessex, and on both sides the hostages were restored to their friends.

The warband of the West Saxons rode after the Army; but cautiously, for fear that some accidental collision might infringe the truce. They encamped five miles behind the heathen, sending forward only a few scouts. It was still dark when Alfred was awakened by an excited sentry.

'The heathen are riding again. They abandoned their baggage and left their fires burning. In the dark we cannot see where they are going.'

It was full day before the West Saxons could take up the pursuit. Though they rode hard they could not overtake the Army. By evening the heathen were safe in Exeter, guarded by water and in touch with the open sea.

'There's one good thing about it,' Alfred told himself. 'They kept the truce until the hostages had been returned, so I don't have to hang innocent men for the bad faith of their comrades. But that's the purpose of hostages, after all. If I can't bring myself to hang hostages there's no point in demanding them. Anyway, every pirate deserves hanging. But I'm glad I don't have to hang a score of them tonight.'

The West Saxons built another palisade, and settled down to besiege Exeter as they had besieged Reading and Wareham.

During Advent a pirate fleet sailed down Channel towards Exeter. But off Swanage a fog came down, and then a sudden squall piled them on the cliffs. The whole fleet was wrecked, to the number of a hundred and twenty ships.

Survivors struggled ashore, to be caught by the fyrd of the countryside. Alfred sent orders that these prisoners should be hanged. It was just, and the fyrd would like it. Besides, he was angry with himself for his qualms over the hostages; and it was easier to hang men he had never seen than to execute famous warriors who had eaten at his own fire.

All the thanes of Wessex went home for Christmas. For eighteen months they had been continuously in the field, and the King could not hold them to their duty any longer. Alfred and his companions manned the length of the palisade, and the local peasants lit deceptive watch-fires; but such measures could not long deceive the veterans of the Army. Towards the end of January 877 King Guthrum led a sally in force, and the King of the West Saxons must retreat.

Beacons told the story, and the warband of Wessex mustered in haste. But the heathen rode too swiftly. Without being brought to battle they reached Mercian Gloucester.

For the rest of that year there was no foe in Wessex. The King and his companions watched the frontier, but the thanes stayed at home.

Every year the Army diminished. From Gloucester King Guthrum sent his orders to the foolish puppet-king of Mercia, and took for his own followers all the eastern half of the land. The despised Ceolwulf might keep the western half; but the pirates held their estates from Guthrum, who remained in Gloucester with his own companions and a few other heathen who would rather fight than plough. Guthrum had no gold to distribute among his warriors, and rude songs were sung about his ill-luck as a war-leader; for at Exeter he had once again abandoned his baggage, and after eleven years in Britain he was as poor as if he had never left the north. But he was still cunning, and ambitious.

At Malmesbury Alfred kept Christmas with his family. The family had been increased by another child, a daughter named Ethelgifu; she kept Elswitha busy and gave him more time to play with the elder children, while Eadburh managed the household. It was almost as good as the old days at Wantage with his brothers. Real peace was so far away that it was futile to hope for it, but undoubtedly things were getting better.

It was a white Christmas, with frost which turned the mud to iron. There could be no hunting on the hard ground, but travel was easy, and a great company came for the twelve-day feast. The abbot of Malmesbury remarked with satisfaction that in this weather it was easy to fetch firewood from the muddiest bottom; Christmas last year had been wet and warm, and by Twelfth Day they had been burning peat for lack of logs.

'Easy journeys make a pleasant Christmas,' Alfred answered, 'but I hope the heathen in Gloucester don't see how good the going is. With all my thanes drunk at the fireside they could raid any part of Wessex without danger.'

'You think always of war,' said the abbot. 'Here we try not to remember it. The heathen don't raid at Christmas time. They have a feast of their own, Yule they call it; and they get just as drunk at Yule as a Christian does in honour of the Nativity. At this season your thanes won't watch the frontier, and I know it worries you. But Guthrum can't get his men to march either, so tonight we may sleep sound.'

'It's ridiculous to worry,' Alfred admitted, 'though that doesn't make it easier for me to stop worrying. Let's see, the Army came to Britain in '65, more than twelve years ago. There is a pattern in its movements. The heathen take up winter quarters after harvest, and never budge until spring. At midwinter we are safe.'

After a pause he added: 'But last summer King Guthrum did something new. He gave hostages, and then he retreated. He might try something new this winter, in revenge. As soon as the holiday is over I shall send scouts to watch him, just to be on the safe side.'

For two days after Twelfth Day everyone was recovering from the feast, and after that it took two more days to summon the local thanes. On the 10th of January, with the ground still frozen, no scouts were watching Gloucester. Alfred was dozing after dinner when the news reached him.

The messenger was the abbey cowherd; he burst in without knocking, pursued by an angry sentry. 'The heathen are a mile away, hundreds of them,' he shouted. 'They are held up at the ford because their horses won't face the floating ice. In a few minutes they will be here. There's just time to run for it.'

From the belltower came the hurrying beat of the tocsin.

Even the small children must be carried on horseback. There was just time to get away, though the baggage must be left in the deserted minster. Monks and peasants, all who could not find horses to carry them, fled on foot to hide among the frozen bushes of the waste.

Two hundred companions, landless young warriors who lived always in the King's hall, formed an escort for the royal family. With such a small force there could be no thought of opposing the invasion. The whole party rode south to the fringe of Selwood. By nightfall they were deep in the forest. Round blazing fires they slept on the bare ground. The glow might betray them to the heathen; but if they slept without fire half of them would be dead by morning, so intense was the cold.

Nearly everyone had remembered to bring something to eat. After twelve years of warfare companion, groom, or nursemaid filled a pouch with bread and meat at the first jangle of the tocsin. They could manage for supper and breakfast, secure in the empty forest. After that they must find peasants to feed them, and the heathen would soon know where they were.

Sitting on the ground under the frosty stars Alfred held a council; not because he needed advice but so that his followers would know his plans if they happened to get separated from the column. Half a dozen captains sat round him, and the ladies Elswitha, Eadburh, and Godgifu; ladies did not normally sit in council, but his family had a right to know their future.

'Because of the weather the Army caught us unprepared,' he began, 'but for the same reason they won't ride far. Even King Guthrum can't keep his men in the saddle during cold like this. What they have really done is to shift their winter quarters; they are not starting a new campaign. As soon as they find a town of warm houses they will halt until spring. We must gather our warband and shut them in before they can ravage the country round their new camp. But until our warband is mustered we must hide. Tomorrow we shall make for the marshes of Somerset. Elswitha knows them, and she will point out a safe refuge. Most of the companions will come with us, but I shall send out some to rouse the country thanes and the landowning companions who are keeping Christmas in their own halls. The place of the muster will be Glastonbury, because everyone knows it; and the day Ash Wednesday, which every Christian notices. That allows a full month for preparation, and no one can mistake the place or the day.'

'It's not the time of year for fighting,' objected Egwulf, captain of the companions. 'The thanes would come more willingly if the muster were fixed for Easter.'

'If the Army can march in midwinter so can the West Saxons,' Alfred replied with a snort. 'Before Reading we kept the field all winter, and again before Wareham.'

'That's just it. Men will fight in winter as a novelty, but not if it is expected from them every year.' But the King did not deign to answer this second grumble.

'The island of Athelney is the best place of refuge,' said Elswitha. 'It's an island in a marsh, not in the sea. It's big enough for all of us, and small enough to defend. You can ride in by a causeway if you know it, but if you try without a guide you drown in the marsh.'

'We'll go there,' the King announced. 'For a month we shall hide, and when I and my companions ride to the muster we shall leave the women and children in safety.'

'It's a desolate marsh,' Eadburh pointed out. 'Nothing grows in it. You will have to collect food from the peasants farther west.'

'There aren't very many of us. The ordinary food-rent of Devon will keep us. We shan't be a burden on a hungry countryside.'

No one else had anything to say. But it was odd and disheartening that the companions drew lots to choose the messengers who must ride with the summons to the muster; as a rule they liked carrying messages, with the hospitality that was the due of a royal messenger. That night only the children slept, under all the cloaks and blankets in the party; adults shivered by the fires under a frosty sky.

On Athelney there were no buildings save a cowherd's bothy; but with rushes and turf and brushwood the fugitives made huts that would keep in warmth and smoke, though they did not always keep out the rain. There was plenty of fuel and no need for concealment. Peasants brought word that the Army had halted at Chippenham; and even if the heathen should discover the King's hiding-place they could not get at him through the marsh.

But it was surprisingly difficult to collect food. The companions who rode westward came back empty-handed, or at most with a horse-load of flour or a single lean cow. The Devonsaetas explained that they had nothing to give, for pirates raiding from Wales over the Severn Sea had emptied their barns. More ominously, the Cornwelsh refused even a nominal tribute. They said that the West Saxons could not protect them from the exactions of the Army, and that their land was too poor to pay rent to two masters in the same year.

It was a very miserable time, but Ash Wednesday was not far off and until then the fugitives on Athelney could endure.

Alfred set out with fifty companions to ride to the muster. Another fifty were left as garrison on Athelney, and the rest were travelling on the King's errands. Even as a young atheling Alfred had led a greater following; things were in a sad state when the King of the West Saxons had a bare fifty men at his tail.

So far the heathen had not ravaged the open country; that would come later in the year, unless the Saxons hemmed them in with a strong palisade. Alfred rode through unburned villages, though at the approach of strange horsemen the peasants hid in the woods so that he could gather no news. On the afternoon of the second day his thin horse brought him within sight of the tower of Glastonbury minster, and he knew that the most sacred shrine in Wessex had thus far escaped the plunderers. But as he came nearer he saw that the buildings were deserted; the community had fled to the woods.

The country was strangely quiet. Even the horses did not prick their ears, though usually horses hear footsteps before their riders. Alfred turned to the chaplain who rode beside him. 'We haven't mistaken the day? You are sure this is Shrove Tuesday?'

'Quite certain, my lord. At the beginning of Advent I got this year's calendar from Canterbury, and I know that Easter falls on the 23rd of March. All the big minsters got the calendar about the same time. Perhaps in the stress of invasion some of your thanes haven't heard Mass very regularly. But everyone knows when Lent begins; you can't be a Christian unless you keep Lent.'

'That's why I chose this date for the muster, because everyone must know it. But we seem to be the first to arrive, though the meeting is fixed for tomorrow. The West Saxons are not often so exactly punctual. There's no doubt that this is Glastonbury, and known to all my people. I don't understand it.'

'Perhaps I can guess the reason, though I hesitate to name it,' answered Duduc the chaplain. 'But here is a man riding to meet us. One of your companions by his arm-rings. Yes, it's Wulf, whom you sent into Kent.'

The solitary rider was nervous. He glanced anxiously up at the Tor, then peered into the woods. When he saw the King and his small escort he gestured violently, obviously urging them to take cover. Then he spurred his tired horse to a gallop.

'Don't halt in the open, my lord,' he called as soon as he was within hearing. 'There may be heathen about.

Get under the trees and post a sentry, and I'll tell you my news.'

'If you say so,' Alfred answered cheerfully. 'But heathen raiders who choose the mustering-place of Wessex for an ambush are likely to get the worst of it.'

'There is no muster, my lord. That is my news. Remember all Wessex knows that on Ash Wednesday the King will be at Glastonbury, so perhaps the heathen know it also. There's great danger here.'

'Then we must come away to the nearest wood, and hide in a thicket while you talk to me.'

As Alfred turned his horse he nearly fell from the saddle; his head was whirling so that he could hardly keep his balance. In a flash he understood. While he lurked cravenly in Athelney he had lost the throne of the West Saxons; some bolder warrior had stolen his people from him.

'Have they chosen another King?' he asked. 'Who is he? Does he come of the right line of Cerdic?'

'They have chosen King Guthrum, my lord,' Wulf answered as the companions dismounted and clustered round to listen. 'That's what it amounts to, though I suppose they won't admit it. At least they won't resist King Guthrum. They say it's useless. They have fought the Army for twelve years, and it's stronger than when it landed in Britain. The West Saxons have had enough. No one will come to the muster.'

'Do you mean that they have deserted God, and Christendom, and civilization, as well as their chosen King?' asked Alfred. 'Will they enlist in the heathen Army, to sack convents and minsters?'

'It's not as bad as that, my lord. They won't fight for King Guthrum, but neither will they fight against him. Those who had silver hoarded have taken it and fled oversea to Frankland. Most of the country thanes plan to offer ransom to the Army, so that their lands shall be spared. King Guthrum has proclaimed that he will take ransom from any village lord, since the King of the land hides instead of either fighting or buying peace from him. Even some of your sworn companions have gone oversea, saying that the oath is dissolved since you do not protect your land. I have come here to warn you, and I shall follow you while you need me. But it will be best for me and for you, and for all the West Saxons, if you take your household oversea and join King Burhed in Rome.'

'But I am trying to fight now. I hid only because the Army had taken us by surprise and I needed time to collect my warriors. I—' Alfred bit his lip and forced his mouth into a firm line, though his cheeks were blushing. It is unseemly that a King should justify his conduct to his companions.

'My lord, you cannot fight. Your people no longer follow you.' Wulf waved his hand at the empty landscape.

Alfred felt too desolate to speak. Then, luckily, he lost his temper. He knew what to say to this little band of loyal companions; he remembered what Ethelred used to say during the battle-winter.

'Get mounted, those of you who still heed the oath of companionship. The *nithings* may leave me now. If ever they return to the land of the West Saxons they will be outlaw. I am riding back to Athelney, and my true followers with me. But I am not going back to hide from my enemies. I can't fight the Army, but I shall harry their outposts and their foragers. I shall fight the heathen so long as I can hold a sword. While the true King of the West Saxons lurks in the greenwood King Guthrum and his heathen can never rule undisturbed in Wessex.'

No one could refuse such a challenge. All the companions made haste to mount. Yet Alfred knew that some of them would slip away later, when they could desert without facing the reproach of their comrades.

They rode back to Athelney, stumbling in the dark over the familiar path. They had not been expected, and for supper there was nothing but a few eels and a little oatmeal.

Alfred ate alone in a little turf hut, for in this refuge there was no building where he might sit among his companions. Then he wandered over to the next mean round hut, which did duty as the bower of the royal ladies. His children slept on the floor under thin and dirty blankets. Elswitha was mending his spare shirt while Eadburh tended the smoky fire; Godgifu was grinding meal on a handquern. This was the royal seat of the King of the West Saxons, he reflected; would he live to see again the decent state of his childhood?

As he entered Elswitha looked up; she had already heard the news. 'So there was no fighting,' she said, as a statement rather than a question. 'It's too early in the year for pirates to cruise the Channel. We can get oversea if we risk a winter voyage.'

'Do you want to live in exile?' Alfred asked her.

His wife shrugged. 'We are in exile now, it seems. A King does not live in this fashion. If we stay here the children will grow up savages. But I won't go without you. I am Woden-born also, and I do not desert my lord in the field.'

'If I am killed you must go oversea at once. That's an order. But if you are not afraid I should like you to stay while I fight this campaign.'

'Then you are still fighting?' asked Eadburh, on her knees to blow at the embers. Godgifu stopped grinding, and sat still to listen.

'I shall fight with my fifty companions. If they leave me I shall fight on alone. I shall fight while the heathen remain in Wessex. Fight them again and again, it's the only way to get rid of them. That's what Ethelred used to say.'

'Keep it up until spring, and you may find others fighting beside you,' Eadburh encouraged him. 'The heathen are taking ransom, but they are not now taking over the land. After a time the West Saxons may choose to fight rather than go on paying. Besides, to pay ransom does not in the end save anyone from heathen plundering.'

'But you must feed your household. How will you do that?' Godgifu reminded him.

'There are not very many of us. We shall hunt. I have never before hunted for food, only for fun. It will be a new experience. If the worst comes to the worst my people owe me food-rent. I shall take it by force from those who will not pay their lawful dues. But I shall never give in.'

There were no hounds on Athelney, and not enough men to beat the woods. The King of the West Saxons must stalk his deer, killing in silence with a single arrow like any lawless poacher. But Alfred knew the forest; even in that bitter season he seldom came back to the island empty-handed.

His handful of men raided lonely settlements, taking by force the food-rent due to the King. Alfred could not bring himself to go with them; a King may command the robbing of his people, but he cannot be seen to rob them in person. Instead he hunted alone, or with a single servant to carry back the kill.

Another trouble, besides the lack of hounds, was the shortage of arrows. In Athelney he could gather only a dozen good hunting-arrows, true flighted. Any man with ten fingers can make a war-arrow, something with a sharp head that will kill at six feet; but only a skilled fletcher can fasten a balanced head to a straight shaft so that the missile flies true for a hundred and fifty yards and lodges in the heart of a deer. Without hounds a wounded stag meant a lost arrow.

In the middle of March, Alfred travelled far to the north-east in search of an undisturbed covert; it was important to bring back a fat buck for the Palm Sunday feast before the rigours of Holy Week. He took one servant, and the six straight hunting-arrows that remained to him. Rain fell incessantly, which made the weather a little warmer; but the wet got the flights of his arrows into a sorry tangle. All the same, on the third day he was lucky. He crept right among a herd of fallow deer to kill a good buck. He cleaned and skinned the carcass where it lay; but even at this stage of his fortunes he thought it unworthy of the royal dignity to carry meat on his own back. His servant set out for home while the King sat under a tree to put his gear in order.

It had come on to rain more heavily than ever. The light was going; water dripped through bare branches. Alfred considered. He had no blankets and no fire, so that a night in the open would be most unpleasant. On the other hand, he was unarmed save for his bow and hunting-knife, for it is impossible to hunt on foot with a sword dangling between the legs; if he sought shelter in a village he would be at the mercy of the peasants.

These fears were absurd, he told himself angrily. He was the chosen King of the West Saxons, and if they wanted to betray him to the heathen the sooner they did it and got it over the better. He would not slink through the woods in fear of his own subjects. He remembered that half a mile away there had been in the old days a lonely cottage, the home of a charcoal burner who had married and settled down to plough a little clearing in the waste. Ten years ago a stag had been headed there, and the day's sport ruined. Perhaps the cottage would still be standing, though the charcoal burner must be dead. (It was odd to realize that ten years ago he had hunted with dear Ethelred; he thought of himself as still a youth barely grown, but on his next birthday he would be twenty-nine.) He tucked his precious arrows under his sheepskin jerkin and set off to find shelter from the rain.

The cottage stood as he remembered it. No one had ploughed the clearing, but that was natural with the heathen ranging at will through the land. At least someone was at home, for a column of smoke told of a brisk fire in the hearth.

He hailed the cottage, to show that he came in peace; but the door remained barred. He beat on it with the

Alfred Duggan

handle of his knife, crying, 'Hail Mary.' From within a
tremulous voice answered: 'Full of Grace,' and added:
'You Christian out there, are you alone?'

'Alone, and wanting to get out of the wet. Let me sit
by your fire while I dry my arrows. I have eaten this
morning and I can manage without supper.'

Eyes examined him from a slit where the thatch met
the wall. The door was unbarred, and an old woman
stood on the threshold.

'Come in. I am alone but so are you, and there's
nothing in here to tempt a robber. My man is going
round his snares. I have a good fire, because I am baking.
But we have very little flour. Nowadays it's hard to come
by, with heathen pirates chasing honest farmers off their
own land.'

'I understood, mother. In these bad times strangers
should not expect food as well as shelter.'

That was a nasty remark; but Alfred was hungry as
well as tired, and the buns baking on the hearth smelled
so good that he longed to taste them. Even a good King
cannot remain the kindly father of his people when his
people have deserted him.

The old woman flared up at the insult. 'We are Saxons
here, not savage Welsh who don't observe the laws of
hospitality. Of course you share our buns, if you come
under our roof. But no one will eat until my man is
back. Nowadays flour is something special.'

She looked at the buns steaming by the fire.

'So special,' she went on with a grin, 'that I had
forgotten how much baking is needed. I must put on
more sticks and I haven't any cut. There's woodstack
behind the hut.'

She glanced towards a hatchet leaning against the wall,
and then at Alfred's belt. He could see the thoughts
chasing through her mind. 'This man has a knife, but no
sword. If I let him have the hatchet I shall be at his
mercy.'

'In this weather you wouldn't find the firewood. I

212

shall go out and cut a few faggots. Just keep an eye on the buns while I am gone, and turn them when they are done on this side.'

Picking up the hatchet she stumped out of the cottage.

Alfred looked at the glowing fire; steam still rose from the buns, and it would be some time before they needed turning. By the hearth lay a billet of wood, the only seat on the bare earthen floor. Sitting down, he drew the draggled arrows from under his jerkin.

Cousin Neot had prophesied that his people would desert him, and the prophecy had been fulfilled. But he had not persisted in the unchristian haughtiness which had shocked Neot, and it had not been suggested that he would end his days forsaken and deserted; if he stuck it out a better time might come. The West Saxons were not angry with him; it was just that they had lost heart. For twelve years the Army had been ravaging in Britain, and no one had been able to withstand it. Presently the Saxons would discover that to offer ransom was no solution. Britain was a poor country, and the Army wanted more than daily food. When the heathen had taken all the gold and silver they could find they would begin to burn and slaughter, hoping to extort more. In the end the Saxons would see that even death in hopeless battle was better than paying ransom. He must keep his little band in arms until his people returned to their allegiance of their own free will.

That might not happen for years, but it might happen tomorrow. Some minor success against a little gang of raiders might make them eager to try the chance of battle once again. Would it do any good if he hunted down a few pirates and hanged his prisoners in some conspicuous place? Not with fewer than a hundred companions to follow him; he could not be sure of exterminating more than a score of pirates. But something might happen somewhere. Vague rumours had drifted into Athelney that Ethelnoth, alderman of the Somersaetas, was at large with a warband beyond Selwood; and the men of Devon and Cornwall, though they would not pay food-rent, had not as yet offered ransom to the Army. If the heathen ventured into the far west the peasants might take up arms against them. Only one success was needed. Then the whole picture might change . . .

His last arrow was smooth. The old woman had been away a very long time. With a guilty start he looked at the buns, and saw black smoking cinders on the hearth.

He was feeling through his empty pouch, to make sure that he had no money with which to pacify his hostess, when she returned with her husband. She must have waited outside the cottage to warn him of the presence of a stranger. The man carried a hare, which would make a good meal for three people; it was more important that he carried a sharp well-tended spear. It gave him the upper hand against a hunting-bow and knife.

After a glance at the hearth the old woman let herself go.

'I know your kind. A lazy, rakish, thieving war-companion, that's what you are. You have never done any useful work, reaped a field or milked a cow. You can't do anything but kill and plunder. You can't do even that very well, for I see you lost your sword running away from the Army. I was too well-mannered to ask, but I suppose you are a follower of that foolish King Alfred, who keeps the war alive though he's been beaten. Why doesn't he go oversea, and let us have peace? Fightingman, warrior, plunderer, that's what you are! A burden to your kin and to every peasant who earns an honest living! You shan't taste this hare that my husband snared in the dangerous forest at risk of his life. Get out of my cottage before I take a stick to you!'

She brandished a besom as though it were a spear; while her husband, ashamed of this breach of hospitality but prudently obedient to his wife, shrugged his shoulders with an apologetic smile and made no effort to restrain her.

Wearily Alfred rose to his feet. That old forester held

his spear very clumsily; a veteran of the battle-winter could knock him off his feet and take over this cottage. The fire was warm; outside cold rain pelted down. Then he seemed to see the stern face of cousin Neot, and put aside the temptation. The old woman was within her rights. He tucked the bundle of dry arrows under his jerkin and stumbled to the door.

Before he could reach it there sounded a thunderous knocking. No one moved, though the churl took a firmer grip of his spear. Then a rat-tat changed to blows, and a well-placed kick splintered the latch. As the door flew inwards a tall warrior stood framed in the opening.

'Have you news of the King?' he demanded. 'Why, there you are, my lord. Were these people annoying you? That's a good fire. Even in this weather the hovel should burn easily. If you like we can chuck the pair of rascals on the embers before we pile the thatch on them. No? Then, you oafs, kneel before the King of the West Saxons and thank him for sparing your miserable lives.'

Alfred recognized the newcomer as a prosperous Devon thane.

'That's all right, Cutha,' he said quickly. 'There has been a slight misunderstanding, but I was at fault. If you have any money please give the goodwife a penny, royal largess you know. Perhaps I shall repay you one of these days; if I don't it will be because we have both gone to a place where money is no use to us. My apologies, madam, for spoiling your supper. As you have just pointed out, I have little skill in the domestic arts. You have horses outside, Cutha? Let me ride behind a groom, and we shall be in Athelney by dawn. We ought to find something to eat there, for I have just sent them a fat buck. You can tell me your errand while we ride.'

The old couple had fallen on their knees. But as the wife caught Cutha's thrown penny she still scowled.

13

Edington

Of course the King did not ride pillion behind a groom.
Cutha gave him his best horse; everyone in the company
moved down one, until the least of the grooms was left
to find his way to Athelney on foot.

As they rode through the rainy darkness Cutha told
his heartening news.

'Ubba Ragnarsson crossed from Wales to Devon with
only twenty-three ships. As you know, the Devonsaetas
are willing to pay ransom to the Army; but with Ubba
and his men there could be no question of buying peace.
Those savages kill and burn for the pleasure of it. In
Wales they had wasted all Dyfed, until hardly a Christian
remained alive. So Alderman Odda mustered the fyrd of
Devon. Then he lost his nerve, and fortified himself on
the hill of Cynwit, by the sea. Ubba thought he had us
cornered, and would not waste lives in an assault. The
heathen surrounded us, waiting for us to yield from
hunger. Suddenly Odda led us in a charge against the
besiegers. The heathen were taken by surprise. By
nightfall Ubba was dead, with forty of his sworn companions and a thousand men of his warband. But that's
not the best of it. When we came to divide the spoil
Odda found a great linen banner worked with the figure
of a raven . . .'

'Do you mean *the* Raven Banner?' Alfred broke in.

'I think so. Ubba was a Ragnarsson, brother to Ivar
and Halfdan. We all know the story, how the daughters
of Ragnar wove the banner in a single night, weaving

spells into it so that the Raven flapped his wings when the heathen would be victorious, and dropped his head when they were in danger of defeat. Ubba did not lead the great Army, he had only twenty-three ships. But King Guthrum is not a Ragnarsson, and King Halfdan has gone to Ireland with only a few companions. When he left Britain he must have turned over the Raven Banner to Ubba his brother.'

'Where is it now?' Alfred asked eagerly.

'Alderman Odda hung it in some church, but I don't know which. I told him he ought to send it to the King, but he answered that it was his own spoil, taken in battle by his own companions, and that he would leave it as an heirloom to his children.'

'That's a pity, but perhaps Odda deserves it. Will the Devonsaetas come to my muster when I summon them?'

'If you summon them soon, my lord, while the great victory is fresh in their memories. It was only twenty-three shiploads they beat, not the great Army. But for the moment they fear no foe.'

'Ah, but they'll have to come, Cutha. Don't you see? The Army will seek revenge. And at bottom Odda is loyal. He deserted me because he thought it was the only way to save his people from pillage, but when he hears of a West Saxon warband in the field he will join it rather than fight alone. What about the other lands beyond Selwood? Is there any news of the Somersaetas?'

'Yes indeed, my lord, and good news. When they heard of our victory at Cynwit they flocked to join their alderman. At present Ethelnoth leads all the fyrd of Somerset, as Odda leads all the fyrd of Devon. What the Cornwelsh will do I don't know. Most will stay at home to guard their land, for they don't care what happens to Saxons. But some will join you. With the Raven Banner taken the whole west knows that the Army can be beaten.'

'I shall have to talk it over in council. We mustn't waste this opportunity, but we must allow time for every willing man to come to the muster. When I have gathered all my force I shall march against the Army wherever it may be, and attack it. That's against the rules, I know. But if we try another siege, with endless hanging about and watching in the rain, my men will grow bored and go home. We shall fight in the open field, and finish the war.'

In the dim starlight Cutha was surprised to see a flash of white teeth as his hungry, tired King laughed aloud.

In the second week of May the fyrd of the West Saxons was gathered on the eastern fringe of Selwood. Alfred had summoned every man who could march, down to peasants armed with slings and ox-goads. Even with these peasants, who could not stand in the front rank, it was not a very great host. Hampshire, Wiltshire and Somerset had sent every man they could, the thanes of Devon had come without their churls, and the Cornwelsh had sent a small contingent. But no warrior came from the dependencies of Wessex, from Kent, Sussex, Surrey or Essex. The men of these harried lands would rather pay ransom than risk their lives in another desperate battle after fourteen years of unsuccessful war.

Alfred must fight without delay, for he could not feed his men. The Army was still in Chippenham, living well on the ransom of despairing Saxons. If the heathen sat tight to endure another siege the Christian host would disperse with nothing accomplished.

Though the Saxons had assembled openly the heathen made no move. Alfred talked over the problem in council. There were ways of getting news from the Army. Every day peasants brought to Chippenham the ransom with which wealthy fainthearts had bought immunity for their lands. But these peasants understood nothing of military affairs, and they never spoke to a heathen of rank. Would the Army march out to fight in the open? Someone must find out.

At the end of a long discussion Alfred spoke up. 'I

myself will visit the Army. I shall go as a man of quality, a warrior who may speak with chieftains. Perhaps I shall see King Guthrum. When I return we shall know their plans.'

There was an immediate outcry. 'We can't spare the King,' said alderman Ethelnoth. 'If you need a warrior of high rank I'll go myself; though how I get in unless I drive a cow I don't know. And if I pass for a cowherd I can't speak with King Guthrum.'

'Do you sing, my dear Ethelnoth? Do you know the old epics? I heard you last night after supper. You would never pass for a gleeman.' In high spirits the King elaborated his plan.

'I play the harp really well, and I know the old poems. Besides, for days past I have been thinking of this expedition, and I have worked myself into the proper frame of mind. This is what I told myself: I am a Saxon of good birth, a poet and singer. I have genuinely despaired of Christendom, and I choose to go back to the ways of my heathen ancestors. I beg to join the great Army as a humble recruit, and to pay my footing I offer to entertain the captains. What do you think of that? Our songs will seem delightfully foreign to the heathen, but they can understand them. Probably they have the same kind of legend in their own tongue. Of course I may not find out the vital plans. I can't ask King Guthrum to tell me his intentions. But by the time I leave I ought to have a pretty good idea of whether the Army is itching to fight or longing to cower behind its palisade.'

'It might work,' said Odda of Devon, weighing the plan in his mind. 'It doesn't seem worth the risk, gambling the life of the King for knowledge of the enemy's plan. But you are our leader. If you want to go we can't stop you.'

'It *is* worth the risk, alderman. This is the last warband of the West Saxons, and if it disperses during the boredom of a hungry siege we shall never gather another. I must know whether the Army intends to fight. And if

King Guthrum is undecided I may help to make up his mind for him.'

The heathen palisade stood on a bare hilltop; the sentry on the gate could see a long way. He was not worried by the solitary warrior in byrnie and helmet, who carried a harp slung on his shield and whose sword was secured by stout peacestrings. The man must come in peace, since he could not defend himself; and it was easy to see that he came alone.

It was presumptuous of the cheeky young harper to offer his sword to the Army, who did not need the help of soft-handed Saxons. But if he could sing there was no harm in listening to him. He brought a purseful of silver as his ransom, and King Guthrum decided that after they had heard him they would let him go unharmed. Life would be less strenuous if Saxons brought their silver into camp of their own accord, instead of running away when decent pirates chased after them to take it.

The harper knew a great many songs, and sang them very well. He began with an ancient poem about the wanderings of Grim, the one-eyed wayfarer who is really Woden in disguise. The wanderer moves up and down the earth he rules, to punish unfaithful companions and reward householders who offer hospitality to strangers. It was a poem appropriate for a renegade seeking asylum; even though Guthrum had already decided to refuse the volunteer he admired his wit. The heathen could hardly understand the archaic language of the song, but to hear it made them feel cultured and scholarly.

Next he sang of what will be, one day when the world shall be ripe for its end. When that time comes Woden and all the Aesir will know themselves foredoomed to defeat, and the heroes of Valhalla will know it also. But because they are Aesir and heroes not one will shrink from the onset. Every doom was decreed long ago, and a good man meets his doom without flinching. The warriors of the Army, aspirants to Valhalla, felt uplifted by thought of the nobility they would display at the end of time; uplifted and mournful and at the same time eager to prove their courage. Death must come to every man, and that is not the end. After death will come Ragnarok. But the heroes of the Army who have ravaged all Christendom will face the Twilight of the Gods with a fortitude that does honour to the whole human race.

Lastly the harper sang of a feud in the royal house of the West Saxons, of the gallant end of loyal companions after a King had been trapped by his enemies (it was the song Alfred had sung at Burhed's wedding, long ago). The audience of captains and famous warriors agreed that these sworn companions had shown a very proper spirit. By the end of the poem they were so exalted that they beat on their shields, boasting of the deeds they would perform in the next battle. While the applause was at its height the harper sang a little extempore jingle, rhyming on the names of the most famous warriors present and suggesting that they should at once march against their miserable enemies. All the company took up the cry, until presently they noticed that the harper had slipped away. He must have changed his mind about joining them, which was rather odd. But King Guthrum had already decided to refuse him, so it did not really matter.

The sentry made no difficulty when the harper left the camp. The man had brought silver, and it had been accepted as ransom for his head. The Army always keeps its bargains. The Saxon might go in peace.

Word came that evening that the Christians were assembled on the fringe of Selwood, mustered in arms to challenge the Army. With his captains in such a warlike mood Guthrum thought it wiser to march against them, though he knew very well that if he sat quiet in his camp the defenders of Wessex could do him no harm.

'Is that all of them?' asked Ethelnoth as the Saxon leaders peered at the hillside above Edington.

'All we have to worry about,' Alfred answered

cheerfully. 'Remember, King Halfdan took a good half of the Army to Northumbria. What was left split again, and half of them settled on their own farms in Mercia. King Guthrum leads only a quarter of the original Army that came to Britain fourteen years ago. But his men are the only warriors of the great Army who still live by the sword. If we can beat them we shall have peace.'

The West Saxons walked slowly up the hill towards the heathen shield-wall.

As he tramped over the green May grass Alfred was aware of an odd silence behind him. It is a mistake for a leader to look over his shoulder too often, but he stole a sidelong glance at the men behind him. They breasted the slope stolidly, breathing through their noses. About this advance there was no exaltation, no excitement, no feeling of death or glory. The close-packed ranks trudged like ploughmen going to work in the furrow. A voice shouted a war cry, but no one took it up and it died away. Yet no one shrank or tried to drop back among the peasants in the rear rank. His companions were packed closely round the Dragon standard of Wessex, with its tall pole topped by a crucifix and its little reliquary below. The Dragon embodied Wessex, its adornments reminded them that they were fighting for Christendom. While they could see it they felt no need to cheer.

He knew in his bones that his warband would give a good account of itself. These men had come out to do their duty, because life was intolerable while the Army ravaged Britain. Before sunset they would end the war, or their lives. Theirs was the silent, stolid courage of men who go into a raging sea or a burning building because honour will not permit them to refuse the challenge. During the battle-winter, he remembered, he had charged with drawn sword, beckoning his companions to the slaughter; now he marched soberly and in silence, his sword in its scabbard and his head bent to pick his way. His only task was to bring these men within reach of the enemy.

Now they were within long arrow-range, and he could see the heathen plainly. They were not so numerous as the Saxons; but every man of them was a picked warrior while his own rear rank was stuffed with peasants. King Guthrum and his companions were grouped round a horse's head set on a pole; the head was still fresh and undecayed, so they must have been sacrificing to their false gods just before the battle. Perhaps they had been a little awed by the chanting and tinkling of bells at the field-Mass; it was known that the heathen feared Christian magic.

Just beyond King Guthrum stood a group of baresarks. He knew more about these eccentrics now than when he had encountered his first specimen at Reading. They were biting the rims of their shields, and in a moment they would charge. Their rush could break the steadiest ranks, but his men knew how to deal with it. It is useless to fence with a baresark; the only thing to do is to let him pass and then stab him in the back. There is nothing dishonourable in this, for the baresark has already taken an unfair advantage by yielding his body to the possession of a demon.

Sixty yards to go, and still utter silence. Alfred settled his left arm in the shield-straps, and drew his sword; he heard the rustle as hundreds of swords were unsheathed behind him. The heathen were restless, but he could see King Guthrum gesturing at them to stand fast.

When the lines were twenty yards apart the heathen charged, shouting their war cry. Alfred just had time to see that they had charged against orders, unnerved by the silent approach of the defenders of Christendom. That was a good omen. King Guthrum had lost control of his men at the outset of the battle.

A yelling knot of baresarks swept down, and his companions jumped forward to guard him. Hairy naked chests were all about him, and the thud of flailing battle-axes. Baresarks do not smell like ordinary heathen; they give off a reek of sweating flesh instead of the stink of dirty woollens. An axe sheared a segment from his shield, and he stumbled to his knees. That bare navel must belong to an enemy. He sank his sword into it and won room to struggle to his feet.

The battle was not five minutes old, and already there was a heap of bodies round him. That is what happens when a baresark charge is held; the madmen cannot last in a standing fight, but they take many foes with them as they are killed.

He glanced quickly to the flanks. Everything was going well. The heathen charge had been raggedly delivered, with the steadiest veterans remembering their orders to stand fast and the hotheads running out without permission. The Saxons had held it. Now the battle was at a stand, as both sides hewed at each other over the war-linden.

Even peasants in sheepskins could be useful in such a fight. Their weight backed up the byrnie-wearers in the front rank, and some of their spears were long enough to reach the heathen over the shoulders of the companions. This would be a long, dour fight. What made it strange was the absence of clamour. There was plenty of noise: gasps, grunts, cries of pain, the thud of stricken shields; but neither heathen nor Christian shouted a war cry or even cheered to encourage his comrades. On both sides thousands of men were getting through an unpleasant but necessary duty.

The heathen fought without their usual dash. They were veterans who never made a mistake, difficult men to kill; but it seemed that they were more anxious to survive than to crush their adversaries. After the first ineffective charge they stood on the defensive, their shields interlocked, their feet braced to yield no ground. They were so reluctant to advance that six feet in front of them a man might feel safe. The Saxon peasants remained in the battle-line, though usually they fled after half an hour of fighting.

Alfred withdrew a little from the front rank to see

the battle as a whole. He could not encounter King Guthrum, who also stood behind the battle-line surrounded by a body-guard of well-armed companions. The mark to aim at was the heathen standard, that bloodstained magic head of a new-slain horse which rose in the centre of their line. The pole on which it was fixed was magic also. It was old and smooth with use but gleaming with gold leaf, and halfway up was fixed one of the magic arm-rings on which the heathen took oath. No one held the standard, for it was firmly set in the ground.

The fighting died down as the Saxons withdrew to regroup. Alfred moved a few paces down the line, and led his companions in a charge against the horse-head standard. The attack made no impression on the heathen shield-wall, for here the bravest of the pirates stood on guard. In the scrimmage a wounded heathen, stretched on the ground to die, drove a knife into Alfred's foot. In itself the wound was unimportant, for his thick boot turned the blade. But now he was too lame to run fast in retreat; at the end of the day he must hold the place of slaughter, or never leave it.

The next attack reached nearer to the standard. The Saxons were doing little more than hold their ground, though it could not be said that the pirates were retiring. During the next lull the heathen took down their magic pole and set the horse's head on a plain spearshaft, an encouraging sign that they feared to be driven back. But the battle had continued for nearly three hours.

There was nothing to do but to continue on the same lines.

Alfred grouped his companions for another charge. His losses were less than he had expected, less than they had been in similar battles. The heathen were fighting mechanically, intent only on preserving their line; so long as they could repel the Saxons from their shield-wall they would not take risks to slay an adversary.

By the middle of the afternoon the Saxons had gained

a technical victory. The heathen retired by detachments, little packets of men running back fifty yards and then forming again, so that they still made a front against their enemies. That night the Saxons would be able to boast that they held the place of slaughter, with all the plunder of the slain and gathering of abandoned weapons that make it valuable. But the Army had suffered little loss. Behind the palisade at Chippenham it would be as formidable as ever.

Now that the battle was on the move Alfred felt the hindrance of his wounded foot. If he withdrew, his men would cease to fight and there would be no proper pursuit. But he could not run after the enemy as they retired. He sent a companion down the hill to fetch his horse.

He was running a risk, and he knew it. No prudent man mounts a horse while there is fighting nearby. Horses are nervous creatures; a rider who gets mixed up in a fight is likely to be stabbed in the back as he wrestles with the reins.

All the same, there would be no pursuit unless the King led it. If he could not run he must ride, trusting to the protection of his companions. He looked anxiously downhill to the Saxon baggage-lines.

Presently he saw a troop of horsemen cantering towards the battle. His message had been misunderstood; no groom would suppose that the King alone would mount, while the rest of his men fought on foot. Someone had sent forward horses for all the King's companions.

Only a hundred yards from the heathen line there was an amazing muddle, as puzzled companions stood by their horses and protested at the supposed order that they should ride off the field. Alfred, safely in the saddle, shouted explanations, kicking out his damaged foot to show his reason. Companions mounted and then dismounted; grooms called to their masters; frightened horses neighed and reared.

Suddenly Alfred heard a great shout of triumph. He

looked at the battle, and saw there was no battle. The heathen line had broken.

The few mounted Saxons rode through the eager pursuers like huntsmen urging on a pack of hounds. This headlong rush was too disorderly to be a feigned flight, and with twelve miles to cover before the fugitives reached their palisade the Saxons had a golden opportunity. But why had the heathen fled so suddenly, when a moment before they had been withdrawing in good order? Could they have been frightened by the arrival of the horses? Alfred recalled that Franks sometimes charged on horseback. That must be the explanation, he decided. The heathen feared this new art of mounted warfare; when they saw the horses brought up to the front line they had expected a cavalry charge. The battle of Edington had been won by a muddle in the horse-lines; but then many battles have been won by a chance mistake.

During the headlong pursuit the heathen lost heavily. Their horses also were tethered in rear of the battlefield, but they were too hard-pressed to seek them out. Though most of their grooms mounted and fled a number of horses fell into the hands of the pursuers. So did all the baggage the heathen had brought with them from Chippenham; though it was poor stuff, for their best plunder was stored behind the palisade. The twelve miles between Edington and Chippenham were covered in less than three hours, and it was still broad daylight when the Saxons halted outside the closed gates of the heathen camp.

The men who had marched to battle in silence were now wildly excited. They clamoured to storm the palisade immediately, before sunset; and Alfred had difficulty in persuading them to encamp and begin to build a counter-palisade before the entrance to the heathen camp. He knew that a siege was inevitable. The pirates might have been defeated, but those veterans were never demoralized. If no way of escape were open they would fight hard for their lives, and a confused battle among their huts might end in the rout of the attackers.

By nightfall sentries had been posted and huts built for the King and a few other leaders. The warband of Wessex settled down to another siege, as in the past they had besieged Wareham and Reading. Those were gloomy precedents, but glory and unexpected success kept the men in good heart. They were singing round the fires long after dark, when Alfred assembled his council.

Odda spoke first, the alderman of the Devonsaetas who had set the ball rolling by his capture of the magic Raven Banner. But now he was anxious to get back to the west, and inclined to magnify the difficulties of their situation.

'I have made inquiries, and so far as I can find out the heathen have lost none of their famous leaders. No one has found any very splendid arms on the field. We can be certain that King Guthrum got away; by now we should have heard if he had been slain. So here we are again, stuck outside a heathen palisade which we cannot take by assault. That's how it was at Wareham, and before that at Reading. In the end we shall have to pay the heathen to go away. Why not offer them a small ransom now, and dismiss our men to get in their hay? Won't that be better than sitting here all summer and autumn, while pirate ships raid our undefended coasts? We can't capture a heathen camp, and we ought to know it. I say, make peace now, while our men still remember their victory. Then they will come willingly to next year's muster.'

'We haven't tried an assault on *this* camp,' Ethelnoth objected. 'Let's attack it tomorrow, as soon as we have our companions sorted out. We might get in, who knows? The Army isn't invincible, we proved that today. But if the first assault fails I agree with Odda. My best men spent a rough winter in the woods, like the King and his companions. If we keep them in the field much longer their allegiance will be very shaky next year.'

'Why do you both talk of a muster next year?' asked Alfred. 'Do you take it for granted that this war will last for ever? Suppose we can beat the Army now, beat it so thoroughly that it never again troubles us? Isn't that worth another summer in the field, to finish this everlasting war?'

'My lord, you are not yet thirty years old,' said Odda stubbornly. 'Today you have chased your enemies for twelve miles. Of course you think that another stout push will finish off the war. So do the rest of the young warriors. But after three months you will be very tired of staring at the closed gates of this camp. Then you will wonder whether it would have been better to follow my advice.'

'I'm not thinking of how the heathen fled today; though it's true they have not suffered such a defeat since Ashdown, and that was more than seven years ago.' Alfred tried to keep his voice friendly. 'I am thinking of the meagre supper we ate an hour ago, and wondering if the heathen had anything better. Don't you see, you cautious old veterans? At Reading the Army had Mercia behind it, and control of the river. At Wareham they were in their chosen winter quarters, and they had taken ransom from half Britain. But this year they left their winter quarters just after Christmas. That's how they caught me napping. They rode to Chippenham too swiftly to bring supplies with them. Since they have been here they have offered peace to the thanes of Wessex, and I'm sorry to say a great many of my subjects paid ransom rather than fight. But this is the hungry season of the year, for pirates as well as for Christians. Harvest is three months away, and most men are finishing their winter stores. I expect the pirates ate their ransom as fast as it came in. They are too frightened to go out foraging, and anyway there is nothing in the fields for them to take. After a week they will be hungry. After a month they will be offering ransom to *us*. If we keep up the siege we may perhaps make an end of the Army.'

'This isn't the great Army any more,' put in Egwulf the chief of the companions. 'Halfdan's men are in Northumbria, and a lot of the others in Mercia. The people we met today didn't fight like the old Army at Ashdown. Our King has beaten the Army, if only his aldermen will do as he says.'

'Egwulf would make a good alderman, if there should happen to be a vacancy,' added a companion from beyond the glow of firelight. Ethelnoth and Odda exchanged uneasy glances.

'I'm glad I have convinced you,' Alfred said quickly. 'We are all agreed then? For the rest of the summer we besiege this camp, unless the enemy should yield before harvest. There is no more to discuss. Tomorrow at dawn we shall muster our men, and count the losses of our last great victory. Henceforth every captain will inspect his followers every morning, and report to me the name of any man who deserts his lord to go home and look after his fields. Now it's time for sleep. I shall see you all in the morning.'

That was how a victorious King could dismiss his council.

Ten days later a single man came out from the heathen camp. He was a tall warrior, wearing many arm-rings and a rich byrnie. After walking a few paces he laid his axe, sword and shield on the ground and waved a green branch as he continued to approach the Saxons.

Alfred gave orders that the envoy should be brought before him. Had there been anything to hide it would have been more prudent to meet him in the open ground between the palisades; but a walk through the Saxon camp would prove to the pirate how the Army was beset.

The man had been searched for hidden weapons, so a group of armed companions twenty yards off was body-guard enough. Alfred received him alone. He wanted to avoid formality, and to find out if possible what the enemy were really thinking.

231

'Where's Earl Oscytel?' he asked pleasantly, to open the conversation on a friendly footing. 'I talked with him before, and we made a good treaty. He and I understand one another. I should like him to be your ambassador.'

'He was killed, and so was Earl Amund,' the envoy replied shortly. 'Our sole leader is now King Guthrum. Here is his sacred arm-ring, to prove that I represent him.'

'Ah yes, I have seen it before. At Reading, to be exact, all those years ago. I don't doubt your credentials. What do you want?'

'The Army is willing to depart in peace. You must give us a little present, just a few pieces of silver for each man, and we shall go back to Mercia and leave Wessex unharmed.'

'You are a good envoy. You spoke that very well, but of course it's not what you mean. You really came to tell me that the Army must get out immediately, or before harvest you will all be dead of hunger. That's the truth, isn't it? Now suppose you explain why I should let you go, instead of keeping up the siege and waiting for you to starve?'

The envoy thought hard, and presently decided a smile. 'We are hungry, that is true, my lord. In another month we shall be starving. But we are still the Army, the great Army which lives by the sword. You can drive us to despair, but Wessex will not be the better for it. If we charge out to die like heroes you will kill us in the end. But how many Saxons will go home to their wives when the slaughter is over?'

'H'm, it would pay me to let you go in peace, if I could be sure you would go peacefully. I won't pay ransom. That's definite, and you need not try to persuade me. All the same, we might find a way to finish the war. Does King Guthrum offer any pledge of his good faith?'

'He will take oath on his sacred arm-ring,' said the envoy. He seemed to be about to add more, and then shut his lips firmly. Alfred guessed that there was another proposal in reserve, if he should refuse this one.

'That's not enough, not nearly enough,' he said testily. 'He swore that oath before, and it was broken. It's not that I doubt his good faith, but he can't always control his men. Once you are riding at large you might ravage Wessex on your way to Mercia, if you didn't seize some other strong position for your next winter quarters.'

'King Guthrum has considered that point. Of course he regrets that his oath was broken, by men who would not obey his commands. He suggests that, in addition to the oath, the Army and the West Saxons should exchange hostages.'

'*Exchange* hostages!' Alfred put on a fine show of outraged indignation. 'Since when has a victorious King exchanged hostages with a defeated foe? If you want West Saxon hostages come out of your camp and take them.'

Gulping, the envoy braced his shoulders.

'Very well, my lord. We shall hand over hostages, in guarantee of our peaceful departure; and we ask for no Saxon hostages in return. But that's my last word. If that's not enough we shall charge out sword in hand. It's what I wanted to do anyway, but I am King Guthrum's sworn companion and I must bear his messages. For myself I prefer death to dishonourable surrender.'

'But you do as your lord commands,' said Alfred with a smile. 'Obedience to your chosen lord can never be dishonourable. Well, that's settled in principle. No ransom. You give hostages and we don't. But there will have to be another meeting to settle the details. Come here tomorrow. I shall want to pick the hostages you hand over. My men will give you a meal before you return to the camp.'

The young envoy was too proud and too angry to eat with his enemies, even though the Army was hungry. After a correct but cold salute he stalked back to his own palisade.

Alfred sat on before his hut, gazing into the fire. It

was too soon to be quite certain, but this seemed to be the end of the long war. The Army genuinely intended to go in peace, or at least that was what the pirates intended at this moment; the trouble was that they changed their minds very easily.

He could make sure of peace by continuing the siege until they were dead of starvation or killed in a hopeless sortie. Why offer any terms at all? Of course there were arguments for making a treaty now. His own men wanted to get back to their farms, and the pirate sortie might be successful. The weaker side sometimes won against the odds, as he should know better than many other war-leaders. But those were not the reasons why he had accepted the proposal for a treaty. He looked honestly into his own heart and understood that he wanted to spare the lives of these pirates, if it could be done with safety to Wessex.

The Army was a curse, the scourge of Christendom; there was nothing to be said for it. But he had liked every individual pirate he had met. That young man today, for example, negotiating against his will in obedience to the command of his lord, and negotiating so badly because he was too honourable to haggle. A man like that was a robber and murderer because he had been reared in robbery and murder. But he followed his own code, he was brave and spoke the truth. It would be a pity to kill him if a way out could be found.

14

Christian Kings

The choosing of the hostages was an empty form. Alfred could not know which warriors were valued by the Army, and had he known and demanded their surrender he could not know that the right men had been sent. But it was important to bring home to the pirates that they were begging for their lives which the mighty King of the West Saxons had graciously consented to spare. For a week envoys considered lists of names, and then there was a formal conference between all the leaders on both sides.

King Guthrum and his councillors came on foot to the Saxon camp. They came fully armed, but surrendered their weapons at the gate. Then they sat on the grass in a semicircle, with the councillors of Wessex sitting opposite. King Guthrum was in his fifties, with grizzled hair and the beginning of a paunch. He sat down slowly, grunting at the pain in his rheumatic joints; there were lines of anxiety on his cheeks and forehead, and his face was drawn with hunger. But his brooches and cloak were very rich. He was obviously a competent war-leader, in complete command of his followers.

The conference nearly foundered at the outset. King Guthrum had changed his plans; he now said that he could not leave Chippenham until after harvest. Alfred suspected that the Army did not feel itself strong enough to conquer fresh winter quarters without a summer of rest and good rations, but he could hardly urge the pirates to invade another Christian Kingdom. Naturally the West Saxons answered that the Army must leave at once or face an assault. It took a whole day of talking to decide that the pirates might stay at Chippenham until autumn, if they promised to leave before Christmas. During the summer the West Saxons would send them supplies, but they must pay for everything on the nail, in silver or gold. Thus the plunder that the heathen had taken in Mercia and Northumbria would be left in Wessex, which was as it should be.

Alfred went to the second day of the meeting full of confidence. He saw that even if the Army might once more become formidable King Guthrum was finished. He had been a clever war-leader. For years the Army had been quartered in Britain, living well but never quite driving the peasants to desperate revolt; its winter quarters had been well chosen and strongly defended; the surprise attack in midwinter which had so nearly destroyed Wessex must have been Guthrum's idea. But now he was admitting defeat, and never again would the pirates follow him to war. Would he step down into the ranks and continue to live by pillage, or would he take his plunder and live quietly at home in the barbarous north?

On this second day Guthrum recognized Alfred, who had been waiting for something of the kind and was not surprised. The heathen chief was grumbling to his followers about the run of bad luck this year, which had culminated in the fatal decision to leave the palisade and fight the West Saxons at Edington.

'It was more your fault than mine,' he said to his councillors. 'The warriors were eager for battle, and you didn't back me up when I advised caution. They had been restless for days, and the incitement of that Saxon harper was the final touch. I wish we had never allowed the man to give his performance. He's more to blame for Edington than I am. I should have hanged him when I had the chance. Where is he now, I wonder?' His eyes rested idly on the Saxon councillors sitting opposite.

He gave a start, and rose to his feet. As he strode across the circle Saxon guards fingered their swordhilts. But Guthrum was unarmed, and Alfred never moved as the heathen stood over him.

'You were the harper, King Alfred. You stirred up my men to that unnecessary battle. I had you in the midst of my camp, and I let you go for a purseful of pennies! If I had killed you there would have been an end of Wessex. No other man could have gathered the force that beat us at Edington. If on that day I had kept my wits about me I should now be King of all Britain.' Then he chuckled, and raised his hand in salute.

'But what a feat, to go unarmed into the camp of your enemies and persuade them to do the wrong thing! It's worthy of the heroes of old. I hope some poet knows the story. If you are too civilized to boast like a true German I shall get one of my own skalds to put it into verse. Perhaps that would be best. I shall see that he doesn't leave my name out of it, and then I shall be remembered for ever. For such a deed will never be forgotten while warriors sing round the fire.'

It was a graceful compliment, and obviously Guthrum meant it. Alfred began to like the man, as he had liked other pirates. What a pity that he should be an enemy of mankind!

'I was the harper, King Guthrum,' he said with a boyish grin. 'I used to wonder whether I sang well enough to pass as a gleeman. My brothers admired my singing. I am glad the pirates admire it also. Even your wicked followers appreciate the good things of civilization.'

'We appreciate the good things of civilization if we can get them without paying for them,' answered Guthrum, also smiling. 'But you can't say your songs were very civilized. They were all about our northern gods, and savage enough to make even veteran pirates clamour for battle.'

'Civilization makes me appreciate savagery the more keenly,' said Alfred, forgetting the negotiations and

237

settling down to discuss something really important. 'I know other stories: about the children of Israel making war on the gentiles, about Romulus and Regulus and Hannibal and Alexander and other heroes of Rome; so that I see the more sharply the starkness of our northern tales. In our stories the hero serves only one thing, his private honour. If you know that other brave men have served greater things, their cities or their laws or the One True God, you can bring out that starkness with greater force. Do you like to make verses? If you stay in Chippenham through the summer you must come to my hall and hear about Joshua and Julius Caesar and a great many more. They were famous in their day, and their deeds would go well into verse.'

'At some other time I should like to hear about them. In fact I have a project which I would like to discuss with you in private. But I see that our councillors are growing impatient. Before we break up today we must settle the price of a sack of barley and a fat ox, or there will be trouble when the West Saxons bring provisions to our camp.'

They went back to the endless intricate haggling which was also good fun in its own way; to get the better of your enemy in a bargain was almost as satisfying as to defeat him in battle. But Alfred had seen a flash of something deeper in Guthrum. He wanted to talk with him at leisure and in private.

Two days later the terms of the treaty had been settled, and the stipulated hostages delivered to the Saxon camp. The pirates threw open their gates, and paid silver by weight for every waggonload of food brought in. Alfred dismissed his thanes to their homes, though he himself stayed with his companions outside Chippenham to make sure that the heathen lived as peacefully as they had promised.

On the evening of the second day Guthrum came to him, unarmed and unannounced.

The King of the pirates wore a tunic of green silk he had taken in Frankland, though it had been woven in Constantinople. His cap was of white bearskin from the far north and the golden clasp of his belt had been chased in Cordoba. His arm-rings also were of heavy gold; but they were not the sacred arm-rings on which the heathen took oath, for these had been delivered to Alfred with the other hostages. A handsome youth carried the King's sword and battle-axe, but he waited at the gate of the Saxon camp while Guthrum continued alone.

Alfred also was alone, sitting on a little stool before his hut. Nowadays he was nearly always alone when he was not working; the last survivor of four united brothers had found no one to take the place of dear Ethelred.

He saw with surprise that Guthrum was feeling shy. It was natural that he should feel shy, coming thus un-invited to the leader of the enemy who had defeated him; but if it made him feel uncomfortable why had he come at all? There was no outstanding business to make this visit necessary.

Alfred made him welcome, calling for another stool and a jug of real French wine. Foreign wine was scarce in Britain nowadays, and even Bishops offered Mass with the nasty vintage of local grapes; but this uninvited caller was a fellow-King, and the West Saxons must show him due hospitality.

Guthrum gulped the wine as though it were beer, which was annoying; until Alfred saw that he drank to screw up his courage, and felt sorry for him. But why had he come, if he didn't like it? Surely not to ask for the return of the hostages? He wouldn't get them, no matter how humbly he begged.

After a few remarks about the weather and the excellent quality of the provisions the West Saxons were selling to the Army, Guthrum got his courage to sticking point. With a bashful smile he stammered out his request: 'I want to be washed in that Christian way of yours. I'm tired of being a pirate. I shall settle down to end my days

239

in some part of Britain already conquered by my Army.'

'Baptism, you mean?' asked Alfred, astonished. 'I'm very glad to hear it, but it can't be done without preparation. There are all sorts of other things that have to come first.'

'Why? I'm a King, and people usually do what I ask of them. If it's a question of money, I have plenty. This washing is done by your priests, isn't it? I know you have priests with your warband. I have seen them making their magic before your array whenever we have met in battle. Fetch a priest now, and tell him to wash me.'

'You don't understand what you are letting yourself in for. Baptism will make you a Christian, bound by all the rules Christians must obey. Only one wife at a time, for example, and you must keep her by you until she dies of old age. On some days Christians eat no flesh, and on others they eat nothing until supper in the evening.'

'Do these rules bind Kings as well as ordinary men?' asked Guthrum with a suspicion of a smile. 'Are all Christian Kings content with one wife, and do they all go hungry on your unlucky days?'

'H'm, I forgot you are widely travelled. All I can say is that I keep these rules myself, that they are supposed to bind Kings, and that the Kings who break them would be more respected by their subjects if they didn't.'

'My subjects respect that battle-axe I left at your gate. There is no need to delay this washing. Send for a priest.'

Alfred considered. He could not turn away a genuine convert, and perhaps Guthrum really wanted to change his way of life; or perhaps he merely wanted to share in the luck of the West Saxons, who had defeated the great Army in battle. He sought for some argument that would be comprehended by this alien mind, and suddenly found it.

'It's like this,' he said patiently. 'When a man is baptized it is more than a lucky washing. At the same time he makes a promise to the priest. In fact he makes quite a lot of promises. Now are you going to promise anything the priest asks of you, without even knowing what the promise means? Would you become the sworn companion of a stranger, a man of whom you knew nothing? It would put your honour into grave danger. No, I shan't ask a priest to baptize you this evening. How would this do? You come and stay with me in some hall of mine, away from our warriors. The priest will explain the obligations you will undertake in baptism, and you and I will talk over the difficulties of ruling as a Christian King. After a day or so the priests will baptize you, and then it is the custom to hold a great feast. I shall vouch for you at your baptism, since every new Christian must have a sponsor; and in accordance with the same custom I shall be host at the feast. We shall be together for ten days or a fortnight, and at the end of the feast we shall part friends.'

Guthrum's little grey eyes twinkled with pleasure. He enjoyed feasting and was gay at the board; otherwise the pirates would never have chosen him for their King. But a King of the pirates must give many expensive feasts. He was glad that for once he was to be a guest.

'You are quite right, King Alfred. If I were to bind myself by oaths I cannot understand I might be shamed. I am a great King and a famous hero. I cannot approach this washing lightly, like the common men of the Army. Some pirates go to the Christian priests whenever they need a clean shirt. I've heard a man boast that he has been washed six times, and that at the seventh washing he walked away in a huff because the shirt they offered him was poorly woven. But he was an outlander from the far north, not an honourable Dane from my own country. We all thought he valued his oath too lightly.'

'Try to say baptism instead of washing. It is the name we use for it, and you are to become one of us. But you will learn this, and many other things, while we feast together in my hall.'

In the long hall at Aller they feasted until midnight; for

the heathen must come fasting to their baptism next day, and the ceremonies would continue until evening. This supper must keep them going for twenty-four hours.

Alfred had chosen this remote royal residence because it stood in country unravaged by the Army, where supplies could easily be procured; but even more because he could see, on the far side of the river, the little hill of Athelney which a few months ago had been all that remained to him of the realm of the West Saxons. If the battle at Edington had gone the other way he would be hiding there now. God had been very good to him.

On his right sat King Guthrum, and beyond him alderman Ethelnoth. But the high table was so crowded that some of the lesser companions had to eat by the door. King Guthrum had brought with him thirty of the most eminent captains of the Army, his own sworn companions, who had agreed to follow their lord into the faith of civilization. Each one had been provided with a Saxon godfather of noble birth, who now sat beside him at the feast and attempted to put into language warriors could understand the complicated truths preached by the royal chaplains. At a side table Elswitha and the royal children, with their attendant ladies, stared in wonder at the savage pirates who tomorrow would be sinless Christians. They looked surprisingly like ordinary men, just a little bit rougher and hairier and more ungainly than polished Saxon courtiers. The pirates were dressed in magnificent tunics, with belts of golden links or at least decorated with gold; but they had brought no weapons save the swords appropriate to their rank, and these now hung among the Saxon swords on the wall. Even well-instructed Christians thought it prudent to sit unarmed for serious drinking.

'In a few hours I shall take oath,' said Guthrum with a beaming smile, 'and still I don't understand half of what I shall be swearing. I don't think the priests themselves understand it. They do their best to make it clear; but all the rules were laid down in a foreign tongue, and it seems to me that the preachers can't put it into Saxon. Perhaps they don't know this foreign tongue as well as they suppose. That man who tried to define the Trinity used phrases from two different foreign languages, until at the end I was utterly baffled.'

'That's largely your doing,' said Alfred with a sigh. 'Fifteen years ago every priest in Britain knew Latin thoroughly and many of them could read Greek. But the Army killed the monks and hermits, who had leisure for study; and we must ordain even ignorant men, or we should have been without the Mass. Now that Britain is at peace I shall try to improve matters. Perhaps learned men will be willing to come here from Frankland and Burgundy. As to the Trinity, my dear Guthrum, no one understands it. How can a man understand the nature of God? We have to repeat the right form of words, or we risk being cut off from the Universal Church. I suppose language is at the bottom of it. Language changes with time. Do you understand all the words of the oath you used to swear on your magic arm-rings?'

'No. Though I had to get them right, or the suitors would have suspected that I was not doing justice. Those words are very old, from the time of my grandfather's grandfather.'

'Well, the Church is eight hundred years old and more, so the language of the priests is bound to be a bit difficult. We shall find learned men to explain it to you. As to our faith in general, never mind the difficult bits. The important thing is what the clergy call the Good News, and very good news it is. God actually loves all mankind, the whole human race. That is news to any heathen, isn't it, and encouraging news?'

'Yes, that's the oddest thing of all,' Guthrum agreed. 'Even odder than God allowing Himself to be killed. No one has ever suggested that Woden likes the human race. We give him sacrifice so that he won't harm us, and perhaps sometimes he helps us in battle against the

Christians. But I have never heard it said that the Aesir are out to help ordinary mortal men.'

'You will understand it better after you have been baptized. Christianity works, you know, for all that it seems so odd. I would rather have dealings with a wicked Christian than with an honourable heathen. At least the Christian will know the rules, even though he may break them. When you are a Christian King you will find it easy to live in peace with the other Kings of Christendom.'

'To live in peace . . .' murmured Guthrum. 'It will be strange at first. I have never lived in peace since I was old enough to carry an axe. War is a good life for the young and strong, but latterly I have not enjoyed the cold and the rain as we rode to plunder. Getting past it, I suppose . . . though yesterday I would have struck down any warrior who hinted at it. Elderly Kings get killed too easily. Look at the sons of Ragnar. They were the most famous heroes of the north, and now the last of them has gone. Odda here killed the mighty Ubba, and I have just had word that King Halfdan has been slain in Ireland. He wasn't killed by the Irish, of course. They can't cope with the heroes of the Army. A rival warband tried to steal his plunder, and he was cut down because he would not flee when his men broke. No more Ragnarssons . . . The world changes every day.'

Guthrum shook his head, mourning the decay of piracy.

'My men will find it strange to live in peace,' he added. 'Some of them nourished great hopes of returning to the north as wealthy heroes. It will be hard to convince them that there's no more rich booty to be had in Britain, though it's the truth and one reason why I am turning peaceable. But the restless can try their luck in Frankland. I shan't stop them.'

'I suppose you have no idea how many will stay with you,' said Alfred. 'We shall have to see you have enough land for them, or they will raid their neighbours. We must fix clear boundaries, too, that everyone can see. Have you made up your mind in which part of Britain you intend to settle? But we can discuss all this later, between your baptism and the chrism-loosening.'

'I had thought of the flat lands in the east, where we killed the brave King who would not sacrifice to Woden. The sea runs up into it, and we are never happy out of reach of the sea. It's the same kind of peat-soil that you get in Denmark, and my men will know how to farm it. Besides, hardly anyone lives there. We won't be bothered by outlaws in the greenwood, plotting to get back their lands.'

Guthrum was genuinely turning over a new leaf, Alfred saw. The pirate was a man of honour, and when he had taken oath he would do his best to keep it. Now, as he sat at the board, he was trying to keep sober. For the last half hour his horn had been full, though from time to time he took a sip when his companions pledged him from farther down the table.

Guthrum's companions were a problem. Their minds were not Christian by nature, and they were following their lord into baptism as they would have followed him on any other voyage into the unknown. Perhaps they would settle down later, but for the moment they were behaving after a very heathen fashion. Foreign priests reproached the Saxons for sitting too long over their drink; but Saxons sat talking with their ale before them, seldom touching it while they boasted at length. These pirates were drinking as fast as they talked, and beginning to be drunk. But while their lord was peaceful they would get drunk and sleepy, not drunk and quarrelsome. Provided none of their Saxon hosts took offence at their boasting they would soon be sleeping quietly under the table. Tomorrow their heads would ache. That was the wrong approach to such a great sacrament as baptism.

On the other hand, baptism washes away all previous sin, not merely original sin, Alfred recalled. These heathen might as well have a last fling tonight; tomorrow they would be bound by the wholesome law that makes drunkenness a branch of the mortal sin of gluttony.

Christendom would be getting some queer recruits. Perhaps the Church would not be greatly strengthened. But God had covered that point, in the days when He walked the earth: 'I come not to call the righteous, but sinners to repentance.' God had the answer to every problem. Alfred signalled to the servants to go round again with the pitchers of strong ale. It was important that these pirates, in the process of reformation, should remember him as a great King and a generous host.

It was late in the following afternoon when they sat down again to break their fast. King Guthrum and his companions wore long white linen tunics, with white woollen cloaks over them. On their heads were white fillets to guard the sacred chrism from the pollution of every day. Whatever their pasts they were sinless now, newborn lambs in the flock of the saved, neighbours and friends to every believing Christian. Their Saxon godparents made much of them. Alfred himself waited on Guthrum, handing him the cup and waiting until he had eaten before breaking his own fast.

There were presents for all the newly baptized. Alfred had given much thought to the matter, and the gifts chosen were harmless and appropriate. Swords, shields, byrnies were the usual gifts from one warrior to another, the kind of thing these northerners expected, the kind of thing their Saxon sponsors would have chosen if left to themselves. Alfred had arranged that they should be given belts, cloaks, tunics; but of such valuable stuff and so richly decorated that they felt the greatness of the occasion.

For Guthrum himself he had a royal gift: all the vessels and vestments needed to equip the chapel of a King. Chalice and pyx were of gold, but the workmanship was more costly even than the material. The copes were worked with the famous English embroidery, the best in the world. The Emperor possessed more of these things, but he had nothing finer in its kind.

'Your weapons are as good as mine,' Alfred explained as he handed over his presents, 'and anyway, I hope you will never need them again. But a great King must have a fine chapel. As time goes on you will collect holy relics, to keep in your chapel. A halidom we call it, and each King tries to have a better one than his neighbour. The King of the Greeks, out in New Rome, has the finest halidom in the world; but then his city has never been sacked since it was founded. My own halidom is fairly good, for a King in a small outlying island, and when next I send alms to Rome I shall beg for a piece of the True Cross. You may begin with some relics of the holy King Edmund, whom the Army martyred. You will be ruling over his land.'

'We must go into that before we part,' answered Guthrum. 'I have taken no land from the West Saxons, but in the north we have a saying: "good fences make good neighbours." We must fix a sure boundary, to avoid quarrels.'

'That won't be difficult in the land you have chosen. I have already worked out a boundary, and I hope you will agree to it. The River Lea, which flows into the Thames, is not much of an obstacle but anyone can see it. You take the left bank and I have the right. Then Watling Street, the great paved road that was built by the old Romans, not by demons as your skalds suppose, runs right across Britain as far as the north-west coast. You have the eastern side of it, until your land marches with that of the settlers from Halfdan's Army. You and they can decide that boundary.'

'That leaves London outside my dominions,' said Guthrum, looking at him keenly.

'It does. London is held by pirates – at present. But they have not been baptized and I have made no peace with them.'

'My men will sympathize with their heathen cousins. It will be hard for us to keep the peace.'

'You have already seen that it is even harder to conquer

Wessex. I am giving you one small province of my dominions, a province which came to me from my father. The land of the East Saxons has been desolated by pirate raids, its royal house is extinct and there is not even a noble of native birth whom I might make alderman. You may keep it and welcome. But I do not give you London.'

'I see. You do not give me a sword either, on this day when you give me gifts. But, after all, I might have been starving in Chippenham. Guthrum and Alfred will remain friends, even while the King of the West Saxons and the King of the Danes argue over their boundary. By the way, the Earl who rules in London is no kinsman of mine.'

'We understand one another. Now let us discuss *weres* and compensation.'

15

Lord of the English

The great minster in Winchester, the hearth and centre of
Wessex, had been decorated for Christmas. Lamps
glowed all down the nave, not merely in the monks'
choir; silver-gilt reliquaries stood on portable altars
against the side walls. All the monks were present in
their stalls, even those whose duties usually kept them in
some outlying grange. A great host of townspeople
shuffled restlessly by the west door. For the King and all
his household had come to keep the Christmas of 887 in
the city of his forefathers, and at the close of the twelve
days of feasting his eldest daughter would be married
with great solemnity.

The monks stood quietly in their places. They were
accustomed to the shadows in the roof and the flickering
of the candles, passing much of every night of their lives
in this echoing gloom. But the townspeople rustled and
shifted; they found it strange to be absent from their
own firesides in the middle of a winter night, strange
and a thing to bring back unhappy memories. But it was
nearly eight years since they had fled from Guthrum's
Army to sleep under frosty stars. King Alfred had brought
them peace and security; it was right that they should
come out at midnight to greet him.

From time to time the Bishop glanced at a candle
burning steadily behind a shield of oiled paper. When
the flame reached the next mark in the wax it would be
midnight, time to begin the first Mass of Christmas. In
the old days it had been very difficult to tell the time in

the dark, especially under a roof where you could not see the stars. The King had introduced this device of marked candles; no one could guess what subject would next occupy the King's extraordinarily active mind. He was a good King, of the right line of Cerdic; it was proper that his monks should wait to do him honour at this great feast.

A clattering at the west door announced the arrival of the bodyguard. They were only a handful, for in this loyal city the King of the West Saxons needed no protection; but they were tall warriors, chosen as much for their looks as for their courage, and they were very splendidly accoutred. In addition to their silver-hilted swords they carried long Danish axes, chased and damascened.

The companions opened a way through the crowd. As the candle burned down to the mark the King arrived, and the Mass began. The King was always punctual at public ceremonies, for he kept a candle of the same kind in his bedchamber.

In his thirty-ninth year Alfred was marked by the hardships of his youth. His shoulders were bowed with rheumatism, his legs bent from long days in the saddle, and his fair hair streaked with grey. But his eyes under tangled brows glanced as keenly as ever, and his hands kept the supple movements of a swordsman. Perhaps this King could no longer feed his court by hunting through the winter woods, but he would still give a good account of himself in the front rank of the warband.

Behind the King followed a group of notables: Elswitha and Eadburh, Ethelfleda and young Edward, the Mercian alderman Ethelred, the West Saxon aldermen Sighelm and Ethelstan, Edwulf the high reeve of Bamburgh and Egwulf the captain of the companions. Such a group could not have been assembled from all over Britain unless the whole land were at peace.

As a compliment to the King the Midnight Mass was offered by his new friend, the Welsh Bishop Asser. The monks of Winchester followed the service attentively, tugging at the markers in their Missals; but the Welshman followed the Roman rite in every particular, so that even the most punctilious Saxon could not protest at Celtic irregularities.

When Mass was finished there followed another ceremony, as had become the custom when King Alfred kept a solemn feast in a great minster. Duduc the chaplain emerged from the sacristy bearing an object veiled in purple silk. Holding it aloft he blessed the congregation, who bowed their heads to venerate the fragment of the True Cross which Pope Marinus had sent to the victorious defender of Christendom. After the blessing Duduc retired with his holy burden, and took it straight back to the royal hoard. The relic was part of the King's own halidom; it was never left in the sacristy of any church, even for a single night, lest some Bishop or his chapter should try to detain it.

At last the minster began to empty. The King and his household marched in procession through the town to the royal hall where the feasting of Christmas would begin immediately, in the middle of the night. For throughout Christmas Eve all had fasted.

Sitting in his high seat Alfred felt a little sleepy, but wholly content. His Kingdom was peaceful, prosperous and loyal; his family was flourishing. At the women's table by the wall sat his wife, whom he liked well enough though he had never been passionately in love with her; and his charming daughter Ethelfleda, seventeen years old and about to contract an important political marriage. Perhaps, if she had been a free agent, she would not have chosen the alderman of the Mercians. But Ethelred owed everything to Wessex, and would not dare to ill-treat her; he was a good man and a practising Christian, so flattered by this great alliance that he would do his best to make her happy.

Also at the women's table was Eadburh, his mother-in-law and dearest friend. It was a wonderful stroke of luck that she should live permanently at his court. He enjoyed the company of learned and witty ladies, and poor Elswitha, though well bred and well mannered, was neither witty nor educated. No one would ever take the place of his dead mother, but Eadburh sometimes reminded him of Osburh.

At the end of the row of magnates sat Edward, his eldest son, and that was best of all. The fifteen-year-old atheling was making his first appearance at a formal feast, and behaving exactly as his father wished. He enjoyed his food, for he was a sturdy youth; but he ate gracefully. He did not drink too much. He spoke respectfully to his elders, who in turn accorded him the respect due to his birth. Edward was of the right line of Cerdic, and all that a young atheling should be. The future of Wessex was secure.

Edwulf of Bamburgh sat in the highest place among the foreign guests, above the three Welsh princelings. He had been looking round the hall, identifying prominent people with the assistance of Bishop Asser beside him. Now he caught the King's eye and inquired respectfully: 'I don't see the atheling Ethelwold. Is he unwell?'

'When last I heard he was in the best of health,' Alfred answered with a frown. 'But he prefers to keep Christmas at Wimborne. He is old enough to have his own sworn companions. Some of them get a bit boisterous when they drink with mine, so I didn't press him to come here. Besides, now that his mother is dead he has taken over the management of his affairs, and he likes to be at Wimborne for great religious festivals to make sure that the monks pay due reverence to his father. That's where King Ethelred is buried, you may remember. Young Ethelwold is always present when Mass is offered for his father's soul, which is very right and proper since really he has nothing else to do.'

The King smiled with patient understanding. That frown had been a mistake, and his habitual self-consciousness was nagging at him.

The frown had been noticed. The high reeve of Bamburgh dropped his eyes to the round of wheaten bread soaked in gravy on which lay his beef; at this great feast even the manchets from which the guests ate were made of the finest flour. 'I see,' he said quietly, 'but I'm sorry not to meet him. I had hoped to have a chat with him before I go back to the north.'

Another voice broke in: 'Oh, he'll come to his cousin's wedding, and of course you will be staying for that. He is often at court. But Christmas is truly the feast of the family, as we say in Wales. A young prince who has gathered a household ought to entertain his dependents on that day. It would not be quite right for him to seek the hospitality of his uncle.'

That was Bishop Asser, explaining the obvious in his lilting Welsh accent. Confound the man, thought Alfred. He's too quick by half, always noticing any unpleasantness; and rubbing it in while he tries to explain it away. The high reeve blushed, and crammed his mouth so full that for a few minutes he could not speak. The kindly and tactless Bishop had made the situation as clear to him as if he had been listening all day to the malicious tattle of the court.

Egwulf, the captain of the companions, began to talk about the weather, a subject to which all could contribute. A green Christmas makes a fat churchyard. Ah, but the swallows flew late, what does that portend? Someone had met a man who had actually *seen* the swallows gather in a ball and sink to the bottom of a pond. The whole company discussed the problem of where do swallows go in winter time.

Presently all returned to the minster for the Dawn Mass of Christmas, which was followed immediately by the morning Mass. A Christian King had done his duty by the festival, and might pass the rest of the day in dozing and drinking.

In the afternoon Alfred slipped away to the bower. His younger children were no longer babies: Ethelgifu was eight, Ethelthryth six, and Ethelward four; but they were still too young to mingle with adults in hall. Five was a small family for a tranquil and fruitful marriage; but Edmund had died in infancy and during the long wars Elswitha had suffered numerous miscarriages. The children and their mother were pleased to see him; but after he had been the affable father for half an hour he excused himself and went to call on the lady Eadburh in her private chamber.

His mother-in-law was as soothing as usual. She sat over her embroidery, white-haired and benignant, while one of her ladies read aloud from a book of devotions. That was just how he remembered his mother. She had been much younger, of course; but in the eyes of a child the lady Osburh had been immeasurably old, one of the grown-ups who have been here since time began. Thus he saw the lady Eadburh at that moment.

As she set a stool for him and dismissed her ladies he picked up the book. It was a handsome little toy, fairly written in clear Carolingian script. The sentence at the head of the page was so clear that without thinking he muttered it aloud: 'Et subito facta est cum angelo multitudo militiae caelestis, laudantium Deum, et dicentium: Gloria in altissimis Deo, et in terra pax hominibus bonae voluntatis.'

'What's the Saxon for that last bit?' asked Eadburh in a casual voice.

'And on earth peace to men of goodwill. There's a catch in it. Some people translate it: "Peace and goodwill to men", which is wrong. God and His angels bear no goodwill to evil men. But why do you ask? You heard it this morning, in the first Mass of Christmas, and I expect you read it yesterday in preparation for the feast. Your Latin is better than mine.'

'It used to be, my dear Alfred, even though I'm no scholar. But lately you have changed. That's the first time I have heard you read Latin aloud, and you translated without effort. Have you gone back to school again?'

'You could call it that. I find it fun, you know. These Latin books are never properly translated. *Militiae caelestis*, for example. In Saxon we say "heavenly host", and that makes me see a crowd of saints in white robes and long white beards. But *militiae caelestis* is quite different. They were warriors. I wonder if they looked anything like the warband of Wessex?'

'I expect they did. You were *milites caelestis* when you broke the heathen at Edington. Angels probably charged beside you, though you didn't see them. I meant something different. I was surprised to hear you read Latin so fluently, and translate in your head. In the old days you couldn't do these things. You must have been taking lessons.'

Once again Alfred felt self-conscious, but by now he was used to it.

'It's that Welsh Bishop, Asser. I want to have at least one educated man always beside me, and I like him personally. Besides, since he's Welsh my clergy can't be jealous of him. He is already a consecrated Bishop, auxiliary in St. David's or something of the kind. You know the way the Welsh run their church, without true dioceses. So my clerks have to defer to his authority and yet they know he can't compete with them for a West Saxon bishopric. Asser will stay with me more or less indefinitely. If he wants regular work I shall make him auxiliary in Sherborne to look after the Welsh-speaking peasants of Devon and Somerset.'

'You don't have to explain away Bishop Asser. He's a good man and a clever man and a nice man, an ornament to your court. But have you also made him your tutor in Latin?'

'Well, while he was with me I dropped my little handbook. the extracts from the Psalms that I always carry for luck. When I was a child my mother started me writing in it, and I kept it up until the wars came. Asser asked me if I could read what was written in it. I explained that I can read my own writing, even in Latin;

and that these passages had been explained to me in Saxon. He thought it a splendid idea, and persuaded me to start a bigger book. Whenever I have time he gives me a Latin lesson. Unless the wars come again I shall soon be able to read everything that was written by the wise men of old.'

Self-consciousness forgotten, he beamed with pleasure.

'I'm glad you have Bishop Asser for a teacher,' said Eadburh. 'You can see the little man really loves learning. It's sad that he isn't a better courtier. Is it because he is too holy, or too intelligent? I suppose a really devout Bishop can't be a man of the world at the same time. At the feast today I overheard him making an awkward topic even more unpleasant. By the way, was he right? Will Ethelwold come to the wedding of my grand-daughter?'

'He was invited, and he said he would come,' Alfred answered stiffly. 'Whether he will turn up on the day is another matter. If I hadn't invited him he would of course have arrived halfway through the feast just to embarrass me. Now he may wait until we have kept a place for him, and then at the last minute send a message that he is unwell, or praying at his father's tomb. The boy delights in making me feel uncomfortable. I don't know why. I have treated him fairly.'

'He isn't a boy any longer. He is a year older than Ethelfleda, who will be married in a fortnight. That's really the trouble, isn't it? You have given him money and land, more than enough for any atheling. But you haven't given him a man's work, and that makes him feel slighted.' Eadburh shook her head with a sigh, then smiled at her son-in-law to show she was still on his side.

'I can't give him responsible work if he won't come to court. He sits at Wimborne and sulks; and they tell me he makes the most disloyal remarks to his new com-panions. If any of my subjects were inclined to rebellion he could make trouble for me, but as things are he can't.

His grievance is that I haven't made him captain of the warband, or at least an alderman. How can I do anything of the sort? He is eighteen years old and he's never done anything. I can't put him over the veterans of Edington, or let him keep the peace in a big shire. He's rich enough to maintain a state worthy of his birth, if he chooses to live in idleness at Wimborne. If he wants to do something useful he must come to court and learn his job from the bottom.'

'Ethelwold is eighteen. By the time you were nineteen you had married my daughter and you were officially second-in-command of the warband of the West Saxons. Perhaps next year Ethelwold will be fit for responsibility. But you know very well the root of the trouble. You won't live for ever. Whom will you nominate to succeed you: your son Edward, or Ethelwold the heir of the right line of Cerdic?'

'I can't bequeath the Kingdom to anyone.' The King answered swiftly, as though he had many times answered the same question. 'The councillors choose the next King, and they can choose any descendant of the great Cerdic. I know that the Franks are beginning to say that an eldest son must come before his younger brothers. But even the Franks don't follow the theory when it comes to the point. Last month Arnulf made himself King of the Austrasians, driving out his uncle Charles. In Neustria and Septimania and Lombardy the Franks have chosen rulers who are not even Carolings. It was a new family anyway, with nothing of the prestige of the Cerdingas.'

'That's got nothing to do with the West Saxons, my dear Alfred, and you know it. The King cannot nominate his successor, but he can indicate his wishes. You are a very popular King, and your wishes will be fulfilled. Have you done anything to show your people that you consider Ethelwold a possible successor?'

'I haven't, for the simple reason that I don't think he would make a good King,' said Alfred in rising anger.

'He's surly and bad-tempered and too touchy about his dignity. But I haven't done anything to spoil his chances either. I deliberately didn't give my eldest son an Ethel-name, to remind the world that he was not heir to the throne of the West Saxons. The succession is completely open. In theory any Cerdinga can be a candidate, in practice they normally choose one whose father was a king. My Edward is a King's son, but so is his cousin Ethelwold. The councillors must decide for themselves. As to your theory about the head of the family, the eldest son of the eldest son, it's not known in these parts. Ethelwold was just as much the head of the family when I was chosen King as he is now. No one mentioned his name. I was chosen unanimously.'

'Of course you were, your brother's second-in-command and the only adult atheling. They couldn't choose a baby while the Army lay at Reading. That quibble shows that your mind is made up. You may be right. Edward may be the best candidate. Play fair, all the same. You loved your brother Ethelred. Don't rob his only son of his birthright.'

There was distress in Eadburh's voice. Her son-in-law was the most famous hero of Britain, a great King and a good man. She could not bear to see any imperfection in him.

But Alfred frowned as he answered.

'As you say, I loved my brother Ethelred. I love him still. There's not an hour of the day when I don't miss him. I look round to consult him whenever I meet a tricky problem, and then I have to remember that he's under the ground at Wimborne. Do you think I want to cheat his only son? But I must think of my people also. I can't saddle them with a bad King, just to ease my own conscience.'

She laid her hand on his arm.

'I'm sorry. We won't talk about it any more. I know you are a just man, or I would not have mentioned it. I don't favour Ethelwold. Remember, Edward is my grandson. There's something else I wanted to ask you. Would it annoy the West Saxons if Elswitha wears a golden circlet at the wedding?'

'Why should it annoy them? Oh, you mean the old custom, that the King's wife is never called Queen. But other great ladies wear golden circlets to keep their veils in place. And even if Elswitha should wear an obvious crown no one would mind. The custom is very nearly forgotten. You have me to thank for that. Among the Kentishmen and the South Saxons Elswitha is given the title of Queen, for they have had Queens since time immemorial. The Mercians also had Queens, I believe; and if Elswitha isn't Queen of the Mercians I can't think of another. With so many foreigners in Winchester all speaking of Elswitha as Queen the West Saxons have grown used to the title. If you like, I shall clinch the matter by getting her to witness a charter as Elswitha, Queen. But that might be going out of the way to stir up trouble. It would be better if she just calls herself Queen, and wears a royal crown whenever she feels like it. Then the sticklers can comfort themselves that she is Queen only in Kent, until Winchester forgets the custom and everyone calls her Queen of the West Saxons.'

'Perhaps they will call her Queen of the English and Saxons. They call you King of them, don't they?'

'Flattering courtiers say so. There has never been a Kingdom of the English and the Saxons, and if I were founding one now I would put the Saxons first. It's a grand title, all the same. I like it, I confess, though it may be childish of me.'

'You have earned it. All the English and Saxons of Britain look on you as their leader, even though for the present they may be under the rule of pirates. There couldn't be anyone more English than Edwulf of Bamburgh, and he comes to your court as though he were your subject.'

'I like that young man. Besides, he is starting from scratch, making a new government for a new people. It's

259

fun to discuss with him the rights and obligations of a ruler.'

'He's your friend because he fought the pirates. In your eyes that's the whole duty of a ruler, isn't it?'

'Eadburh, that's not fair. Edwulf also leads a decent private life, whereas some of those northern English are no better than pirates themselves. But fighting the pirates is important. I wish I could meet some of those burgesses of Paris, though there's nothing to bring them to Wessex.'

'It was a gallant defence, and I'm glad you sent alms to help them rebuild their churches. But in the end the pirates were paid to go away.'

'Not by the Parisians. For a year they held their wall, and they would be holding it yet if their foolish King hadn't paid ransom to the Army. His cowardice cost him his throne, and serve him right. But the really important thing is that the defence of Paris may mean the end of the Army. A siege of a year, and at the end of it a trifling ransom, less than they would have won from the pillage of the open country. When next the pirates go home they may stay there. But then the Franks have these great Roman walls round their cities. I wish my mighty ancestor Cerdic had left more of them standing in Britain.'

'Today you have London, with its Roman walls. What will you do with it?'

'Give it back to its rightful owners. London has never been reckoned part of the realm of the West Saxons. Until the heathen came it was a city of the Mercians. I have turned out the heathen, but I can't keep for myself the spoil they took from my fellow-Christians.'

'That sounds very high-minded, but does it mean anything? How can you give it back to us when we have no King to rule over the Mercians?'

'Ethelred the alderman rules all the Mercians who are not subject to the pirates. I don't know how he became an alderman, and I don't propose to inquire. Perhaps he promoted himself; and if he got his office from Ceolwulf,

King by favour of the heathen, that isn't much better. But I found him an alderman when Guthrum made peace, and as far as I am concerned he represents Mercia. When he marries he shall have London as a wedding gift.'

'That really is generous, and tactful as well. We Mercians will obey any Christian King rather than a pirate, but it's not so long ago that we were the foremost realm in Britain. My kin would not take kindly to being a mere province of the West Saxons. All the same, is Ethelred strong enough to hold London against the heathen – or should I say against the Christian followers of the Christian King Guthrum?'

'Guthrum is genuinely a Christian, you know, odd though it may seem. He venerates the memory of King Edmund, who was martyred by Guthrum's own war-band. He does justice and keeps his treaties as well as many Christian Kings, though that isn't saying very much. His companions were baptized with him, so we mustn't call them heathen; and it isn't really fair to call them pirates, when for much of the time they behave quite honestly. In formal documents I try to call them Danes; most of them came from Denmark, unless they were born in the Army. The Danish Kingdom among the East English is an odd style, but I can't think of a better.'

'They may be excellent Christians even though it came suddenly. The English also changed from heathen to Christian in a single generation, and the conversion seems to have stuck. But you haven't answered my question. Can alderman Ethelred hold London against these Christian Danes?'

'With help from the West Saxons, he can. He is not my subject, but neither is he my equal. I am a King and he is an alderman. We are allies, I suppose, not lord and man. But I shall offer him advice, and my advice will carry great weight with him.'

'That's a good answer, and all the better for being indefinite. Let my people call themselves free, so long as you can be sure they will do what you tell them. But you are generous, all the same, and you must not think I am making fun of you. In your position a great many Kings would have styled themselves lords of London for the mere honour and glory of it.'

'I like honour and glory, but holding back the Danes is more important. A walled town will hold them back, if there is always a garrison in it. London blocks the mouth of the Thames, and makes it difficult for the Army in Frankland to get in touch with the Danes of Britain. The Mercians will defend their own city of London; they might yield it to the Danes rather than hold it for the West Saxons.'

'As you say, honour and glory are not everything. A King should deal fairly, even if he is strong enough to do wrong. That's my last word, for it's time I got ready for supper.'

Over supper Alfred examined his conscience. On the evening of a day which had begun at midnight there was little conversation, and he could think in silence over his ale. He was genuinely being fair to Ethelwold, he decided; in fact he was being remarkably patient.

Godgifu had been dead for some years. It could never be right to rejoice in the death of a sister-in-law, a pious lady who was also the widow of a dearly-loved brother. But it was just as well she had died before he was driven to take action against her. Her foolish fancies, her bad advice to her only son, had been the root of his troubles; or perhaps the deepest root of all had been the un-alterable fact that she was Mercian.

That was it. Ethelwold was half Mercian, lacking the inborn fidelity of a genuine. West Saxon. Long ago the Mercians had deserted their true royal line; they bowed to the rule of any ruffian who could seize the throne. In Mercia they had forgotten the tradition that the true King must be chosen, from the true line, by the voice of his people.

Godgifu had impressed on her son that he was head

of the house of Cerdic. On his father's death the throne should have come to him. Alfred's usurpation might be excused by the difficulties of the times; a child could not rule while the Army lay in Reading. But Alfred was bound in honour to make Ethelwold his successor, and to make public his decision.

That was how a Mercian saw the problem. But the custom of the West Saxons left a free choice to the council whenever the throne was vacant. Alfred had no power to nominate an heir.

That was a comforting explanation of the trouble; but soon Alfred's common sense reminded him that he was cheating. He could not lawfully nominate his successor, but there were ways in which he might indicate his wishes. His own path to the throne had been cleared when Ethelred made him the second man in the Kingdom. He in his turn might summon Ethelwold to court, give him a command in the warband, encourage him to preside in the shirecourts, train him in the business of government. If the West Saxons were content with his rule they would choose his chief lieutenant when the time came.

Well, he had begun to do his part, striving to keep the promise he had made to his dead brother. He had summoned young Ethelwold to court – and the boy had answered by laying down conditions. He would come if he were granted a great command in the warband; above all, he must have more companions and a higher seat in hall than Edward his cousin.

That would be to make him heir to the throne, an untried youth of eighteen. He might be a drunkard, he might be a rake, he might be utterly incompetent. (With his ancestry, he could not be a coward.) The sensible course was to bring him to court and see how he shaped. The silly boy had refused to leave Wimborne unless all his demands were granted; and he had made matters very much worse by hints to his companions, which he would not confirm when challenged, that he feared poison if he dined at his uncle's table. The only way to deal with these vapourings was to leave Ethelwold at Wimborne and make much of young Edward.

Besides, young Edward was an exceptionally promising prince. At the age of fifteen he had beautiful manners, excellent self-control, and remarkable skill with his weapons. Everyone agreed that Ethelfleda was the wisest and most discreet maiden in Christendom, a princess who would help her husband in the government of the Mercians. She was seventeen, old enough for men to judge her quality. When Edward grew up he would be as wise and virtuous as his sister. He would make a fine King of the West Saxons.

Like Ethelwold, Edward had a Mercian mother. But then Elswitha was not a typical Mercian. She was so quiet and dutiful and influenced by her surroundings (and, if the truth be told, insipid and uninteresting) that she was not typical of anything. Her mother had taught her to revere the ancient Woden-born families which had a prescriptive right to rule; she did not hold the wicked Mercian theory that the throne was the prize of the strongest sword. She worshipped her glorious and successful husband, who was also kind and considerate and chaste. She had become, after years of marriage, more Saxon than English. She would never plot to set a nephew against his uncle and lord. She was not related to the cowardly and usurping line of the unfortunate King Burhed.

In bringing young Edward to court he had done right. When the boy was older he would give him a chance to distinguish himself. If he proved a failure he would be sent back to his estates, for the West Saxons must be ruled by a competent King. But all the signs promised that to bring him forward was to do the best thing for the future happiness of Wessex.

The wedding of the lady Ethelfleda, princess of the West Saxons, to Ethelred, alderman of the Mercians was as splendid as the Christmas festivities which had just ended. Once more the Bishop and chapter filled the choir of the minster, once more the True Cross dispersed its blessing over the congregation. In another respect Christmas was repeated: the atheling Ethelwold remained at Wimborne, sending word that he had a cold and was unfit for winter travel. Yet now that he sulked at home he was beginning to be forgotten by the public. Alfred and Eadburh noted his absence, but the only magnate to inquire after him was the provincial and tactless high reeve of Bamburgh.

Ethelfleda held herself proudly, and looked happy as she walked stiffly to the altar. Was she in fact happy, Alfred wondered as he watched her smile up at her stalwart husband? Had he sacrificed his daughter to ambition, giving her to a stranger so that he might call himself King of the English as well as the Saxons? Before he could make up his mind the True Cross was unveiled and he cleared his mind of all secular thoughts.

Walking to the wedding feast he considered the matter again. He decided that on the whole he had dealt justly with his daughter. Ethelfleda was not in love with anyone else. She would rather be a wife than an abbess, the only alternative for a lady of her birth. By the same token, there were not a dozen men in Britain noble enough to be her husband, and of this handful of wealthy and powerful magnates Ethelred was the most worthy. She was marrying a stranger. But her mother had married a stranger, and so had both her grandmothers. It was the fate of ladies of high birth.

Ethelred was a gentleman of decent private life. That he had never tried to call himself King of the Mercians was a proof of his fundamental honesty. London, that splendid marriage-gift, could be taken back as easily as it had been given. The alderman would not be so rash as to ill-treat a wife who had brought him such a magnificent dowry.

He had done right by Ethelfleda, his first-born. Now it was time to do something for Edward, his elder and beloved son. His brother King Ethelred had been a worthy ruler and a loving kinsman; but claims such as these were personal and did not descend in the family. Ethelwold had his due; there was no obligation to give him more.

16

The Obligations of Duty

Alfred had passed his forty-second birthday, and must acknowledge that his youth was ended. At the close of a day's hunting he was eager to get home and change into dry clothes; his whole body ached from the jolting of the saddle. But still he hunted as strenuously as ever; for hunting was considered the supreme amusement of every great lord, and though he might not enjoy it at the time he thought of it in prospect as a great pleasure.

In the autumn of 891 he rode west to hunt among the moors of Cornwall. It was an out-of-the-way corner of his dominions, only to be visited when no danger threatened Wessex. But this year there was every hope of peace. The Danes of East Anglia were quiet. The Army remained in Frankland, ravaging the rich towns of the Low Countries. No one could foretell the future, but it seemed that this autumn the King of the West Saxons would not have to take the field.

He brought only a small household, for the Cornwelsh never had much food to spare. Most of the companions who had fought with him in the great wars were now settled on their own land, and he had arranged that any courtier might if he wished spend eight months of the year in his own home; every second month his whole household changed over. Nowadays young warriors came from all parts of Britain to serve him. By keeping them on duty only two months out of six he made room for these welcome volunteers.

The weather was fine, even on the high granite wastes

of Cornwall. Sometimes Alfred might forget for a few minutes together that he was on the verge of old age. On a fine sunny evening he rode back to the little hall in a fold of the moor where his servants would be cooking supper. Hounds had run well, and his own shooting had been as straight as could be expected. It was a day whose memory he would treasure during the approaching gloom of winter. And this evening he would have a cosy chat with Bishop Asser about the wonders of the ancient world. Queen Elswitha and all the ladies of the royal household had been left behind in Wessex, which added to the attraction of this brief holiday.

As he rode into the yard Asser came out to meet him. The little Welshman was excited, hopping from leg to leg in his eagerness to tell something important. To a King important news is nearly always bad news, but Alfred noted in a quick glance that the captain of the companions had not bothered to come to greet him; besides, Asser was grinning all over his face. Something pleasant must have occurred, though it was hard to think of anything that could add to the pleasure of a good day's hunting.

Pushing through the servants, Asser himself held the stirrup for his lord to dismount. It was the Welsh habit to treat bishops as nothing more than clerks with unusual faculties, useful for ordination and confirmation; Asser could never remember to behave with the gravity expected from a Saxon Bishop. That was part of his charm, and in remote Cornwall it did no harm. Alfred smiled at him in inquiry.

'Visitors, lord King,' called the Bishop happily, 'unexpected visitors from oversea. Luckily they speak Latin, so they can tell you their story – such a story. You must bid them welcome as soon as you have seen to your horse. They are now resting by the fire, recovering from the toils of their journey.'

Dear little Asser was acting in character, Alfred reflected. He gave orders to his King, and took it for granted that Alfred would himself superintend the rubbing down of his horse. So he would, of course, unless urgent business called him away. The King's staller, who oversaw his stables, was a nobleman of such high rank that he often neglected his duties.

It was getting dark when Alfred left the stables. There had been hounds to look over besides the horse, and the head falconer wanted advice about a moping bird. It was all part of the pleasure of the holiday. Among the Cornwelsh he might live like a sporting young atheling, not like a King burdened with all the public cares of Britain.

All the same, his mind had been busy with Asser's news. Who were these visitors whose coming brought such joy? Since it was no concern of the warriors they must be peaceful envoys. Who would be sending envoys to Britain at this time?

The Pope sent envoys frequently, to acknowledge the annual alms given by Alfred in gratitude for the conversion of the West Saxons by papal missionaries. But Asser would not leave envoys from Rome to rest by the fire while the King looked to his horse; the holy men would be greeted by all the local clergy in clean surplices, with incense and the statues of the saints. Envoys from a King of the Franks, or even from the Emperor, would not cause Asser such keen delight. If the pirate who ruled in Northumbria were offering permanent peace the news would have reached him from his companions, not from the bishop. Who else was there? Only the Welsh. That must be it, though the explanation was not very exciting. Welsh chieftains seldom led as many swords as followed a Saxon alderman; but they claimed descent from mighty Roman rulers of long ago and other Welshmen took them very seriously. Some lord of three Welsh valleys and a barren mountain-top, with a pedigree going back to Julius Caesar, had sent to offer friendship and alliance; and to dear Asser it was the greatest event in modern diplomatic history.

In the hall Asser met him; and led him past the benches to the dais of honour. So these visitors had been given the highest seats, even though they had been left to rest unattended until the King should hear their story. Squatting on the edge of the dais, warming themselves over the fire-trench which ran the length of this old-fashioned hall, were three shabby figures. They sprang to their feet as the King approached, and he saw that they were dressed alike, in long gowns of coarse grey cloth; apparently they wore nothing under the gowns, for their bony calloused shanks were bare. They were very hairy, with ragged untended beards; but the shock of hair above was shorter on the crown, as though at some time it had been tonsured.

So that was it: three holy hermits. Probably they had seen a vision which concerned the welfare of Britain. In Cornwall, as in Wales, you found such people under any flat stone. What was there in this to excite even the excitable Asser?

'These holy men have come across the sea from Ireland,' said Asser proudly, 'and I thought their boat so curious that I had it brought here to show to the King. See, my lord.'

He stooped to gather up an armful of hairy cowskin.

'What do you mean? How can that be a boat? Dozens of holy men have voyaged from Cornwall to Brittany, but not even the holiest hermits float about on leather blankets,' said Alfred in astonishment.

'It's a boat all the same, my lord. There was a wicker frame, but we didn't bother to bring it. The Irishmen say they fold up their boat when they come to dry land, and make another frame for the next voyage. That's easier than carrying the whole vessel. But ask them to tell you of their journey. As I said, they speak fluent Latin.'

Alfred paused to collect his thoughts. He also could be fluent in Latin; but the language was so different from Saxon, not only in vocabulary but in the structure and balance of the sentences, that he must think himself into

270

a Roman frame of mind before he could speak it correctly. He looked again at the folded cowskin, and the first question came into his mind.

'Isn't it very hard work to row that thing?' he asked. 'You can't sail in a flat-bottomed bowl, and it has nowhere to step a mast. I don't see any rowlocks either. How did you manage?'

'We hoisted no sail and we took no oars,' answered one of the hermits in a queer singsong Latin. 'God called us to be missionaries to the heathen, but He did not tell us which heathen. So we stitched together this boat and embarked in it, trusting that God would send us to a land that needs us.'

'I see. Did you take any supplies, or did you leave that also to God?'

'We took water, and food also, enough for seven days. Men who run great risks may incur the guilt of suicide. Besides, we are hermits, not heroes, and anything rash would be foreign to our natures. As it happens, our precautions were reasonable without being over-careful. We took supplies for seven days, and on the seventh day we came ashore in this land.'

'I am glad you were so prudent. Since your voyage ended safely I must not call it hazardous; though if you had drifted west instead of east you would now be thirsty. But if God has called you to convert the heathen you have not yet reached your goal. The Cornwelsh were all Christians when St. Patrick landed in Ireland. All Britain this side of Humber has been Christian for two hundred years and more, nearer three hundred. Even the heathen who rule in Northumbria may become Christian as suddenly as did King Guthrum and his companions.'

'Perhaps I expressed myself badly. We did not set out with a firm intention of converting the heathen, but rather to put ourselves completely into the hands of God. Since God has set us ashore in a Christian land we may as well continue our journey to the centre of Christendom. We were discussing it on the strand when a shepherd found us and brought us here. We shall voyage on to Rome, and afterwards to Jerusalem. We thank you for your hospitality. When we are rested we shall pick up our boat and carry it to the Channel. If you give us alms you will be assisting pious pilgrims on their journey, which is a work of charity.'

'I understand. You trust wholly in the will of God, but you reserve the right to change your plans from time to time.'

'We trusted our lives to a boat without oars because that seemed to us to be the will of God. We thought God had commanded us to convert the heathen. But since God has sent us to a Christian land we may as well go on and see Rome. Our own sinful mortal desires have nothing to do with our journey.'

'That is a complete explanation, which you put very clearly. I shall help you on your way, for you are worthy pilgrims. For the present you need food and rest. When you are recovered I shall send you to Frankland. After that you must apply to the Kings of the Franks, and I am sure they also will be pleased to help you. Now I shall leave you to rest. At sunrise Bishop Asser will offer Mass in my chapel, and places will be kept for you within the chancel.'

Alfred continued to his private chamber behind the hall, beckoning Bishop Asser to follow him.

As soon as they were alone he chuckled. 'That's a fine early morning I have arranged for you. You raise my hopes of an important embassy, and it turns out to be three dotty Irishmen. But they were amusingly dotty, so my time wasn't completely wasted. That's why your Mass tomorrow is at sunrise, and not at dawn.'

'I never mind early rising,' answered the Bishop. 'I shall breakfast all the sooner. Perhaps I have been at fault. When I heard that these men had come from Ireland in a cowskin without oars or sails I naturally thought of a miracle. It wasn't until I heard their story that I realized they were as much sightseers as missionaries. None the less, it's a remarkable exploit. God must really have been on their side or they would not have got here in the end.'

'Odd people, and the last of a long line. Three hundred years ago these seas were crowded with Celtic saints, some floating on millstones, some in ordinary boats; but all going wherever God might direct them. Lately there's been no point in it, now that Britain is Christian. These Irishmen are like heroes in peacetime – since there's nothing useful for them to do they must invent useless exploits. It's a landmark, the last of the wandering Irish missionaries. I shall tell my clerks to put down their arrival among the events of the year. Now what shall we read this evening? Will you help me to construe Eusebius?'

They settled down to the lessons which were now Alfred's favourite pastime. He was beginning to read Latin at sight, even the Latin of genuine ancient Romans who had not composed in their heads in German as did the moderns. He had a wonderful sense of being on the verge of the vanished civilization whose ruins he had seen long ago in Rome. To hear the melody of Claudian, to catch every nuance of Orosius, was worth the effort of poring over crabbed letters by candlelight. Asser, who could read fluently but who lacked enthusiasm for the majesty of civilization, was a partner in the task rather than a teacher.

Tonight Alfred could not banish those mad Irishmen from his thoughts. What had persuaded them that they were obeying the voice of the Holy Ghost, when obviously they had merely left home to see the wonders of the world? But then, why did anyone do anything unpleasant? Why had his companions endured the hardships of the battle-winter? Why had he himself lived like an outlaw on Athelney when he might have enjoyed a luxurious exile? Why had Guthrum given his word and kept it, when he might have gone plundering in Frankland? Why was Alfred a King, with men to die for him? Why was Burhed reckoned a bad King? Why did churls pay food-rent and warriors fight for their lords? Why? Why? Why?

'Never mind the *History of the Roman People*,' he said suddenly. 'Instead you shall tell me what duty is, and why good men obey it.'

'A big question,' answered Asser, playing for time. 'I don't think I could answer it from my own unaided wisdom. Luckily the wise men of old thought about it, and we may consider their answers.'

'Which wise men, for example? I'm not interested in the views of some soft-handed scribbler of the old days, who sat in his warm study and told the hired soldiers of the Emperor to do their duty and preserve him. That Horace, for instance, who sang that it is sweet and fitting to die for the fatherland, and in another poem admits that when he himself went into battle he dropped his shield and ran away. I want to hear the advice of a wise man who himself did great deeds.'

'Then Boethius is the man for you,' said Asser, with the delight of one who has found the perfect solution to a tricky problem. 'He was a man of action as well as a scholar, a Roman who was chief minister to Theodoric, the first German King of Italy. Boethius was a faithful Christian, but his lord was an Arian heretic. Jealous rivals whispered against the minister, until at last he fell from power and was condemned to death. But even while he awaited the executioner he was consoled by the promises of God and the knowledge that he had done his duty. He put down his feelings in a book, and the book has survived to this day.'

'If Boethius writes about duty I want to read him. Duty is really the oddest thing in the world, when you come to consider it. We are fallen children of Eve, full of sin and selfishness; and yet nearly everyone of us follows some duty to his own hurt. Of course the duty of a Bishop is higher than the duty of any layman. All the same you must sometimes have marvelled at the sight of sinful laymen doing their duty all around you.'

Asser preened himself, gazing modestly at the floor. 'Yes, the duty of a Bishop is the gravest charge that can be given to a mortal man. In kind it is the same duty as falls to the Pope of Rome, no lighter. As a matter of fact the standard work on the subject was written by a famous Pope. It's the *Cura Pastoralis* of St. Gregory the Great. He wrote it to show the heavy responsibility borne by every Bishop, and to explain his own reluctance to accept the Papacy.'

'Then we shall read it together, as soon as we have finished this book by Boethius.'

Alfred's eyes gleamed. He had set himself to learn Latin so that he might know the past, and especially the deeds of the famous heroes of old. Suddenly he saw that learning might help him to understand the present. These ancient authors were more than an enjoyable field of study; knowledge of what they had written might actually help him at the present day.

'Tomorrow I shall send a messenger into Wales to fetch your copy of Boethius,' he said. 'I have had enough of Eusebius and the greatness of Rome. Rome was great once, I know it; but we can't recapture that mighty past. Tonight I shall teach *you*, for a change. I shall expound a famous German epic. I shall put it into the modern Saxon you can understand, the language you hear spoken at my court.'

That proved to be more difficult than he had supposed. The German poem was full of strained metaphors and echoes of other poems, hard to comprehend unless you already knew a lot of German verse. It seemed absurd that he must stop and explain that the war-linden was another name for the shield-wall, because the best shields are made from linden-wood, which does not split. For that matter the shield-wall is not exactly a wall; the shields are not locked together, merely held side by side. But an attacker will see the defending shields as a wall, and the poet who coined the metaphor must have led many a charge. It was strange that even a Welshman could not see that the swan's bath must be the sea, and that the coursers of the swan's bath are warships. Woden's messengers are the birds of prey who feed on a battlefield; that must be explained to a foreigner whose ancestors had never worshipped Woden.

'In fact a German bard never calls anything by its right name if he can think of another,' said Asser with a sniff. 'It seems to me that listening to German poetry must be very hard work, even for Germans.'

'Listening to poetry ought to be hard work,' Alfred answered.

'Among the Welsh the poet does the hard work. Our verse is more carefully wrought than yours, but it is quite clear to its hearers.'

'That's not true of the poems you translate to me. Everything goes in threes in them, and there are perpetual references to legends I have never heard.'

'You see, my lord,' the Bishop smiled in triumph. 'A poem cannot be rendered into another language. That holds good of any deep work, even one written in prose. That's why you must learn Latin to appreciate Boethius or even Orosius.'

'You are right about poetry. Perhaps works of instruction can be translated. It must be so, since the same truths hold for men of every tongue. It would be fun to try to translate Latin truths into German language. One day, when I have the leisure, I may try it myself.'

'We have come a long way from the mad Irishmen, and the compulsions of duty. I never thought to hear the warlike King of the West Saxons seeking a hobby to occupy his leisure.'

'I'm not warlike. I wasn't warlike even as a young man. The Army was *there*, and I had to fight it. Now the Army is in Frankland, and Guthrum's men keep the peace. But the old wars were interesting at the time. Even you, a man of peace, like to hear of them. We rode miles out of our way so that I could show you the thorn tree of

Ashdown. But that's over, and I may well have time to spare in my old age.'

'But today you have been hunting, and it is getting late. I must visit the Irish pilgrims before I go to bed. Will you excuse me?'

Alone in his chamber, Alfred returned to the problem of duty. Duty had guided his life, and it would be comforting if he could get to understand it before old age overcame him.

In September it was time to return to Wessex for the Michaelmas sitting of the lawcourts. The Irishmen were safely on their way to Rome, and at home everything was going smoothly. But this was the time of year when pirates sought fresh winter quarters, and it would be as well to keep an eye on the restless settlers in East Anglia. King Guthrum was lately dead, and it was not at all certain which ruler controlled these English Danes. After a pious end Guthrum had been buried with Christian rites at his royal hall of Hadleigh. His conversion had been genuine, and for ten years he had kept the peace in his new Kingdom. But many of his companions had followed their lord into his new religion from no higher motive than personal loyalty, and now they might go raiding again.

As Alfred reached Winchester a messenger rode in from the south. He was the master of a roundship which traded across the Channel, but what he had heard among the Franks seemed to him so important that he left his cargo at Southampton and hastened to the King.

Standing in the hall he recited his message at the top of his voice; for good news should be widely known, and the cheers of the excited companions encouraged him.

'The Franks have gained great victories over the heathen,' he said with a broad smile. 'Haesten and his followers have been driven from the Loire. It is said they are about to sail from Frankland, and perhaps they will

Alfred Duggan

come to Britain. Yet they are frightened, beaten men, who cannot harm us. But the most important battle was fought far inland. On the River Dyle, near Louvain, the heathen built a strong camp, intending to winter there. The fyrd of the countryside attacked them, and were beaten with heavy loss. Then King Arnulf rode up with a great host of Austrasians, Saxons and Bavarians. King Arnulf advanced on foot against the heathen rampart, and stormed it after a bitter fight. In one assault, without a siege, he captured the heathen camp. Most of the pirates were killed, and the rest fled in disorder. Today there is no Army, no Army anywhere in Frankland!'

'But the veterans of the great Army which fought us from Reading to Edington now call themselves Christian and farm among the East English,' said Egwulf the old captain of companions. 'I hope they also remember that the Army is finished.'

17

The End of the Wars

Exeter was safe. Alfred rode through the abandoned camp of the besiegers, noting the number of fires and the quantity of rubbish. The pirates had been fewer than he had been led to believe, and perhaps he had been wrong to leave the campaign in eastern Britain and hasten to the defence of his western lands. The pirates had fled when they heard of the approach of the King and his warband; there had been no fighting.

But in this renewed war the resistance of Wessex, the resistance of Christian Britain, no longer depended on Alfred's personal fortitude. He had a colleague, a young second-in-command who did more for him than he had ever done for his brother Ethelred. Last year his son Edward, just twenty-one years of age, had led the main warband of the West Saxons against the Army. They had encountered at Farnham in Hampshire, and the young atheling had driven the pirates in headlong flight. That might have been luck, but then came the skill which proved young Edward to be a great war-leader. The fugitives were edged away from their natural line of retreat and shepherded northward until they fetched up against an unfordable reach of the Thames. Unfortunately it was very hard to get the better of the veteran pirates of the Army. Somehow they crossed the unfordable Thames and holed up with their desperately wounded King on an island of the River Colne. Then had followed the usual anti-climax which so often lost the reward of a Christian victory. The thanes of Wessex wanted to go home; the pirates swore peace and were permitted to depart to their cousins in East Anglia.

So of course this year they had linked up with Haesten's band, reinforced from East Anglia and Northumbria. Alfred had been marching to attack them when he heard of the sea-borne descent on Exeter. He had hurried west with his own companions and the fyrd of Devon, leaving young Edward and alderman Ethelred to defend the south-east.

Now there was no enemy in the west, and the King might return to his main warband. On the other hand, it was still necessary to keep a small force in Wessex west of Selwood. The Danes of Northumbria were cruising off every coast of Britain, and with friendly harbours so near they could keep the sea all summer. The raiders who had fled from Exeter would return as soon as they knew the King was back on the lower Thames. Alfred was forty-four; he had no need to earn further glory, and he no longer enjoyed the thrill of hand-to-hand combat. As he rode over the rubbish of the deserted camp he made up his mind to stay in the west and leave young Edward to guard the richest and most civilized part of his realm. It might come to the boy one day; it was his duty to defend it.

Almost at once he was sorry that such a thought should have entered his head. His conscience began to nag at him. As always, the concept of 'duty' had set his mind racing. It was the duty of Edward to fight in defence of the West Saxon people, as it was the duty of any other West Saxon of noble birth. But to say that the boy ought to lead the warband, that he had a special duty to defend what would one day be his own, was to beg the whole question of the succession.

When a King died the council chose his successor. That was the law of the land, as it had come down from the days of the first conquerors. Hitherto the choice had always fallen on an atheling of the right line of Cerdic, but that was only an unspoken convention. If there were a better candidate, even of undistinguished ancestry, the councillors would be within their rights in choosing him.

That was an exploration of constitutional law. Law is a fascinating subject for thought, and a wise man will never neglect remote contingencies. But in practice when King Alfred was dead the council must choose between Ethelwold and Edward.

Both were King's sons, of the right line of Cerdic. Ethelwold was the elder, representative of the senior line, wealthy, a brave warrior followed by a band of dashing and faithful companions. On the other hand, at this moment Edward led the chief warband of Christian Britain. He had been put into his command by his father at the age of twenty, when there was nothing to show that he knew how to manage a campaign.

His promotion had been naked favouritism; but it happened to have turned out well. He had covered himself with glory, and in the relentless pursuit after Farnham he had proved his great capacity. Alfred acknowledged that he himself at the age of twenty would have thought only of pursuing the heathen wherever they might flee; Edward, in the excitement of his first victory, had remembered the lie of the country and contrived to push the foe against a deep reach of the Thames. The boy's young shoulders carried an amazingly mature head.

Long ago dear Ethelred had begged him to look after his infant son. He had promised to look after him; and at the time, he reminded himself honestly, he had meant that he would train Ethelwold to be his successor. But at that time he could not know that his own Edward would promise to become the greatest war-leader in Christendom. He would be failing in his duty to the West Saxons if he did not give young Edward a fair chance of ruling over them.

There was nothing that you could put your finger on against young Ethelwold. The atheling was an up-standing young warrior, recklessly brave and much loved by his reckless companions. Everyone said he was magnificent in the front rank of a charge. But he was a champion, not a war-leader. Though he had fought under Edward's command, he would never have thought to edge a fleeing foe against an impassable obstacle. And there was something in his character that Alfred distrusted. In battle he would distinguish himself, but could you be sure he would always fight for Wessex? There was nothing blatantly wrong with his private life; he heard Mass when he should and kept the law. But there were rumours of too many girls and too much to drink. If he were given his head he might sink into debauchery.

The final decision lay with the councillors, and he must leave it to them. He must treat these two young men on their merits, forgetting that one day they might be rivals for his throne. While pirates were raiding from Devon to Kent he needed a lieutenant to take command in his absence. Edward was a good leader, brave, energetic, and loyal. If he had been a stranger instead of a son he would still have been the best lieutenant available. So what was there to worry about?

Besides, Ethelwold was the son of the Mercian Godgifu. There was something Mercian about his reckless swashbuckling bravado. Mercians rebelled against their Kings and fought each for his own hand. It was bad blood.

Edward also had a Mercian mother. But obviously it had not affected him. He was through and through a Woden-born Cerdinga, of the right line of Cerdic, the destined King of the West Saxons.

But Ethelred, looking down from Heaven, might not be pleased at the way his brother had kept his promise.

There was no enemy near Exeter, but all the seas were crowded with pirates. At a little harbour on the south coast Alfred found the fishermen standing on the cliff, watching a single heathen longship.

'Why don't you man your boats and go after her?' he asked.

'We would never catch her,' answered the village

shipwright. 'Pirates fight for plunder, not for glory. They won't waste time on poor fishermen.'

'If one of my longships were here she could catch the pirate,' said the King, half to himself. 'But of course the pirate might win the fight. How can I make sure that my ships are more formidable than any pirate?'

'That would not be too difficult, my lord,' said the shipwright. 'Your ships never sail far from harbour, but the pirates must come from the Baltic north-about round Scotland to the Channel. They carry food for a month and water for a week. Your ship could fill all that space with armed men; and there's no reason why it shouldn't be bigger than the pirate. I could build a ship twice as long as that heathen in the offing; and it would be seaworthy provided it never made a long passage.'

'But who could sail her? Would I have to hire Frisians?' asked Alfred with a smile. 'It's odd, isn't it, how we Saxons have forgotten the open sea? At one time our ancestors were the most daring sailors in the world. The ancient poet Claudian describes their ships, which could turn and back in weather that sent the Romans into harbour.'

'There are men in Devon who can sail the open sea,' said the shipwright, angered at the slight. 'What about Edgar, over to Barnstaple? Three times he has sailed in his own ship to Frankland, and once to Spain. He can sail anywhere, and his crew can defend themselves from pirates.'

'Indeed. And where is this famous warrior to be found when invasion threatens his own shire?'

'Why, he mans Barnstaple palisade, of course. That's his duty. He's no thane, to go riding with the warband. The noble companions might be offended if he offered to join them. He's the son of a churl.'

'So are some of my best companions,' answered the King. 'In this war we fight where we are most useful, not where our ancestors fought. Three voyages, you say, and defending his cargo with his own men? I shall tell him to buy a good horse, and to ride with the warband when next we go to battle.'

'His duty as burgess is to hold the palisade. Must you put an extra burden on a churl just because he prospers?' asked the shipwright angrily.

'He will not be a churl when he rides with the warband. He will be a King's thane, with the place in my hall and in the shirecourt that is the due of his rank. That's it. At the next council I shall issue a decree. Every merchant who has sailed three voyages in his own ship must take up the obligations of a thane, and in return he will have a thane's honour. Thank you, my good man. You have given wise advice to your King, as though you were a councillor of noble birth.'

There were other plans in Alfred's mind, plans to improve his realm without changing the fundamental customs of his people. But changes like this could not be introduced in the middle of a desperate campaign. He must wait until Britain was at peace, if he should live to see that happy day.

Then a courier came galloping in from the eastward. He shouted the good news of victory to every passer-by, but his written message was for the King's eyes only.

Edward had drawn a cross beside his name to authenticate the letter. At a pinch he could have signed in full, or indeed written the whole message. But the copying of an official dispatch was the duty of a clerk, whose professional script would be easy to read at the other end.

'We have stormed Haesten's palisade,' the despatch began. 'But do not think of it as a great victory like Ashdown or Edington. We waited prudently until Haesten was raiding in Mercia, though he had left a garrison to hold his camp. I marched against it with my companions. Alderman Ethelred led the men of London and part of the warband of the West Saxons. We took the palisade by assault in a single day, without formal siege. We have all the plunder taken by Haesten in

Britain, and some of the plunder he won from the Franks. Many Christian captives have been set free. We have destroyed many pirate ships, and taken to London as many as we could move. I have given my warriors a fitting reward, and sent the rest of the spoil to your hoard in Winchester. But I don't know what to do with certain trophies found in the camp – the wife and two young sons of Haesten himself. She is his real Danish wife, not a concubine. Shall I hang her and her brats, or sell them back to Haesten for a heavy ransom? Please answer at once. My men dislike pirates, even women-pirates and boy-pirates. They will die suddenly if they remain with my warband.'

Alfred rewarded the messenger with a gold arm-ring, and enough ale to keep him drunk for a week. How right he had been to give command of the main war-band to that splendid son of his! At twenty-one Edward was already the most cunning and successful war-leader in Britain. The King's son had not been unfairly favoured above the King's nephew; the King had merely chosen the best man to carry the heaviest responsibility.

That same evening he sent another messenger to Essex, commanding Edward to send Haesten's wife and sons immediately to Winchester. At the same time he summoned alderman Ethelred, for between them they must solve a difficult problem.

Alfred sat with his son-in-law in a carrel of the new scriptorium at Winchester. The light was fading, and the clerks had finished their copying until tomorrow. The place of the interview had been chosen with care. This scriptorium was a new venture, started by royal command to make good the loss of service-books destroyed in pirate raids. It was an obvious echo of the famous scriptorium of Charlemagne, and would remind the alderman of semi-independent Mercia that his people had not really surrendered their freedom when they came under the protection of Wessex; they were cooperating

285

in the restoration of civilization in Britain. The clerks wrote as much for Mercians as for West Saxons.

'Well, what shall we do with these little pirates?' asked Alfred, when Ethelred was comfortably settled with a jug of ale at his elbow.

'Does it matter very much? If we hang them we shall give a lot of pleasure to a great many people. If you don't like hanging children you can keep them as slaves and give them a sound Christian training. Or you could sell them back to their father for a good price. But if Haesten is as clever as they say he is he will cheat you over the deal.'

'You don't remember them, I see. I myself wasn't sure until I had seen them. What in your opinion is the obligation of a godfather to a godson who has fallen into captivity?'

'Good God, how silly of me to forget. You mean that Edward has captured my little John and your little Peter? Haesten has so many wives, and so many children, or so they say, that I never thought of the brats we sponsored.'

'But they are the same brats. I haven't spoken to them, for fear their mother should make a tiresome scene; but I had a look at them from a window as they were taken to prison. Only a few weeks ago we became their godfathers. Haesten got the better of me in that deal, but I don't regret it. Baptism is always worth trying. With Guthrum it worked, you remember. He was a reasonably good Christian until the day of his death. Yet on the morning of the battle of Edington I am sure he had no intention of deserting the gods of Valhalla.'

'But at Edington you defeated him and chased him for miles. When we blockaded Haesten in Kent there was no real fighting. Out of a blue sky Haesten offered to turn Christian and to live in peace with you. He wasn't baptized to save something from the wreck of defeat, only to snatch some small advantage in a campaign which was still undecided.'

'At the time I thought he was lying, and now I know

it. All the same I did right to believe him. Imagine the fate of a heathen who really wants to be a Christian, and dies unbaptized because no one will trust his sincerity! I wouldn't care to have a thing like that on my conscience.'

'Well, there it is,' said Ethelred casually, not very interested in the fate of two young Danes. 'They are Christians, but undoubtedly they are also pirates. After you have hanged them perhaps they will go to Heaven. Real heathen pirates have no chance of salvation. I shouldn't try to do a deal with Haesten if I were you. He has already proved himself too slippery a customer.'

'Have many of your godsons been hanged, and did you do anything to avenge them?' asked Alfred in a carefully neutral tone of voice.

'Of course no one has ever hanged a godson of mine, and if anyone did I should kill him unless first he killed me,' Ethelred answered with heat. 'But that wasn't a proper baptism, so I am not really a godfather. Haesten never meant it. He was only trying to get away without a battle.'

'The baptism of those children was valid all the same; though whether today Haesten is a bad Christian or an impenitent heathen is a question to puzzle theologians. The boys are too young to understand what was done to them, which puts them in the same category as infants. No one disputes the validity of infant baptism. You are a godfather, and young John Haestinga is your godson.'

'Then he is under my protection and you must send him back unharmed to his father. Is that what you want me to say?'

Ethelred stared in bewilderment at his strange father-in-law, who was always turning questions upside down until the answers came out different.

'Of course we send back the boys. I would have done that anyway, whatever you advised. I shall tell you a secret. I have never yet hanged an innocent hostage, and I never will. I must keep that a secret, of course, because if everyone knew my hostages would be no use to me.

We must send back the mother too, because as their kin in blood she is our spiritual kin. In Wessex we take godparents seriously. Perhaps you don't know that by the old law of King Ine the godfather of a slain man is entitled to the same compensation as his lord.'

'I'm not sure we had that law. During my lifetime there has been very little law in Mercia. But it seems a sound idea. Very well, the boys and their mother go back.'

'Oh, but we do more than that. When your godson visits you, you do more than return him unharmed to his father. I shall give my Peter a good horse and a strong byrnie and a damascened sword, and a chalice for his chapel if he seems to know what it's used for. You must give your John rich presents, that's why I wanted to talk it over with you beforehand. If ravaged Mercia can't afford handsome presents I shall be happy to lend you anything from my hoard.'

'Mercia has indeed been ravaged, but I can still give gifts to my godson,' said Ethelred stiffly. 'I will not be outshone in generosity by any Saxon. All the same, my companions will laugh at me for making presents to a pirate who hasn't even asked for them, a pirate who has already cheated us once by falsely pretending to turn Christian.'

'We shall be laughed at, but we are doing what honour demands. The best thing of all is to behave like a saint, but I'm not cut out for that. If you behave as a man of honour you never seem foolish to yourself, whatever the neighbours may think. That's all that really matters. I'm glad you see it in the same light. Remember, there's always the chance that Haesten may genuinely change sides. Guthrum came over to us and never afterwards betrayed me, though he had been as bloody a pirate as any of them.'

But though Haesten sent a polite message of gratitude when his wife and sons were returned to him, decked with rich jewels and mounted on fine horses, he remained the bloody pirate he had been all his life.

The pirates who had threatened Exeter were still cruising in the western sea, and Alfred returned to guard Devonshire. Then Haesten and his Army rode westward up the Thames so swiftly that the defenders could only ride after them. Alderman Ethelred commanded the pursuit, for the atheling Edward was holding his marriage feast in Winchester. His bride was a West Saxon lady of good birth, Eadgifu the daughter of Sighelm the King's thane who ten years ago had carried the alms of the West Saxons to Rome and far beyond. She was a suitable bride for an atheling, and there was no reason why they should not like one another.

The pirates could ride anywhere in Britain, but they dared no longer stay to plunder. Haesten and his men rode up the Thames to its source, and then northward up the Severn. Though they had no shipping they clung to rivers, perhaps because where a river runs there is always a way through the hills. Ethelred came pounding after them with the mounted thanes of Wessex and Mercia, but he could not catch up and bring them to battle. But when they reached the upper Severn the pirates were brought to a halt, for all the chieftains of Wales came to the help of King Alfred the champion of civilization. With the spearmen of Wales barring the way the pirates took refuge on a little island in the river. There Ethelred besieged them until they had eaten their horses. In the end they fought their way out, though with heavy loss, and the survivors struggled back to their cousins in East Anglia.

After harvest the pirates set out on another raid, according to their old habit of seeking winter quarters in an unravaged land. But now there was little unravaged country left in Britain, and the Army rode right across Mercia to the deserted fortress of Chester beside the Irish Sea. When Ethelred came up with them he found the steep Roman walls too strong to be attacked, but he wasted the countryside so thoroughly that very soon the pirates were starving. As usual, they endured starvation that would have killed a Christian; but immediately after Christmas they broke out southwards into Wales.

It seemed that the Army could ride through Britain wherever it willed. But now it must ride very swiftly, with avengers coming after. Haesten had pressed on so hard to Chester that his men had no time to plunder and the country suffered little harm.

In the winter, at long last, the luck began to turn. The fleet which had been cruising off Devonshire returned eastward towards Guthrum's land, but pirates who landed to ravage on the way home were cut off and routed by the fyrd of the South Saxons. Then storms arose and the ships were wrecked on the chalk cliffs of the south coast.

The danger had lifted from the south-west. Haesten was ravaging in Wales beyond the Severn Sea; but there was no reason to fear that the Welsh would make common cause with the heathen, as sometimes they had done in the past. Alfred, and Ethelred his alderman, had shown that Saxons and English could be good Christians and good neighbours. The Welsh were now firm on the side of civilization. The King of the West Saxons might keep his Christmas peacefully in Winchester.

In the cloud of thirsty flies the horses stirred restlessly. Since early morning Alfred had been in the saddle, and at the age or forty-six he found it tiring to sit a restless horse all day in the same place. But while he led the whole warband of his dominions, in the presence of the enemy, he must remain on horseback so that his men could see him. The hot sun made him sleepy, and for a moment he relaxed his attention. At once the dancing stallion whipped round to kick at Egwulf's mount, dancing restlessly beside him. Alfred swallowed the oath that rose to his lips; at any moment he might find himself fighting a battle and it was important to remain in a State of Grace. Then, as he wrenched the horse round again, it passed through his mind that perhaps he ought to be grateful; for the movement had shown him a strange picture, a picture he would long remember.

Behind him the fields shone golden in the setting sun, golden corn and golden stubble, with the reapers moving forward in line like warriors in array. Waggons lurched behind the reapers, their oxen bellowing in the torment of the flies; some waggons were actually pulled by horses, for it was urgent to get the harvest behind strong walls before the pirates could take it. In the distance a column of loaded carts crawled along the paved road to London.

Behind him all was peaceful industry, a pastoral scene from Vergil. In front, half a mile of grey ungathered hay ended in the weathered logs of the Danish palisade and the cluster of dragon-heads where their longships were beached. It was an allegorical picture of Peace and War, the dividing line the long ranks of his warband, standing in bored idleness behind the shield-wall.

'Another blank day,' said old Egwulf, moving his horse cautiously out of reach of bad-tempered heels. 'While we are here the pirates won't come out to fight for their supper. But presently we must go home, unless you propose to sit out another battle-winter; and then I suppose they will win their corn from the barns where we have stored it.'

'Not another battle-winter. One is enough for a lifetime,' Alfred answered absently. 'There's no point in laying siege to their camp, either. They have had a full year to strengthen this palisade. Honestly, I don't know what to do. But I feel I ought to do something, after bringing such a great host within half a mile of the Army.'

He might say what he liked to old Egwulf; no need to maintain his royal dignity with a companion who had been a veteran when his lord first drew his sword.

'We can't catch them on the move,' he went on. 'We can follow them closely and make them hole up again, but that's not good enough. We stand over them and they grow hungry; but we grow hungry also, and I can't keep the men under arms when they want to be sowing next year's corn. But we ought to be able to do *some-thing*, if only I could think of it.'

'Artful scoundrels, aren't they?' replied the old companion. 'I have followed the wars for fifty years, and never in my life did I think of the upper Lea as a navigable river. The people here use nothing but tiny barges. But the pirates bring long-ships up to the camp without any trouble at all.'

The curious scene of harvesting and war had already set Alfred to making pictures in his mind. These words brought up another picture, of something he had often heard told but never seen: the embattled bridges of the island-city of Paris, with Christians dropping stones on the pirate longships below.

'That's it. My dear Egwulf, you have given me the plan. Look, two miles downstream the river narrows. We build a bridge there, with a palisade on either bank. If our men can hold the bridge the pirates must leave their ships to rot!'

Once more Alfred heard the heathen war cry, and saw the line of brandished axes as the enemy charged. But he did not draw his sword, for he stood on the watchtower which guarded one end of his new bridge. His companions had told him that he was too old to fight, unless things were going badly and the thanes needed the inspiration of his leadership. It seemed strange to be standing idle while his people did the fighting for him. But he was not missing anything important; this was not really a battle.

The pirates had been slow to discover the new bridge, when ditch and palisade were already formed and strongly garrisoned. Seeing their ships bottled up, the Army was making a demonstration to frighten away the builders. When they recognized that the palisade was held by warriors quite willing to defend it they withdrew in good order to their own camp. A formal siege might have reduced the bridge; but since the expensive failure before Paris nine years ago the Army had grown wary of formal sieges.

Next day the pirates broke out westward, in a headlong dash to reach fresh hunting-grounds before winter. Alfred's warband was not strong enough to bar their way; but West Saxons and Mercians rode after them, gathering the fyrd of each shire as they passed through it. The pirates dared not challenge battle in the open; riding day and night they reached the Severn and fortified a strong position at Bridgnorth. They were still looking for unravaged Christian land; surely in such a large island as Britain there must be plenty of it, if only they rode in the right direction. They were slow to understand that all Britain had already been plundered. On their hurried journey west they had been too hotly pursued to spare time for foraging. They settled down to endure a hungry winter.

Meanwhile the Londoners had marched in triumph to the deserted camp on the Lea, and fetched back great numbers of abandoned pirate longships. At a great *Te Deum* of thanksgiving Alfred sat on a throne facing the high altar of St. Paul's, as was the due of the King of the West Saxons who was also the chosen lord of all the English; but by the King's command alderman Ethelred dedicated the tithe of the spoil, and himself took the remainder for the hoard of Mercia. For the ships had been captured in the dominions of Mercia, and London itself was a Mercian city. Alfred was determined that the Mercians should acknowledge his protection of their own free will, and that their independence should be shown publicly to all men.

In the summer of 896 Alfred prepared with some reluctance to celebrate his forty-seventh birthday. A hundred tiresome little weaknesses, when he rode a hot horse, when he tried to run or to climb a steep hill, reminded him that he was getting near the end of his life.

The short time left to him was being wasted by this

everlasting and futile war. Now that the thanes of the West Saxons were well mounted and trained to ride hard the passage of the Army did little harm. The pirates would burn any building they passed and kill any peasant they met; but as a rule they were in a hurry to reach a safe camp, and had no time to plunder aside from the line of march. All the same, there seemed to be no way to get rid of the Army. Time and again the West Saxons had faced them in battle; at Ashdown and Edington heathen dead had covered the field; they had been routed, they had been starved in their camps, their ships had been towed in triumph to London. But still the Army flourished, replacing its losses with fresh recruits from the heathen north.

The Army lay secure in its strong camp at Bridgnorth on the Severn. The Christians were weary of the war and might disperse after a severe defeat. Tomorrow a messenger might warn Alfred to mount and flee, as he had fled to Athelney more than eighteen years ago. It was just thirty years since the Army had come to land among the East English, and still the Christians of Britain had not discovered how to get rid of it.

Then news came that the Army had broken out from Bridgnorth, riding hard to seek refuge in the heathen Kingdom of York. In Wessex they waited for the next invasion; until slowly it became apparent that there would be no more heathen invasions. While the English and Saxons still kept the field the Army had sickened of the endless war. Some pirates settled down to farm among their comrades in Northumbria and East Anglia; others, still eager for a roving life, crossed the sea to try their luck in Frankland. After thirty years of plunder the Army had disbanded. The Kingdom of the West Saxons was free, independent, and at peace.

18

The Lawgiver

This was not a meeting of the council. That would be held tomorrow. It was just that the King wished to talk things over beforehand with his mother-in-law and a chosen group of intimate advisers. Most of these advisers happened to be foreigners, and so might not sit in council without giving offence to old-fashioned Saxon thanes. The Mercian clerks who had begun the whole affair, founding the palace school and encouraging the Saxon clergy to brush up their Latin, were not exactly foreigners nowadays; though when they were born Mercia had been a foreign Kingdom and it would be tactless to make them councillors of Wessex.

Asser, now Bishop in the western Welsh-speaking parts of Sherborne, acknowledged Alfred as his King. Ten years' residence among the Saxons had left him as Welsh as ever; he still spoke Saxon clumsily and ungrammatically. But John the Old Saxon and Grimbald of St. Bertin had spoken German from their cradles; any West Saxon could understand them, though they would never pass as natives.

Abbot John was the hero of the little gathering. They all stared at him as he shifted uneasily on his stool, conscious that recently he had not behaved in all respects like a monk of St. Benedict. But Alfred would not let him off; he must tell the full story of his adventure, though he feared Bishop Asser would put it in the book he was writing.

'It was really nothing extraordinary,' he mumbled.

'Starting a new minster is always a tricky business. Of course the King was right to found one on Athelney, the scene of his exile; but it's a desolate site, and very wet in winter. Monks who volunteer for a new foundation come as a rule because they are dissatisfied with their communities. They think all will go well in a fresh place, but perhaps they are unsuited to the monastic life anywhere. It's hard for a grown man to admit his whole life has been a mistake. Most of my brethren are Franks. The country is strange to them, and perhaps they resent being put under the rule of a German abbot. That part of it is all quite understandable and forgivable, especially since at the foundation of a new minster you must enforce the letter of the Rule, with no mitigations.'

'Yes, but tell us of your adventures,' said the King. 'If the monks had asked for another abbot I might have listened to them. That isn't what they did.'

'Well, as I said, they are Franks, ignorant of my life in the world before I entered religion. What they did was very wicked by any standard; it happened to be foolish also, because they didn't know me. Mind you, only a small minority was concerned. Most of them are good monks, though they might prefer a more lenient Rule.'

Abbot John looked round with a smile, to emphasize that he was being fair-minded.

'This small and wicked minority got in touch with a couple of robbers; and if you stop to think, that's the oddest part of the whole queer business. They were strangers on Athelney, unable to speak the local language; and monks under my charge don't stray from the enclosure to gossip with villagers. I suppose there must be some affinity that makes very wicked men recognize each other at sight. Of course my monks have no money; I look after it for them. But wicked men will always find a way. Somehow they offered a bribe to these two robbers. It was arranged that they should attack me while I prayed alone in the chapel between Nocturn and Prime. That's the whole story, and a sad one. The faithful brethren came to the chapel when they heard us scuffling. We bound the robbers, and the King hanged them.'

'That's not the whole story. Come, John. We want to know why the two robbers didn't kill you.'

'There were only two of them, my lord. In my youth I fought the Wends. This miserable pair were robbers, not warriors. They carried swords, but no shields or helmets, I suppose because on their journey they hoped to pass as honest men. They crept out of the shadows very clumsily, and I heard them; and then they didn't know how to begin. Even a wicked man hesitates before cutting down a monk at his prayers. While they gaped at me I picked up that big Missal you so kindly gave us. I whacked one robber over the head with it. He didn't get up for some time, so I took his sword and went after the other. Then this second man fell on his knees to beg for mercy, so I couldn't hit him. At the moment I felt disappointed, but it was all for the best. No blood was shed in the chapel, so there was no need to reconsecrate it. Then all the community arrived, awakened by my war cries. That was where I committed a grave fault. The war cry of my family calls on a famous ancestor who used to be worshipped as a heathen god. I ought not to have shouted his name before the altar. But I don't think my Frankish monks understood the ancient German war cry, so in the end no harm was done.'

'I expect your ancestor is the same as mine,' said Alfred gently. 'All his children are rightly proud of their descent from Woden, but luckily I never called on him while I was leading the Christian host against the heathen. That might have led to a misunderstanding.'

'So the robbers were taken, and afterwards hanged,' said Eadburh. 'What happened to the wicked monks who had plotted the murder?'

'The King hanged them also,' answered John, and tightened his lips so that he should say no more.

'Oh, Alfred, you hanged professed monks? Wasn't

there some other punishment you could have given them?' Eadburh was distressed.

'Abbot John was their lord and they betrayed him. There can be only one punishment for such grave treason. That's why I asked John to tell us the whole story. Tomorrow I make public my new code of laws, and in it I have laid down that treason to a lord is bootless.'

The foreigners looked puzzled, and Alfred hastened to explain.

'*Boot* is the compensation due to a ruler for a breach of his peace, as *were* is the compensation due to the kin of a slain man. When one West Saxon kills another, and they do it constantly, he pays *boot* to me and *were* to the dead man's kin. But if the kin refuse compensation and prefer to kill the slayer they owe *were* to his kin but no *boot* to me, since my peace was broken before they killed him.'

'A complicated subject,' said Grimbald the Fleming with a shrug. 'In Frankland also they pay compensation for murder and a fine to the lord of the land. But I took my vows too young to share in any bloodfeud, so I never had occasion to learn all the details.'

'Those details are most important,' Alfred declared. 'Free men who carry swords must be allowed to maintain the bloodfeud. I couldn't stop it anyway, even if my law should forbid it. But we must make it easy for an honourable man to offer compensation if he would rather pay than fight. The law lays down how much he ought to pay, so the avengers of blood can't bully him into offering more than the slain man was worth. But it's even more important that warriors should see it as honourable to pay up and end the bloodfeud. I hope to persuade some great man to accept the *were*; then ordinary warriors can do it without being called cowards by their neighbours. But the murder of a lord by his man is bootless.'

'That's an innovation, surely,' said Eadburh. 'We didn't have that law in Mercia in the old days, before the Army had smashed up everything. The *boot* for the killing of a great man was more than for a peasant, of course; but it was the same whoever killed him, his own companion or a stranger. The laws of our ancestors did not recognize these oaths of vassalage, which are quite modern anyway. It seems to me that you are trying to alter the laws of the West Saxons. Is it possible to change the laws of a people, the laws that have come down from the ancestors? And if it can be done, can the King do it by his own authority?'

'Oh, laws can be changed,' said Archbishop Plegmund at once. 'There can be no doubt of that. The laws of *boot* and *were* and bloodfeud were fixed by Woden, so they say. But the other laws that punish sacrilege and breaches of Christian conduct must have been introduced after St. Augustine had converted us.'

'The Romans used to decree new laws in their assembly, in the days before they had an Emperor to do it for them,' Alfred explained. 'I used to be terribly puzzled by that early Roman history, until Bishop Asser here gave me the clue. Every Roman had three names, and he might be called by any one of them! Isn't that extraordinary? But once I had grasped that Marcus and Tullius and Cicero are all the same man the whole story became clear, and very interesting it is. Now, if the Roman people could make new law, and bind themselves by it, why shouldn't the people of the West Saxons? That is what I shall suggest at tomorrow's council. Of course I may not get my own way.'

'You will get your way, King of the Saxons and of the English and of all the Christians of Britain,' said Eadburh a trifle sardonically. 'Will you also take this opportunity of recommending to your people the King who should succeed you when you are gone?'

'I shall leave their choice unfettered. Anyway, a decision now would not bind the council after I am dead. When they have buried me they may choose among the athelings.'

Eadburh snorted.

'You mean you will leave them a free choice between Edward who has led the warband to victory, Edward who has been second-in-command to his father since he was twenty years old; and Ethelwold who lives quietly at Wimborne. You can call that a free choice if you like. I say you have already chosen for them.'

'Ethelwold does not live so very quietly. He has gathered a great band of companions, and I have done nothing to hinder him. He could have had a command against the Army if he had been willing, but he chose to sulk because I would not give him a greater command than I gave to Edward. When I was tied down to the defence of the west I sent my best war-leader against the pirates in Essex. As it happens my best war-leader is also my eldest son. Should I have allowed the Army to win the war for fear of seeming unfair to my nephew?'

'What you did was best for your people, and for the Mercians also,' said alderman Ethelred. 'But tomorrow you ought to declare your wishes openly. Anyone can see that you want Edward to succeed you. If you leave the question undecided Ethelwold may give trouble.'

'To fight for the throne was the Mercian custom, when the Mercians had a throne to fight for,' said Alfred savagely. 'It's not a thing we do in Wessex. Here we keep to the right line of Cerdic, and disappointed athelings accept the verdict of the council. Besides, I can't come out openly for Edward. To do that would be unfair to Ethelwold. I promised my dead brother that I would protect the interests of his son.'

For a full minute no one said anything. The Mercians were bitterly offended, and the other councillors waited for the King to recover his temper. They knew why he was angry. He was a just man, but there had been a flaw in his justice. He pretended to himself that he was holding the balance level between Edward and Ethelwold; but he could not deceive his own conscience, and the memory of past injustice made him miserable and abusive.

Asser turned the conversation from this painful topic. As a Welshman he had an open mind about the succession to the throne of the West Saxons; but he was interested in law as an object of speculation, and he thought he saw the germ of a new principle in what Eadburh had said earlier.

'So the old law of Mercia did not recognize treason to a private lord? That is most curious. Sworn companionship is a very ancient institution. We Britons have known it since Rome ceased to rule us, and Tacitus records it as flourishing among the Germans long before the first Saxon came to Britain.'

In the interest of the discussion Alfred forgot his grievance.

'War-companions have been with us from the beginning,' he said. 'But that's not quite what I meant. A war-companion never betrays his lord, or if he does the other companions kill him immediately. There's no need to fix a penalty for such an unlikely crime. No, I was thinking of this new system of vassalage; where unwarlike men, peasants and petty farmers swear to serve and uphold some thane in return for his protection. It's a good thing in itself. It makes for order. Suppose there is a killing. The lord of the slayer is rich enough to pay the *were* of the slain man at once; later he collects it by instalments from his man. The kin of the slain probably accept a good lump sum, when if they had been kept waiting they might have carried on the bloodfeud. But I want vassals to understand that they can't get protection for nothing. The oath they swear puts them on the level of honourable companions, and they must be as faithful as any warrior. But it's a new system. When King Ine issued his code he had never heard of it. We must make room for it in the laws I issue tomorrow; or the thing may get out of hand, with timid vassals switching from one lord to another in their search for protection.'

'Then you ought to add a regulation that a vassal may change lords only at a meeting of the shirecourt, in the presence of the alderman,' said Asser, with a glow of pride in his accurate use of these barbarous technical terms.

'Yes, we'll do that. It's a good idea. But the other still stands. No man may buy his way out of the grave crime of killing the lord who holds his oath.' Alfred was now quite calm and good-tempered.

'There's one other point, about inheritance,' he went on. 'All these nuns who ran away with handsome scoundrels during the confusion of the wars. No child of a nun may inherit anything from his father. I don't suppose he would have the impudence to claim anything, but we ought to make that clear.'

The discussion meandered over various contingencies of law.

They considered at length the problem of the kinless refugee who might be an honest man but had no one to vouch for him; after the long wars Wessex and Mercia were full of such men. The solution proposed was to form artificial groups, on the lines of the old drinking-guilds. But would men bound together only by decree of the shirecourt, not by any tie of common ancestry, genuinely stand by one another in the bloodfeud, or suppress the occasional black sheep among their members? Alfred thought it might work, if the new groups were encouraged to receive Communion together; the Frankish clerks, unfamiliar with the clubbable habits of Saxons, were more doubtful.

When everyone was working in harmony, in the kind of hopeful detailed intellectual planning that Alfred enjoyed almost more than hunting, they were interrupted by Elswitha.

The Queen of the English and Saxons, who was not exactly the Queen of Wessex, was never invited to take part in a serious discussion; though afterwards she might be present to grace the formal meeting which ratified and published whatever the real governors of Britain had worked out in private. Elswitha was a good woman, who had been a very good mother. But she could not take an interest in any group larger than her family, and now that all her children were settled in life she had really nothing to do.

Ethelfleda helped her husband to rule the Mercians. Edward, a grown man and father of a family, was war-leader of Wessex. Ethelgifu had been installed as abbess of the new foundation at Shaftesbury. Ethelthryth had gone oversea to marry Baldwin of Flanders, who was not exactly her kinsman though he was the son of her father's stepmother. Young Ethelward the scholar was studying in Winchester, though he had not been tonsured in case one day he should be called on to marry and continue the line of the Cerdingas. They had all escaped from the kindly but stifling care of their mother.

Nowadays Elswitha had no occupation but to pray in the chapel, to brood over the adventures of her youth when the Army ranged at large in Wessex, and to interrupt serious meeting with everyday trivialities. Alfred loved her as much as he had ever loved her, and he had never in his life been physically unfaithful; but in the daytime they had very little to say to one another.

Under her arm Elswitha carried a bundle of dusty silk. She beamed nervously round the company.

'Oh, Alfred, I hope I don't interrupt anything important, but I felt I had to show you this,' she said breathlessly. 'Look, it's a little tunic and cloak of the finest purple, and in the middle of the bundle this tiny sword. You'll never guess where I found it. But what I want to ask is – couldn't little Ethelstan wear them tomorrow, at the great meeting of the council? They are just the right size for him. He would look splendid, and wearing them would give him the confidence to behave as an atheling should in front of all the great men of Wessex and of Britain. I had to come and ask you at once, with the meeting due to begin at sunrise tomorrow. But go on with your discussion. I'm sure it's too deep for me to understand, and I shan't offer an opinion. I just wanted Alfred's permission for Ethelstan to wear these dear little clothes.'

Her shyness made the others feel shy. Eadburh her mother was scowling at her to go away.

But Alfred was too interested to feel his usual self-consciousness. 'I know that tunic and cloak,' he said quickly. 'Where did you find them?'

'An old reeve died in the west, and when his heir went through the house he found a bale that had been stored there since the battle-winter. It had been sent off from Wantage when the Army first came to Reading, and kept in store until it was forgotten. The rest of the bale was old hangings and bed linen, not worth keeping. But right in the middle I found these things, which must have been put there to hide them. Wrapped in the cloak was a little white-and-gold headband, too short for any woman to wear. But the whole outfit is just the right size for little Ethelstan, Edward's son.'

'Of course they will fit him,' Alfred answered. 'They fitted me when I was his age. That's the sword, cloak and tunic I wore when the Pope made me a Roman Consul. I brought them home and kept them among my treasures. I'm glad someone remembered to save them when the heathen were raiding round Wantage.'

'Well, can Ethelstan wear them tomorrow? That's what I came to ask.' Elswitha could not be interested in anything that had happened to Alfred before their marriage, or in anything that had happened so far away as Rome. But her eldest grandson was in her bower at that very moment, and she had promised to beg this treat for him.

'Ethelstan may wear any jewellery or robes that his grandfather chooses to give him, so long as he is careful not to spoil the King's gifts,' said Eadburh at once. 'But whether he should appear at tomorrow's law-giving in the state of a Roman Consul is an important question, which should be discussed by the King's advisers. Why can't he dress up in the bower to amuse his play-fellows, instead of intruding on an important adult function?'

'He wants to show himself to the bishops and

aldermen, and the other great men among the West Saxons. I promised to ask his grandfather. You know, mother, I never like to disappoint a child,' said Elswitha pettishly.

'Ah, but a grandmother must yield to the authority of a great-grandmother,' Eadburh answered in triumph. 'I can't expect to see Ethelstan a grown man, but while he is a child I have some say in what he shall wear. I think he is too young to appear at a formal council. He won't know how to behave, and he will waste the time of his elders. But this is a matter of state, and the King must make the final decision.'

'Let the boy wear the fine clothes the Pope gave me so long ago,' said Alfred with a smile. 'I never thought to see them again, and I should like to see them worn by a handsome young atheling. The councillors must listen for hours while my code of laws is read out to them. They will endure the tedium more patiently if they have something striking to look at.'

'Do you see what that means?' When Eadburh was cross she looked a tiresome old woman, all her charm and intelligence hidden by her frown. 'The people will suppose you are putting him forward as the future King of the English and Saxons. Well, why not,' she went on with a sudden smile. 'He's my great-grandson and a nice little boy.'

'Nonsense, my dear. If he wore my own crown and regalia that wouldn't make him King, until he has been chosen by the people. In this realm there is no such thing as an heir to the throne. When I die the throne will be vacant until the people appoint my successor.' Alfred also was smiling; but he knew the weakness of his argument and went on to elaborate it.

'That sword and tunic did not make me heir to the throne. I never was my father's heir anyway. I succeeded only after my three elder brothers had each reigned in his turn. Ethelstan won't even get the Roman Consulship as I did, since it is not in my power to confer it. They are

305

very nice clothes, meant to be worn in a great assembly.
Ethelstan is the only atheling small enough to wear them.
He shall wear them tomorrow, for as long as he can sit
still. I suppose his nurse will take him away when he gets
restless.'

'Then I may tell Ethelstan that he will have his way?'
asked Elswitha in a puzzled voice. She could hear that
there was friction in the council. But she made no effort
to understand the cause of it, because long ago she had
made up her mind that politics were beyond her. 'That's
all that really matters, isn't it? Not to disappoint a little
boy.' With a bright smile all round the company she
ducked out of the room.

In November of the year 899 Alfred lay on his bed
staring at the rafters. The Bishops had been with him,
but after they had done all that the Church can do they
had left him to think undisturbed. He knew he was
dying; but he had passed his fiftieth birthday, and that,
for an atheling of the right line of Cerdic, was a
considerable achievement. His father, who had never
campaigned in winter, had lived only two years longer.
He had been granted a long reign, more than twenty-
eight years, and he had done most of what he had set
out to do.

The great heathen Army was finally dispersed. There
were still plenty of Danes in Britain; but those south of
Humber had been baptized, and they lacked a leader. In
East Anglia there was a Danish King of sorts, a less
important successor to Guthrum; but in the boroughs of
the midlands each warband lived independently. York
was the prize of victory in the wars of Ireland, and its
King had no authority over the Danish settlers in the
south. Already Ethelred and Ethelfleda were beginning
to expand the dominions of Christian Mercia.

He had failed to make Wessex into a new Rome, but
he left his ancestral Kingdom in better shape than he had
found it. A small fleet guarded the coast from pirates; his

thanes came willingly and well-armed to the muster, mounted on good horses; fortified boroughs kept the country secure, for the garrisons actually lived in them and repaired the palisades. In every minster, and in many parish churches, were priests who could read their Missals and render into Saxon what they read. The Church flourished because at last it had been properly endowed. He had abated the scandal of private minsters, mere estates bequeathed by lay abbots to their lay kin; pious and useful minsters had been revived by donations from the King's own purse. The alms of the West Saxons, heavy pennies of pure silver, flowed in a plentiful river through Christendom. The Saxon School in Rome had been freed from toll, in token of the Pope's gratitude; in Ireland and Frankland and Germany monks serving altars refurbished after the ravages of the pirates remembered in their prayers the generous King of the West Saxons. Even in fabulous India they prayed for him, if the tale of his envoys was true; how they had met in Rome Bishops from Mesopotamia, and had given them money to continue their journey to India in comfort. Little provincial Wessex, the remote Kingdom in a corner, was known throughout the civilized world. And he, Alfred, was something that his ancestor Cerdic had never aspired to be: he was the chosen lord of all the English and Saxons of Britain, save for those who were not yet liberated from the Danish yoke.

Best of all, when he made the world aware of Wessex, he had also made Wessex aware of the outside world. His people felt themselves to be part of the community of civilized men, colleagues of the Franks and Germans and Spaniards and Italians and Greeks who also were driving back the barbarians and enlarging the bounds of the true world, the world where proper men might live as they should.

In his dominion laymen knew their duty because he had translated the writings of Boethius; they knew the deeds of their mighty ancestors because he had collated the old legends into a coherent book. The book was brought up to date annually, so that posterity also should know its duty. Clerks knew their duty because he had translated Pope Gregory's *Pastoral Care*. The aldermen knew their duty because he had published the laws of his realm in writing. They had to read these laws, too, or they would be dismissed. In every shire, so Asser had told him, you could see bearded veterans struggling with their hornbooks. He looked back on his work and saw it had been good.

His people could grasp the physical shape of their world, because he had added to his translation of Orosius an account of the lands from whence the pirates came. Othere and Wulstan, what marvellous tales they had told. . . . Staring again at the rafters, he saw in his mind's eye those bare rocky uplands where the summer sun rode high all night, peopled with crooked little men who lived by the milk of their deer. Eastward in the Baltic he saw the mouths of wide frozen rivers, with voyagers waiting for the thaw so that they might journey south through grassy plains to Micklegard the golden. And the pirates' Micklegard, he knew, was also New Rome, the city of the Emperors, which could be reached by sailing east through the Middle Sea as well as by rowing south up the great rivers. In his mind he held the whole world, and he understood it.

Presently, when Purgatory had washed away the stain of his sins, he would look down in actual truth and see this whole world; and standing beside him would be Ethelred his dear brother.

In the next world Ethelred would still be his friend. He had not cheated Ethelred's son, nor deprived him of his inheritance. The envious blamed him for showing favour to Edward and Ethelstan; but he had made no public pronouncement, he had left the question of the succession to be decided lawfully by the council. If Ethelwold blamed him it was because that untrustworthy young man was at bottom half a Mercian. Any Mercian might leave you in the lurch. His people knew it. That was why they preferred Edward.

He had *not* cheated Ethelred. His conscience was at rest. The room grew darker.

Epilogue

Extracts from the *Anglo-Saxon Chronicle*.

N.B. The Chronicler begins his year at Michaelmas, so that events which we should consider to have occurred in the autumn of 899 are chronicled under the year 900.

900. In this year died Alfred, son of Ethelwulf, six days before All Saints. He was King of the whole English people, except for that part which was under Danish rule, and he had held the Kingdom for one and a half years less than thirty; and then his son Edward succeeded to the Kingdom.

Then the atheling Ethelwold, his father's brother's son, rode and seized the residence at Wimborne against the will of the King and his councillors. Then the King rode with the host until he encamped at Badbury near Wimborne; and Ethelwold stayed inside the residence with his companions who had given allegiance to him; and he had barred all the gates and said that he would either live or die there. Then the atheling rode away by night and went to the Danish army in Northumbria, and they accepted him as King and gave allegiance to him . . .

902. In this year Ethelwold came hither with all the fleet he could procure and Essex submitted to him.

903. In this year Ethelwold seduced the Army in East Anglia to break the peace. . . Then King Edward went after them as soon as he could collect his warband. . . And there were killed alderman Sigewulf and alderman Sigehelm, and Edwold the King's thane, and abbot

311

Cenwulf and Sigebert son of Sigewulf and Edwold son of Acca and many besides. And on the Danish side King Eorhic was killed, and the atheling Ethelwold whom they had chosen as their King . . . and a great slaughter was made on both sides.

METHVEN'S CLASSIC HISTORICAL NOVELS

Methven's Classic Historical Novels are available exclusively from branches of Methven's Booksellers and the Methven's web site (for a listing see over the page).

Methven's is a chain of quality bookshops in the south-east of England founded in 1993. We aim to provide our customers with a wide and interesting range of titles in all major categories, and first-class service, based on the knowledge and enthusiasm of our booksellers.

In 1998 we wondered what we might do for the National Year of Reading that was more than just a window display or a series of one-off events.

As keen readers of history, and from our experience of helping customers, we think that good historical fiction can help to fill gaps in historical knowledge, stir the imagination and start a wholly new line of reading. You might end up thoroughly disagreeing with the novel's point of view but be grateful to the author for getting you started.

At the same time there was concern in the press about the awareness of history amongst the young and our own experience of interviewing bright young graduates was that their historical knowledge was surprisingly sketchy.

As a contribution to turning the tide, at last running strong again through the fine work of Patrick O'Brian and others, we have begun the Methven's Historical Novels series with the English histories of Alfred Duggan. No better choice could be made to encourage the historical imagination.

Alan Clifford
Managing Director
Methven's plc

METHVEN'S CLASSIC HISTORICAL NOVELS
by
ALFRED DUGGAN

THE LITTLE EMPERORS
Britain and the Collapse of the Roman Empire
ISBN 1 902894 00 6

CONSCIENCE OF THE KING
The Saxon Invasion of Britain
ISBN 1 902894 01 4

THE KING OF ATHELNEY
Alfred the Great and England in the 9th century
ISBN 1 902894 02 2

THE CUNNING OF THE DOVE
Edward the Confessor and England before the
Conquest
ISBN 1 902894 03 0

GOD AND MY RIGHT
The Life and Death of Thomas Becket
ISBN 1 902894 04 9

£6.95 each

Available from our web site at **www.methvens.co.uk** and from
all branches of Methven's Booksellers:

AYLESBURY: 19 High Street, Aylesbury, Bucks, HP20 1SJ

CANTERBURY: 28 High Street, Canterbury, Kent, CT1 2RY

COBHAM:12A Anyards Road, Cobham, Surrey, KT11 2JZ

HERTFORD: 12-14 Bircherley Green, Hertford, Herts, SG14 1BN

ORPINGTON: 202 High Street, Orpington, Kent, BR6 0JN

ST ALBANS: 17 The Maltings, St Albans, Herts, AL1 3HL

WINDSOR: 26 Peascod Street, Windsor, Berks, SL4 1DU

WOKING: 46 Commercial Way, Woking, Surrey, GU21 1HW

WORTHING: 22-26 South Street, Worthing, W. Sussex, BN11 3AA